Mike Tiernan

To Paul

Happy Birthday

Hope you Enjoy.

Mike.

Best Wishes

Mike Tiernan

25.4.09

First Published in 2003

This edition is published in 2008, by Ickenham Publishing Co.

Printed in the U.K. by: The Creative print Group limited, London NW10.

The Profanity of Eagles

By

Mike Tiernan

In memory of James Tindall
A big man in every respect

Then

In the early hours of 6 June 1944, 4,000 allied ships, in three main lines, forced their way through a squall in the English Channel, their destination occupied Europe.

The German Army Group West, under the command of Field Marshal Gerd Von Rundstedt, waited in prepared positions around the Pas de Calais with the bulk of its armour, confident that they would push the British and Americans back into the sea. They were wrong – the Allies would not land at Calais, but in the Bay of the Seine, on the beaches of Normandy – D Day had arrived.

The Allied intelligence services had mounted a series of highly sophisticated deception plans that had led Hitler to believe that Calais was the objective. His own beliefs confirmed by German intelligence operations, Hitler refused to move any troops, even as the boats came ashore.

This is the story of a brilliantly conceived German intelligence operation, 'Operation Golden Egg', which, due to a twist of fate, was cunningly adapted by British Intelligence to completely fool the Germans as to the exact location of the invasion.

NOW

An elderly man stood alone at the Polish war memorial situated on the outskirts of London. His body was held at attention, his head bowed in respectful remorse. Two young women sat in a bright red BMW a few pace away, watching the old man. Like him, they were tall, blonde and blue eyed.

The old man stooped to lay a wreath of bright red poppies at the foot of the plain white cross. He straightened his back, bringing his right arm level with his shoulder, the tips of his fingers touching his temple, in salute. He stood quietly looking at the names carved into the memorial. Faces he had met over 50 years ago came to him briefly before fading, returning to the recesses of his mind.

He turned to walk back to the car where the girls sat, a small tear rolling down his proud, still handsome face.

"Everything ok, grandfather?" the younger of the two women asked as he took his place on the back seat.

"Yes, my dear," he said quietly as he wiped his eyes.

The other woman watched the old man's face in the rear-view mirror as she started the engine, satisfied that he was all right; she turned her concentration to the road. The BMW pulled away towards the A40 heading west. As the car descended the slip road, the old man gazed at RAF Northolt, the runways, the hangars, little changed by the passing of time. His memories came flooding back and he touched his right knee, instinctively, remembering that day.

CHAPTER 1

Day one (1944)

The door closed with a gratifying clunk. Christian sank deeply into the cool leather of the driver's seat, worn but comforting, like an old pair of shoes. He reached for a cigarette from a silver case, took out a Players, closed the lid with a clench of his fist, noticing another reassuring metallic sound. He liked things solid, well built, like a Spitfire.

Christian cupped his hands around the flame of the lighter out of habit, taking a long deep draw at the cigarette. He held the mixture within for as long as possible, before letting the blue-grey smoke waft slowly into the confines of the Morris, watching it roll like breakers over the windscreen. He smiled to himself, placed the lighter and cigarette case inside his tunic, tapping the breast pocket, the way a man might pat a small child, re-assuringly.

Christian was happy; the base medical officer had passed him fit, he would be flying again. He pressed the starter motor and the engine responded, bursting into life. He selected first gear, easing the Morris from the parking space and slowly making his way towards the main entrance of RAF Uxbridge.

The Corporal at the gate lifted the long barrier, saluting smartly as the car drew alongside. Christian wound down the window, smiling contentedly at the recognition of his rank. He returned the Corporal's salute before turning right onto the Uxbridge Road.

Christian drove the car through Uxbridge town centre, his mood elevated by the MO's decision to pass him fit. His eyes noticed things in a brighter more objective way, the greyness that had clouded everything since his accident was gone, and his mind now reacted in a positive light to the world about him.

The sun was still warm; the cold of winter, with its long dark nights, had passed long ago. The trees, resplendent in their new foliage, cast shadows, the flowers bathed in the sunshine, and the air was fresh and clean.

Christian drove to the A40, turned right heading east towards Northolt airfield and the city of London. It was only a short journey, but already his right leg was beginning to stiffen. The tension that had rested in the pit of his stomach all day began to rise. Christian tried to calm himself, telling himself it was only a reaction caused by the vigorous attention of the MO. However, he knew deep down that, no matter how he might try to convince himself, the problem was not a temporary one - it would remain with him always.

Flight Lieutenant Christian Kawolski, fighter pilot, DFC – a hero of the Battle of Britain, he had eighteen kills to his name before an ME109 had clipped the tail of his Spitfire as Christian attempted an unorthodox rudder turn. With the loss of control, the aeroplane had plummeted towards the patchwork quilt that was England's countryside. Christian contemplated bailing out of the stricken aircraft, but decided not to do so; he trusted the aeroplane, trusted his ability as a pilot. The Spitfire came out of the spin too late and too low to avoid a crash landing, which tore the heart out of his kite, together with the ligaments of his right knee.

Two farmers, who had been working in an adjacent field, pulled Christian from the burning wreckage. Critically ill, he was rushed by ambulance to a local hospital, where he spent the next three months hovering on the borderline between life and death. Only his inner strength, and a determination to survive, kept Christian alive.

Gradually he began to recover, much to the amazement of the medical staff. When he was able to fend for himself, Christian was transferred to an RAF hospital where he spent a lonely and frustrating eighteen months in torturous recuperation. Now fit and able to fly, according to the MO, Christian's spirits soared. It wouldn't be Spitfires, but it was still flying, he told himself.

Christian Kawolski was tall, athletic and muscular in all the right places, like a tennis player. His blond hair, deep blue eyes and generous smile displayed white teeth, despite the nicotine that had swirled over them. Christian was handsome, yet slightly boyish in appearance; he had the overall appearance of a mid European, and would have made a good Aryan in Hitler's new order, except for the fact that Christian was Polish and hated Germans.

Christian had lived in a small suburb of Warsaw with his wife Monica and two daughters - Maria, six, and Anna, now five. Anna had only been a baby when Christian had left to join his squadron in those dark days of 1939. Christian needed to fight the Germans and fly – Monica knew that if Christian could not fly then his spirit could not fly, and that would eat away at him like a cancer. Monica knew she could not hold him, so she agreed to his needs reluctantly, and took the children to her parent's house, assuring Christian that they would be safe.

Later that summer, Christian escaped to Sweden by smuggling himself aboard a freighter together with a friend, Eric Bem. By the spring of 1940 they had made their way to England, where they both joined the RAF. Christian and Eric were sent to Northolt airfield on the outskirts of west London, joining the RAF Polish Squadrons based there. After the initial period of training, which allowed them to familiarise themselves with the versatile Spitfire, both pilots were given their RAF wings. Christian's friend Eric was to die horrifically in his flaming Spitfire, on only his second sortie.

Christian turned off the A40 and headed towards Ruislip. He slowed the Morris as he approached the main gate of RAF Northolt. When he reached the barrier, he showed his pass to the Corporal on duty, who signalled to an MP to raise the barrier, and then saluted smartly. Christian returned the salute in a perfunctory manner, before turning right towards the administrative buildings and parking the car in the allotted space. Christian switched off the engine.

Christian's earlier euphoria had waned as the pain in his knee had slowly increased in intensity during his relatively short journey to the airfield. He tried to ease the pain by massaging the knee; the way the pretty little RAF physio had shown him. He opened the door and with both hands supporting his knee, swivelled on his buttocks, guiding his right leg out of the car. Christian reached for his cane, and with its assistance he placed both feet firmly on the ground and hoisted himself upright. He straightened his tunic, and slammed the car door before making his way, more confidently now, towards the Adjutant's office.

Christian did not take too much notice of the office, or the warm handshake of the Adjutant as he welcomed him. His mind and senses were pre-occupied with the pain in his knee. The chattering and ding of a typewriter reaching its margin brought Christian back to reality, he apologised to the Adjutant, like a schoolboy in front of the Headmaster. The officer's obviously sincere smile forgave Christian's lapse.

"Not to worry old chap, probably a bit low on fuel, Airman Book will show you to your quarters, maybe see you a bit later in the mess." The words the Adjutant had spoken were not condescending, but honest and typically English. He liked the English, they genuinely believed they could win the war and had done so right from the start, despite being almost totally alone in their struggle. Christian admired and respected them for that. He thanked the Adjutant, saluted sharply, turned and followed the Airman out of the office.

As he left the building Christian noticed the air had become chilly, and the sun was low towards the end of the runway, casting shadows over the small hamlet of Ickenham visible beyond. His eyes scanned the airfield, identifying the aircraft that lay scattered about the field, or in the main hangars located to his right. There was a variety of craft, highlighting Northolt's diversity of operations: a Dakota, a couple of Ansons, two squadrons of Spitfires - not as many as there had been in the earlier days of the Battle of Britain or during the blitz on London - and a lone Blenheim.

It was then that Christian noticed the Lysander, its distinctive shape silhouetted against the gathering gloom. His eyes wandered over the full length of the aircraft longingly: this was to be his new ship, his new craft, his new aeroplane. Christian's duties would involve flying the Lysander deep into occupied Europe, delivering S.O.E. agents to operate clandestinely behind the German lines. Christian felt better, more alert, the sight of his new aircraft had re-juvenated his spirits, he stared appreciatively at the silhouette of the Lysander until it disappeared from view.

Christian followed the Airman down the length of a dimly lit corridor before they stopped and entered into a small comfortable room. Christian's eyes surveyed the interior of his shared quarters. There was a window, as yet without its blackout screen drawn, a small wash hand basin with a circular mirror above, two bunks, one as yet unmade, two small cabinets and a dark panelled wardrobe.

The Airman drew the curtains before switching on the light and attending to his duties as Christian's orderly. Christian noticed a picture frame on the bedside cabinet next to the made up bed, he picked the frame up and stared at the photograph within – a young Flight Lieutenant with a huge schoolboy grin had his arm around a pretty WAAF.

"That's Flight Lieutenant Moreland, sir," said the orderly, noticing Christian's interest in the photograph.

"Freddie to his mates, sir," added the Airman, "Nice young gentleman he is too, sir, he'll be your room mate and your instructor on the Lysander sir. The pretty one's his young lady, Cathy."

Christian turned to the orderly, noticing him for the first time. Airman Book was about 35 years old, small and slight in stature. A short pointed snout of a nose separated the dark eyes, which were highlighted by the thin spectacles that he wore. Airman Johnny Book was a cockney from Barkingside, who would act as orderly to both Christian and Freddie Moreland; over the weeks and months he would come to be known affectionately by both officers as Birdy.

Airman Book finished making the bed for the new officer. He carefully hung Christian's uniforms in the dark old wardrobe and placed his smalls, shirts and ties in the bedside cabinet, before placing his hygiene articles, toothbrush, razor and brush on the shelf over the wash hand basin. When he had finished settling Christian into his new surroundings, Book turned his attention to the new young officer, noticing his Polish insignia.

"Will that be all, sir?" Book asked.

"Er, yes, um that's fine thank you, Airman," Christian replied.

"Right sir, I expect you want some kip, so I'll be taking my leave now, sir."

"Yes, what? Oh yes, of course," Christian stammered, his mind elsewhere.

"Goodnight sir, Oh! Breakfast is at oh-seven-thirty sharp," book added as he turned and made his way out of the door, closing it softly as he went.

Christian decided to take Book's advice. He unbuttoned his tunic and loosened his tie, undoing the top button of his shirt at the same time. Finally, he removed his shoes without undoing the laces, the lazy way a child might. He instantly felt relief as he did so, the cool air wafting over his tired, sore feet. Christian sighed, sat on the bunk and gently ran his hands over the problem knee.

When the ache subsided, Christian placed both hands under his thigh, lifting and manoeuvring his leg on the bunk, he lay back with his hands behind his head and thought about the day. All in all it had been a good one, better than he had experienced for a long time. He could allow himself to think about flying again; in a couple of days he would be able to do the thing he loved most. With these thoughts still on his mind he drifted into a deep sleep.

Sean Duffy stared out of the grim office window for perhaps the fiftieth time that day. Duffy had chosen this office when he had become the manager at Rawlingson's Dairy back in the heady days of 1940. Duffy had not selected the office for its size or grandeur, since it was smaller and sparsely decorated in comparison with the previous manager's room. However, its windows allowed an uninterrupted view of the fields and hedgerows that dipped gently towards the main East-West trunk road, the A40, and to RAF Northolt beyond.

Duffy methodically scanned the airfield in the fading light, his eyes alert, trying to discern anything different or unusual since his last routine observation. Everything seemed normal, just as it had been all week. Duffy glanced at the clock on the yellowing wall, and noted the time and in a large black diary, next to the time, he wrote one word – Negative.

Duffy rose from his seat, his chair scraping on the wooden floor as he did so. He moved towards the office door that led to an outer office occupied by his vigilant secretary, Mrs Flack. Standing by the door, he waited and listened, but all was silent except for the noise of his breathing. He gently opened the door and peered through the exposed gap. Duffy's eyes scanned the outer office for signs of activity, but all was quiet. He had heard his secretary, tap on his door and mumbled a grudging farewell at about six; she hadn't waited for an answer, she never did.

Satisfied that all was well, Duffy returned to his desk, picked up the diary that lay on the surface and moved towards the wall that housed the small paraffin heater. Slipping his hand behind the fire, he unloosened a panel in the wooden fascia, and placed the diary into a recess between the fascia and the wall. Once he had wedged the book into its secret hiding place, he replaced the panel and returned to his desk.

After a final look around his office, Duffy picked up his jacket from the back of the office chair, retrieved a brown leather satchel from his desk top and made his way to the outer office. He descended the stairs into the main office and reception, and exited into the cool fresh air.

Duffy walked across the gravel to where he had parked the Austin van that displayed a Friesian cow and the name of his official employer: 'Rawlingson's Dairy'. Duffy sat behind the wheel silently for a moment collecting his thoughts, before taking out a cigarette and lighting it. Drawing deeply on the tobacco he waited for the buzz the nicotine would bring, before exhaling loudly and watching the smoke drift lazily out of the open window.

The rage came as it always did at this time, a small movement in the pit of his stomach, which grew in intensity. He thought about the frustration of it all. 'Five bloody years,' he murmured to himself, 'why don't they call? Have they forgotten me? Are my dispatches read? used? What's the point of all my labour?' The questions kept coming to him.

During the first couple of years, Duffy had felt elated, thought that the precise data he had forwarded to Dublin was of importance, helping to rid his country of the oppressor. Now he wasn't even sure who the oppressor was anymore.

In the early days many people had supported the movement against its traditional adversary the British, the high command openly accepting the advances of its newfound friend Germany. Duffy, who had first hand experience of the Nazis, was not convinced that Hitler would honour Ireland's neutrality; sure, they supplied the boys in Dublin with military merchandise in exchange for information on the Brits, but should Germany defeat Britain, he couldn't see Hitler allowing Ireland to exist in its present form. Just like almost everywhere else in Europe, he would invade. Ireland would have swapped one evil for a more dangerous, more sinister alternative.

The Army Council did not realise the danger of the game they were playing. Like them, Duffy had taken great delight in assisting Britain's misery, but that had faded over the years. Now he was convinced that Germany must be defeated first; if that could be achieved whilst fooling them into supplying the merchandise needed, then that was all well and good. The merchandise itself now only came ashore in small quantities, matching the meagre information sent to Germany. What Duffy and Dublin needed was something big, something so important that the Jerries would not be able to resist.

Duffy finished his cigarette. The anger had subsided; he felt more in control, more composed. He turned the key, pressed the starter motor, and heard the engine respond and drove out of the yard, turning left onto the track that led to the Ruislip road. When he reached the junction, Duffy again turned left, gunning the Austin down hill towards the A40.

Police Inspector Tommy Boyle finished reading the report that lay on the desk in front of him and replaced it in the brown cardboard folder. He walked to the bank of grey metal filing cabinets that stood against the far wall of his office. Boyle opened the top drawer marked 'unsolved', and placed the folder into the file named 'Molly Redburn, Hammersmith,' before closing and locking the cabinet.

Boyle glanced at his watch, it was 7.30pm, so he just had time for a quick wash and shave before he left to conduct what had become a regular Friday night vigil. He was hungry, but he knew it would be sometime before he could eat. Tommy Boyle said goodnight to the desk sergeant, left the police station and got into his indistinct small black saloon. Boyle drove through the winding streets of the town, and entered the car park of the public house.

The Six Bells was not the sort of hostelry that Boyle would normally frequent. Boyle had joined a colleague here for a birthday drink with his wife Mary, about six months before. He had spotted a face in the crowd, a face from the past, a face he had seen in Hammersmith during an investigation in 1939. The man was older, more subdued perhaps, but Boyle was convinced it was the same man. Ever since that day Tommy Boyle had watched the public house, it didn't take long to find out that the only time he needed to continue his vigil was Friday nights, that was when Emily worked.

Boyle parked the car and entered the pub via the rear entrance door, and made his way to a bench seat in the snug close to the front door, a newspaper tucked under his arm. From that position he could survey the whole bar, whilst still remaining fairly inconspicuous.

"Good evening Tommy, the usual?" the landlord greeted him.

"Yes please, George."

The landlord took a pint jug from one of the hooks suspended in the ceiling; he poured the dark brown liquid expertly into the glass. Boyle paid, took the drink and sat down at his usual seat, unfolding his paper and beginning to read.

Boyle had just finished reading the headlines when Emily stepped into view, from the direction of the kitchen.

"Evening Tommy, anything of interest in the posh paper of yours tonight?" she beamed as she placed a tray of clean glasses on the counter in front of him.

"I don't know yet, Emily," he replied, "I've only just arrived."

"Not got stuck on that crossword of yours yet, then?" Emily said with a cheeky smile.

"No, not yet Emily, I haven't had a chance to look at it yet, and I probably won't if you keep pestering me, now get on with your work and serve somebody. There's a bloke over the other side of the bar, who looks parched."

Boyle regretted his harsh words the moment he said them, Emily's smile disappeared, her eyes showing the hurt Boyle's words had brought. She felt rejected, and rejection was something that Emily had known all her short life. Boyle tried to smile apologetically, it was too late, Emily turned on her heels and moved to the other end of the bar to serve the thirsty customer.

He had made a mistake and he knew it. He turned the pages of his newspaper annoyed with himself; part of his self-imposed vigil was to protect the girl. He had failed in that duty, failed just like all the other well-intentioned people Emily had met during her lonely 19 years on this planet. Emily was a sweet girl, blonde, blue eyed, very pretty, quite brash and hard on the surface, but with a bubbly sense of humour, the type that was expected from an attractive young barmaid. Yet underneath the veneer that was publicly on display lay a hurt and very vulnerable little girl.

Emily Cassidy was abandoned as a baby, and brought up in the orphanage across the road from the Six Bells. Emily had been fostered on many occasions and her hurt would sometimes surface in down right disobedience and terrible temper fits. Her last foster parents had finally abandoned Emily when she was sixteen, because she had reported the nightly intrusions into her bedroom by her drunken foster father to the police. The family closed ranks, and the case was closed.

Emily totally lost faith in the system that had failed her yet again; she distrusted the police and hated them with a vengeance. This relationship had not been helped when, having run away from home, she was charged with prostitution as she desperately tried to survive on her own. The charge was dropped on the proviso that she broke away from that phase of her life.

Since that awful day, Emily had managed to secure a job as a receptionist at a local building firm. Her boss was so delighted with her aptitude that he had promoted her to secretary, before finally making her his personal assistant. Emily spent her Friday nights working at the Six Bells. For the first time in her life she felt accepted and Emily was a girl who needed to be accepted and loved.

Boyle watched as Emily glanced at her watch, which she seemed to be checking with the pub clock. Boyle did the same; the pub clock was exactly five minutes fast. It wouldn't be long before the man he was waiting for arrived, the man responsible for his Friday night vigils, the man he had seen in Hammersmith all those years before.

Emily smiled at him and he saw the nervous anticipation in her eyes, he smiled back warmly. Emily's face lit up as she returned Boyle's forgiving smile, now happy and content again, Emily carried on with her duties. He studied the girl for a moment; she was the image of Molly, could almost have been her double if Molly had not left this earth in a prolonged and violent death.

Captain Ernst Mosel sat in the rear seat of the black saloon as it approached German Naval Intelligence headquarters in Berlin. Mosel had been summoned by his master, Unter Admiral Carl Heinz Reitzer. Mosel passed efficiently through security, the Admiral's limousine in which he travelled being recognised immediately. The driver opened the door for Mosel, saluting smartly as he did so. Mosel returned the salute and moved purposefully to the steps that stood before him. Mounting the steps, Mosel entered by the open front doors, passing two guards, resplendent in their black uniforms, black helmets and highly polished boots.

Mosel entered the bustling foyer, handed his coat to an orderly, and straightened his tunic and his tie, feeling the Iron Cross First Class at his throat.

An orderly approached. "Captain Mosel?"

Mosel nodded.

"This way, sir."

Mosel picked up his briefcase, gripping the handle firmly and followed the orderly's back as he made his way up a vast, gently curving staircase to the first floor landing.

He was shown into a large comfortable anteroom where he was met by a Leutnant who gestured towards two large brown, deep-buttoned leather chairs, separated by a grey marble table with a small gold lamp stand. Mosel seated himself in the deep cool leather, as the Leutnant approached two giant mahogany doors. Two guards, identical to those at the main entrance, snapped to attention, their shiny machine pistols coming to the present in total unison. The Leutnant hesitated for a moment before knocking on the door and then confidently marching in. When the doors closed behind him, the two guards snapped back into a stand easy, maintaining their menacing stare.

After a few brief moments, the huge doors parted and the Leutnant beckoned Mosel in. Picking up his briefcase, he entered into the Admiral's office. It took Mosel's eyes sometime to adjust to the difference in light; whereas the anteroom had been bright and purposeful, the Admiral's office was dimly lit in comparison, with subtle light emitting from two lamps. He took a pace forward and felt his boots sink into the dark red carpet. The Admiral sat behind the vast desk, framed by a huge picture of the Fuhrer that adorned the wall behind him.

"Take a seat Captain, I won't keep you a moment," the figure behind the desk said without looking up from the papers he was attending to. Mosel sat directly in front of the desk. His eyes roamed across the desk coming to a halt at the brass nameplate, which displayed the Admiral's, full name and rank, 'Unter Admiral of Naval Intelligence, O.K.W., Special Operations'. The Admiral had been outranked in the service only by old man Canaris himself, until Himmler, spurred by jealousy, had removed Canaris from office in February of that year.

When the Admiral had finished reading the report, he collected the papers and tapped them together on the table. Satisfied, he placed the papers in a large black folder marked 'Top Secret,' closed the cover and pushed the papers to one side, then removed his gold rimmed spectacles, rubbed the tiredness away and placed the glasses on the table in front of him. Mosel saw the strain in the red-rimmed eyes, the stress lines on the forehead and the greying temples. The Admiral had been put under enormous pressure since the removal of Admiral Canaris, Himmler, his new superior, distrusted the ABWEHR and was continuously trying to usurp the department with his own service, the S.D.

The Admiral looked at Mosel and spoke.

"This plan of yours Ernst, will it work?"

"I am confident it will, sir, providing the last two pieces of the jigsaw fall into place."

"And how are those areas coming along?" asked the Admiral.

"I expect operational readiness in the next three weeks, four at the most, sir."

The Admiral stared directly into Mosel's eyes, searching for any hint of uncertainty, or nervousness.

"Good proceed as planned and keep me up to date with all developments." The Admiral paused, still staring at Mosel. "And Ernst, this scheme or yours, only you, department III and myself know about this, even O.K.W. are in the dark, keep it that way."

"Yes sir," Mosel replied firmly.

"Should your plan fail," the Admiral continued, "yours, Ernst, will be the first head to roll, do you understand?" Mosel swallowed hard before he spoke.

"Yes sir."

The Admiral reached into a desk drawer and handed Mosel an envelope.

"Your authority, Captain, this should satisfy any needs you may have. Use it wisely."

"I will, sir."

The Admiral replaced his spectacles, picked up a gold fountain pen and started to write.

"Good luck, Captain Mosel." He said without looking up from his writing.

Mosel stood up, came to attention and saluted.

"Thank you, sir." With that Mosel turned and left the Admiral's office.

Once again he found himself seated in the soft leather of the Admiral's personal car. From the corner of his eye he saw his reflection in the small courtesy mirror, situated in the rear of the big saloon. Mosel stared for a moment at his image, before turning his attention to the small mahogany drinks cabinet, which was fitted, to the rear of the front bench seat. He pulled the brass handle and watched as the cabinet unfolded before his eyes revealing a mirrored interior. He took a small crystal glass and poured a generous measure of Schnapps, which he swallowed in a single gulp. Mosel felt the warm liquid slip down his throat before it exploded inside his stomach. He stared at the empty glass for a while before returning his gaze to the vanity mirror.

'My God, Ernst, what have you started?' he said to his reflection.

The driver interrupted his thoughts.

"Are you ready, sir?"

"What…oh yes, drive on."

The driver eased the big saloon forward; the car followed the long drive to the main gate. Mosel poured himself another drink, slipping it slowly this time. He reached to the iron cross which hung around his throat, sank back into the deep leather and smiled to himself. 'It's started, Ernst... there's no going back now.'

The vision of Monica disappeared – Christian tried desperately to bring it back but it was gone. Christian lay on the bed trying to remember parts of the dream as best he could. He had been with Monica beside the lake; they had decided to go for a picnic and had borrowed Eric's motorcycle and sidecar. They had driven to the country, Christian on the bike, Monica and Maria in the sidecar.

The early summer sun lay gently on their exposed skin as they lay side by side on the blanket that they had laid on the sweet smelling grass. Maria, just two, played by the waterside, as the gentle ebb and flow of the lake lapped on the shore. Christian stared at the small child, as only a father would, watching her innocent play, oblivious to everything but the game her imagination had concocted.

Maria wobbled on her firm little limbs, her determination alone keeping her balanced. Christian took in the whole of her being. Maria had long curly golden hair; huge deep blue eyes that sparkled, those she had inherited from Christian, the rest of her features were all Monica. She was petite, feminine, broad mouthed with thick lips and a wicked little giggle that made his heart soar. Christian watched the child for a while before turning his attention to Monica.

He stared longingly at his wife, her beauty had never waned, and her figure had remained perfectly balanced, even after the rigours of childbirth. Christian became aware of his heartbeat, which had risen in tempo. Monica noticed Christian's attention, and smiled warmly at the man she loved. His physique excited her; her eyes scanned the body that lay next to her. Strong athletic legs, the flat stomach, the rise of his chest, scattered with blond hair of which Christian was so proud. Monica continued her surveillance of his tanned, muscular body, the strong jaw, the generous mouth and the eyes... those beautiful big blue eyes. She saw the tenderness and love in those eyes, and she felt happy and secure in Christian's love for her.

Monica moved her eyes to Maria, before returning her attention back to Christian. He was smiling at some vacant thought that made him look totally at one with the world. Christian lay on his back, his hands behind his head, staring at the azure sky. He was as happy as any man could be, he had a beautiful wife and daughter and he was a pilot.

Christian sensed rather than felt Monica's shadow move over him, felt the firmness of her breasts through the thin cotton dress that she wore. Her warm damp lips touched his, her tongue gently persuading his mouth to open. Christian's hands went to her face; gently he pulled her deeper to him, the blood rushing to his loins, the stiffness growing. Monica felt the swelling as it pressed against her hip, she pulled her mouth from his; staring intently into the deep blue eyes and smiled girlishly, highlighting her perfectly presented white teeth. Christian placed both palms on the swell of her bottom feeling the outline of her panties underneath the cotton of her dress.

"Christian." His name only a whisper.

"Yes, darling."

Monica's face became more serious. Christian noticed the hesitant tone in her voice.

"How do you think Maria would feel about having a little sister?"

Christian didn't take it in immediately, but when the realisation did come he jerked his head back, his eyes studying hers, it was then he saw the sparkle.

"You don't mean…?"

"Yes," she said proudly, as she turned to look at her flat tummy. Christian followed her gaze. "Soon, darling, very soon," she said patting her tummy.

Christian inserted his fingers into her hair and cupped her face, his thumbs stroking the soft pale skin.

"How do you know it's a girl?" he asked questioningly.

"I just know, I'm a woman…women know these things." Monica pulled her head back slightly, "you don't mind do you…I mean another girl…that's alright, isn't it?"

Monica looked slightly hurt.

"Yes, of course it is, silly." Christian pulled her to him again, gently kissing her eyelids in turn, whilst turning her head so that her face could nestle on his chest, her hair lying against his face. Christian stroked her hair with one hand as the other caressed the mound of her bottom, gently exploring the two taut round orbs. The swelling in his groin grew as her hip ground deep into his swollen member. There would be plenty of time for a boy later he decided….

Then it was gone, the mental picture disappeared…almost as if a light had gone out.

Duffy pulled up outside the front of the Six Bells, parking the van in a service space. Since it was a Friday he had purchased fish and chips in Ruislip Manor on his way home from work, his staunch Catholic upbringing still ruling him. After consuming his supper, Duffy had washed and changed then selected his attire for the evening.

He shut the van door and looked at his reflection in the window. He was dressed in brown brogues, brown corduroy trousers, a beige lightly checked shirt complimented by a pale yellow tie, a brown sports jacket with leather arm patches completed his dress. Duffy grinned, winking at his reflection.

'Sean Duffy,' he said to himself, 'you are a mighty handsome feller, so you are.' Smiling happily, he entered the bar by the front entrance.

Emily noticed his entrance immediately. Duffy saw her look, noticed her uncertainty, his mouth breaking into a huge grin, his eyes smiling as only an Irishman's can. Emily saw the infectious grin; the smiling truthful eyes and her mouth blossomed into a beautiful smile. They both fought their way through the throng of bodies until they met face to face by the till, separated from bodily touch only by the expanse of the wooden bar.

Boyle had taken in Duffy's arrival as he had all comings and goings that night. He watched the couple's amorous stares for a moment before returning his attentions to his crossword.

"Good evening, Mr Duffy, and how are you?" Emily smiled, hardly able to contain the feminine instincts inside her.

"Better for seeing you, Emily, and how are you this fine evening, darling girl?"

Emily's fingers nervously played with the bodice of her gingham dress where it met the exposed flesh of her bosom and the gold heart shaped pendant that hung between the swelling of her firm breasts.

"Your usual, Mr Duffy, sir?"

"If you please, girl," Duffy said, as his eyes followed Emily's movement down the length of the bar, watching the contortions of her bottom as it moved within her dress provocatively. Emily could feel Duffy's eyes on her as she took a glass from the lower shelf, shamelessly exposing the full shape of her rear. Emily slowly poured the black liquid into the glass, when the glass was three quarters full; she waited, allowing it to settle, before topping it up, the white creamy head foaming at the top of the glass. Emily wiped the small overflow with her index finger, she then slowly put it in her mouth, licking it clean.

'The little bitch is teasing me,' Duffy thought to himself.

Emily returned to where Duffy stood and placed the beer in front of him before blowing a secretive little kiss. Duffy raised the glass to his lips noticing the heart shape pattern she had put on its surface. He took a large sip, his eyes glancing over the rim; he returned the compliment with a huge grin before returning the glass to the bar.

"Gorgeous."

"Me or the Guinness?" Emily giggled mischievously.

"Both." Duffy replied.

Boyle had seen the little game being acted out. He raised his eyebrows and studied each of the lovers in turn, before returning his attention once again to his crossword.

It was late by the time Mosel returned to his office, he picked up the phone and dialled a number, and waited for a response. When it came he spoke briefly.

'Fertilise the egg,' was all he said. Mosel picked up his briefcase from the desk and left.

Christian's thoughts kept returning to Monica, unable to relax, he had washed, shaved and headed towards the mess. When he reached the entrance, Christian heard the muffled sounds of tomfoolery being conducted from the other side of the wooden door, he changed his mind and walked to where he had parked the car. He couldn't face the familiarity of the officers' mess just yet, too many bad memories stalked his mind, the ghosts of too many faces no longer of this world still haunted him.

He drove out of the main gate, and turned left and headed toward Ruislip. He did not know where he was going or why. His thoughts still on Monica, Christian was oblivious to everything in his transient state. The sign of a pub brought him back to reality. He pulled the Morris off the road and parked. A simple twist of fate occurred the moment he passed through the doors, and now his life would change forever.

Boyle saw him enter, noted the Polish insignia, before returning his attention to the newspaper. Emily also saw Christian enter, her eyes betraying her sudden interest. Smiling, she approached the handsome young officer at the bar.

Duffy saw the smile, noted the reaction and felt the hurt. He turned to look at the tall handsome man who now stood next to him. Admitting to his good looks, he shrugged his shoulders and returned his gaze once again to the pretty young barmaid with a knowing look. Emily had seen Duffy's reaction, ignored it as fair game and stood blushing slightly now at the Adonis that stood in front of her.

"What can I get you?" She smiled.

"Beer, please."

"Haven't seen you here before, new to the area are you?" Emily enquired as she poured the beer.

"Sort of," Christian replied. "I've been in the area before…but…but I've been away for a while."

Emily brought the now full pint of bitter to Christian, setting it down in front of him.

"Pilot, are you?" Emily said, feeling silly in her nervousness, as the wings were prominent on his breast pocket.

"Was…am…sorry," Christian mumbled.

"Of course you are, silly me," Emily patted his hand, her blush taking on a deeper hue. Christian put some change on the bar to pay for his drink.

"I'll get that," Duffy interjected.

"No, no, please don't worry…."

"Not at all, a little token of our undeniable appreciation and respect for our gallant men in blue, I insist."

"Thank you," Christian said.

"Not at all," Duffy smiled and extended his hand. "Sean Duffy."

"Christian…Christian Kawolski," Christian shook hands with the mercurial Duffy.

Emily glared at Duffy, annoyed at the intrusion. She took the coins from Duffy, deposited them loudly in the till and slammed the drawer shut, folding her arms, she stood sulking by the bar. Duffy noticed the tantrum and waved his arm in Emily's direction.

"And this beautiful specimen of young womanhood is our own Emily, Emily Cassidy."

Christian smiled at the girl; Emily returned the smile and made to move. Duffy immediately turned to Christian, dismissing the girl once again. Emily's little girl attitude returned.

"So I guess you're in Spits then?" Duffy continued.

"Pardon? Oh, yes… well I was…"

"Was?" Duffy inquired.

"Yes until the crash, a bit of trouble with an ME109."

"Not flying now?" It was more a question than just normal conversation.

"Er yes...actually I start re-training tomorrow."

"What will you be flying?"

"Lysanders."

"Cloak and dagger stuff,." Duffy continued the mild interrogation.

"I really can't say." Christian replied firmly.

"Of course you can't, I understand, can't be too careful can we?" Duffy conceded. "Anyway, nice to meet you Christian, cheers." he said, raising his glass, noticing that it was almost empty he turned to Emily.

"Another pint of Ireland's finest, girl," His smile a wicked grin. "Forgot myself so I did."

Emily, grateful for her inclusion dropped the sulk, her femininity returned. Her movement, the almost sensual act of pouring the Guinness, did not go un-noticed by both men. The conversation melted into small talk between the three of them, interrupted on Emily's part by her other duties.

Tommy Boyle emptied the last dregs of his pint, picked up his newspaper, and left unnoticed.

In a suburb on the outskirts of Berlin a phone rang. Gunther Schloss was in a deep sleep as the RAF had not visited that night. The intermittent drone of the telephone bell brought him to consciousness, the pyjama covered arm reached out of the covers to switch on the bedside table lamp. Schloss half sat up, putting on his wire spectacles, and answered the phone.

"Schloss." He answered.

"Herr Schloss, Lieutenant Steiner, ABWEHR, Captain Mosel has a job for you."

Schloss sat up.

"What is it?" he questioned.

"No time now,' the voice was curt, to the point. 'A car will pick you up at 9am tomorrow morning…don't be late!"

Schloss heard the click as the device at the other end disconnected the line. He put the receiver down, took off his spectacles, rubbed his eyes in disbelief and switched off the light. As Schloss snuggled once again beneath the covers his thoughts turned to the brief conversation.

'At last,' he said, turned and drifted back to sleep.

The pub was empty now save for the three of them. The landlord came into the bar refreshed from his night off, listening to the wireless and reading the paper in his flat above the bar. He noticed Sean Duffy and the young pilot before turning to Emily.

"I'll lock up for you Emily, all ok down here?"

"Fine, George, I'm finished here."

"Time I was off." Christian said.

"Me too," Duffy added as he drained the last of the Guinness from the glass. Duffy and Christian shook hands, exchanging farewells. Christian smiled intently at Emily as he left.

Christian started the Morris, swung the car in a wide arc and made his way to the car park entrance, waving to Duffy as he passed. Seeing the road was clear, he pulled out and sped up the hill towards Ruislip. Duffy returned the wave, opened the door to the Austin and sat heavily in the driver's seat, his mind on the young pilot and what he had heard.

His concentration was interrupted by the thought of Emily, her reactions to the pilot had disturbed him. The desire he felt for her, so long contained within the depths of his inner being was now in conflict. He felt the anger rise. Duffy lit a cigarette to calm the tension. The nicotine, which invaded his senses, slowly began to take effect.

Duffy saw the lights go off, heard the muffled voices.

"Goodnight, George."

"Goodnight, Emily."

He saw the girl as she came out of the bar's front door. Looking up, Emily noticed the van and walked towards it. Duffy threw the cigarette butt out of the window, leaned across the seat and opened the door for her. He waited until she sat down before he started the engine and headed in the direction of Emily's home.

When they reached the flat where she lived, Duffy switched off the engine, sat back and put his hands on the steering wheel. Emily touched his thigh.

"Are you alright, Sean?" She asked, her voice sincere.

"Yes, fine thanks." He replied slightly off hand.

"Have I done something wrong…have I upset you?"

Duffy turned to look into her eyes; the genuine sorrow he saw melted his frustrations.

"Of course not, Emily." His grin not as full as normal, he reached over and kissed her soft cheek.

"Oh Sean, I'm sorry…" Emily put her arms around his neck. Duffy pulled her close to him and hugged her, his arms tight in loving security.

CHAPTER 2

The car arrived exactly on time, Schloss was ready. The man who came to the door was sombrely dressed, his mood as colourful as his attire.

"Herr Schloss?"

"Yes."

"Come with me, please." The man turned and walked back to the car without waiting for a reply. Schloss, bewildered, followed the figure meekly, and silently entered the rear door of the car. A uniformed man in the front seat did not turn when he spoke.

"Herr Schloss, Leutnant Steiner, we spoke last night."

"What's all this about?" Schloss asked nervously.

"No questions, just sit back and enjoy the journey."

Schloss could see the man's eyes looking sternly at him from the reflection in the driver's rear view mirror.

The journey was anything but enjoyable for Schloss, his feelings of unease, coupled with the sights that met his eyes at the destruction of his beloved capital, made him feel vulnerable and insecure. The carnage wrought by the intrusions of the RAF by night, the USAF by day was evident. Bedraggled, lifeless citizens of this once proud city sloped amongst the ruins as scavengers flitted between the stark walls. What had once been homes and businesses now resembled something out of an apocalyptic novel. Tears began to form in his eyes.

The car had stopped to allow a home defence truck to pass. As he waited and watched, Schloss began to stare at the sobbing figure of a woman. Probably younger than she appeared, her clothes dirty and torn, her face smudged with grime. She held a silent, lifeless bundle of a child in her arms, her moaning as she rocked to and fro haunted him. With tears now rolling down his face, Schloss turned and began to weep. Steiner watched the reactions of the old man in the mirror, but felt no sympathy, his hardness bred from long experience.

By the time the car pulled up outside ABWEHR headquarters Berlin, Schloss had composed himself. After the routine security checks, Schloss was shown into Mosel's office, the gruff young leutnant by his side.

The room was businesslike, if a little dull. A senior naval officer sat behind a desk, a mountain of files almost obscuring him from sight.

"Herr Schloss, Captain." Steiner snapped as he announced the Captain's guest. Mosel stood to greet the old man his eyes surveying the appearance.

"So good of you to come, please take a seat." Mosel pointed to a chair.

Schloss sat down, awed by the presence of the man.

"That will be all, Hans." Mosel dismissed his aide.

"Yes sir." Steiner snapped to attention, turned and left the office closing the door behind him.

"Sorry to bring you all the way here," Mosel said cordially, "You must be wondering why I sent for you Herr Schloss?"

"Yes, yes it was a bit of a shock…after all this time." Schloss mumbled.

"I assure you Herr Schloss, your presence here is of the utmost importance to the Fatherland…and perhaps the future conduct of the war."

Schloss felt the importance of the words Mosel had spoken. He felt more confidants, but still confused.

"But what can I…a simple, loyal German citizen offer which is so important to you and my country?"

"More than you could imagine, my dear Gunther," Mosel paused. "It is Gunther isn't it?

It was a rhetorical question, Mosel knew everything about Gunther Schloss, more than the man knew about himself. Mosel knew about his parents, his real parents, his false identity, his admirable but false allegiance.

"But first I would like to show you this." Mosel passed a plain brown envelope to Schloss and waited for the reaction. Schloss put his spectacles on, opened the envelope and slid out the single photograph. Mosel saw the reaction immediately. The lips aquiver, Schloss felt sick, his mind spinning, comprehension clouded.

"But…no…it can't be." He stammered, "I never…no, no it's not me…how did you do this? This is preposterous…a lie!" Schloss slammed the photograph on Mosel's desk.

"Calm down my dear Schloss, let me explain." Mosel said gently patting his victim's hand.

Schloss sat and listened for the next hour as Mosel unfolded the history, revelations, coincidences and plain facts about his life. Gone was the earlier arrogance, in its place meek acceptance. Mosel was happy, everything was going to plan. Like a poker player, Mosel was leading his victim, waiting until his opponent was coerced into following his every move, enhancing the deception, waiting for the right opportunity to strike – then laying down the winning hand.

Gunther Schloss was lost for words. No questions came, as no answers would be welcomed, he meekly accepted Mosel's rationale. Mosel did not show any sign of emotion, he had won, cleaned the man out; destroyed him. Whatever beliefs he had possessed, now was the time to re-build, to re-invent Gunther Schloss…Patriotism, Mosel knew, was the key. Mosel set to work.

After a detailed account of the role Mosel envisaged for Schloss, his responsibility – his duty, he now brought the man to the point of no return.

"So you see, my dear Gunther, the Fatherland is in need of your services, of course, I cannot order you to accept my proposals." Mosel hesitated, his voice becoming less supportive.

"Then again, I can't protect you should you refuse. I would, as a matter of departmental orders, have to pass the details of our conversation to the S.D., and Himmler, of course." Mosel let the words sink in; the mere mention of the S.D. and Himmler in particular, brought untold fear into the man's eyes. Mosel smiled, "So Gunther, what is it to be?"

"Yes, yes I will accept. If the Fatherland is in need of my services, then I shall not falter. I am a German, and proud, regardless of what you have told me today." The arrogance had returned, much to Mosel's delight. Arrogance would be a necessity if Schloss were to perform according to the script Mosel had set.

"Excellent! Gunther, I assure you, Germany will be proud of you." Mosel congratulated the man on his brave decision - not that he had any choice in the matter. Mosel leaned forward pushing the intercom button.

"Hans."

"Sir?"

"Come in will you?"

"Yes, sir."

Mosel turned his attention once again to the pathetic figure that sat in front of him. It would take a great deal of hard work to convert Schloss into the role, he thought. Steiner entered the room, and stood silently awaiting orders.

"Hans take Herr Schloss to his quarters."

"But…" Schloss stammered, "my home…my clothes…what…"

"Steiner will see to everything." Mosel's voice was authoritative.

"But my…"

"My dear Schloss, you must understand that we cannot let you leave these premises until you are operationally ready and, with due respect, you have much work to do, no further questions, Hans will see to you." Steiner stepped forward, his hand on Schloss' shoulder. Mosel ignored the man's plaintive look and carried on with his work.

"Good day Herr Schloss," he said without looking up.

Schloss meekly stood, realising any objections to his temporary imprisonment would be to no avail, dejectedly he followed Steiner out of the room. When Steiner and the disillusioned Schloss had left, Mosel sat back in the deep-buttoned cushions of his chair and smiled.

Christian spent a boring, frustrating weekend in the classroom at Northolt, familiarising himself with the instruments of the Westland Lysander. Although the basic instruments of flight were the same, each aircraft had its own idiosyncrasies, take off, speed, rate of climb and so on, altered dependant upon the aeroplane.

The Lysander was a versatile aircraft, much slower than the new breed of single seater fighters and with its fixed wheel frame it had been taken out of front line duties for more sedate roles. Its forte, due to the very short take off and landing specifications, made it ideal for covert operations. Throughout the 1940's until the end of the war it would become synonymous with that role.

Christian, like all pilots, wanted to fly and decide its capabilities for himself, but he was experienced enough to understand his need for research. It was simple, as the English said. "You can't put the cart before the horse."

Christian's instructor was Freddie Moreland, an excellent pilot in his own right. Freddie, like Christian, had suffered during the Battle of Britain. Unlike Christian's more obvious, physical suffering, Freddie's was mental. The stress and strain of operating non-stop throughout the battle, making four or perhaps five sorties a day, had taken its toll. Freddie was the 'old hand' of the mess in terms of actual flying hours and combat experience – the only survivor from those early days, which was a great deal to handle at 23 years of age.

Freddie proved to be an ideal instructor, not only because of his vast knowledge of the aircraft, but also for his understanding of what the pilot felt. Added to that was the fact that the two men, although from entirely different backgrounds, seemed to gel. Gel into an understanding that would lead to friendship.

The attentive Airman Book had formally introduced Christian to Freddie. The initial nervous small talk, with the addition of Book's humour, had cemented the relationship from the start. Book had been busying himself with his duties whilst the two officers made their acquaintance.

"Will you be taking breakfast, gentlemen?" he had asked. They both agreed. "Well as you know," he continued, "only operational crew are entitled to the 'full monty', bacon and eggs like, but as it's the young gentlemen's first day," he said looking at Christian, "I expect we can bend the rules a little…and anyway, Doris owes me a favour…I might even be able to get you an extra rasher of bacon each."

"Can he do that?" Christian asked.

"Birdy can do anything." Freddie grinned.

True to his word, the two pilots sat down to breakfast with 'the full monty', as Book had put it, an extra rasher of bacon on the side of their plates. Other men sat before their meagre breakfast envious of Christian and Freddie, envious of their orderly, the conniving Airman Book.

The two men had eaten their feast hungrily, the conversation less formal, less timid. From that moment on a friendship formed, a friendship that would end only in adversity.

US Major General Alexander Popowski was typical of the new breed of staff officer in the US army of the period. Brash, aggressive, overconfident and totally lacking in actual combat experience.

Popowski was born in Lubeck of Polish origin. His father was a baker, who had worked hard to provide a basic living. His doting mother also worked in the shop until the birth of their son. In 1890, when Popowski was only two, the family emigrated to the United States of America, as so many Europeans had done. Depressed with the old order in Europe they longed for the adventure and opportunity that the new world had to offer.

Hard work, combined with perseverance and the outstanding quality of the product of his labour, meant his father was able to secure small premises in the south side of the Bronx area of New York. His reputation spread, and within five years there were five shops, all in the Bronx area. Within fifteen years he had a chain of sixty, which had expanded into the more affluent areas of New York and Boston.

His father had hoped young Alex would join the business, but the young man had only one dream, that was to be an officer in the brave new United States Army. Popowski graduated West Point, third in his class, in 1910. By 1915 he was a Captain. Upon the entry of the United States into the Great War in 1917 he was a respected staff officer. Sent to France in 1918, he joined Pershing's staff as a major but was too late to see any action.

Between the wars Popowski spent most of his time in Washington where his now affluent, powerful father, introduced him into the proper circles on Capital Hill, hoping one day to use his network of friends in high places to advance the career of his son into politics. Alexander, however, had no such ambitions; his dedication was channelled only into military activities, and becoming an expert in European tactics. In 1942 he joined Eisenhower's staff. He was nicknamed Popeye due to his similarity in appearance to the cartoon character, with huge arms developed in his early years whilst working in his father's bakery, and the ever-present pipe only adding to his caricature.

In 1943 Popowski was seconded to Montgomery's eighth army as US liaison officer to the Polish divisions under his command. Respected by Monty for his excellent staff work and dedication to duty, Popowski had now risen to be a full General, and was responsible for all staff work relating to the Poles. With the invasion of Italy having taken place, Popowski found himself in 1944, under the overall command of the British General Alexander, Montgomery having been returned to England to plan the invasion of occupied France.

Despondent that he had not been recalled by Eisenhower and Montgomery to play an active role in the planning of D.Day, Popowski along with 50,000 Poles sat behind the line at Cassino, desperate for action. Major General Alexander Popowski, frustrated at his lack of activity, would become a thorn in the delicate balance of the

Allied High Command. Using his father's powerful position, he would seek the glory that his destiny demanded.

In the vast complex of ABWEHR Headquarters in Berlin, Popowski's name would become known to Captain Ernst Mosel. Mosel, a meticulous intelligence officer, would use the friction caused by Popowski's insubordination, together with a full history of his background, to mount the most audacious plan ever conceived by German military intelligence. By an incredible twist of fate at birth, Popowski would become the goose that laid the golden egg.

Christian woke early. The tedious studying in the classroom was over for the time being, and today he would be taking his Lysander up for the first time. Christian breakfasted with Freddie at his side. Unable to swallow any food due to the excitement in his stomach, he pushed the meal to one side. Freddie, not affected, scraped Christian's remains onto his plate and ate the lot.

Sipping coffee and chain smoking did not alleviate the tension, which had now spread to Christian's injured knee. He started to massage the problem joint, knowing it was only psychosomatic since it always troubled him at times of stress. Freddie noticed Christian's anxiety, and looked directly at him sympathetically.

"Steady on old boy, at this rate you'll have used up all your ration before we take off, I know how you feel, or at least I can guess," Freddie added. "I've been there too, it's no big deal, you're an excellent pilot and the Ly's a great lady to fly, slower than you're used to but she can do things even a Spit can't, you'll be fine, I know." Freddie patted Christian on the shoulder as he rose from the table. "Come on, it's time we got suited up." As the two men exited the dining room into the clean fresh air, Christian stopped and turned towards Freddie.

"Thanks for that, Freddie, I appreciate it." Christian said honestly.

"No problem, old boy. Now then, show me what you can do."

Christian climbed into the cockpit, adjusted his parachute harness, strapped himself in and waited for Freddie to do the same. Once Freddie was seated, and the canopy closed, Christian did a quick check. Satisfied all was well, he signalled to the aircraftsman to swing the prop. The magneto fired, and the power plant of the radial engine burst into life. Christian adjusted the mixture allowing the propeller to settle into a rhythmic hum, then tested the rudder, flaps and aerodynes. Satisfied with his pre-flight check, Christian opened the throttle allowing the Lysander to taxi to the runway.

Christian turned the aircraft onto the runway and opened the throttle fully, felt the shudder as the engine increased in tempo and released the brakes. The Lysander reached its take off speed quickly. Christian pulled back on the stick, felt her nose rise as she gently left the tarmac of the runway. Christian climbed to 500 feet, passing over the small hamlet of Ickenham that nestled at the end of the runway, retracted the wing area and settled into level flight by easing the throttle back. Christian checked the airspeed indicator, the horizontal horizon and altitude before letting out a huge sigh – he had done it – he was flying again.

He took the aircraft up to 2000 feet to begin a series of circuits to familiarise himself with the way the Lysander handled. She was totally different to the Spitfire, slow to turn, her instruments less responsive to change. The fixed wheels caused a certain amount of drag, which Christian soon overcame. Within five minutes he had got the hang of her perfectly.

Freddie spoke, his voice filling Christian's ears.

"OK Christian, that was good, let's try a landing."

Christian headed the aircraft towards Harrow before making a tight turn and beginning his descent. The flaps were lowered, the throttle eased, the rudder adjusted to compensate for the slight crosswind. He brought them in low and level. Just before the tyres touched the tarmac, Christian raised the nose slightly and settled gently on to the runway. Without bothering to stop, Christian increased the throttle, pulled back and allowed the Lysander to take off again.

"Excellent, let's try it again," Freddie said, "this time much shorter." The whole process was repeated another three times. Each landing and take off being much shorter than the previous one.

Christian was about to make his fourth approach when a voice in his earphones startled him.

"Hello Batsman – Hello Batsman, Umpire calling, are you receiving me over?" It was the voice of the traffic controller in the tower at Northolt. Christian responded.

"Hello Umpire, Batsman receiving you loud and clear, over."

"Hello Batsman, this is Umpire, we have a spin bowler coming over the wicket, do you receive over?" This was typical RAF jargon but it did serve a purpose. The tower was informing Christian that a slower, heavier aircraft was approaching from the Harrow area over the gasometer that was used to line up the aircraft ready for descent to Northolt.

"Hello Umpire, this is Batsman, I have him in sight and I will make an extended turn and follow him in, over." Christian had seen the aircraft as it approached. Initially a small dot, it had grown in size as it made its way towards Northolt. Christian followed the aircraft, a Dakota, in, landing once again perfectly.

Once the Lysander had come to a complete stop, both Christian and Freddie extracted themselves from the aircraft. Grinning at each other, congratulatory handshakes were exchanged before Freddie, picking up Christian piggyback style, carried him towards the main building, both men in fits of raucous laughter.

"Bloody pilots," an aircraftsman mumbled under his breath as the two men departed.

They ate lunch, this time Christian scraping the plate clean, smoked, drank tea and chatted about the morning's experience before returning to the aircraft and repeating the whole process for the remainder of the afternoon.

Duffy watched the air display from his office window at the dairy. He had arrived early as it was Monday, there was always somebody skiving on a Monday. Much to his surprise all the floats, cars and vans were out on their rounds, so he decided to make himself an early brew. Duffy went into the small kitchen, filled the kettle with fresh water, lit the gas stove and put the kettle on the blue flame. Duffy waited until it finally boiled, poured the water over the leaves he'd put into the pot and let it brew.

When the tea was ready he poured some into a thick enamel mug and added a little milk, stirring the thick brown liquid as he did. Once in his office he removed the diary from behind the panelling, put it in his desk drawer and locked it.

He heard his secretary arrive. After a minute or so she poked her long neck round the door, greeting him in her monotone voice with all the enthusiasm of someone who had been sentenced to death. Duffy returned the greeting with a smile, which was wasted, for as soon as she had uttered the forced communication, she had retracted her long neck, disappearing into her own office. Within seconds he heard the familiar tap, tap of the old Imperial typewriter.

Duffy finished the rest of the tea whilst looking lazily out of the window. His mind wandered. She was a funny old bird his secretary, she had a long face, small mouth, thin lips, all seated under a mattress of grey hair. Her body, if you could call it that, was long, thin and totally featureless. Still, she left him alone, not bothering him unless it was important.

The noise, faint at first but clearly audible, of an aircraft taking off brought his attention back. He opened a desk drawer, took out a pair of binoculars, small but very powerful and followed the aircraft as it climbed. Duffy watched the plane, a Lysander, fascinated by the series of circuits, take offs and landings. It must be an instrument check he thought. Lysanders were used exclusively for nigh time operations for S.O.E. cloak and dagger stuff, then it came to him in an instant, Christian Kawolski had told him that he was retraining on a new aircraft.

Duffy watched in admiration; if the pilot of the Lysander was Kawolski then he was good, very good indeed. But why Lysanders? Duffy asked himself, Kawolski had told him he was in Spitfires before, surely the British still needed good fighter pilots. He must be good, you don't get a DFC for nothing, Duffy thought, remembering the medal ribbons on Kawolski's breast pocket. Duffy considered his findings. He must have been chosen, he decided, but for what…? Then it came to him clearly. Kawolski had been chosen to fly the Lysander on a special mission for S.O.E., a mission of great importance to British Intelligence. A mission that would require a pilot of exceptional skill and daring.

Duffy sat back in his chair, a huge grin on his face. Dublin would be pleased, and so would Jerry. This news might even speed up the delivery of merchandise. Now all Duffy had to do was somehow get close to Kawolski. Duffy thought back to Friday night, he remembered Emily's reaction to the handsome pilot. The way she had looked at him, the way he had looked at her.

Duffy had been jealous at the time, but if he could use Emily to get close to Kawolski, he would be able to discover more about the man, why he had been chosen and, more importantly, what he had been chosen for

Duffy did not like the thought of Emily showing her affection to anybody else, he wanted that privilege for himself. He was the only person who really loved the girl, he told himself. Doubt began to infect him. What if she fell for Kawolski? No, he couldn't let it happen, there must be another way, he told himself, but there wasn't. Duffy knew he would have to sit back and watch, possibly even assist in the liaison!

At lunchtime Duffy drove his van to Ruislip Manor, parked outside a telephone box and made a call. When the phone answered he pushed button A and spoke.

"It's Duffy." He said, "we need to meet, usual place in thirty minutes." He put the phone down then called his office. Duffy waited as the tone rang. 'Come on, come on,' he said agitatedly.

"Rawlingson's Dairy, Mrs Clack speaking, how may I help you?"

"Mrs Clack, its Duffy," silence, "I'm afraid I'm having a spot of bother with toothache…I may be a little late coming back to the office…"can you manage without me for a while?"

"Of course I ca,." she almost spat the words down the line. Duffy had obviously offended her by challenging her professionalism.

"I'll try not to be too long."

"Is that all, Mr. Duffy?" she said curtly.

"Yes, yes that's all Mrs Clack, i'll..." The line went dead. Duffy felt like a schoolboy who had been caught misbehaving in class and being sent to the corner by the school marm.

"The old bitch." He cursed slamming the phone against the mirror in the booth, which reflected the anger on his face. The mirror shattered into bits, pieces littering the floor of the booth. Duffy dropped the phone allowing it to swing wildly on its cord. He stormed out of the booth, nearly knocking a passer-by to the floor. Duffy glared at the man for a moment then turned and stormed back to his van. Duffy slammed the door as he sat behind the wheel.

The anger inside of him rose, its intensity frightening him. Beads of sweat formed at the temples. 'For Gods sake, Sean, calm down,' he told himself. Duffy lit a cigarette to calm his nerves. Still fired with rage, he started the van, gunning it down the Manor towards Ruislip, the engine screaming.

By the time Duffy had parked the van behind the Great War Memorial he was calmer. He decided to go for a drink and crossed the road to the Swan. He felt like he needed a whisky but decided to order a Guinness instead. Duffy took a large gulp swallowing almost half the pint before he settled the glass back on the counter, wiping the creamy head from his mouth as he did so. He lit another cigarette, drew heavily before letting the blue smoke billow out, sensing the nicotine's calming influence. He sipped the rest of the pint slowly, calming himself as best he could.

When he'd finished, Duffy left the Swan and entered the teashop across the road. He ordered coffee, selected a corner seat with a view of the front door so he could watch the comings and goings. He made the coffee last as long as was needed. Constantly looking at his watch, Duffy awaited the arrival of the man he had spoken to on the phone.

The bell on the teashop door jingled as it was opened and Duffy looked up. He saw the short stocky man in the baggy trousers enter, a folded copy of the Mirror stuffed unceremoniously in the jacket pocket. Duffy waited for the man to be seated before he stood up. He paid the jolly woman behind the counter for the coffee, purchasing some breadcrumbs at the same time.

When Duffy left the teashop he crossed the road to the Memorial, and passed through the gardens walking towards the duck pond. He selected a quiet spot, away from the main feeding area, opened the breadcrumbs and began to feed the greedy birds.

Duffy saw the man with the Daily Mirror approach, pass him, select a bench about twenty feet away, take out his newspaper and begin to read. Duffy glanced around. An old couple passed by hand in hand, the woman chatting busily, the man silent, gaunt. Duffy waited until they had trudged out of sight before taking another look round. Two boys were playing cowboys and Indians on a mound of grass that protruded towards the pond. The man with the newspaper seemed oblivious to his surroundings, the broadsheet covering most of his face.

Duffy edged closer to the man, feeding the noisy ducks as he went along, the greedier ones following his trail.

"Good afternoon." The man said softly, just audible over the chattering of the ducks, his eyes never leaving the paper.

"Good afternoon Francis." Duffy replied. His back still facing the man.

"Well Sean, what's so important that you had to drag me all the way out here on a Monday afternoon?"

The man was Frankie Cavenaugh the IRA's quartermaster in London, and therefore, technically Duffy's boss. Duffy told Cavenaugh all he knew – the chance meeting with the Polish pilot, the Lysander flights that morning and the conclusions he had come to. Cavenaugh listened to Duffy for a good ten minutes evaluating all the information that he had heard before answering.

"If what you say is true, and I do mean if, Sean, then I think this information you have could be important, very important." He paused. "Dublin needs something good to give our Jerry friends, they've been a bit miffed with our offerings recently. If there is something worthwhile in what you've said, then they might speed up the flow of merchandise to us. God only knows we need it, those bastards in the Dublin Government are getting too pally with the Brits."

Cavenaugh stood up and approached Duffy, standing to his left but still not looking directly at him.

"Listen, Sean, I'll get this information of yours off to Kilbride in Dublin by tonight, in the meantime, you keep pressing, find out as much as you can about this Polish fellow, use whatever resources you need, but don't let him out of your sight." Cavenaugh put his hand on Duffy's shoulder. "We can't screw this one up, Sean, it's only a morsel, I know, but maybe, just maybe, there's more to it." Cavenaugh threw his eyes to the heavens. "The Army Council desperately needs something to give the Jerries. If they back out on us now it could put us back twenty years!" With that Cavenaugh departed, speaking without looking back. "Good day to you Sean."

"Good day to you Francis." Duffy replied as he continued to feed the ducks.

Christian practised short take-offs and landings for the remainder of the day. When he finally touched down for the last time that session he was tired. He had passed the first test with consummate ease, and now only had the night flying exercises to go. If he passed that hurdle with any semblance of ability, then he would be passed for operations. That meant getting back into the fight, being of use once again.

Tommy Boyle was looking forward to his supper, Mary had somehow managed to get a little lambs liver for him. Boyle tidied his papers on the desk, collected his hat and coat from the chair, switched off the light and made his way to the entrance of the police station. On the way out he stopped at the front desk to bid goodnight to the duty sergeant.

"I'm off, Brian, anything interesting happen today?" Tommy said making conversation.

"Not much, Tommy, fairly routine for a Monday so far." Boyle was about to turn to leave when the sergeant spoke again. "There was one thing, now you come to mention it, hardly earth shattering, though." Boyle stopped.

"What's that then, Brian?" He asked.

"Oh, nothing to bother you sir" the sergeant said, wishing he had kept his big mouth shut. "Probably a job for those lazy sods in CID." He said nervously compounding his earlier gaff.

"Those lazy sods are my CID."

"Sorry, sir." He said apologetically.

"Tell me." Boyle almost demanded.

"Well, as I said sir, not that important…bit of vandalism in a phone box in the Manor, sir."

"Kids?" questioned Boyle.

"No sir, a bloke sir…according to the witness."

"We have a witness?"

"Yes sir, it's all in the statement, sir."

"Where is it?" Boyle demanded. He was becoming annoyed with the sergeant's casualness.

"Right here, sir." The sergeant passed a buff folder to Boyle. He read it.

Liam Kilbride received the information Cavenaugh had sent via the safe route late that night. He read the short transcript several times before coming to the conclusion that it wasn't important enough to call a meeting of the Army Council, but it was interesting enough to pass onto his ABWEHR contact in Dublin. He could include it in his weekly report; at least it would fill out the meagre offerings they had assimilated from the other live units. Maybe, he thought, it could be of more relevance to the Nazis than it was to Sinn Fein.

Kilbride opened the door that led to the mêlée of Rileys Bar on the north bank of the Liffey. He poked his head into the throng searching for O'Brien. When their eyes finally met, he signalled O'Brien to come, then returned to his desk once again. O'Brien tapped on the door entering without waiting for a response.

"You wanted me, Liam?" O'Brien said in his Belfast drawl, a dialect not pleasing to the ears of the uninitiated.

"Yes, Patsie...something interesting from London, nothing we can use at the moment," Kilbride paused before saying almost perfuntionarily, "but it might be of some use to Rudy."

Kilbride passed the document to O'Brien, then continued.

"Oh! And Pat, make sure he gets it tonight."

"Ok, sure Liam, I'll do it straightaway." O'Brien said, then left.

It was three o'clock in the morning, German time. Mosel had been working late again; the bunk in the small anteroom to the side of his office had hardly been used since it had been erected. Mosel was tired, he had sensed his concentration lapse over the last hour or so, and so he decided to take a short break. He stretched his legs as he entered the communications room. It was quieter now due to the hour, he took a large metal jug off the stove and poured himself a mug of coffee. The Ersatz coffee substitute was thick, bitter and stale to taste, but it would help to keep him awake.

A teleprinter started to tap, tap. Mosel went to the machine, watching unemotionally as the data appeared line by line. Something caught his eye, immediately bringing the alertness back. The communiqué was from the Rudy network in Dublin. Mosel tore the flimsy sheet from the machine.

"Get Steiner, send him to my office immediately!" Mosel barked at a corporal.

"Yes sir."

Mosel strode purposefully back to his office the flimsy still in his hand. Steiner entered, his salute as sharp as ever.

"You asked to see me, sir."

"Yes Hans, get me the files for RAF Polish section, anything we may have on a Flight Lieutenant Christian Kowolski, newspapers, everything you can lay your hands on."

"Yes sir."

"Oh, and Hans, send in some fresh coffee, black and lots of it, it's going to be a long night." Steiner turned and left the office, closing the door behind him.

At Bletchley Park, Britain's secret code breaking centre, Wren Officer Julie Parker was on duty in the communications centre. Julie came on shift at ten o'clock expecting a fairly quiet night, she wasn't wrong, the hours dragged. Then at two o'clock things started to happen. A message in German code was picked up at British Intelligence MI5 section in Belfast and relayed to her station at Bletchley Park. The message contained within the cipher had been sent by Rudy a known German agent operating in Dublin.

Rudy was well known to British Intelligence, they knew of his activities in the republic, his IRA connections. S.I.S. had passed a significant amount of information, most of it completely useless, via a double agent within the ranks of the IRA's London Brigade. The IRA would then pass the data to Rudy who would in return, send any relevant data via the German black code, which had been broken earlier in the war, to the desk of his controller at the ABWEHR, Captain Ernst Mosel.

Julie, realising the possible importance, took the flimsy directly to her supervisor. He read the document, dismissed it as low priority, placing it into the non-critical file. Julie was put out by her supervisor's casualness. The cipher was more detailed than anything Rudy had sent recently, Julie stood her ground. The supervisor looked up from his paperwork, flashing a condescending look at the young Wren officer before he dismissed her.

"That will be all, Parker."

Julie shrugged her shoulders, then returned to her station.

One hour later the teleprinter started again, another message from Belfast. They had picked up a transmission from Willy as they called him, a well-known operator who worked within Mosels department, details to follow.

Thirty minutes later the de-code was transmitted. Julie read the document, tore the flimsy from the machine, marched towards her supervisor's desk, slamming the document in front of him. The supervisor gave her a cursory look, picked up the flimsy, and then began to read. Julie watched as the supervisor's face changed. He took the phone in his right hand, dialled a short number, and waited for an answer.

"Commander, it's McClain here sir, Julie's picked up something on the Rudy line…I think you ought to see this sir." He paused for the reply before continuing. "Yes sir, I'll come straight up…Yes, she's here…yes sir." He put the phone down, then looked into the young Wren's eyes, saw the look of triumph. "He wants you to come along as well…get Marjorie to cover your station."

Mosel researched the files Steiner had brought to him. He found what he was looking for. Mosel placed the cutting from the London Evening News on his desk. He studied the young face in the photograph that stared back at him, before pressing the intercom button.

"Hans, any news on that address in Warsaw?"

"Yes sir…Bad news, it's empty, has been for some time."

"What about relatives, parents?"

"Nothing on him, but we're checking on the other side, should get some feedback anytime now, sir."

"Keep me informed Hans." Mosel released his finger on the intercom button, then continued to read what information they had so far.

Mosel was a brilliant Intelligence Officer, his bright analytical mind was complimented by an ability to think laterally. His attention to detail was almost manic. Small snippets of data, easily overlooked by someone of standard intelligence, would be categorically filed and cross-referenced. This dedication now produced results. In front of Mosel lay an almost complete history of the life of Christian

Kawolski, who would become a cog in the greater machinery of Mosel's plan, the most audacious plan ever devised by German Intelligence, 'Operation Golden Egg.'

Should Operation Golden Egg succeed, then the Allies would have to delay any invasion for at least a year, or perish on the landing zones. The political and psychological repercussions would reverberate throughout the corridors of Whitehall and Washington. Unable to mount a second front, the allies would squander their resources on less profitable sideshows. That would allow Germany to recover sufficiently enough to transfer a vast amount of men and materials to the Eastern front to destroy the Bolsheviks.

Steiner interrupted Mosel's thoughts.

"Sir, we have the address…the targets are resident."

"Excellent, Hans, proceed, use our best people…and Hans, make it look like a Gestapo operation."

"Yes, sir."

CHAPTER 3

Commander Peter Thompson had read the report sent by motorcycle from Bletchley Park. He stood by the window of his office in Baker Street staring out of the glass frame at the business of London below. Remarkable, he thought to himself, you can bomb them by night, destroy their homes, their businesses, but come the light of day, the proud industrious people of London would shake themselves down and continue with everyday life. The cauldron of destruction wrought by the Luftwaffe over the last four years had taken its toll; the skeletal grey gaunt structures of bombed buildings dotted the skyline.

The phone rang. Thompson moved to his desk to pick up the receiver.

"Good, send him in," he said.

"You wanted me sir?" Harry Milburn said as he entered.

"Yes Harry, come in. What have we got on the IRA in London, who's running the show at the moment?"

"Cavenaugh, sir."

"Good, tail him Harry, don't let him know we are onto him, but stick to him like glue."

"Yes sir, anything else?"

"Yes, our man, make sure he's not compromised - and another thing Harry,"

"Sir."

"Get me everything you can on a Polish pilot based at Northolt – Flight Lieutenant Christian Kawolski, I believe he's one of S.O.E's taxi drivers."

"Yes sir." Harry Milburn left Thompson to his thoughts.

Thompson pushed the button on the intercom and spoke to his secretary.

"Alice get me an appointment with 'C' and have a car ready, oh, and a cup of tea please."

"Yes Commander." The secretary replied.

Commander Thompson continued his observations from the office window.

A black saloon with three men inside pulled up outside a small chalet style house in a smart suburb on the outskirts of Warsaw. Two men in dark suits and hats got out of the car, went to the door, knocked and then went straight in. The driver, the engine still running, stayed in the car.

Five minutes later the two men emerged from the house, one escorting a young blonde woman with two crying children, the other carrying two small suitcases that he put into the trunk of the car. The woman and children were shepherded into the car. Both men got in, one in the back, the other in the front. Two elderly civilians watched as the car sped off, tears in their eyes. A child's pram, which had been knocked over in the process, lay on its side, a wheel spinning wildly. The doll, which had been in the pram, lay in the mud.

Duffy arrived early that morning. One of the vans had been playing up, and if it refused to start he would have to assist the milkman with his round. Doing the rounds was a chore to a man of Duffy's intellect. The sight that met Duffy's eyes was a completely empty yard, devoid of all forms of transport. Duffy raised his eyes to the heavens, thanking his God.

With plenty of time now on his hands Duffy decided to make a brew. When the coffee was poured, he took the steaming mug upstairs to his office. He had just sat down at his desk when the phone rang.

"Please dear Jesus. Don't say the van's broken down." He picked up the receiver.

"Rawlingson's Dairies."

"Sean?"

"Francis, what is it?" Alarm spread through his mind, direct contact was only to be used in an emergency.

"Meet me at the usual place." Cavenaugh said. The phone went dead.

Duffy held the phone, staring into space.

"What the Feck…"

Commander Thompson sat across the desk from the most powerful man in British Intelligence, Sir Stewart Menzies, or 'C' as he was known. 'C' had the power to destroy careers and in some cases, lives. He had a direct line to Winston himself – not a man to trifle with. Thompson felt compelled to speak first.

"You have read my report, I see sir." Thompson noticed the document in front of the Commander.

"Yes," 'C' answered, his fingers interlocked, his eyes staring.

"I know it's only supposition at this stage, but it definitely smacks of something big. I know Mosel… he wouldn't be involved unless…unless it was important."

"Agreed." 'C' confirmed.

"With your permission sir, I would like to put some resources behind this. Watch it, see how it progresses."

"You want the department to set up an operation?" 'C' asked.

"Not exactly sir…I was thinking more of letting S.O.E. take control."

"Lucian, you mean?" 'C' leaned forward.

"Yes sir, perhaps we can let something slip to S.O.E. about our concerns over Lucian, they would naturally have to react."

"So what your saying Commander, is that I sanction the passing of MI6 data to S.O.E., knowing full well that they will waste it on some harebrained scheme of their own making…and…should it fail, as it probably will do, S.O.E. will bear the brunt of the responsibility."

"Yes sir, basically that's it." Thompson said lightly.

"Good, carry on, let me know the full scenario before it goes public."

"Yes sir." Thompson stood to leave.

"Thank you Peter Good day to you." 'C' said.

"Thank you, sir."

It was a worried Duffy who drove the Austin van towards Ruislip that lunchtime. He had made another excuse to visit the dentist, complaining that the fictional visit of the other day had not resolved the problem. Mrs Clack had shown him a disbelieving look as he had explained to her the necessity of revisiting the 'tooth mechanic,' as he called them. He cursed the mean old bitch, together with Cavenaugh who had instigated the whole problem.

Duffy parked the van in the George car park, just off the High Street. It offered an uninterrupted view of the duck pond, as well as the gardens of Manor Farm, with the great barn and the Manor House in the background.

Duffy walked around the corner, entered the Swan and ordered a Guinness. He sat by a window seat that overlooked the teashop where he had met Cavenaugh before. Several minutes passed by before Cavenaugh came into view, strutting confidently, he entered the teashop, his stocky frame stretching the fabric of his worn jacket. Duffy sipped the Guinness and waited.

After about five minutes, Cavenaugh appeared again, scratching his head as he looked up and down the street, across at the War Memorial and then back again. Duffy could see the frustration grow; Cavenaugh began to bang the newspaper he carried repeatedly against his thigh. 'Not so cocky now, are you, Francis?' Duffy said to himself as he watched the man squirm.

Finally Cavenaugh had had enough, he stuffed both his hands together with the newspaper in his pocket then set off heading towards the duck pond. Duffy waited, his eyes now trained on the man in the raincoat with the trilby hat he had seen following Cavenaugh when he had arrived. The man stopped as Cavenaugh entered the teashop, waiting in a nearby doorway. When Cavenaugh had come out again, the man in the raincoat had looked into the baker's window, peering at Cavenaugh from the corner of his eye, amused at his antics. When Cavenaugh had stormed off in the direction of the duck pond, the rain-coated man had followed him.

Duffy finished his beer, left the Swan, and then followed the raincoated figure as he cut through the War Memorial gardens, a hedge separating him from Cavenaugh's view, as the two walked in parallel. The man watched as Cavenaugh sat down on a green bench close to the duck pond, he selected a bench on the other side of the hedge before he also sat down - a gap in the foliage giving a clear view of the hapless Cavenaugh.

Duffy studied the scene for a few moments wondering if the man was Cavenaugh's back up or something else. Either way he would have to take him out. Duffy could not afford any slip-ups, security was essential, so far Cavenaugh had screwed it up at every turn. Duffy approached the raincoated figure.

"Do you have a light, good sir?" Duffy said waiving a cigarette. The man had not seen Duffy's approach; he was startled, off balance.

"Eh, yes…just a minute..." The man fumbled in the pockets of his raincoat, realised the matches weren't there so he began to search his trouser pockets, his head twisting slightly, exposing the neck. That was the moment Duffy had been waiting for. His clenched fist thundered into the man's head like a cold hammer, hitting him hard just behind the ear where skull met neck. The man crumpled to the floor, shock and nausea giving way to blackness.

Duffy quickly glanced round to make sure there was nobody in sight. He grabbed the lapels of the man's raincoat and hauled him up and sat him on the bench. He steadied the man, placed his hands flat on his knees then, for good measure, pulled the trilby down over his eyes. To all intents and purposes the man would look, to any curious passer-by, as if he were asleep. Duffy retraced his steps, calmed himself down, before walking with a slight stagger towards the impatient Cavenaugh.

Unbeknown to Duffy, Mrs Clack had seen the stagger as she made her way to her own dental appointment, the office junior manning the phones in both her and Duffy's absence.

'Typical,' she thought, 'he's drunk.'

Cavenaugh had also seen Duffy's approach and noticed the slight stagger.

"Jesus Sean, you're late, and drunk into the bargain." Cavenaugh spat. "Dublin will hear of this, mark my words."

"Calm down, Francis." Duffy could see the stress, the anger in the man. Duffy always called Cavenaugh Francis, as he knew it irritated him. Cavenaugh preferred to be called Frankie, it went with the gangster image he had of himself. "I'm not drunk, I've been to the dentist." Duffy continued his hand going to his face to soothe the imaginary bad tooth. "Admittedly, I've had a pint of Ireland's finest, but I'm perfectly sober – it must be a reaction to the cocaine the dentist gave me."

Cavenaugh seemed to accept his explanation.

"What in Gods name, Francis, is so important that you have to drag me out of the office two days in a row, that old hag of a secretary of mine is getting very suspicious, I had to use the dentist as an excuse to get out."

"I'll tell you what's so bloody important!" Cavenaugh paused, calmed himself and began again more slowly, more in control. "What's important, Sean, is that Jerry has got het up over this Polish pilot feller, they want everything you can get on him, want him pumped for information, put in a corner." Cavenaugh smiled, more confident now. "I thought you could use that little tart you've been screwing with, get her to make eyes at the pole, get him in the sheets, a bit of pillow talk." Duffy could feel the anger rise.

"She's no tart." He spat, his eyes dark and menacing.

"She's a prostitute, for God's sake."

"Was, Frankie, was – she's not now."

"OK Sean o.k. she's not a prostitute now, but she has the looks, the wile and the experience necessary to do the job. To get what I want…we wan," Cavenaugh corrected. "Dublin and Adolf will be very pleased with us Sean me boy, could be the making of us, don't you see?"

Duffy thought hard about what Cavenaugh had said, he didn't like it, but he knew it made sense; anyway the girl was half way there, Duffy remembered the way Emily had looked at the pilot. He would have to use her, just like everyone else had used her during her short unhappy life…poor Emily.

Cavenaugh put his hand on Duffy's shoulder. Duffy lifted it away with his fingers and let it drop, staring hard into Cavenaugh's eyes.

"OK Francis, I'll do it."

"Good man, Sean." Cavenaugh smiled

"Oh, and Francis."

"Yes, Sean?"

"Don't call me at the office again." Duffy raised his finger to Cavenaugh's face threateningly, "and don't call Emily a prostitute again."

Duffy strode away. He retraced his steps, checked on the slumbering figure in the raincoat then doubled back to where he had parked the van. Duffy sat quietly watching Cavenaugh as he disappeared back the way he'd came, this time he wasn't being followed.

The morning's flying had gone as expected. Freddie Moreland was almost envious of Kawolski's flying skills, the Lysander seemed to be an extension of Christian, performing feats that even Freddie did not think it was capable of.

"That's it for the day." Freddie said as Christian landed the Lysander yet again.

"But why Freddie? There's plenty of time left."

"Get your flying suit off Christian and meet me in the car park in twenty minutes."

"But…"

"No buts, Christian, I've got some good news for you."

"What?" Christian asked.

"I'll tell you in the car." Freddie said, "and look smart, Cathy's coming too."

Christian said hello to Cathy as the three of them jumped into Freddie's small red roadster. Both Cathy and Christian looked embarrassed as Cathy had to sit on Christian's lap for the journey. When they arrived at the Plough, Freddie brought the car to a standstill.

"Come on then, you two, let's have a drink." Freddie beamed.

"Freddie, I can't." Christian said.

"Why not?"

"Because I'm flying, remember."

"Not for the rest of today you're not."

"What do you mean?"

"Tomorrow you start night flying exercise – three days, that's probably overdoing it in your case." Freddie grinned. "Day off Saturday, briefing Sunday afternoon, take off Sunday night."

"What?" Christian looked totally lost.

"You've got an op old boy."

Christian let Cathy out of the car then threw his arm around Freddie's shoulder, his elation evident.

"Steady on old boy, you'll make Cathy jealous." Freddie grinned.

"Sorry Cathy," Christian turned to Freddie's girlfriend.

"Don't be silly Christian," Cathy smiled, and then planted a big kiss on his cheek.

"Come on, let's celebrate." Freddie said.

"The drinks are on me!" Christian said as the three friends entered the pub.

"Champagne." Christian demanded as he reached the bar.

"You'll be lucky," answered the dour barman.

'Then two and a half pints of your best bitter, my good man." The three giggled as the barman raised his eyes before setting off down the bar to pour the drinks.

"What's the occasion?"

Christian turned to see where the voice had come from.

"Emily, what are you doing here?" Christian's face let up as he saw her.

"It's my friend's birthday." She smiled, we were just having a drink to celebrate."

"Bring her over," Christian said. Emily signalled to her friend to join them. Both Emily and Christian made the introductions before peeling off to one side.

"So what's the celebration for?" Emily asked her eyes smiling at Christian.

"Looks like my training has paid off, they're putting me on ops."

"Not Spitfires again?" Emily's eyes betrayed her feelings.

"No, Lysanders…just a glorified taxi driver really." He reassured her.

Emily saw the excitement in his face, could see the love he had for flying. She blushed slightly, annoyed at her jealousy.

"Not much danger." Christian added.

"So you won't go off and get yourself killed then?" Emily's eyes began to moisten.

"Of course not." Christian shrugged his shoulders, "but if it happens, it happens. It doesn't matter, the risk I mean," he continued, "as long as I'm flying again."

"It matters to me," Emily said, her lip quivering slightly. Christian saw the hurt in her eyes, he put his arms around her, pulling her close to him.

"I'll be fine, don't worry," he said, hugging her tightly, feeling her trembling body close to his.

"Hey you two! That's enough of that." Freddie interrupted as he passed the drinks to Emily and Christian. "Hey, I've got a great idea," Freddie continued, "look there's a dance at the church hall tonight, why don't we continue the celebration there? It might be a fit of a whiz." He beamed.

"And what celebration might that be?" It was Duffy, annoyed by the conversation with Cavenaugh; he had decided to have a pint so he had stopped off at the Plough where the Guinness was better.

"Sean, good to see you again." Said Christian shaking the Irishman's hand.

"You too, Christian." Duffy's eyes went to the girl.

"Emily."

"Sean."

"Well," Christian said breaking the silence that had followed, "what will you have to drink?"

"A Guinness please." Duffy answered, his eyes still fixed on Emily who returned the look, slightly sulkily, annoyed at Duffy's intrusion.

Tommy Boyle sat at his desk at Ruislip police station. He had made a call to Irish Special Branch in Dublin once he had obtained clearance from his superiors. The phone had been answered in a sweet Dublin accent.

"Special Branch, Good morning to you, how can I help?"

"Police Inspector Noel Riordan please.

"Who shall I say is calling?"

"Police Inspector Tommy Boyle, Metropolitan Police in London." Tommy had replied.

"Hold just one moment…you're through," the voice said.

"Tommy, how the devil are you?"

"I'm fine Noel, thanks, and how are you, Patricia, the kids, all well I hope?"

"They're fine thanks Tommy, and how is your lovely wife?"

"A devil in a skirt still, Noel," Boyle replied. They exchanged small talk for a while before Noel came to the point of the call.

"So, what can I do for you Tommy?"

"I'm following a lead that's come to light," Tommy explained, "It's regarding the murder of Molly Redburn, a prostitute, that happened back in England in 1939, do you remember?"

"Yes, I do," said Noel, "Hammersmith wasn't it? Similar to the case we had here in Dublin as I recall."

"Listen Noel, I need a favour," Tommy said. "I need some information about a possible suspect, it's a face that's appeared here in Ruislip recently. A face I've seen before in Hammersmith," Boyle continued, "and Noel, he has a Dublin accent, although I believe he's from the North, somewhere near the border." Tommy hesitated. "Noel?"

"Yes Tommy?"

"He was in Dublin at the time of the murder you investigated."

"I see," Noel, said, his mind wandering back to that awful case. Mary McGrath, nineteen years old, a prostitute also, brutally murdered at such a tender age.

"Look Noel," Tommy broke Riordan's thoughts, "I've got a couple of days leave owing, thought perhaps I could pop over, providing they give me clearance, see what information you might have on this feller – work together on it if you like."

"Sure Tommy, what's his name?"

"Duffy…Sean Duffy."

Emily arrived at the church hall on her own. Duffy had called her office explaining that something had turned up; he'd join her later, if he could. Emily had taken the bus then waited a short while outside trying to decide if she should go in or not. It wasn't the done thing for a young lady to enter a dance on her own. Finally she made her mind up. "What the hell," she said, shrugging her shoulders as she entered the hall.

Emily handed her coat to the girl in the foyer, put the ticket into her handbag before entering the main hall. The dance was in full swing, the band playing a Glenn Miller tune. Nervously Emily's eyes darted to and fro, searching the mêlée for any sign of Christian or the others. Realising they were not on the dance floor, she made her way to the small room to the side of the floor which served as the bar area.

Emily spotted the group immediately. Christian's broad shoulders, filling his tunic perfectly, caught her eye. Christian was leaning on the bar, facing her, casually chatting to Freddie, probably about flying she decided looking at Cathy who was toying with her drink, obviously not part of the men's conversation. Christian saw her as she entered; he interrupted Freddie's conversation.

"Freddie, would you excuse me," he said not waiting for a reply. Christian moved towards Emily. He held out both his hands taking Emily's slender fingers in his, his eyes never leaving hers.

"Emily, I'm so glad you came." Christian kissed her cheek gently as he glanced over her shoulder, "Sean not here?" he asked.

"No, he phoned…something came up…he might be along later." She said before hesitating, "I hope you don't mind me being here, on my own…I don't want you to think…" She felt embarrassed, "I shouldn't have come…I should go…what must you think of me." Emily turned to leave.

"Not at all." Christian said, both hands gently on her shoulders. "I'm so glad you came, Emily." His voice was soft, gentle, and kind. Christian took Emily's hand, "May I?" he asked gently. Emily, re-assured, smiled a soft, girlish smile, her eyes sparkling, her heart beating so loudly that she was convinced Christian must be able to hear it. Christian stared at the girl, gone was the brashness, the cheeky, provocative barmaid, instead he saw the real Emily, a beautiful, shy, sensual young woman.

Emily was dressed in a pretty magnolia coloured print dress, patterned with tiny pink flowers. The dress exposed her bare shoulders, its bodice edged with delicate lace. A small gold heart shaped pendant nestled between the swell of her breasts, the gold chain disappearing into her wheat coloured hair, which waved gently to her shoulders. Christian's eyes followed her beauty; the dress was fitted to her waist before flowing over her hips, coming to rest just above her knee. The whole ensemble was finished off with tan coloured stockings, red shoes and a handbag to match.

Christian couldn't take his eyes off her she looked so beautiful.

"I'm sorry," he apologised, "I can't help it… I just can't take my eyes off you. You look so…so…"

Emily put a finger to his lips, touching them gently. "Don't Christian…don't apologise."

Christian looked all around nervously, sensing that everybody must be staring at them, they weren't. The noise of chattering came back to him. People were immersed in their own conversations, glasses chinked; laughter came from a corner near the bar. It was as if he'd been in a trance, then somebody had turned up the volume again.

"We had better get back to Freddie and Cathy, would you like a drink?" Christian asked, still captivated by the girl.

"Yes please, if I may." Emily smiled, "A martini."

"One martini coming up, madam." Christian took her hand, gently leading her to where their friends stood at the bar.

The four friends chatted happily at the bar for sometime, before taking their drinks into the dance area. Christian found a table close to the band. The bandleader sensed the mood of his audience, seeing the floor was packed with couples wanting nothing more than a chance to embrace. He signalled to the band to change the tempo, slow things down. The leader mouthed the name of a song to the players who noticed his command and began to play a slow dance tune. The dulcet sweet tones of Lavender Blue filled the room. Couples, singles who had surreptitiously glanced at each other, men who had spent all night trying to catch a girl's eye, girls who wished for recognition of their femininity, made their moves.

Much to Emily's delight, Christian made his.

"Emily, would you like to dance?" he asked. The confidence of his infatuation dispelling his natural shyness.

"I'd love to, Christian." The word Christian rolled off her tongue like a kiss. Christian took her hand, led her gently to the floor. He took her to him; their fingers interlocked like a carpenter's joint, together, his other hand on Emily's waist, just above the swell of her bottom. He touched the fabric of her cotton dress; sensing the pale skin beneath, felt her golden hair caressing his face. Emily reciprocated, her other hand on his firm broad shoulders, the material of his collar, the soft skin of his neck, as soft as a summer's wind to her touch.

They moved rhythmically to the music, dancing as one. They each felt the other's hot breath on their necks and hair. Christian pulled her gently but firmly closer to him; his groin felt the pressure of her thighs, as Emily responded. For them, at that moment, their bodies entwined, they were two lovers, two bodies as one.

They continued to dance long after the music had finished, noticing nothing except each other, as their hearts pounded in harmony, each guiltily expecting the other to notice. The noise of clapping a sign of recognition to the bandleader's intuitive selection of music brought them briefly back to reality, slowly from their secret place. Christian kissed her neck gently just before their faces parted.

Neither spoke, each captivated with a desire for each other, then returned to their friends. Small talk followed as both Emily and Christian held their eyes on each other, just as if the dance had been a dream, neither wishing to lose the moment. Neither listening properly to the conversation, regardless of whom it was directed at.

The music changed again, the audience controlled by the master with the baton, now gyrated to the jitterbug, couples swapping their partners for dances, as young couples do. The four friends did as the others had. Christian danced with Cathy, Freddie with Emily, Christian's eyes following her, hers following him.

"Listen, Christian," said Freddie. "Cathy and I are going to make a move, sorry to break up the party." Freddie winked at Christian. Both girls saw the glance and felt slightly embarrassed, yet both were grateful for the interruption.

"But how will you get back?" Christian asked.

"Don't worry old chap, Cathy's cadged a lift."

They said their goodbyes, each couple delighted with the compromise, but neither showing any sign. Christian took Emily's hand, guided her to the foyer, where they both picked up their respective coats and left.

Christian drove Emily to her home, a flat on the first floor of a semi-detached house in an attractive tree lined street. He parked the car, switched off the engine before sitting back in the leather of the driver's seat. They both sat silently, neither knowing what to do next. Like strangers or teenagers on a first date, their minds were racing, their bodies longing to touch, their mouths unable to speak.

Finally Christian made the first move. With his mouth and throat dry, he leaned toward Emily. She met him halfway, their faces only inches apart. Their eyes firmly fixed on each other's. Christian paused; he noticed her eyes close, moved his mouth to hers, felt the warmth of her lips on his. The two young lovers kissed, slowly, deeply, and beautifully.

"I...I'd better go Christian," Emily lied, not really wanting to spoil the moment, only her conscience persuading her to leave. "My landlady, she..."

"I understand Emily," Christian said as he kissed her again.

Christian got out of the car, went to Emily's side and opened the door; she smoothed her dress with her hands outlining the curve of her bottom as she exited. Christian walked her to the front door, where they both stood silently for a moment.

"I've had a wonderful night." Christian said softly.

"So have I." Emily breathed.

"I want to see you again Emily...soon... I can get Saturday off... perhaps we could go to the country...or the..."

Emily kissed her index finger before gently laying it on Christian's lips.

"I would do it sooner," he added excitedly, "but I've got night flying exercises to do, I could..." He didn't finish the sentence; her lips were on his again.

"Goodnight Christian," she whispered. Then she was gone.

Christian almost skipped back to the car. He started the engine then drove off towards Ruislip and his base at RAF Northolt, his heart filled with her whole being.

Sean Duffy stepped out from the hedge that had concealed him. He lit a cigarette, raised his eyes as he heard the curtains being pulled across the bedroom window where she slept. Duffy cursed under his breath. 'Jesus, girl, what are you doing to me?'

Duffy shrugged his shoulders, took one last look at the bedroom window, thought about Emily's naked body alone in her bed. Her thoughts not of him, but of the young handsome Polish pilot. Duffy pulled up the collar on his jacket as the light rain began to fall. Turning, he headed back to where he had parked the van, some distance away. By the time Duffy reached the Austin he was soaked by the heavy rain.

Tommy Boyle had received confirmation of his travel arrangements for his trip to Dublin. Scotland Yard had provided the dispensation he needed. It was a contented Boyle that slept that night, his loving wife asleep beside him.

Boyle took the train to Liverpool, which took ten hours due to the Luftwaffe's interruptions from the night before. The raids were infrequent these days; having received a bloody nose from the RAF they were more selective in their targeting. The object of the night's raid had been on the marshalling yards that handled the vast majority of the ordnance that was moving south, ready for the invasion. Tracks were strewn with rubble, engines were out of synch. Boyle slept when he could. The passage to Belfast on an ageing steamer which ran a shuttle service between Belfast and the mainland, delivering raw materials, carrying a few passengers for additional revenue was rough, sleep impossible, the threat of U boats constant.

He finally arrived in Belfast at six in the morning, waited for the eight thirty train to Dublin, actually boarding at ten thirty. The train seemed to stop at every station, spending forty-five minutes at the border alone, before it finally picked up speed once in the Irish Republic. Boyle stared out of the window; he had forgotten how simple and beautiful Ireland was. When he reached Dublin he took a taxi to a small hotel a couple of streets behind the south bank of the Liffey, registered, then went straight to his room, sleep beckoning.

At six thirty the following morning he woke, bathed, dressed then took a short invigorating walk along the banks of the Liffey. The weather was cloudy, rain threatened. The buildings, which followed the contours of the river as it cut thorough the capital on its endless rush to the sea, were grey, gaunt, and practical. Tommy selected a small café, breakfasted, then returned to his hotel. His thoughts now preoccupied with his meeting with Noel Riordan and the information he would gather on Sean Duffy.

The taxi pulled up outside the Irish police headquarters, after a brief wait Boyle was shown to the office of police inspector Noel Riordan.

"Tommy! How are you?" The welcome was warm, friendly. The men exchanged pleasantries shook hands and sat down to business.

"So what have you got on Duffy for me, then, Noel?"

"Quite a lot, Tommy." Riordan took out a buff folder, and opening it, began to read almost as if he was talking from a script, interjecting his own thoughts when he felt them relevant. "Sean Michael Duffy, born September 26th 1919. Father, Michael Patrick Duffy, served with the British Army in the Great War 1916-1918. Fought on the Somme, Passchendaele – mentioned in despatches. Joined the army of occupation until his demobilisation – met a girl, Marta Siegle who was married to a German Corporal. He was killed, by the way, Tommy at the Somme in 1916," Noel interjected before continuing his soliloquy, "She, Marta, was a Pole originally, a catholic. Michael Duffy paid her passage in 1919; arrived in Ireland in May of that year, they married the same month. Sean Michael Duffy was born in the September in County Armagh."

Riordan looked up from his reading, his eyes scanning Boyle's attention, before he spoke again. The next sentence was said with some degree of compassion. His father was killed by a British bullet during the troubles in Crossmaglen in 1920."

"Jesus!" Tommy said, "The Somme, Passchendaele, he went through all that only to be shot by what was, in effect, his own side, in his own country!"

"That explains a lot about Duffy's later life, Tommy, shall I go on?"

"Please Noel." Boyle shook his head at the irony of Duffy senior's death.

"Anyway, where was I? Oh yes…mother and son moved to Dublin same year. She took up a position as housekeeper to a wealthy couple on the South Bank. Duffy was educated at the Sacred Heart, then Dublin University. A degree, a first in history." Tommy raised an eyebrow at Riordan's disclosure. "He then seemed to go off the tracks a bit, spent a lot of time in the North of the city. A few misdemeanours, nothing serious. Then…and here's where it gets interesting, Tommy, believed to be recruited by the IRA whilst still at Dublin University. He's described as an avid supporter of the IRA, suspected in certain instances north of the border, on the RUC's wanted files. Duffy has an hatred of all things British…understandable when you think of his father." Tommy nodded in agreement. Riordan continued. "Disappeared in 1939. Believed to have gone to England."

"Was that before or after the death of Mary?" Boyle asked.

"After," Riordan said, "and Tommy, Duffy knew Mary, he was seen with her on several occasions."

"Was he a suspect?"

"Yes, very much so, but…we had no real evidence to hold him, nothing we could pin on him directly. Before you ask, Tommy," Riordan said noticing Boyle's body language, "yes, he's still a suspect. As you know, we have never closed the file on Mary's death, just like you with Molly's. As you are aware Tommy, the two murders were almost exact in detail. One more thing, Tommy."

"What, Noel?" Boyle looked directly into his friend's face, and did not like what he saw.

"We know for a fact Duffy was in Hammersmith at the time of Molly's death.

"The bastard." Boyle said as he sat back in his chair.

"Exactly!" Riordan said, then he leaned towards Boyle.

"What is it, Noel?" Boyle sat forward.

"Duffy's mother."

"Yes?"

"He despised her because…she had been a prostitute."

Boyle looked shocked at the revelation. "Molly, Mary…both"

"Yes," Riordan interrupted, "Molly and Mary were both prostitutes."

"My God, Emily!" Boyle said aloud.

Commander Peter Thompson RN was putting the final touches to the report he had complied for S.O.E. when the phone rang.

"Thompson." He answered.

"Sir, Operation HQ Italy has intercepted an American cipher that our US general friend is trying to transmit," said the voice on the other end of the line, "its in open sir," he continued.

"What's in it?" Demanded Thompson.

"Lot of non descript stuff but, and here's the interesting bit, he's complaining to the folks back home in Washington that he's got zero to do. Lots of senators on the list. Seems his Poles, two divisions at the ready, rest in reserve, total 50,000 troops are being held in reserve. Armour is being siphoned off to assist the American push. Wants pressure put on Roosevelt, Eisenhower and Monty to use him and the Poles more positively…Blimey sir!" The voice said.

"What?" Thompson asked.

"He's demanding to be used in the planning stages for the invasion, sir."

Thompson paused for a moment, thought hard then responded.

"Send it."

"Sir?"

"You heard me, send it."

"OK, if you say so sir…I'll send it for re-code." The voice added.

"No! Send it as it is."

"Yes...yes sir." The line when dead.

Thompson dialled a number.

"Ah, Tim, I've got a driver for you, he'll pick Lucien up on Sunday, usual time OK?" Thompson did not wait for an answer; he disconnected the line, then dialled again. "Put me through to 'C' will you? Ah, Sir, Thompson here, I've got something..."

British Intelligence was used to the Americans' naivety and disregard for proper channels. During the early part of the war, America, young, adventurous, brash even, had great belief in anything American and that unfortunately included their estimates of the enemy. Having never fought a major action against a sophisticated and resolute intelligence system, they assumed their ciphers were foolproof. British Intelligence knew better. During the early stages of the North African campaign, the British were in awe of Rommel – the desert fox seemed to anticipate everything the British tried, out manoeuvred them and hit at the weakest spot.

It wasn't until the Allied Command structure was brought under the control of a single headquarters staff, overseeing all of the different armies, nationalities, religions etc., together with their own localised HQ Staff that the mistakes were identified. Rommel wasn't the genius he was reported to be, quite simply he had just followed the mass of information German Naval Intelligence was sending him and altered his plans accordingly.

The Americans were guilty of sending all the data relevant to both their own and British dispositions, on open ciphers to the United States, and particularly Washington. Bletchley Park, the Allies' main code breaking centre, were able to identify the source of the leak and eventually to use it to their advantage, culminating with the defeat of the Afrika Korps in the Middle East. The main protagonist in this whole episode was an American Colonel who, when he was deemed no longer effective, was returned hastily to Washington, where he spent the rest of the war in a low priority desk job.

General Popowski's use of cipher (which he was unaware had been compromised, then used by British Intelligence with Eisenhower's full knowledge) was a carrot that Thompson hoped German Naval Intelligence could not refuse. Ernst Mosel in particular, as it had been Mosel's department that had broken and used the code so effectively in the earlier part of the war.

All Thompson could do now was sit and wait...

CHAPTER 4

Schloss felt more like a prisoner than a good German patriot, for patriot was how he saw himself.

Gunther Schloss was born in 1888 in a cottage hospital on the outskirts of Lubeck, a port on the northern shore of what was now Hitler's 1,000 year Reich. His German parents were wealthy and middle class. Gunther, the only child, was wilful and spoilt. He served with gallantry during the First World War, wounded twice, once by the Russians and once by the French. An Iron Cross, first class, an indication of his patriotism. He was to lose his parents in the great influenza epidemic that swept all Europe in the aftermath of the Great War.

Despondent in the aftermath of Germany's defeat, and reckless with his inheritance during the depression that gripped Germany during the post war years, Gunther sought passage to America, where he quickly settled down and became a teacher. In 1930 he was Professor of European Studies at Boston University.

He had a love and respect for his adopted country but in his heart he was German. With the outbreak of war in 1939, he had given up his professorship and returned to the Fatherland. Desperate to prove his loyalty he tried to enlist in every service and government department but was refused by all. He almost resigned himself to the fact that the new order had no place for an old veteran and hero until he received that fatal phone call.

His initial excitement at being chosen had lifted his soul, made him feel wanted, needed, and worthwhile – that initial euphoria had waned with reality. He was confined to a comfortable set of rooms but he could not go anywhere within the complex without armed guards. He could not speak to anyone within and was allowed no contact whatsoever with the outside world.

His day began at 7.30 with breakfast, then it was a tyrannical endurance briefing on all things American – latest films, stars, fashion, foodstuffs, Wall Street financials. If this wasn't enough to bear, he was forbidden to speak in his beloved German tongue, each transgression being dealt with by a punch to his body from a sombre, sadistic sergeant. He had to learn by heart the hierarchy of the Allied Command structure from photos, newsreels and the foreign press. Not only names, dispositions, characters, likes, dislikes but mannerisms, preferences and attitudes to all things.

This punishing routine was everyday until 10pm, only punctuated by meal breaks. The food, despite Germany's own rationing, was excellent, All-American, even the coffee. The one thing Americans do well, he thought, as nigh time brought sleep and relief. 'Just what in God's name did Naval Intelligence want from him?' Gunther Schloss thought bewilderedly every night. 'He was a good patriot,' he told himself repeatedly, yet his mind told him that he would betray something that was sacred to him, what? he did not know.

Major General Alexander Popowski was frustrated with his inactivity at the sharp end of this war. If things didn't happen soon the war would be over and just as in 1918 he would have missed the combat, the chance to lead men in action, yet again.

He had made a nuisance of himself at divisional, army and corps levels, pleading with everybody to give him the chance to prove himself. He had lobbied visiting officials and dignitaries at various functions. Explaining to anybody who would listen his plans for ending the war in 1944. General Alexander, as overall Allied Commander in the Italian campaign, found his work with the Poles professional, dedicated and at times inspirational, yet felt the man a bore.

The low priority use of the Polish divisions in combat led to Popowski's frustrations being viewed from above as bordering on insubordination. Montgomery, who Popowski respected, Eisenhower, Patton and the congenial Bradley were all back in the UK planning the great invasion of Europe against Hitler's Atlantic wall. Even if the Poles were finally to be used in adversity, Italy would still only be a sideshow.

His willingness to put his opinions and feelings of self-importance above his duties made him potentially a loose cannon. His direct lobbying of Eisenhower, Montgomery and now Washington made him dangerous. They would have to involve him even if only on the periphery, or replace him.

The open cipher picked up by British Intelligence and allowed to be transmitted would by a series of events and coincidences seal his fate. From that moment on Major General Alexander Popowski, United States Army; would have no say in his own destiny.

Christian Kawolski was a superb pilot; the Lysander was like an extension of himself, like a skin surrounding him. It didn't seem to worry him what type of aircraft he flew. The speedy, dynamic Spitfire, dependable Hurricane or the flimsy bi planes in Poland. Flying was second nature to him and the Lysander was an aeroplane, it was that simple.

Freddie was in awe of the man, at times genuinely frightened at the audacity of some of his approaches, if you could call them that. A steep dive, levelling out above the treetops, sudden dropping of wheels on the ground, coming to an absolute standstill in a matter of yards. Take offs below the normal rate of knots, tyres dismantling the newly formed foliage of treetops. This boy could fly anything, even tissue paper driven by a rubber band; if it had wings Kawolski could master it.

Christian was enjoying himself. Night flying brought no fear. Flying on instruments was a challenge, fun, excitement. He used his six main instruments as an extension of his feelings, to confirm what his senses were already telling him. He practised hard every night, using a small flying club's strip near Denham, just on the border of Middlesex and Buckinghamshire and on one occasion a short par three on a local golf course. That had earned Christian a ticking off from the station commander, and a sulk from Freddie who was a member.

When he wasn't flying, his thoughts were about Monica and his two daughters - Anna, who had only been a baby last time he saw her, and Maria. It saddened him sometimes when the pictures of their faces would not appear. He'd have to concentrate his mind so much that his temples pulsed. The image slowly came into focus, like a photograph slowly developing in a darkroom. When the visions finally came, it brought mixed emotions, relief and sadness. Then his vision would disappear, like a light being switched off, when the light was switched on again they were gone and Emily would appear.

Was it lust? Loneliness? Need for affection or something else? Could he love two women, really love two women at the same time? That question filled his thoughts, made proper sleep impossible. The only time Christian wasn't at odds with his conscious was when he was flying. Then the sole thing that mattered was his aircraft and his job. Not even Freddie, whom he liked very much, was relevant in the seat behind him; he was literally, just a passenger.

Mosel read the de-coded American cipher that Steiner had brought to him.

"Hans, it seems our goose is getting restless, this message he sent to Washington, it's fairly explicit."

"Surely that's good, sir." Steiner said.

"I'm not so sure Hans." Mosel looked troubled, "what Popowski is doing borders on insubordination, what if they replace him?"

"I think that's highly unlikely, sir." Steiner said encouragingly.

Mosel looked at the young man as a father might do to an enthusiastic son. "The confidence of youth," he said under his breath, just audible enough for Steiner to hear.

"Sir, if I may," Steiner hesitated, "Sir, Popowski's father has close ties to Roosevelt's government, he donated huge sums of money to get him elected, also he has many friends in powerful positions in Washington." Steiner could see he was getting through to his superior.

Mosel leaned forward to listen more closely to the young leutnant. Steiner continued with his thought process. "Popowski is an American staff officer, highly respected by Montgomery by all accounts, add to this the fact that he has had a remarkable effect on the morale of the Polish troops, taking them from a defeated rabble to a professional fighting force.

"Carry on, Hans."

"Well, sir, we know Montgomery, Eisenhower and Patton are in England, have been for some time. That can only mean one thing."

"The invasion." Mosel interrupted.

"Exactly sir, also we know most of the allies best troops have been withdrawn from the Italian front. Alexander is faced with a stalemate at Cassino, yet he hasn't used the Poles. According to our intelligence reports there are over 50,000 Poles behind the lines in Italy."

"What are you getting at Hans?"

"Sir, the British declared war due to the Polish question, they are morally bound by that declaration. The Polish government in exile have become frustrated at the opportunities the Polish troops have been given; they want their soldiers to be used to free Poland, not to be used piecemeal in what is essentially a sideshow. Add to that, sir, the fact that there are over five million Poles in America, most of them in Roosevelt's own back yard.

"I see, I see what you mean Hans." Mosel said his mind racing now. "The Poles will be brought back to England ready for the invasion, and Popowski, a Pole himself, will lead them."

"Yes sir, that's exactly what I think."

"Hans, what would I do without you?" Mosel smiled.

Commander Tim Brethwell, head of F section S.O.E. was a worried man. S.O.E. had been having a hard time of it recently; agents critical to the invasion had been compromised or rolled up by German Intelligence. The problem facing him now, with the invasion deep in the planning stages, was to replace those agents that had been lost, and above all to maintain security. Brethwell's adversary, the man responsible for all of his problems of late, was Captain Ernst Mosel. Somehow the wily old cruiser Captain seemed to outflank his every move. He was adamant that Mosel had been involved in the break up of the Victor network.

The network in question, run by one of S.O.E.'s best operators, had been lost in December 1943. Victor, real name Captain Charles Hockey, had been captured and executed by the S.D. His agents scattered or lost. S.O.E. should have seen it coming; security had been broken. Agents, operators and couriers had all disappeared, many on the actual drop zones. Phil Morrison, a radio operator, had tried to warn S.O.E. that all was not well. Morrison, probably under torture, had tried by the use of deception to warn his controller in London.

A young Wren radio officer, Florence Kirby, first noticed it. Florence had noticed a deliberate mistake in all of his transmissions since November 1943. She knew his touch, his fingerprint; it was different. She was convinced that Morrison was trying to warn her that something was wrong. Three successive drops were blown, Jerry was up to something and Morrison was the key. Florence reported the anomalies to her supervisor; however, her concerns were lost in the bureaucracy of the department that was in total confusion at the time.

The last report from the Victor network had omitted the mistake. Florence was now certain that the signature on the other end was different, a slight deviation in touch and speed. That could only mean one thing; the finger tapping out the code on the transmitter was not that of Phil Morrison. She reported her concerns again, this time going over the head of her supervisor, direct to Commander Tim Brethwell.

S.O.E. decided to test the possible security breach by sending a special code, one that was only to be used in an emergency. There was no reply. Morrison, despite his terrible suffering, had omitted to pass that information to his captors. A brave man he had died in the agony, not only of physical abuse, but also in the mental agony of knowing that S.O.E. had failed to heed his warnings. The Victor cell was disbanded immediately.

If the Lucien circuit, S.O.E.'s only other network in the invasion area, had also been compromised, the whole secret front, vital to disrupt the enemy during the landings would be in jeopardy. Brethwell had to know if Lucien was still intact, and to confirm that he would have to bring its leader, Henri Dacourt, back to London for interrogation. If Lucien had been compromised, was being used by Mosel, then S.O.E. would have to know now.

Brethwell signed the operational order to extract Lucien from France. All he needed now was a pilot of exceptional skill and courage to do it. The answer now lay in front of him, provided by of all people Commander Thompson S.I.S. MI6. But why? At the end of the day, Brethwell thought, what option did he have? He would have to take the offer MI6 had given him. He had to get Lucien out and this Polish pilot...Kawolski was his best bet, possibly his only option – he would have to trust him.

Duffy drove through the blackout to the White Hart public house in Hanwell, parking the van a couple of streets away. As he walked through the rain he looked toward the sky, low black clouds obscured the night. The rain became heavier; he pulled the collar up on his coat, feeling a rivulet of cold water run down his neck. "At least it will keep fat Goering's boys away," he mused, "but not the doodlebugs."

The pilotless flying bombs known officially as the V1, colloquially by the resilient Londoners as doodlebugs, which fell towards London day and night regardless of the weather. What a terrible way to go, he thought, not being able to see death – just the drone of an aircraft engine – then silence except for the multitude of prayers asking God to make it fall somewhere else, the anticipation, then....nothing.

It made him shiver. If he had to go, he hoped to God it was a bullet in the brain, a gun in his hand, enemy dead around him. The chamber devoid of shells, like a Viking or a hero in one of those Hollywood films. A wide grin spread across his face, done to death by a doodlebug in London! Now that, Sean, would be ironic.

He entered the noisy, bustling interior of the saloon, it was already full of customers, mainly Irish. A gaunt looking man seated in one corner played a penny whistle. Some of the crowd mouthing the words to the rebel tune, others tapping their feet. Thick blue smoke hung in the void between heads and the nicotine stained ceiling. Laughter from some corner, the chinking of glasses, a girlish giggle. His brain intercepting each perceptive sound, registering, analysing, aware. He identified the bar by the density of the throng and made his way through the mass of shoulders, and ordered a Guinness.

He waited until the dark liquid settled. He knew Cavenaugh's eyes were on him, sensed the stabbing pain of hatred between his shoulder blades. Duffy turned, identified an unoccupied table in the corner near the window. He negotiated his way through the milling human mass and seated himself facing the approaching bulk of Cavenaugh's frame. Cavenaugh's face betrayed the annoyance he was trying to conceal, he paused, forced a smile and made his way to the table.

"Sean, me lad, what brings you here on a night like this?" Cavenaugh spoke, trying to seem complacent.

"Well, I was just passing, and I thought why don't you pop in and see your friend Francis. See how life is treating him. Any how it would have been rude not to, since I was in the area." Duffy grinned.

"Cut the bullshit, Duffy. What the hell are you doing here?" Cavenaugh demanded, his face reddening with rage. "You know the rules, the procedure."

"Sorry Francis, did you not have time to get a Daily Mirror?" The sarcasm was evident.

He saw Cavenaugh make a fist, saw the eyes narrow. "Go on, just try it. Nothing would give me greater pleasure than to bust your ugly conceited head," Duffy said. Cavenaugh saw the animosity in the eyes and like the coward he was, he backed down, a false smile, a relaxing of the muscles, the fist going limp.

"Listen Sean, what is it? It's obviously important otherwise you wouldn't have broken security, come all this way in a bloody downpour." His voice trying to sound concerned, but failing miserably.

"It is important, Francis, we need to talk." There was seriousness in Duffy's voice.

"Here is fine," replied Cavenaugh, "we're among friends." He waved his hand, his head turning slightly. Duffy looked around him; nobody seemed to be taking any notice of the two men in the corner. The penny whistle man was in full flight, blowing on the haunting little instrument, his long and bony fingers doing a jig on the surface of the small silver tube, his feet tapping out the tempo. The crowd sang in chorus, "and the rifles crash to the echo of a Thomson gun."

He turned his eyes towards Cavenaugh, "It's the Polish flyer, Francis, he's gone operational." He let the statement sink in.

"What…when?" Cavenaugh stammered.

"I found out the other day, he had a bit of a celebration and told me they passed him ready for ops."

"Did he say when?"

"Yes, he let it slip, it's Sunday."

"This Sunday?" Cavenaugh became excited.

"Yes, probably briefing Sunday morning, take off about 1am and land in France before 3am. It will be quite dead by then, Jerry will be off his guard."

"Do we know where?" Cavenaugh was using the royal 'we'. The conceited fool, Duffy thought.

"My sources reckon north of Bordeaux, my guess is their going to pick up Lucien."

"And what sources are these?"

"That's on a need to know basis, Francis," Duffy's eyes narrowed, the intent clearly shown.

"But I'm your bloody controller! I've a right to know." Cavenaugh was agitated, off balance, hurt again.

"My sources are mine, and that's the way there going to stay, not you, not Dublin, not anybody will make me reveal them – do you understand Francis?" the voice was calm, forceful. The eyes menacing.

"But...but . . ."

"No buts, Francis," Duffy said flatly. He continued once Cavenaugh had calmed. "The Brits are getting nervy with Lucien... after the debacle with the Victor operation. It's understandable – they want him back, want to find out if he's safe, if the network is intact.

"But if they get him back, it's...it's . . ."

"They won't get him back."

Cavenaugh understood. "Poor bastard." He said quietly, almost sympathetically.

Duffy looked at Cavenaugh. Dublin's quartermaster in London. The Boss, The IRA's most potent weapon. A means to destroy the Brits' war. You're just a petty gangster, a pawn, and a glorified messenger boy...if you only knew. He broke the silence.

"Get details of our conversation to Dublin tonight. Get them to let Jerry know what's happening." The words came out as an order. Cavenaugh, deep in thought, accepted them as just that; unaware that it was Duffy that was controlling him.

"Yes...yes of course, I'll see to it straight away."

"And Francis . . .don't contact me, I'll contact you if I need to, understood?"

"Yes, Sean. Yes."

Duffy made to leave, content that the meeting was over. His control of Cavenaugh was complete. He stopped – the crowd were shouting the words to Molly Malone, the skeleton with the penny whistle blowing and sucking, his feet doing a jig under the table.

All of a sudden the volume became less audible, and trailed off into a murmur. A new sound filling the ears. Low, faint at first, slowly growing to a crescendo. The drone of a single aircraft engine. A sound they all recognised. Silence fell, except for the mumbling of an old woman saying her rosary, the beads flicking through her fingers. Suddenly she stopped, a look of horror on her face, as if she had been frozen in time. The engine had cut out.

People stared at the nicotined ceiling, muscles tensing, hearts pounding, the silence deafening now. They all felt the shudder, moments later heard the explosion as the warhead on the silent missile made contact. Windows rattled, a sudden wind slamming against them...realisation came slowly, but thankfully. The doodlebug had exploded some distance away; they were OK...safe...this time.

The penny whistle started to play. Throats were cleared, voices became audible again. Duffy cleared his own throat, swallowed the rest of the Guinness in one mouthful, pulled his coat tightly around him for security and left the pub. The rain was heavy now, almost a relief Duffy thought. The tinkling of an ambulance bell hurtling down the Uxbridge Road on its way to the scene of impact came to his ears, 'Jesus!' Duffy thought that was close.

CHAPTER 5

Tommy Boyle said his goodbyes to Noel Riordan at the station. Noel had commandeered a car to drive Tommy to meet his train, and both men used the opportunity to discuss the two murder cases. Boyle sat back in his seat as the locomotive began to pull away, the waving figure of Riordan fading as the train gathered speed. Noel had mentioned the name of another character that could have figured in the Dublin case, a criminal of some distinction. His name was Frankie Cavenaugh.

Cavenaugh, Noel told him, had known IRA connections. He was believed to have been the bagman for the north Dublin cell, collecting money from the various IRA rackets. That, Noel thought, would have brought Cavenaugh into contact with prostitutes and possibly Mary McGrath. Boyle had asked Riordan if he knew the whereabouts of Cavenaugh, but all Noel could tell him was that he had left Dublin about the same as Duffy. His new address was unknown. If Boyle could locate Cavenaugh, perhaps he might be able to assist him in his endeavours to catch the suspect in the Hammersmith murder.

The steam from the locomotive passed the window in intermittent puffs. The urban sprawl of Dublin began to fade, and fields dotted with small white stoned cottages came into view. Boyle leaned back into his seat, his mind now focussed on the long arduous journey ahead, before he drifted off to sleep.

Mosel received the de-coded message from the Rudy network in Dublin that morning. Fitful from lack of sleep, he had dressed early, his attention focussed on the never-ending stream of paperwork that passed through his officer every day. Steiner had brought the message to him as soon as it had been de-coded. Mosel smiled with satisfaction as he read the flimsy.

"British Intelligence have fallen for our plan, Hans, they're picking up Lucien on Monday morning, probably during early hours. Make all the necessary arrangements, will you?" Mosel hesitated for a moment, "and Hans?"

"Yes sir?"

"Make sure the S.D. Gestapo in particular get to hear about it, then proceed as planned."

"Yes sir," Steiner acknowledged, snapping to attention.

Mosel put his pen down and smiled "It's started." He said to himself, he picked up the pen again and continued to write.

Emily found it difficult to control her feelings, her heart fluttering every time she thought about Christian. Her work, normally of the highest standard, suffered, much to the annoyance of her boss. Emily had miss-directed calls, made basic typing errors then filed purchase ledgers in the sales ledger files. Infuriated, her boss had sent her to make the tea, re-type the letters, and, most of all, concentrate.

Emily pouted as she apologised to her boss, using her femininity to its full. The little girl look defused his anger. As she left the office he knew she had manipulated him. He fancied her and she knew it. She could wrap him around her little finger, as most pretty young girls could do to their elderly bosses. Her boss knew he would never sack her; Emily was the best thing that had happened to the small business. Everybody, staff and customers alike all adored her, so did he.

She wanted, needed to see Christian now, today. She couldn't wait until Saturday and her boss reluctantly gave her permission to call Christian at Northolt. Emily telephoned the airfield and was put through to the adjutant's office. The adjutant had explained to her that Christian was unable to come to the phone. He could not be disturbed, however, he did agree to help by leaving a message for Christian, telling him that Emily had called. She thanked him for his understanding, gave him the details then thanked him again.

"Don't worry, miss," The adjutant had assured her. "I'll make sure he gets the message."

At lunchtime Emily made her way to the Plough, this time without her friend. Emily ordered a lemonade, taking the drink outside she selected a table in the garden facing Bury Street. She sat down, her thoughts of Christian.

Ten minutes passed without distraction save for the persistence of a wasp, which was scavenging for food to take back to its hungry grubs. Emily watched as the wasp settled on a droplet of spilled lemonade. Picking up a beer mat, her hand hovered over the annoying insect; she was just about to swat it when a hand appeared over her shoulder. Emily looked up and Christian's hand came down on the unsuspecting insect, squashing it.

"Christian." She almost shouted as she sprang to her feet.

"I thought it was bothering you," he smiled.

"My hero," she giggled as she almost jumped into his arms, planting a huge kiss on Christian's mouth as she did so. "Oh, Christian, I'm so glad you could come." A happy smile spread across her face.

"I can't stay long, I've got to get back to the base."

"Not to worry, just as long as you're here now." Emily's smiled faded, but her eyes didn't. "Oh, Christian, I've missed you so much."

"I've missed you too, Em." Emily hated people calling her Em, but when Christian said it, it was like candyfloss at a fair, sweet and exciting.

They sat down facing each other, her hands in his, their eyes locked on to each other.

"Oh, I'm so happy…just being with you…it does funny things to me." Emily smiled. "You must think I'm a silly girl, but I just can't help it. Christian," Emily continued. "I think I'm…"

Christian touched her lips gently with his finger, 'don't say it Em, not here…not now." Christian took Emily's hands in his; gently he kissed each one in turn. His eyes went to hers; he saw the hurt in them. Emily's eyes began to moisten, a small tear formed. Christian watched as the tear hung desperately to the lashes that outlined the huge blue eyes. He saw it loose its fight with gravity, fall then roll gently down her cheek. Christian was annoyed with himself; he had done the one thing he had tried to avoid. He'd upset her, hurt her.

"I feel the same about you, Em," Christian said honestly, hoping the guilt he felt about Monica and the girls, which were eating away at his insides, didn't show. His hands gently cupped Emily's face, his mouth, his lips catching the runaway tear, the soft salty taste filling his senses.

"Let's go for a walk." He whispered.

"OK," Emily said quietly.

They walked silently hand in hand, as they stepped into the dark woods they looked up at the sunlight peeping through the canopy of tress, glistening and twinkling like stars. The sun, when they came to a break in the trees was unusually warm for the time of year. Gently it caressed any exposed skin. The bluebells littered the ground. Daffodils, risking the threat of a late frost, opened their petals like the arms of lovers, while bees, gratefully accepting the gesture buzzed frantically above the sweet smelling pollen.

Christian touched Emily's hand, she turned to face him, her head slightly bent, her eyes lowered towards the ground, her foot nervously digging at the soft soil. Christian put his finger gently under her chin; slowly he raised her face until their eyes met. Emily could see Christian was about to say something important. Deep down she knew it was going to hurt.

"Emily…I have to tell you something." He hesitated; the words were slow to come. "This isn't easy for me." Emily could see the distress in his eyes, she tensed waiting for the bombshell that would shatter all her feelings, destroy her. "Emily, I can't go on like this, it's tearing me apart, I have to tell you the truth."

"You're married." Emily said softly.

"How…how did you know…what made you…?" Christian was lost for words.

"I knew you were married, well, guessed. I'm not some stupid little girl with a crush, Christian, I'm a woman." She said firmly, the hurt evident.

"Is it so obvious?" Christian asked.

"Afraid so. It came to me while I was waiting for you. A handsome man, a pilot, a bloody hero to boot, you just had to be married. Your eyes confirmed it just a few moments ago."

Emily turned to face away, the tears began to form. Christian turned her head back towards him. He looked deeply into her eyes, watching the tears roll down her cheeks. He gently leaned forward to kiss them. He felt her body tremble as he pulled her close to him. She responded, and he held her tightly for a moment before pulling away to face her.

"I'm so sorry Emily…I didn't try to deceive you…I didn't mean to fall…" the words trailed off. Emily looked into his eyes and saw the honesty there.

"Christian," the way she said his name was so tender, so loving. "Christian, it doesn't matter." She kissed him softly on the mouth.

"There's more Em." Christian said. Her body shivered as he said her name.

"What?" she asked as she kissed his neck and ear lobes.

"I've got two children, girls, five and seven years old." The words were almost blurted out.

Emily pulled back from him, the shock registering.

"Oh, I see…I see." She spoke softly.

"That's just it, you don't," he said. "I love Monica and the girls but…but I love you too Emily. I just can't help it…I'm so sorry." Christian turned to go.

"Wait, wait." Emily said. "Christian I love you too, don't you know that. I have never loved anyone the way I love you, Oh, Christian." Emily ran to him. Christian hugged her tightly, her breasts flattened against his chest. They stood silently hugging each other for a moment both their necks damp with tears. Neither speaking. A squirrel watched inquisitively from a tree.

Eventually, after what seemed an eternity, they parted, kissed and began walking back the way they had come; their hands intermingled. Emily stopped, turned to Christian and spoke.

"Christian, you and I are now, this war is now, let's just live what time we have together…for the now, when it's all over. . . " She paused, her lips trembling,

"I'll understand…till then its just you and me, we love each other, lets just enjoy the moment."

"Yes, Em." He knew she was right; she was brave and strong where he had been a coward, weak. He held her hand as they left the woods.

Major General 'Popeye' Popowski was in the Polish army group divisional headquarters far behind the Rapido River and the Monte Cassino front line. The Allied armies - predominately British and American - under the command of Alexander, were stuck in a ferocious stalemate in Southern Italy that spring morning. Anzio had failed in its objective as an operation, the hammer against the anvil vision for crushing the majority of the German army in Italy was in tatters, the belligerents were facing a war of attrition in the mountains and river valleys.

He was putting the finishing touches to yet another cipher, this one to some Senator friends of his father when his aid entered.

"What is it, Thomas?" he said in Polish.

"There's a jeep outside General, Alexander wants to see you at his headquarters now, sir."

During the journey he sat in the front of the jeep, he wiled away the time by imaging he was an Emperor, a Caesar, reviewing his troops. He saluted every soldier he saw, grinning hugely at the weary men, who when he had passed swore under their breathes at the skiving staff officer.

By the time he reached Alexander's headquarters his initial euphoria had waned. The early spring thaw, the rain torrents, followed by the inevitable hot sun, had turned the tracks into nothing more than ruts in hard mud. The jeep had bounced and banged its way through the valleys like some obscure ride at a fair. His thoughts at that moment were exactly at one with Alexander's, namely what to do with the pain in the ass.

General Alexander was seated at his desk, a myriad of reports from the front lay before him. Popowski entered the sparsely occupied room, noticed the pile of data the man behind the desk was attending to. He had no animosity towards Alexander or the Limeys, they had after all, stood up to Hitler alone for over two years. He had tremendous respect for Montgomery, had seen his abilities, his dedication, his regard for his troops, more importantly, he had regard for their lives. Meticulous to the point of frustration he was a thorn in the side of Eisenhower, Churchill and most of all Patton. Eisenhower, ever the diplomat, rode a very fine line between appeasement and bullying – with Patton and to some extent Bradley and Roosevelt on one side, Montgomery and Churchill on the other.

To Popowski, Alexander was of the same ilk as Montgomery. Too much Britishness on one side, a soldier's soldier on the other.

"Sir, you asked to see me?" It was Popowski who broke the silence.

"General Popowski, so good of you to come." He stood to greet the American officer, his handshake firm and honest. "Please take a seat." Popowski obliged. "Would you care for some refreshment after your journey?"

"No thanks, General, I'm fine."

"Good, good. You're probably wondering why I asked you to come all this way?"

"The thought had crossed my mind." Popowski smiled a toothy smile, gone was the brashness, the gung ho attitude he had displayed to his aide Thomas. He was after all in the presence of his commanding officer, overall Allied Commander in Italy.

"Yes, quite so. Your men, the Poles, what's your impression of them?"

"As a people or as a fighting unit, sir?" Popowski had slipped back into the role of the professional soldier with consummate ease.

"Both."

"Well, as a people and as a fighting unit they're basically the same, sir. Proud, brave, tenacious and above all, they have a hatred of Germans, Nazis and all things German – they invaded their country, sir."

"Yes quite, I suppose neither of our countries know what that feels like." Responded Alexander honestly.

"If you're asking me can they fight, the answer is yes. They've already proved that on many occasions in this war. If you're asking will they fight? The answer is yes, anywhere there's a German, the Poles will go. If…" He hesitated, giving time for Alexander to fully appreciate his next statement for it was as important to him as it was to the whole Polish nation. "If you're asking how should they fight? Then the answer is simple sir…as a unit, as a nation under Polish officers, under a Polish flag."

"I see." Alexander was thoughtful. "Yes I really do see."

Popowski sat back in his chair, so far, so good, he thought.

"They're ready?" It was Alexander again.

"They're ready, sir, in fact they're over ready, sir."

"What do you mean?" The British general asked.

"Sir…the way the Poles feel right now, they've got to get into this war, and into it properly. They're desperate to fight and kill the Nazis, but they've got to do it as Poles, sir, otherwise they feel like their letting the folks back home down. That could lead to a loss of morale, sir."

"Will it?" asked Alexander.

"It will unless we give them a job sir. A Polish job sir."

"I see, yes…yes I think you're right, General Popowski." Alexander was analysing the information he had been given, before moving to the next part of his rationale in sending for Popowski.

The man had been frank, honest and sincere. Now was the time to build upon the confidence before achieving the other reason for the meeting – to bring Popowski back into line – before the whole thing became too political.

"General Popowski."

"Sir."

"It seems Monty's fairly keen to have you back in the UK." He let the statement sink in before continuing. "As you know Monty's heavily involved in the planning of the invasion of Northern Europe. He, like myself, has the utmost respect for your professionalism, he's been delighted with your inside knowledge, together with the excellent work you have done with the Poles. My feeling is he could send for you at any moment."

"Sir," Popowski was dumbfounded. Alexander's subtle pandering was working on the American. "Almost a certainty, I would say." Alexander paused. "Look Popeye, I don't want to lose you and I don't want to lose the Poles. You're right, they are good soldiers and God only knows I've lost most of our best units, British and American, to Monty. I can't afford to lose either of you, not if I'm going to beat Jerry in Italy before the summer."

Popowski was elated by what he was hearing. Alexander continued.

"We need to bring the two Polish divisions up to the line." Alexander, ever the skilful commander, could see the effects he was having on the man opposite.

"There's a bit of a show, an attack being planned at the moment, mainly an American affair in the west. The British units to the east will act as a diversion to the main US thrust." Alexander paused yet again; it was imperative that he let Popowski down gently.

"We've got to fool Jerry into thinking that our troops are still massed in the Cassino area and for that we need you and your Poles." He could see Popowski's whole body deflate. "Personally I don't have too much hope for this plan, it's been tried before and failed. That's where you come in."

"Sir?"

"What we're going to need, and soon, is fresh troops, experienced officers and men, to play a significant role in defeating Jerry at the right place and at the right time, that General Popowski is Cassino. I plan to give you the monastery itself."

The balloon had been re-inflated, now was the time to put down any insurrection by the American.

"Putting the Poles into the line now will give them the opportunity to familiarise themselves with the objective, bloody them so to speak, but, more importantly, allow them to punch a hole right where Jerry won't like it." He let Popowski wallow in the glory a little before delivering his vital sentence, before bringing the war back into line. 'Of course, if Monty takes you back to England before…or if your government or Eisenhower judge your ciphers to Washington of late to be politically incorrect…maybe you could be back in Washington… and that's no good to me, Monty, you or the Poles."

He'd done it, the man was cornered, he had a choice, toe the line, be professional, a chance of possible glory, an opportunity to serve not only his adopted but also his birth nation, or to be sent back to the US to live out his career in total obscurity…he knew which way the man would respond.

Cavenaugh was delighted by the news from Dublin; the Germans were convinced that the information sent by Duffy was of the highest quality. In return, a new shipment of merchandise had been authorised, and the submarine would land the goods as soon as Mosel confirmed that the pigeon was safely in their hands.

What had excited Cavenaugh more than Dublin's praise was the appendage that followed the communiqué. Duffy was in serious trouble. One of the IRA's men, a mole in Irish Special Branch, had information that a British policeman was interested in Duffy's movements. They suspected that Duffy had been complicit in the murders of two prostitutes, one in Dublin and one in Hammersmith in 1939. Duffy had known both women and had been in situ at the time. Dublin demanded that Duffy be protected. The operation concerning the Polish pilot, Mosel's requirements, and above all the shipment of the merchandise, must not be compromised.

Cavenaugh laughed aloud, he had Duffy just where he wanted him, under his control. Cavenaugh knew he could call the tune, Duffy would need him. He smiled to himself, if he could pressurise Duffy it could leave the way open for Cavenaugh to pursue his interest in the pretty girl Duffy had in tow…what was her name? Ah, Emily, that was it, and a prostitute to boot. Cavenaugh's mouth spread in an evil smirk.

Duffy had his own problems that day. Arriving early as usual, he had discovered that one of the milkmen had called in – following a death in his family, he would be unable to do his round today. Duffy swore, since he would have to do the man's round.

By the time Duffy returned from the round it was midday. He made his way to his office to start on his normal tasks. As he entered he found a suited stranger in his chair.

"Who the hell are you?" Duffy demanded, still tired from his exploits on the round.

"My name's Henshaw…Head office…sorry, your chair." The suit pointed to Duffy's chair as he rose from behind the desk. "Sorry to arrive unannounced." He continued, "your secretary told me to wait in here, I understand you've been out on the rounds."

"Yes, we're a man down today, what can I do for you Mr…"

"Henshaw, Barry Henshaw." The suited man put out his hand.

"Henshaw…I haven't heard of you before." Duffy said ignoring the hand.

"No, no you probably haven't, I'm new, only been in the job a couple of weeks. I thought I ought to visit the local branches, get in at the deep end."

Where were you before?" Duffy asked as he sat behind his desk.

"Oh, er.er, United Dairies actually." He replied.

"So what can I do for you, Mr. Henshaw…Barry?" Duffy smiled.

"Er, um…nothing at the moment," the suit replied, "your secretary was most helpful…I just wanted to introduce myself…well I must get on." The suit said, nervous now.

"Must go, others to see…you know the form…well it's been good to meet you, Mr Duffy."

"You too, Mr Henshaw, Barry. Now if you will excuse me?" Duffy said, "I must get on, a mountain of paperwork, you know how it is Barry."

"Yes of course, well goodbye, Mr…"

"Duffy, Sean Duffy." Duffy watched as the suit stumbled out of the office.

Duffy was confused. "Think, Sean, think." He looked at his desk, and saw something was wrong. The paperwork had been moved, not put back in the correct order. Duffy checked the drawer. It was still locked.

Duffy's secretary was still at lunch. The old witch had probably shopped him to head office, Cavenaugh and his bloody meetings, that's probably why the old hag had done it Duffy told himself. He picked up the phone and dialled head office.

"Hello, Rawlingson's Dairies." The voice answered.

"Hello, you don't know me," Duffy lied, "but one of your managers…a Mr Henshaw, Barry Henshaw has left his briefcase in the back of my cab."

"Hold the line please." Duffy waited. "Hello." The voice came back. "I'm sorry we do not have a Mr. Henshaw, no one of that name works for Rawlingson's Dairies, could anyone else help?"

"No, no that's alright, probably my mistake…thank you." Duffy disconnected the call. He flicked through the telephone book. He found the number he wanted and dialled.

"Hello, United Dairies, Maureen speaking, how can I help?"

"Barry Henshaw, please." There was a short pause.

"Sorry sir, no Mr Henshaw listed."

"Oh, he left a couple of weeks ago, sorry my mistake, I forgot." Duffy lied.

"Well, I've been here for five years sir, I've never heard of any Mr Hen…" He put the phone down. Duffy sat deep in thought; he tried to find some logical explanation. A dreadful thought came to Duffy. He sprang to his feet and went to the loose panel behind the paraffin heater, searching the void – it was empty. The diary, all the information he had sent to Dublin was gone.

Emily was wiping some glasses when Boyle arrived.

"Hello Tommy…usual?" she smiled brightly.

"Yes please, Emily."

Boyle still tired from travelling, noticed something different about the girl. Twenty years in the force had taught him to notice things. What Boyle saw was a change. Gone were the provocative blouses, tight skirts, and high heels. That wasn't all; Emily's whole demeanour had changed. Gone was the tarty attitude, in its place a new image. The girl next door, a beautiful daughter, the sort of daughter any parent would be proud of.

Her hair was fresh, bright, the colour of corn. Her make up virtually non-existent. Her teeth white like ocean spray, surrounded by coral lips. Her smile like sunshine. Emily had changed, or somebody or something had made her change herself. Tommy Boyle took his pint to the usual spot, opened his newspaper and took out his pen ready for his Friday night vigil.

It didn't take long for the pub to fill. Virtually every customer that came in complimented Emily, the perceptive ones like Boyle realising that this was the real Emily. Every time the door opened both Boyle and Emily would look up. If it was obvious to Boyle that Emily was waiting for somebody to turn up, then to an onlooker, Boyle would appear the same. Boyle would have to be more professional, more careful.

Duffy arrived later than usual; as he entered Emily looked up and saw the huge grin. Slightly disappointed, she half smiled. Duffy noticed, he was slightly taken aback, hurt. By the time he'd made his way through the crowd to his normal place by the till. Duffy's pint was settling on the bar.

"Good evening, and how are you, darling Emily?" Duffy smiled to restore his pride.

"I'm fine Sean, thanks." Emily held out her hand for the money.

Duffy counted out the coins, passing Emily the correct amount.

"You look different tonight, Emily."

"Oh, really?" she said, the smile she gave him was still edged with disappointment.

"Don't get me wrong girl, this fool is saying you look beautiful, no more beautiful."

"Thanks, Sean." She answered sweetly as she turned on her heels to serve another customer, the wiggle not on show.

"Yes, sir, what can I get you?"

Duffy watched her as she served the customer, "She's in love and not with you, Sean." He told himself. Duffy picked up the stout, sipping the bitter tasting liquid. His mind on Emily: He'd lost her and he knew it.

Duffy saw Emily's expression change, something was wrong. Emily stood frozen, as if turned to stone, gone was the cheerful smile, the sparkle in her eyes. Emily's face showed disgust, her eyes narrowed, the pupil's smaller. Duffy had seen that look many times in his life, it was hatred. Duffy turned to identify the source of her hate. Standing in the doorway, the familiar stocky figure, the smug smile, framed by two mountains of beef, was Cavenaugh. Cavenaugh saw Duffy and with the aid of his two minders he pushed his way to the bar. Duffy felt the anger rise within.

"Sean, how are you?"

"Francis."

"You know Porrick, Seamus."

"Yes."

The two thugs nodded toward Duffy - probably all they were capable of, Duffy thought.

"What do you have to do to get a drink in this joint?" Cavenaugh spat, now in his gangster role.

It was Emily who spoke next. "Just ask politely…the way other people, human beings would." She said, her voice sharp, curt.

"And what if I don't" Cavenaugh's words were a threat.

"Then I'll bar you!" Emily said with conviction.

"Why my dear, sweet Emily," Cavenaugh's tone was nasty. "My, my, haven't we grown up," he continued, "and dressed like a lady to boot, business must be good these days, how's your back."

"You bastard!" Emily spat under her breath just audible enough for those in the immediate vicinity to hear.

"You little whore." Cavenaugh was rattled, "You little…"

"Cut it! Francis," Duffy interjected.

Cavenaugh turned to face Duffy. His eyes quickly checked to see if Porrick or Seamus were close.

"What did you say?"

"You heard me Francis." Duffy sniped.

Cavenaugh was indignant. He was about to emphasise his annoyance when he saw the look in Duffy's eyes. The look that any man might see only once in his life, the look that tells him he's about to die. Cavenaugh backed down.

"Sure I was only having a craic, Sean." Cavanaugh's eyes went to his two gorillas for support, they smirked in unison. Cavenaugh turned to face Duffy again. He saw the mood, his eyes flicked toward Emily. "Emily, my dear, my sincere apologises…drinks on me, and one for yourself, Emily." He said like an outsider trying to impress strangers, except that Emily and Duffy weren't strangers.

The drinks arrived, although Emily had declined. The conversation with time became less tense, almost pally. Emily was not impressed. Tommy Boyle having seen enough, left unnoticed by all, just as he had wanted. In his newspaper by the side of the crossword, Boyle had written three names joined by an arrow. Duffy – Cavenaugh – Emily. There was a fourth name, Christian Kawolski – pilot.

The conversation, assisted by the alcohol, became more pub-like, more ribald. Only the two gorillas remained impassive. Duffy had noticed the copious amount of alcohol consumed by Cavenaugh. It's only a matter of time, he thought. Nature took course, Cavenaugh's bladder was full, and he needed to empty it.

Cavenaugh almost stumbled as he got off his barstool. He made his way gingerly towards the toilets that were situated at the rear of the public house. Duffy feigning drunkenness, staggered after the stocky frame of the departing Cavenaugh. He glanced over his shoulder towards Porrick and Seamus.

"I'd better go after him boys, in his state he might fall." Duffy slurred.

Porrick made a move, Seamus put his arm in front of him, his look telling Porrick to wait, see what happens. Both minders remained where they were, their eyes firmly fixed on Duffy as he rounded the bar and staggered down the three steps to the toilets. All the time he could feel the two pairs of eyes on his back.

When he was out of sight, Duffy straightened himself, then followed Cavenaugh into the Gents. When Duffy opened the door he saw the struggling Cavenaugh.

"Frankie, fancy meeting you here." Duffy giggled, closing the door and sliding the bolt unnoticed.

He sidled up to Cavenaugh who was desperately trying to undo the fly buttons on his trousers. Duffy saw Cavenaugh was off balance, pre-occupied. He moved quickly, his fist slammed into Cavenaugh's stomach. Phlegm exploded from Cavenaugh's mouth. Shock, pain, all came at once. Cavenaugh's knees buckled under him, and he began to drop. In a single movement, Duffy grabbed his lapels and held the huge weight. Lifting the torso at the same time, he slammed Cavenaugh into the tiled wall.

"What the Feck are you doing here, Francis? I told you not to contact me, I would contact you." There was no disputing the venom in Duffy's voice.

"Dublin." Cavenaugh spluttered. The agony in his stomach spreading, intensifying.

Duffy eased the grip, allowing Cavenaugh's feet to touch the ground.

"What about Dublin?"

"They told me to keep…keep a close eye on you."

"Why?" demanded Duffy.

"This thing with the p…pilot…Jerry…Dublin's convinced its big…I'm supposed to keep a watch on you…protect you…make sure you're OK."

"So that's why you brought those two gorillas with you?" Duffy released his grip.

"Yes, yes…for your protection, Sean." Cavenaugh wiped the spittle from his mouth.

"I don't need protection, not from you. not from Dublin, and certainly not from those two goons you brought here tonight, do you understand Francis?"

"Yes Sean, yes… . . But Dublin."

"No buts, Francis." Duffy straightened Cavenaugh's clothes, looked down at the large wet patch on Cavenaugh's trousers and tutted, "I think you've had an accident Francis," He grinned.

Cavenaugh had just about regained some composure when Duffy spoke again.

"Oh, and Francis…"

"What?" Cavenaugh spat.

The words had barely left his mouth when his vision became blurred just as Duffy's fist smashed into his face. Cavenaugh felt the impact, the flow of blood and heard the bone disintegrate. He knew his feet were no longer in touch with the ground and that the solid tiled wall would break his fall, his back and head impacting first.

"That's for Emily," Cavenaugh heard Duffy say, then the blackness came.

Duffy slid open the bolt on the door. He sat Cavenaugh up, his back against the wall. Duffy took some of the oozing blood and smeared in on the tiled wall. When he had finished he took a towel, poured cold water on it and proceeded to wipe Cavenaugh's face. The door burst open and the two minders filled the frame.

"Lads, lads I'm glad to see you. Frankie's had an accident, slipped on somebody's piss, smashed his poor nose on the wall, how unlucky can you get?' Duffy slurred pretending to be the drunk again. Seamus and Porrick studied the scene, hesitating just long enough for credibility to sink in. The blood on the wall, the wet patch, Duffy attending to the stricken Cavenaugh sympathetically. No sign of a weapon…it looked plausible.

"I thought he'd drunk too much but this…poor, poor Frankie. Listen guys," Duffy continued, "give me a hand to get him up."

The two gorillas still confused, obliged.

"Better take him home or maybe to hospital, that nose, I think he may have broken it when he slipped."

Duffy outlined the course of events that must have led to Cavenaugh's unfortunate accident. Seamus and Porrick eyed each other; Seamus shrugged his shoulders, Porrick nodded. The two huge men lifted Cavenaugh with ease, carrying the still unconscious Frankie to their waiting car.

"Bye- bye, fellers. I hope you feel better Frankie. What a shame we were having such a good time," Duffy grinned, his face showing only pretend concern.

When they had gone, Duffy returned to the bar, sitting on the vacant bar stool, he ordered a scotch. When Emily returned with the drink Duffy downed it in one.

"Where are your friends?' Emily said with contempt.

"Oh, they've gone…poor Frankie had an accident, he slipped, I think his poor nose is broken." Emily looked at Duffy, her eyes quizzing his doubtful sincerity. Emily's eyes went to Duffy's hands and she saw the grazed knuckles. She knew then what had happened. She smiled at Duffy, a knowing smile, a thank you.

"I could have handled it you know."

"Like you did a couple of years ago," Duffy snapped.

"That was different, I was different…I was naïve, he took advantage."

"He could have killed you, Emily."

"I know, Sean, I know."

"He's still dangerous. You need to take care girl, people like Cavenaugh don't forget."

"Yes, yes you're right Sean, thank you…have that one on me." Emily knew Duffy had saved her again, just like he always did. She felt ashamed of her treatment of him, he deserved better.

"I'd be telling a lie if I said it wasn't a pleasure, anyway, enough of him, get me a pint would you sweetheart, I suddenly have a terrible thirst," He grinned.

Emily leant over the counter and kissed Duffy gently.

"Thanks, Sean." She smiled, then went to get his pint.

Duffy studied her; Emily was beautiful. He wanted to tell her, show her how he really felt but he couldn't. "Jesus, girl, what are you doing to me," He whispered.

When they left that night there was no lovemaking, just a cuddle and a kiss, like a brother and sister parting. Emily was in love – but not with Sean Duffy. He'd blown it, lost her and in his heart he knew it.

CHAPTER 6

Like Mosel, Commander Thompson was also at his desk that morning, trying to make sense of the information in front of him. Mosel was up to something and something big. Before he drew any conclusions he wanted to go through everything again.

The intercom sounded.

"Yes, Grace,"

"Harry Milburn to see you sir."

"Thanks Grace, send him in."

"Commander, you sent for me." Milburn said as he closed the door.

"Yes Harry, come in, take a seat, how's Nick's head by the way."

"He's still a bit sore, sir, seems he took a bit of a whack."

"Listen Harry," Thompson, the nicety over was back on track. "I've been going over all the information we have. Something's missing, I'd like you to give me your impression."

"Well, sir. Let's start with what we have already, Cavenaugh is the IRA's quartermaster in London, Nasty piece of work, came over in '39, based in Hammersmith. Moved to Hanwell in 1940."

"There's a fairly large Irish influence in Hanwell?" Thompson asked.

"Yes sir, seems Cavenaugh likes to be surrounded by his own kind."

"A face in the crowd?"

"Yes sir, exactly, well as I was saying, he's based in Hanwell. We've pushed some fairly useless stuff his way, nothing of substance, until…"

"Carry on Harry."

"Well, as you know sir, everything Dublin gets, it passes on to the Rudy network, from there direct to Mosel. The IRA were getting a bit desperate for something good to give Jerry. Supplies of weapons, ammunition, merchandise as Dublin calls it, were drying up. Mosel put a stop on any further transactions, then we received a communiqué about a Polish pilot, Christian Kawolski, Hero in the Battle of Britain, DFC shot down in 1942. Returned to active duty this month after a long convalescence."

"And Mosel gets interested?" questioned Thompson.

"Yes sir, activity between Dublin and Mosel's department goes into overdrive."

"Why."

"He's a Lysander pilot now, sir, dropping S.O.E. agents into France and the Low Countries. SOE have lost a lot of agents recently, we know about the Victor network, got our suspicions about Lucien. SOE has too, sir."

"So why is Mosel interested then, Harry?" Thompson was leading the man on.

"Well, he's an expert pilot, can fly anything. Takes risks. Too many according to those that know him. S.O.E. want Lucien home – want to find out what's going on. They can't afford another Victor scenario, especially with the invasion imminent. Seems he's the best man for the job."

"So back to Mosel." Thompson gave Harry time to think.

"Well, sir, we've suspected Lucien for sometime. Jerry seems to be one jump ahead of S.O.E. we reckon Mosel's turned him.

"Good, Harry, continue."

"Well, Mosel won't want to lose Lucien to S.O.E., not now."

"What would you do if you were Mosel, Harry?"

"I'd pick up Lucien and the Polish pilot, sir."

"Then S.O.E. would know for definite that there's a leak?" Thompson was guiding the man, "come on Harry, think," he said to himself.

"Yes, I see what you're getting at, sir, if I was Mosel I would have to fool S.O.E. into thinking that the Lucien cell is still OK."

"What would you do then, Harry?"

"Kill Lucien…make him into some sort of hero." He said matter of factly.

"My thoughts exactly, Harry…" Thompson hesitated let the information sink in, before continuing, "what else have we got?"

"Well sir, we know Cavenaugh has to have an operator, that's close in someway to this Polish pilot."

"Who have we got in the frame?"

"Sean Duffy, sir, has known IRA connections. His father was shot by the Black and Tans on the border in 1920. He moved to Hammersmith in 1939 and on to Ruislip in 1940. Has a job as a manager at Rawlingson's Dairies in Northolt.

"Why him? This Duffy chap."

"Most of the information Cavenaugh's put across to Dublin recently is about the Polish pilot. Checking back, Dublin's been getting a steady flow of reports regarding aircraft and personnel movements at Northolt airbase, most of it about squadrons, numbers based at Northolt, sir." He waited seeing if his boss got the connection. He did.

"S.O.E. agents."

"Yes sir…there's something else sir…"

"What Harry?"

"Christian Kawolski was based at Northolt during the Battle of Britain, the Polish squadron flew from there, sir."

"And now he's back. . . and flying Lysanders."

"Yes sir." Harry Milburn was pleased with his assessment so far.

"Back to this Duffy chap, Harry, what's his involvement? Have we got any proof?"

"I was coming to that. As I said sir, we've had our suspicions for sometime, a lot of it circumstantial I agree, we've got Duffy, IRA no doubt; motive his father's death. His movements follow that of Cavenaugh exactly, then there is his move to Ruislip, digs in Ickenham, right at the end of the runway. Ideal position for surveillance and his job at the dairy."

"What about it?" Thompson asked inquisitively.

"Rawlingson's Dairy, and particularly Duffy's office window, looks directly over Northolt airport, sir."

"I see, Harry, so the information Cavenaugh sent to Dublin…He'd need a man in, or close to the base."

"Yes, sir."

"Anything else?"

"Yes, I decided to do a bit of further investigation. I sent Henshaw to his offices at the dairy posing as some busy body from Head Office, fortunately Duffy was out, his secretary, Mrs Clack was very helpful, almost pleased."

"And…"

"He found this, sir," Harry passed a large black book to Thompson.

Thomson took the book "What is it…a diary?"

"Yes, sir. But that's not all, it's a logbook as well, dates, times of aircraft movements, numbers etc. It all corresponds with everything Cavenaugh was sending to Dublin, sir." Thompson flicked through the pages of the large black book.

"Where did you get it?"

"From the office, sir, Duffy's office, hidden in a loose panel behind a paraffin heater."

"Very astute of your man." Thompson was questioning the ease with which Henshaw had found the incriminating book.

"Not really, sir the office is fairly sparsely furnished. Any trained operative could have found it."

"There's something interesting in the last few days sir." Harry leant towards Commander Thompson. "Look here sir, he lists his meeting with Kawolski, and here's the best bit…" He flicked over a page in the diary Thompson was holding and jabbed his thumb at the handwriting.

Thompson stared at the words. " 'Met pilot again, has an op planned for Sunday night, inform Dublin.' I see," said Thompson "and did he?"

"Yes sir, and Dublin passed it that same night to Mosel."

Harry Milburn sat back in his chair, a sense of supreme satisfaction on his face. Commander Thompson looked at Milburn and smiled to himself. "OK Harry, don't get conceited, it's me that's pulling your strings as well, son."

"Right. That's confirmed – Duffy's the linkman, obviously knows this Polish pilot, and is able to get information out of him. Well done, Harry, what else have we got?"

"Well," Harry sat well back in the chair, confidence written all over him. "This American General – the one that's been sending the open ciphers complaining to all and sundry about his lack of employment."

Thompson nodded. "What about him?"

"Sent to North Africa in 1942, seconded as American Liaison Officer to Montgomery's HQ. Lifer, professional soldier, excellent Staff Officer. No direct combat experience but highly thought of by Monty, followed him to Sicily and Italy, now directly under Alexander's control."

"And?" asked Thompson

"He's got some very powerful friends in Washington, he's trying to put pressure on Eisenhower to use him, probably wants to be back with Monty, wants to be involved in the invasion sir. Seems he desperately wants to see some action, bit of glory before he's too old."

"What's the relevance?" Thompson already knew in his own mind the answer to his question.

"Mosel's interested…we know that from de-coded German Enigma codes, broken by Bletchley Park.

"Why?" asked Thompson.

"Don't know yet, but it might have something to do with the IRA and the pilot, sir."

"What makes you think that, Harry?" Thompson was startled by the imposed connection.

"Well, sir, he's Polish. His family came from Poland and he was born there, the only survivor of twins."

"What happened to the other one?"

"Died at birth sir, a boy apparently." Harry had done his research. "Not only that sir, he speaks fluent Polish, so does Duffy by the way."

"Duffy?"

"Yes his mother was Polish and this American General is seconded by Alexander to the Polish divisions in Italy."

"So what you're saying is we have the IRA, Duffy, a Polish Pilot, an American General who's Polish and Mosel all possibly in the frame."

"Yes sir, that's about it…circumstantial I admit, but there is a link, do you see, sir?"

"Yes Harry I see…I see. But what is it, what is Mosel up to?"

"I'm afraid I don't know the answer to that sir." Harry seemed a little dejected now.

"We'll just have to wait and see what Sunday brings then." Thompson was bringing the conversation to an end. "Couple of things I want you to do, Harry."

"Sir?" Harry sat forward.

"One, keep tabs on Duffy but don't get too close. Choose another man, someone Duffy hasn't seen, change them daily so he doesn't know he's being watched."

"Yes sir."

"Two, find out more about this Polish pilot's background, family, wife, if he has one. Get back to me as soon as you've got it ok?"

"Yes sir, what about the American General and Mosel's interest, sir?"

"Leave that to me, Harry. Right you'd better get on." Commander Thompson's concentration was back to the papers in front of him. Harry Milburn realised it was time to leave, he got up, stared at the head of Commander Thompson as it was bent over the papers.

"Oh, Harry,"

"Sir,"

"Well done Harry."

Harry Milburn left the office a little happier. When he had gone, Thompson waited until he was sure Milburn had left the outer office before tapping the intercom button on his phone. "Alice?"

"Sir."

"Get me 'C' urgently." He asked.

He continued to read and think about Harry's assessment. It was good, more importantly; it was what Commander Peter Thompson knew to be true. The phone rang, he picked it up.

"Thompson here…yes sir… I need to speak with you urgently…yes sir right away. I'll be there in about ten minutes…thank you sir."

Mosel Escorted by Steiner, arrived outside the door of the small annex that in peacetime had served as the servants' quarters. The sight that met Mosel eyes as he entered the room pleased him. The man who stood before him was tall, well built. His hair was cut in a crew cut, fashionable in the American movies of the time. The greying temples added to the authoritative appearance. His jaw was firm, honest and square.

Mosel's eyes took in everything, the uniform, well tailored, expensive. Mosel looked into his face, the blue-grey eyes set astride the proud nose.

"Excellent Hans," Mosel turned to leave, he hesitated turning his head back towards the man in uniform, "and congratulations to you." He smiled.

"Dankeschon, mein Herr." The man's heels clicked together.

Mosel smiled, but his eyes did not.

"He's not ready, is he, Hans?"

"No sir."

"Carry on." Mosel said as he exited the room.

Steiner turned to the man in uniform, the look of disgust burning in his eyes.

"OK mein Herr, let's start again shall we, and this time no German, you idiot."

It was a beautiful Saturday morning in England's southern counties. The sun high, was set in an azure sky. The flowers in a rainbow of colour filled the neat gardens, the trees were heavy with new foliage. Springtime was at its height. Daffodils crowded at the base of the trees, cow parsley filled the hedgerows. It would be a good summer.

Christian drove to Ruislip in Freddie's red MG roadster, which his friend had kindly loaned to him. The cool wind in his face stimulated his complexion, adding to his handsomeness. He tooted the horn as he drew up outside Emily's flat. He saw the window open, saw her face, his heart began to pound.

"Won't be a minute," Emily called. Christian smiled as her face disappeared behind the net curtain. While he waited, he looked at Freddie's car. The bright red paint glistened in the sunshine, and its chrome fender reflected the light. The headlamps, either side of the grill, looked menacing, ready for the road ahead. No wonder Freddie had been reluctant at first to let Christian borrow it. She really was a beauty.

Christian heard the front door close, and looking up, the sight that met his eyes made him forget about the car. Emily was radiant. She wore a white cotton dress with tiny yellow flowers. Two straps revealed her bare shoulders, the hemline trimmed with lace broderie anglaise, like a petticoat, sat just above her knees. On her arm she carried a pale yellow cardigan that matched the low-slung sandals.

Christian's eyes went to her face, which was shaded by a straw hat complete with a yellow ribbon, a small flower clipped to one side. From under her hat, her hair fell like golden summer rain to lie gently on her bare shoulders. Her eyes as blue as the deepest mountain lake.

"Emily you…you look so beaut…" the words did not finish, Emily kissed him gently on the face, smiled that girlish smile and whispered in his ear, "I know Christian…I know, and it's all yours."

Christian swallowed hard, his Adam's apple sinking in his throat. He saw her mischievous smile as he took her arm and led her to the passenger door. She waited by the door a moment, every bit a young lady, as he opened the small wing door. She passed her cardigan and bag to him while she smoothed her dress as she seated. Christian handed back the bag and cardigan, sprinting round the car and leapt into the front seat.

He fired the motor, heard the roar of the precision internal combustion engine, slipped her into first and powered the roadster away from the kerbside.

"Where are we going?" Emily asked.

"You'll see." Christian grinned; the MG sped towards the junction.

They drove along the A40 to Uxbridge, turned towards Iver, crossed the River Thames at Datchet and followed the open road through old Windsor before pulling off to the right at a teashop, close to the river at Runnemede, which had the huge green hill of Englefield Green as its backdrop like curtains at a theatre. Christian parked the roadster and they both walked hand in hand to the small pale-bricked building.

The teashop was bright and airy; the tables were linened in perfect order as if on parade. They selected a table close to the window overlooking the road and the great expanse of the river as it lazily made its way towards London, spreading its width at Southend before mingling with the North Sea.

A waitress, her white starched apron spotless, came to their assistance. They ordered two coffees and a slice of lemon cake. They held hands, fingers barely touching across the table, they engaged in small talk, the weather, and the warmth of the sun, giggling at each other's response the way young lovers do.

The waitress returned, Emily ate her lemon cake with a fork, the white napkin on her lap, chatting busily, occasionally removing a small crumb from the corner of her sweet mouth with a little finger. Her eyes bright, happy, girlish. All Christian could do was smile and stare at her, like a small puppy, hanging on every word she spoke. He was totally consumed by her.

When they had finished, Christian paid the bill. Not in a rush they studied the plaque, books and tapestries which lined the walls of the tea shop which had dual function as a museum to 'The Magna Carta' Christian studied the transcripts 'in 1215 on this site, the barons of all England met and forced the autocratic King John to sign the Magna Carta, there instilling the first democratic state in Europe.'

"Crazy." Christian thought, all these years later here he was on this site, like a warrior, a baron of the skies. Trying, like millions of other people, to bring an end to a totalitarian state led by a despot who had engulfed not only England, but the peoples from the four corners of the world, in a war of global consequences.

Emily noticed the concern in his eyes, and tore the hat from his head, turned and ran out of the shop giggling. Christian, grinning from ear to ear, chased her to the car park. They played catch me around the MG, Christian finally outwitting her by doubling back and grabbing her. Emily just managed to throw his hat at the last minute.

"Why you wicked, naughty little..." He didn't finish, her arms came up around his neck, her eyes wide, expectant, her lips touching his. His arms fell to his side, lightly holding her hips before pulling her sweet smelling warm body to him. Their mouths kissed gently, lovingly, the lips parted slowly, the skin sticking trying desperately to stay in contact with each other's. Barely inches apart her eyes looked up to him

"Oh, Christian." The words rolled off her tongue. He pulled her firmly to him, her head resting on his shoulder; his face nestled in her sweet smelling hair, like fresh harvested wheat. They held each other for a moment before parting. Christian reached into the back of the roadster and took out a blanket. Hand in hand they crossed the road to stroll by the sun sparkled waters of the Thames.

When they found their idyllic spot close to the wide sweep of the river's bend, Christian laid the blanket out on the soft green carpet of grass close to the water's edge. They sat in the warm sunshine, Christian laid his hand delicately on the cool skin just above Emily's knee. They glanced at each other, smiling, before turning their attention to the river and its wildlife. The ducks and moorhens busily scuttling across the water, a mother duck with six little ducklings in line crossed the river from the far bank.

"Oh look, Christian, aren't they lovely?" Christian's thoughts were different. The boy inside the man saw the mother duck as a battleship escorted by a little flotilla of destroyers in line. From the surface of the river broke a pike, raising its snout above the surface for a moment before sliding below the water again like a U boat on the prowl.

"What are you thinking about?" She asked.

"Oh, just how wonderful and beautiful everything is." He paused looked at Emily, removing her hat, watched as the golden hair flowed to her shoulders and kissed her gently on her forehead, "but not as beautiful as you, Emily."
Their lips met, their bodies, as if in slow motion, gently falling to the blanket. Their mouths came together, tongues touching, and they kissed warmly.

They lay together on the blanket, happy in each other's company.
After perhaps half an hour, Christian sat up slightly restless, fidgeting with anything within reach. Emily smiled and sat up. Flicking her fingers through her hair, put her hat upon her head and rose to her feet.

"What's wrong?" Christian asked.

"Nothing – come on, you're bored, lets go back to the car and find a pub for lunch, I'm hungry."

Christian picked up the blanket, as he was bending, Emily raised a foot to his backside gently shoving him so that he fell spread-eagled on the grass. She laughed aloud, turned and began to run giggling and shrieking in a girlish way. Christian chased after her, by the time they reached the car, both were hot, sticky, their throats sore with laughter. They hugged and jumped into the car driving towards the exit.

Christian turned left then left again. Navigating the sharp incline of Priest Hill, he dropped the engine to a lower gear then gunned the accelerator throwing the MG up the hill. When they passed the brow, the road levelled out, they cut between tall tress before breaking into the wide expanse of the village green dotted with figures in white playing cricket. The wind in their faces had cooled their bodies now.

Christian circumnavigated the green parking the roadster outside an idyllic country pub called The Barley Mow, its bright paintwork standing out amongst the other properties that snuggled around the periphery of the green. Its cool dark interior was welcoming. They ordered beers, the condensation clinging to the glass in miniature droplets, giving a frosted appearance. To follow, they ordered fresh bread, cheese, tomatoes and sweet pickle for lunch.

Christian escorted Emily out into the warm sunshine selecting a table overlooking the cricket field to wait for their food. He held the chair out for Emily, waiting for her to sit, before seating himself. They sat staring into each other's eyes, their concentration broken only by the slap of leather on willow, the slow polite hand clapping, recognition of the batsman's ability to propel the ball towards the boundary.

The food when it arrived was fresh, appetising and well presented. They ate hungrily, sipping the cool beer intermittently to clear their mouths. When they had finished, they sat for a while watching the game, their hands in each other's.

It was Emily who became fidgety now. "Lets go for a drive Christian."

"Ok" he said.

"The hillside, the view must be fantastic from there."

They finished the last dregs of their beer, stood up and walked to the car. The seats were warm from the midday sun.

"Ooh." A little gasp escaped from Emily as her bare skin touched the leather covering. She wiggled her bottom trying to cool the surface.

Christian drove the way they had come, just before reaching the brow of the hill, he turned right into Coopers Hill. He followed the winding English lane, both of them admiring the whitewashed properties, which peeped at them through the spring foliage as they passed. The road became narrower, the hedges, neatly trimmed, began to close in on them. The huge arched windows of a convent framed the road, which appeared to come to an end. Just prior to coming to the solid stonewalls; Christian turned the roadster into a gap in the hedge on his left before coming to a halt.

"Look Christian, look." Emily shouted with glee. She jumped from the car and ran towards the edge of the hill. Christian followed her. They stood in silence for a moment, their hands in each other's, their eyes wide, alert; scanning the vista in front of them.

The hillside dropped sharply beneath their feet, its sides smothered in the bright alternating shades of green from the canopy of trees, small patches of open land lay sunlit between the copses. As the gradient began to level, a small patchwork of fields clung to the winding river, its surface glistening in the sun, as it snaked on its journey to the sea. In the near distance a flight of Spitfires were taking off from the small airfield of Heathrow, their vapour trails pointing to the outline of Staines and the City of London beyond.

"Oh Christian, it's beautiful." Emily gasped as they sat in silence, his arm around her shoulder. Their eyes scanned the distance spotting landmarks in the hazy sunshine. Christian watched the Spitfires climb and bank overhead, their Merlin engines settling to a lower tone. He almost felt envious of those pilots before his eyes that were following them fell upon Emily. She was still smiling and staring at the wonder before her. He knew then that all the pilots above would wish to be where he was now...with Emily. His brain finally came to terms with what his heart already knew: he loved her.

The sun was quite low when they decided to leave. Christian held her hand gently in his; they both took a last look at the wonderful view before turning and walking back to where they had parked the car. Both of them thought what a beautiful spot this would be to build a little cottage with white walls full of ivy and clematis, which would cling to the brickwork.

The journey home was quiet and thoughtful, Christian's eyes darting between the road and Emily. She silent, hardly speaking at all, her hand occasionally flicking her hair. It wasn't until they approached the familiarity of Ruislip that Emily spoke.

"I'm hungry again, what about you, Christian?"

"Me too." He responded. "Fancy stopping at the Plough for a quick bite?

"Yes why not." Emily smiled. When they reached their destination they ordered the fish together with an acceptable medium dry cider. It was approaching eight o'clock when the reached Emily's front door, the sun dipping in the west caused long shadows, which crept up on them.

Christian switched off the engine and sat quietly, wishing the day wasn't coming to an end. Emily saw his mood, smiled, got out of the car and waited. Christian followed her. He was about to kiss her when she took his hand and led him towards the door. She opened the door with her free hand and led him through the small entrance door and proceeded up the stairs.

"What about . . . ?" Christian whispered.

Emily stopped him. "Don't worry, they've gone away for the weekend. Gone to her sister's in Brighton." Emily was referring to the couple that lived downstairs - the small semi had been divided into two flats, her door was at the top of the stairs.

Emily opened the door, putting her finger to her lips "Don't say anything, Christian," she whispered as she led him through the neat little apartment to the bedroom. She let go of his hand as she stopped in front of the window, the dim evening light silhouetting her form. The curtains were still drawn from the morning, the nets crisp and white.

Christian looked around the bedroom. It was comfortable, feminine and smelled of honeysuckle. When his eyes returned to Emily she smiled nervously before slipping the straps of the dress from her shoulders, disturbing her golden hair. In the same movement her hands went to her back neatly easing down the zip on her dress, it slithered soundlessly to the floor, lying delicately at her feet. She stepped from her shoes, her eyes meeting his.

"Christian," she breathed. He came to her and took her in his arms, his mouth on hers, his hands exploring the cool skin, touching the satin material of her bra and French knickers, which were edged with silk. Christian's hands cupped her face, their mouths working intensely. He slipped his hands gently down the contours of her body, resting for a moment on the swell of her bottom before continuing to follow her curves. At the top of her thighs, his hands increased the pressure as he gently lifted her into his arms, turned and walked to the bed, lowering her on the soft surface. Christian kissed her long and deep, Emily responded, her tongue flicking at his.

When their mouths parted for air, he looked into her eyes; they were moist, not borne of sadness but tears of happiness.

"Christian," Emily whispered. "Take me…love me…please." It was almost a plea.

Christian kissed her eyes. His mouth moved to hers briefly, her lips trying to catch his before they moved softly to her neck. Christian adjusted his position so that he was beside her, his shoes scuffing together before falling to the carpet. Emily's hands went to his shirt, almost tearing the buttons as she exposed his chest. Her fingers began to massage him, while her breasts heaved in the bra, which fought to contain them. Suddenly they were naked, his mouth kissing her hard as her hands went to his back, her nails clutching at the flesh.

Christian turned Emily on to her flat smooth stomach. Lifting her hair with one hand, he began to kiss the nape of her neck, as she let out a small moan of delight. Christian's mouth now moved down her back, exploring the bare flesh, nipping the soft skin occasionally. Emily gave little cries of pain and pleasure, her nails digging into the ruffled sheets. Christian's mouth gently followed her thighs, kissing the flesh as he did so. When he reached her toes, his hand reached up to her hip and, realising his intention, Emily slowly rolled on to her back.

Christian repeated the kissing, this time moving up her body, his lips caressing the inside of her thighs before coming to rest on her mound. Emily's knees pressed against the side of his head as her hands reached for his hair. Emily slowly guided his head to hers, their mouths met again. His hips rose then settled between hers.

He entered her slowly and deeply. Their lovemaking was tender, purposeful and beautiful. When they finally came to rest, their sweat soaked bodies fell on each other, their chests heaving and falling, their hearts pounding, hot breath on each others necks, they lay together.

Christian turned onto his back, pulling Emily gently to him, her head on his chest, his mouth kissing her golden hair.

"Christian."

"Yes, Emily."

"I love you, Christian Kawolski."

"And I love you, Emily Cassidy." Christian kissed her head softly. "Now rest, go to sleep."

Emily giggled, "Christian?"

"What." His voice gentle.

"It was a lovely day, wasn't it?"

"Yes, Em, wonderful."

"Christian?"

"Yes, Em?"

"You do love me…really…don't you?"

"Yes Emily, I do love you…now go to sleep." Christian said as he gently slapped her exposed bottom.

"Ooh, that's nice." Emily whispered wickedly.

"Go to sleep." Christian smiled, pretending to be stern.

"Yes, sir!" She giggled.

Slowly with their bodies providing the soft warmth, they drifted into happy sleep.

When Christian awoke the room was filled with darkness. Emily deep in sleep lay on her tummy, her naked body rising gently with each breath. Christian slipped from the sheets the covered Emily. Adjusting his eyes to the gloom, he dressed quietly. Finding some notepaper on her dressing table, he scribbled a note using an eyeliner pencil. Kissing her forehead gently, he left the note on the pillow, before leaving the flat and making his way to where he had parked the MG.

Christian didn't bother putting the hood up on the roadster. He lit a cigarette, drew deeply, then let the smooth smoke exhale. Christian started the car, cursed at the throaty roar of the engine, slipped into gear then gently pulled away. He headed back to Northolt, his mind on tomorrow's mission, his heart still lying next to Emily.

Sean Duffy had seen Christian pull away. "A curse on you Christian Kawolski." He breathed. Duffy looked up towards the bedroom window, imaging Emily naked in her bed, her body and soul contented in soft sleep. He was jealous.

Emily was awoken by the early spring sunshine filtering through the net curtains of her bedroom window, still drawn from yesterday. Her hand reached for Christian, searching the pillow for his face. All she found was a note written in eyeliner pencil. She read it in her sleepy state – "To my darling Emily, Love always, Christian." She smiled a sleepy smile, putting the note under her pillow, turned and fell back to sleep.

CHAPTER 7

Mosel was also awake early that morning. He was fully dressed in his official uniform when Steiner arrived.

"Good morning, Herr Captain."

"Good morning, Hans, is the car ready?"

"Yes sir. The plane is also ready at the airfield, I've managed to second a Junkers for you sir, should get us to Paris ahead of schedule."

"Good Hans." Mosel stopped, noticing the awkward look on his aide's face. "What is it, Hans?" He questioned, Mosel had known and worked with Steiner since 1939. He trusted the young man, if something was troubling Steiner it would sooner or later trouble Mosel.

"It's Herr Schloss, sir. He's demanding to see you." Steiner was embarrassed by the demand. The man was weak, a fool, not worthy of the honour that was being bestowed on him.

"Where is he, Hans?"

"Outside sir, shall I show him in."?

"Yes, and get the car started now, I shall follow you in a brief moment." Steiner showed Schloss into the room before leaving to make sure the driver of Mosel's car was ready. At the same time he ordered a soldier to stand guard at Mosel's door.

"Herr Schloss, what's the problem, can't this wait? I'm on my way to an important meeting."

"Herr Captain, this plan, this façade, theatrics you are planning, I will have no part in it, I…I…wish to speak with someone in higher authority." Schloss weakly slapped the table trying to emphasise his newfound confidence.

Mosel rose to his full six foot, his fists clenched in anger at the fool in front of him.

"Herr Schloss," he calmed his rage. "My dear Herr Schloss, the mission to which we are working towards is of the utmost importance to the Fatherland. The Fuhrer himself has taken a personal interest in its progress," he lied, "and you Herr Schloss, Gunther," he softened his tone, "you my dear Gunther are the essential cog in the whole machinery of this plan. You, Gunther Schloss, are the most potent weapon in our arsenal, a weapon which if used properly will win the war and win it this year, this year, Gunther." That statement was not a lie, he genuinely believed it.

Schloss stuttered, lost for words.

"So my dear Gunther, please return to your work… and Gunther, work hard, work hard!" Mosel picked up his briefcase and made for the door. "I have an important meeting with the Fuhrer, I must not delay any more." Mosel lied again.

"Yes, yes of course…" Schloss was dreaming of his self-importance. As Mosel passed the guard he barked an order, "Escort that man back to his quarters."

A car pulled up outside the building near the naval dockyard. The driver got out went into the front door, the engine still running. He returned a few minutes later with another man dressed in dark coat and hat. With the two men was a young blonde woman, who was clearly agitated. She was carrying a small suitcase. The three got into the car, the man in the dark clothes and the woman getting into the back. A third man appeared at the doorway, holding two young children, the girls were crying, holding out their arms. Both the young woman's arms reached out of the window of the car as it drove off.

Sir Stewart Menzies (C.), Head of MI5, was working that Sunday. The visit by Commander Peter Thompson RN, and the scenario he had depicted, needed careful thought. He had called his opposite number in MI6 and given him a brief synopsis of Thompson's report, negating to inform him of those areas of MI5's interest of course. They had both decided not to inform S.O.E. but to sit and wait, see what happened.

After careful consideration, he realised that something of this potential magnitude could not be kept from Winston. He dialled the number of the safe line.

"Prime Minister, Good morning to you, it's C. Yes, I do appreciate the time. Yes, Prime Minister, it is urgent – I need to see you on a matter of the utmost importance. The conduct of the war may depend on it," he added. There was a short silence before C continued. "Yes sir, I will be there in one hour, Thank you Prime Minister."

Christian Kawolski awoke early also, his body still aching from the rigours of his lovemaking with Emily, his mind on the operation ahead. He found himself unable to finish his breakfast, despite the extra rations of bacon and eggs since he was on Ops that day. The briefing was set for 4pm, until then he was supposed to busy himself. He asked the adjutant if it was possible to visit his girl. The request as he expected was denied, he was not allowed any contact with the outside world in any form, no visits, no telephone calls, no letters. He was confined to base until his departure late that night.

When Emily was fully awake she re-read the note from Christian and was worried. Her mind fully functioning now had gone into overdrive. She wouldn't be able to see him before the operation, she knew that. But what if something went wrong, he was shot down, captured, or…? No, no that could not happen to Christian, he was an excellent pilot. She tried to reassure herself, but what if…?

Her mind was in turmoil, her stomach tight, her heart saddened, she would have to see him, speak to him, get a message to him somehow! She dressed quickly, her mind made up. Emily was dressed in shorts and T-shirt with white socks, low casual shoes and the obligatory bag to match. Her hair was worn up, exposing the fine bone structure of her face, she wore no make up. Most girls would feel vulnerable, self-conscious, going out at warm sunny Sunday morning without their full ensemble. In Emily's case it didn't matter, she had other more important things on her mind besides her appearance. To anyone who saw her that day she was just Emily, beautiful.

She went to the call box opposite the Plough and phoned the base, waiting nervously for an answer.

"Yes, Hello, Flight Lieutenant Christian Kawolski, please."

"Just one moment, madam." The male voice answered. There was a short delay.

"I'm sorry that's not possible. No calls to be put through to the officer."

"But its very important, I must speak to him." She pleaded.

"Sorry, love, there's nothing I can do."

"What about the station commander. Can I talk to him?"

"Just a minute, miss." Another long delay, she started to panic, the money was running out, Emily searched her handbag, found another coin, and inserted it into the infernal machine. Her heart beating loudly, her body shaking in anticipation.

"Sorry miss," the voice again. "No can do, try again tomorrow."

"But…but I must…" she stopped as the line went dead. Emily began to cry.

Christian tried desperately to busy himself; he had chatted to the mechanics about his aircraft, questioned every detail of its readiness. Then he visited the CO asked if he could do an instrument check, but the request was denied. He tried to find Freddie but was told he was in meetings regarding the op, not to be disturbed. He had gone to the mess, which was empty. He tried to read a newspaper but could not concentrate; the words were just a blur. He had walked around the base trying to talk to anybody that would listen. He was becoming annoying and he knew it. God it was still only 10.30, he still had five and a half-hours before the briefing.

Emily had composed herself, she decided to go to the base, she had to see Christian. She caught two buses, finally reaching the bus stop outside the main gates to Northolt air base. She approached the soldiers on duty at the gate.

"Er, Corp take a look at this." Both studied the pretty girl as she approached.

"Yes, miss what can we do for you?" He scanned the whole length of her form, a lustful look in his eyes.

"Flight Lieutenant Christian Kawolski, please."

"Just a moment, miss," The lustful guard dialled the number.

Emily waited impatiently, not noticing the guard's stare.

"Sorry miss, no can do."

Emily was beside herself with pain and frustration, tears beginning to form again.

"But I must see him." Emily tried to push past the guard. He caught her; her arms struggled to free her from the man's clutches. He held tight. Her anger through denial was reaching fever pitch. Emily kicked the guard hard, catching him on the shin, his grip loosened.

"You little bitch." He screamed in pain. He grabbed at Emily again, caught her hand and pulled her back.

"What's going on here Corporal?" A voice of authority demanded.

Emily freed herself from the man's clutches, recognising the voice.

"Freddie, oh, Freddie," she ran to Moreland and flung her arms around him.

"Emily." The shock on his face when he identified her. "Emily, what's the matter?" His voice was calmer now, concerned for the young girl.

"Oh, Freddie, they won't let me see Christian…I…I tried to call but…I had to come Freddie. I love him…I must see him." She was sobbing now.

"There, there, I know Emily, I know." Freddie consoled her "Corporal?"

"Sir?"

"Get this young lady a cup of tea."

"Tea! Sir…but." He stammered.

"You heard me Corporal."

"Sir!" He returned indignantly as he limped away, "Tea, fucking tea…where am I supposed to get fucking tea, at this time." He mumbled.

The other guard was smirking at his mate's misfortune. His eyes on the girl.

"Come on Em, can you talk." Freddie's voice was slow, steady.

"Oh. Freddie, I'm sorry for causing you so much trouble, but I just had to try and see Christian, nobody will let me see or even call him." Emily was becoming calmer.

"It's impossible, Emily, security, you know the form."

"Yes Freddie, I know, I just had to try."

"I understand sweetheart, but…I'm afraid there's nothing I can do, a message perhaps."

"Oh yes Freddie please."

"No problem Emily, what shall I tell him?"

"Tell, tell him I love him, love him no matter what…and Freddie?" Emily's hands went to her neck; she undid the little clasp, took off the chain with the little heart pendant.

"Give him this please Freddie."

Freddie took the chain and looked at the golden heart. Simple, sweet, just like you Freddie thought.

"I'll make sure he gets it Emily." He studied the beautiful young girl for a moment.

"Can I get you a taxi."? Freddie turned from Emily to the corporal who had miraculously returned with a cup of tea. "Corporal get a taxi for the young lady, if you please."

"No…no…it's ok Freddie, I need to walk, sometime to think, please, please I'll be ok."

"You sure Emily?"

"Yes Freddie, and Freddie?"

"Yes."

Emily kissed him on the cheek "Thanks Freddie."

Then she turned and walked away. Freddie watched her go, saw her disappear around the corner. He turned to face the Corporal, saw the tea in his hand, his mouth open. He took the teacup and saucer, finished the contents, replaced both back in the corporal's still outstretched hand.

"It's stewed corporal, It's stewed." Freddie turned then sauntered off in the direction of the CO's office. The corporal stared at the teacup and saucer still in his outstretched hand, now devoid of liquid, stared at the departing officer and just shook his head.

The German Naval Staff car pulled up directly opposite the waiting Junkers aircraft, the door was opened, Mosel followed by Steiner go out. Mounting the short steps to the aeroplane they disappeared inside. The three powerful engines of the Junkers were rotating, the noise a steady throb. Mosel together with Steiner was seated in a comfortable cabin in the front of the aeroplane just behind the pilot. The cabin was separated from the rear section, which contained the luggage and any freight. There were two additional seats fitted in the aft for the purpose of the flight.

The Junker JU52 had originally been used as a passenger aircraft; it was not until Hitler brought the world to the verge of war that the JU52 was converted to a long-range bomber. Today it would be used for its original purpose, carrying passengers.

A second car approached the waiting aircraft, the driver pulled up to the rear and a man in black coat and hat got out followed by a young, blonde woman carrying a small suitcase. The man ushered the woman into the rear, the steps were pulled away and the doors shut. The engines increased in noise; slowly the converted bomber moved beginning to taxi. The pilot came on the intercom.

"Ready for take off, fasten seat belts please. Flying time to destination approximately two and a half hours, weather fine, enjoy your flight." The pilot was careful not to mention any names or any form of salutation. The longer the woman seated in the rear was confused, devoid of reason or explanation, the better the effect, Mosel had decided.

The huge craft turned on the runway, a brief last minute check from the pilots completed. The three massive BMW132L radials powered the Junkers down the concrete, their propellers spinning furiously, the noise reaching a crescendo. The nose lifted and the wheels left the ground, it was airborne.

Freddie found Christian in their room, Airman Book was laying out his flying suit ready for the evening's flight.

"Christian, its time."

Kawolski straightened his tie, took a last look in the mirror, put on his hat and adjusting his tunic said, "ok Freddie, let's go."

Silently he followed Freddie to the briefing room. Freddie opened the door and announced him.

"Flight Lieutenant Christian Kawolski."

Christian studied the small room, which was dark, shadowy, the only light coming from two lamps either side of a large oak desk, behind which sat three men. Christian's eyes scanned the room a second time taking in every detail. Next to another chair on the left was a projector, a box of slides by its side. It faced the left-hand wall upon which a white screen had been placed.

The man in the middle of the three seated behind the desk spoke first.

"Good afternoon, Flight Lieutenant, please be seated." The man pointed to the seat directly in front of the table. Christian approached the seat pulled it back slightly before seating himself as comfortably as possible. Freddie Moreland closed the door, without waiting for any command or signal he seated himself in the chair to Christians left near the projector.

"Let me introduce you, Flight Lieutenant, My name is Colonel Buckmaster. I am head of S.O.E. (f) Section France, This.." he pointed to his right, "is Commander Peter Thompson SIS, Special Intelligence service. SIS contains two main areas, MI5 UK mainland intelligence and MI6 who are responsible for intelligence gathering."

"Flight Lieutenant." Was all Thompson said. His eyes firmly fixed on Christian.

"And this..." Buckmaster pointed to his left, "is Commander Tim Brethwell, S.O.E. F section controller for the Paris Bordeaux region." Brethwell nodded. "Oh, and this I'm sure you know is Flight Lieutenant Freddie Moreland, sorry Freddie." Buckmaster apologised. Christian nodded acknowledgement. "Freddie is your flight controller on this mission."

There was a short pause allowing Christian time to take in the introductions before Buckmaster continued.

"I suppose your wondering what all this is about?"

"Yes, sir." answered Christian honestly.

"Well, if these gentlemen don't mind, I shall give you some background." Buckmaster turned to each of the men seated beside him. They each nodded in turn their approval.

“Some time ago we discovered the fact that one or two of our operations had been compromised by German Intelligence. We lost a good number of agents as well as the whole of our Victor network. This as you may appreciate, has caused S.O.E. some considerable headaches. The man responsible for the break up of Victor is one Ernst Mosel, Captain, and Head of the ABWEHR’s department III counter espionage/counter subversion. We believe this Mosel has turned another of our networks code-named ‘Lucien’. Lucien covers the area to the south of Paris as far as Bordeaux. It is of critical importance to the war effort, if it has been compromised we need to know and know now. Your job, Flight Lieutenant, is to pick Lucien up from occupied France tonight and bring him back here for questioning.”

Kawolski nodded.

“Commander Brethwell will give you the full details, Commander?’ Buckmaster turned to face the man on his left.

“Freddie, if you would.” Brethwell turned towards Moreland. Freddie turned on the projector, its light flashed onto the screen by the left-hand wall, Christian’s eyes followed. Freddie inserted a slide. The picture of a Gallic face appeared, the man’s face was dark, swarthy looking in appearance, the eyes hard, unforgiving.

“Code name Lucien – head of the network, real name Henri Dacourt, age 31, born La Rochelle, joined British forces from Vichy French forces in North Africa. Brought to England 1941, trained with S.O.E. and returned to France where he joined Victor network operating out of Northwest Paris 1942-1943. Headed up and expanded Lucien network covering the area of South Paris, Normandy, Brittany. He’s operating out of the Rennes area on the borders of Brittany and Normandy. He will be in Fougeres, a small town to the North east of Rennes today.”

Brethwell looked again at Freddie, who put in a second slide depicting a map of the Brittany area, then he spoke. “Your job, Flight Lieutenant, is to fly your Lysander to a wooded area here.” Freddie pointed to the spot on the screen, “west of Fougeres, near the Fougeres Vitre road, north east of Rennes, keep away from Rennes by the way, there is a German Army HQ, divisional level here, a Jerry airfield and a lot of flack.”

Freddie inserted a third slide showing the southern coast of England, the channel and the French coast, south of Paris to Bordeaux. Freddie continued his delivery.

“Your flight path will take you from Northolt, over Poole in Dorset, into the Channel. Here you fly southwest, skirting the coastline of Normandy, Brittany. Fly south east of Jersey line up with Mont St Michel on the Brittany coast here.” Freddie pointed. “From Mont St Michel head inland towards Vitre, here you should be able to recognise the Chateaux, a former castle. Fly to the north of this following a northeasterly line, the woods should be about 10 miles to the east of Vitre.

Sir.” Freddie looked back to Brethwell, who glanced towards Kawolski and spoke.

“Thank you, Freddie. Your signal lights, four in all, will be in an L shape. The bottom of the L showing you wind direction for approach, the tail of the L showing ground wind direction. Two further lights away from the L will show you the farthest extent of the landing zone. It is believed the landing area, that is to say the clearing in the woods, is about 450ft by 100 yards.

‘Not much space to land,’ Christian thought.

Brethwell continued, “Lucien will be ready for you at 1.30am French time. 0.30am GMT. Your password will be Patriot – the response Re-patronisation.”

“Sir,” Brethwell turned to Buckmaster.

"Any questions, Flight Lieutenant?" Buckmaster asked.

"No sir…well actually just one, sir."

The three men looked perplexed, Buckmaster spoke, "Yes?" Was all he said.

"Why me, sir?" asked Christian.

Commander Peter Thompson spoke for the first time.

"May I?" He looked at Buckmaster.

"Yes of course," Buckmaster conceded.

"Quite right, Flight Lieutenant, a good question." He hesitated. "Well, firstly you're an excellent pilot, ex Spitfire, so you know German fighter tactics. That can only help protect you on your long journey. According to Freddie here," he nodded, "you can handle the Lysander better than anyone he knows, and finally you're Polish!" He watched the expression form on Kawolski's face.

"Polish, what's that got to do with it sir?" Christian was confused for the first time.

"We have put an agent into the Lucien network via another source." Thompson continued, "one of our people from SIS." Now it was the turn of Buckmaster and Brethwell to look shocked. "Her codename is 'Yvette', and her job is to watch what happens. If Lucien should fail to turn up, if you should be compromised, taken prisoner, her job will be to contact you. Try to get you out, report to us on Lucien himself." He let the uncertainty of it all sink in. "Yvette is Polish." He added.

"I see…Thank you sir." It made sense to Christian.

Trying to regain his composure Buckmaster spoke.

"Anything else?"

"No sir." Responded Kawolski.

"Thank you, Flight Lieutenant, and good luck."

Kawolski saluted turned and left, Freddie following.

Yvette, full name Yvette Granville (her English codename) had been recruited by SIS in 1940. Her original function had been to arrange escape routes for Polish servicemen to England. In 1943 SIS brought her to England to co-ordinate British/Polish operations in Eastern Europe. Educated at University in Warsaw she studied modern languages, she spoke French like a native.

Yvette had joined S.O.E.'s (F) Section France in 1944 with the full knowledge of SIS, in the 'beggar' circuit operating in the Northwest Paris sector. On April 11th 1944 she joined the Lucien network as a co-ordinator, go between, with the beggar network. Lucien, Henri Dacourt was not informed of her transfer, believing her to be a courier from another cell visiting the area to look after a sick relative.

The JU52 made its approach to the airfield just outside Rennes. The tower had been informed of its arrival and told to clear all eyes from the aircraft. The controller informed the pilot of the eight-knot side wind and watched as the plane touched down onto the smooth surface of the runway.

A fuel truck together with two black saloons approached the Junkers. One car went to the front of the aircraft, the second to the rear. Two men in military uniforms exited the aircraft and got into the first car. A man in dark civilian clothes and a blonde haired woman got into the second car. The two cars sped off taking the road to Vitre via the service entrance to the airfield. The fuel truck continued to fill the tanks on the Junkers.

Christian and Freddie went over the practicalities of the flight, weather, fuel load, consumption with the increased load for the return journey. The weather in England was predicted to be fine with a clear sky and a full moon. A bomber's moon as they called it. Over the channel and around the Bay of Biscay, a front was moving in. Cloud base was expected at 2,000ft with headwinds of 50/60 knots, possible sea mists from the Cherbourg peninsula down to Bordeaux, which according to the experts at the met office should clear inland from about two miles, giving a clear moonlit sky for approach to the landing zone. It would be a bit bumpy but ideal conditions for the op, with the Luftwaffe expected to ground as many aircraft as possible.

Kawolski ate a good meal before changing into his flying gear presenting himself for final briefing at 21.30, one hour before take off. There were last minute checks on the weather and the aircraft. The list was finally completed and signed by the RAF corporal mechanic. At 22.15 hours the small two-seater truck arrived to take Flight Lieutenant Christian Kawolski to his waiting aircraft.

At 22.00 hours GMT the Junkers 52 lifted from the airfield at Rennes fully fuelled. It carried no passengers, its destination restricted by German naval intelligence. Its flight plan the general area of the North Brittany/Normandy coast.

CHAPTER 8

Christian sat in the cockpit of the Mark III Westland Lysander. He was strapped in, his parachute underneath him. He hoped to God he would not have to use it. Flying an aeroplane was second nature to him, jumping out of one terrified him. He fired the magnetos and the Bristol XII radial piston power plant burst into life. Christian adjusted the mixture, allowing the 890 horsepower engine to settle into a rhythmic throb. He tested rudder, ailerons, and flaps - all hydraulics seemed normal.

Christian tested the VHF TR1143 voice communication radio, checked with the tower via his headphones

"Ready for take off."

"Clear to taxi," came the reply.

He pushed the throttle forward, the engine increased in noise, and the Lysander eased forward on its taxi run, its wing tips flexing. At the end of the runway, the Lysander turned and straightened. Christian spoke to the tower.

"Hello tower, this is Patriot."

"Hello Patriot, this is Northolt tower. Clear for take off, crosswind left to right 3 knots. Good luck."

"Thank you, tower. Patriot rolling, climb 10,000 vector, 220 degrees over and out."

Christian gunned the throttle. The Lysander steadily picking up speed accelerated down the runway. At the required speed he pulled back on the controls. The aircraft gradually left the earth.

Christian adjusted the rudder to counteract the yaw caused by the crosswind. At 1,000 feet he decreased throttle allowing the Lysander to continue to climb at a lower angle of assent. The Lysander banked to the left as it passed over the small hamlet of Ickenham before continuing to climb.

There was some slight bumping as the aircraft encountered some turbulence at 8,000ft. At 10,000ft he levelled the aircraft, checked his controls, the artificial horizon was dead centre, level and true, the trim setting perfect. He checked his compass and settings, his air speed indicator, he was flying at 190mph-39mph below maximum at 10,000 ft. the weather was fine and smooth.

In order to maximise oxygen he took her back down to 9,000ft, since there was no turbulence at that height. All Christian could do now was sit back, scan his instruments and make sure he kept on the correct heading, with his magnetic compass showing him the way. The Lysander's 50ft span gave him a slowish but comfortable ride. His take off had been longer than in practice, the auxiliary fuel tank adding to the weight. He had climbed to 10,000ft in just over six minutes before dropping to 9,000.

Captain Ernst Mosel had eaten a superb meal at the Chateau in Vitre, together with his aide Hans Steiner. Formerly a castle, it had been added to and extended over the centuries. It sat on higher ground to the North west of the small market town like something out of a Robin Hood story. As far as Mosel was concerned, it was comfortable and ideal for his purpose.

In a small room in one of the towers, the young blonde woman sat at a small wooden table, a plate of cheese, ham and bread in front of her, a glass of wine next to it. The door of the room was locked, outside sat the man in dark clothes and hat, a machine pistol on his lap, a walther in his shoulder holster.

Kawolski passed over the shoreline and the small harbour of Poole, the black water of the English Channel below glistening in the moonlight, interspersed with grey patches of cloud. After about ten minutes of flying the weather began to worsen. The cloud had become a blanket obscuring the water, while the expected headwinds increased in velocity, buffeting the aircraft.

Christian knew he could climb to 16,000ft and hopefully avoid the worst of the weather. However, that was the altitude where German night fighters would expect him. Up there he would stand no chance. He decided that soon he would have to drop lower so as to be able to dive into the cloud if spotted, regardless of the comfort of the ride.

At 11.22 GMT the pilot of the Junkers 52 reported engine trouble to the tower at Rennes. He told them he was returning to the airfield. Rennes tower acknowledged the voice, gave the pilot details of approach. Thirty seconds later the Junkers disappeared off radar.

Mosel stood with his back to the fire in the great hall of the chateau at Vitre, a half empty glass of Schnapps in his hand, the crystal glass twinkling, reflecting the light and colours from the fire. He glanced at his watch…

"You informed Sirherheitsdienost?" (German military intelligence security service, the dreaded S.D.).

"Yes Captain," responded Steiner, still seated at the dining table, "they should be at their destination by now." Steiner checked his watch.

"Who has that megalomaniac Himmler sent for the task?"

"SS Obergruppenfuher Manfred Von Ebstein himself."

"Perfect." Mosel whispered as he finished his Schnapps.

The weather was very rough now, Kawolski fought with the controls to maintain some semblance of level flight, he checked his instruments continuously.

Realising that he must be close to the Cherbourg peninsula, he knew he would have to establish a landmark. He eased the throttle back, reducing airspeed and allowing the Lysander to descend towards the thick layer of cloud. He watched the altimeter spin in an anticlockwise motion as the aircraft lost height. 5,000, 4,000, 3,000 . . . still no break in the clouds. The weather was heavy, with rain on his windshield and heavy turbulence. 2,500, 2,000, 1,500, 1,200 . . . then a break. The buffeting eased at 1,000 ft; he could just make out the coastline ahead about three miles.

On the horizon was Cherbourg. Christian let out a sigh of relief; he felt little concern for the weather that was part of flying, part of the thrill. It was his navigation that he was uncertain of, but as usual he had got it right. Christian banked the aircraft to his right, taking a south westerly heading towards Brittany and the Bay of Biscay. He climbed to 8,000 ft above the clouds and relaxed.

Emily tossed and turned in her bed, sleep would not come to her. Emily's thoughts were on Christian alone in his plane, danger all around him. She gave up her fight with the bedclothes and standing up, walked to the window of her bedroom. She drew the curtains, opened the window and breathed in the fresh cool air. Emily looked at her watch, it was midnight, and she had been in bed since ten o'clock. She gazed up at the sky, it was black but with a moon. The moonlight cast shadows amongst the silhouettes of the houses and trees. At least the weather was calm, good for flying she supposed. "Oh Christian, please come back to me." Her hands were in a praying position. Emily Cassidy had not prayed for some time, the last time she recollected was when she was sixteen, praying that her foster father would not come to her bed that night.

Sean Duffy sat in the van a short distance from the small semi detached house where Emily lived, as vigilant as ever. He noticed the drawing of the curtains; saw Emily's naked form silhouetted against the darkness of her bedroom, the moonlight highlighting the shape of her body, the skin pale and smooth. He saw her put her hands together and raise her eyes to heaven as if she was praying. After a few moments she disappeared from sight, but the curtains remained opened.

Duffy wondered if Emily had returned to her bed, praying to God that the handsome, young pilot would return safely to her. Were her eyes focussed on the night sky, protecting Christian Kawolski and the small plane he flew?

Duffy lit a cigarette, blew the smoke out of the van window. "May your God be with you tonight, Emily girl."

Kawolski, by his reckoning, was at a point in the flight where he would have to turn south towards Jersey in the Channel Islands and head for the coast of occupied France towards whatever destiny God had set for him. Another ten minutes he thought. Then he would have to take the Lysander down to the water again to check his position. If he was correct, Jersey should be to his right. It was the main island in the group, as English as Kent or Yorkshire, but unlike England, occupied, under the boot of Nazism.

The controller in the tower of the airfield just outside Rennes watched as a Storch, a German light aircraft took to the skies. The Storch was used by the German as a light reconnaissance aircraft. It had similar capabilities as the Lysander, tonight its function was very similar to that of the Westland's versatile role, namely that of search and rescue. The Storch was looking for the missing Junkers 52.

Christian had taken the Lysander down to 1,000ft and found Jersey to be where he expected. He kept the aircraft low for his approach towards his intended-landing zone. The coast of occupied France was a few miles distant. He knew he wouldn't be able to see it, he'd have to feel, sense it, for in front of his windshield was a blanket of cloud, probably the sea mist he had been warned about.

As he approached the wall of cloud he knew it would be impossible to use visual control. He would have to rely solely on his instruments. Christian set the zero indicator that displayed his height above sea level on his altimeter to 100 ft. That should give him an additional clearance should he encounter the unexpected, power lines, or an unmarked hill. His eyes peeled towards the altimeter and the artificial horizon. The little plastic plane in the bubble was to all intents and purposes his plane.

His eyes were becoming tired; the constant movement from instrument to visual sighting back to instrument again had made his eyes heavy. His temples throbbing, his heart clearly audible. Christian saw a gap in the mist, peered hopefully through the billowing, swirling greyness. He let out a sigh of relief. The mist had parted just long enough for him to spot Mont St. Michel, its dark form silhouetted against the sea. Christian was only about a mile off course.

"Not bad, Christian," he congratulated himself, "not bad at all."

He adjusted his course and direction, and in a few minutes would prepare the aircraft for his final approach. Provided the wind was in the right direction, he could go straight in. His mind came back to the instruments as the mist enveloped the canopy again.

SS.Oberstleutnant Carl Metzer received his final instructions from his superior, SS Obergruppenfuehrer Manfred Von Ebstein. Von Ebstein told his junior that matters of state had precluded him from being present.

It would not be matters critical to the third Reich that kept Von Ebstein away from the Rennes area that night, for in his bedroom in a hotel across from the Opera House in Paris, a young Parisian girl lay tethered to the bed naked, lying face down, the marks from the riding crop Von Ebstein patted against the thigh of his cavalry trousers still evident on her body.

Sir Stewart Menzies sat across the table from the Prime Minister in his subterranean office far below Whitehall. Winston, C thought, looked pallid, not the picture of health or determination that the carefully orchestrated newsreels had portrayed him to be. His eyes were heavy, not though drinking as one might suspect looking at the half empty brandy bottle that sat on his desk, but with the sheer weight of responsibility that had been thrust upon him. Winston, C thought, was simply worn out. Like Churchill's famous speech in the Commons after the victory at El Alamein…he believed Winston was at the beginning of his end.

Winston spoke first, the ever-present cigar clamped in his fat fingers. "I see your man has done his homework."

"Yes sir, It's conjectural at the moment, open to interpretation I know, but. . ." C hesitated, knowing Winston's appreciation of the theatricals "But if he's right sir…if his homework, as you put it, is on the right track…if his assumptions are correct…then sir, I believe we've got something. Something that at worst, can only enhance Operation Fortitude."

"Do you play poker, C?" Winston asked, his eyes wide, cunning.

"No sir." C answered honestly.

"When playing poker," Winston continued, "sometimes you have to force your opponent to show his hand, cajole him into matching the stakes, in simply terms, bluff him. Make him move before he's ready. Assess his boldness…I think it's time we played a card, C."

"Sir," C pretended confusion, willing the PM to authorise what he already knew. Get the PM's approval; an approval based upon Winston's own conclusion, in short his idea.

"This American, the fellow who's causing a murmur of discontent within in corridors of Washington, what's his name?"

"Major General Alexander Popowski, Prime Minister."

"Yes. . . yes that's the chap…a Pole I believe. Montgomery speaks highly of him. A good staffer."

"Yes sir, so I believe." C was delighted with the way the conversation was going.

"The Poles, they are in the line, opposite Cassino, ready to go on the offensive with Alexander's plan. Jerry must know they're there. Will probably move troops from his reserve to supplement the line…suppose," Winston took a huge draw on his cigar for effect, "suppose we bring him back." He waited gauging C's response.

"Sir, I don't know what you're getting at."

"Suppose we get Monty or Eisenhower to bring him back to England…We could shoot two birds with one shot."

"Sir."

"The Jerries, informed of his departure, would naturally assume that the planned Alexander push had been delayed…thus, thus fooling Kesselring into the assumption that the attack was postponed. Letting him weaken his centre whilst believing this Popowski character was somehow relevant to the invasion of Northern Europe. That would allow us to smash the Gothic line at Casino in Italy, whilst fooling Adolf as to our intentions in France."

"Sir." C assumed dismay.

"That could only enhance our operation."

"Yes Prime Minister…I see where you're going with this. What should I do, sir?"

"Nothing!" Beamed the PM, "leave it to me…I'll speak to Monty and Ike." Churchill puffed at his cigar, the eyes alert, the brain fully functional.

"Thank you sir." Sir Stewart Menzies, head of SIS, was ecstatic inside. On the outside no emotions were shown.

"Like a game of poker, C." Churchill continued. "Sometimes truth should be accompanied by a bodyguard of lies."

CHAPTER 9

The mist began to thin out, and Christian was able to use his power of vision again. He spotted to his right the chateau of Vitre standing tall like a guardian over the small town. Christian followed the road from Vitre to Fougeres; it was straight simplifying navigation. He dropped the nose of the Lysander levelling out at four hundred feet, skimmed over the hill, flew over wooded land-then he saw it.

In the distance there were five lights in an L shape. The bottom of the L facing him. Its tail slightly above the level. He was heading directly into the wind, with a slight crosswind. Christian eased the flaps down, reduced power allowing the Lysander to begin to descend. At 150 feet he levelled the aircraft, cleared the trees saw the clearing and dropped sharply pulling the nose up slightly before the wheels touched the soil of France. Christian eased right back on the throttle and applied the brakes. As he felt the Lysander slow to taxi speed, he turned the aircraft 360 degrees and started to head back to the point at which he had landed. Kawolski was 100 yards short of the two lights, which marked the end of the clearing. "Not bad, Christian" he told himself, "not bad at all."

The L shaped lights had been extinguished now; only the intermittent flash of a torch guided him to where his passenger should be waiting. Another 360 degree turn, load his cargo, charge down the improvised runway, then he would be back where he felt safe, secure, where he belonged. Three minutes should do it.

In the great hall of the Chateau at Vitre Captain Ernst Mosel glanced at his watch for perhaps the tenth time that evening. He smiled.

"Hans," Mosel looked towards his aide.

"Sir." Steiner had also heard the aircraft noise as it flew close to the chateau.

"Prepare a room for our guest."

"Yes sir," Steiner saluted, he left the great hall, gently closing the tall double doors behind him.

Mosel poured himself another measure of Schnapps; everything was going according to plan.

Christian eased the Lysander into position ready for take off, the single radial idling. He stretched his legs, accidentally knocking against the bottle of brandy, which Freddie had given him for his maiden op in the Lysander. Freddie had grinned at him, 'take a nip, Christian; it might keep you warm in the freezing cold at altitude'. Christian would never dream of drinking whilst flying, but he appreciated the gesture. He sat the bottle on the seat next to him, thinking his passenger might welcome the Napoleon on the long flight back. The passenger, 'where was he'? Christian scanned the darkness. 'He'd better hurry up', he thought.

A man's dark shape ran from the edge of the clearing, Christian pulled back the canopy of the pilot's area allowing him to give the passenger verbal instructions before take off.

"Hurry up", he called to the approaching figure, turned his attention to the controls. Christian was busying himself ready for take off; the man was now beside the cockpit. "Jump in as soon as …." Christian stopped his sentence; he felt the cold steel of a gun barrel against his temple. Sickness came to him, the type of sickness that starts in the pit of your stomach, spreads through every channel, every sinew of your body. Drying the throat and mouth, sending pulsating strands of pain, deceit, to the brain – the sickness of betrayal.

The man, recognisable now as an SS officer, spoke, his mouth in a twisted smirk, the lips thin, cruel, the eyes burning with a mixture of satisfaction and hate.

"So good of you to come, and on time, Flight Lieutenant Kawolski. Hande hock!"

Christian raised his hands; this was no time to be a hero.

Two German soldiers now stood behind the SS man, their machine pistols aimed at Christian's head. The SS man released the pressure of the Luger from his temple and took three steps back, the gun still trained on Christian.

"Out, schnell." The officer commanded.

Christian looked at the SS man, recognised his rank as an SS Oberstleutnant. He turned his vision panoramically to take in the two soldiers, shrugged his shoulders portraying his willingness to obey the command, unbuckled his straps then hoisted himself out of the aircraft.

What he did in the cockpit with the brandy had gone unnoticed. Before he left his seat, whilst unbuckling the straps he had unscrewed the top of the brandy and as he began to climb from the aircraft, he had kicked the bottle over, the liquid escaped onto the seat spilling to the floor.

Christian stood in front of the SS officer; his hand went to his pocket. The German raised his pistol in alarm. "Cigaretten," Christian said, pointing to his pocket. The officer nodded. Christian took out his lighter and lit the cigarette. Keeping his finger on the Zippo lighter, he maintained the flame. Christian stared hard at the SS man, before exhaling his smoke.

"The engine."

"What?" asked Christian.

"The engine, turn it off, if you would be so kind," smiled the cruel lipped man.

"What? Oh yes, yes of course."

Christian leaned into the cockpit pulled the fuel mixture control lever open as far as it would go before turning to the SS man again. Christian grinned back at the Oberstleutnant, saw his pupils dilate, saw the realisation on his face. Christian turned and threw the still flaming lighter into the cockpit. The alcohol ignited instantly, mixing with the fumes from the open mixture control. The SS officer sent the Luger crashing into Christian's head. The intensity of pain spread, Christian's eyes watered, his knees buckled, his body slumped and fell towards the ground. Christian had just enough consciousness left to feel two pairs of uniformed arms grab him, stopping his fall and dragging him backwards, his feet scraping against the grass and mud of the field.

They dragged him perhaps twenty paces, his rolling eyes tried to focus, he saw the flames rising from the cockpit, smiled, then heard the rush of wind. The noise of the explosion blew the two men dragging him to the ground and he felt his aching head hit the earth as the blackness came. Christian had passed out.

Christian came to consciousness in the back of a German army truck, the bumping stirring his senses; the natural human response was to let out a low moan. All this gave in return for his endeavours to regain some sense of normality was a sharp kick to his shin from one of the disgruntled guards. The excruciating pain brought him to reality. 'Christian', he told himself, 'Show them you're awake and they will hurt you. Pretend, feign unconsciousness, then they will get bored, leave you alone, Concentrate, Christian'.

Christian lay quiet, playing dead. To concentrate his mind he noted the turns of the truck, the distances between turns. By the time the truck finally came to a halt he had forgotten most of the information he had gleaned. The pain in his head the throbbing in his shin had been too much to bear . . . the darkness had come again.

Yvette Granville had watched from a distance, saw the capture of Kawolski, the blowing up of the plane and the beating Christian had received for his bravery.

When the truck carrying Christian had pulled away together with the German staff car Yvette had hopped onto her cycle and pedalled to the cross roads, waited for the truck to arrive and watched it and the staff car turn toward Rennes. They were probably taking him to the local army barracks, to work on him tonight before taking an early flight to Paris tomorrow.

Yvette knew Von Ebstein was in Paris, knew he would want to be involved, not only in the praise that would be bestowed upon him, but also in the sadistic nature of the interrogation. She knew she wouldn't be able to inform London whilst at the same time finding out where and when Christian would be moved. Yvette decided to stick close to Kawolski, then let London know when she had more information.

When Christian came round it took him a few moments to establish where he was, his body movement was restricted, the pain in his head and shin accompanied somehow by pain in his ribs, hands and thighs. Christian realised he was tethered to a chair, his hands tied behind him. There was a table in front of him, the dark shape of a man seated behind a bright light shinning in his face.

"What is your name?" the shadow was speaking.

Christian recognised the voice as the German Oberstleutnant with the Luger.

"You know my name, my rank and probably my serial number."

"Answer the question."

"Go screw yourself." No sooner had the comment left Christian's mouth when the back of a hand slapped his face, he felt the warm blood trickle from the corner of his mouth, instinctively his tongue went to the area of pain. The salty taste of blood filling his senses.

"I am a British officer. I demand to be treated as a prisoner of war." Christian turned to the soldier who had slapped him, a sergeant, "and tell this thug he should salute officers."

"You are a filthy Pole, you could have stolen that uniform." Swore the SS man.

"Oh, I suppose I stole the plane as well, flew it all the way to occupied France, blew it up just so I could wonder at the greatest set of criminals the world has ever seen." The sarcasm was working, the SS man shot out of his chair, all control of the interrogation gone, he lashed out at Kawolski striking his head with some blunt instrument. Christian smiled just before he blacked out again

At 4.30am a truck pulled out of the gates of the chateau of Vitre in the front was Hans Steiner together with a naval marine driver. In the back of the truck were two men in civilian clothes each carried a pistol with silencer attached.

Christian Kawolski could not remember how many times he had blacked out that night. Everytime he came to, the questions started, counteracted by his defiance followed by the beatings and their inevitable consequences.

He knew he had to hold out as long as possible before giving a snippet of information away, that would, he hoped, ease the punishments allowing a chance, an opportunity for him to escape. He must, however, make sure he was mentally and physically capable of seeing an opportunity for he knew such options were available only for a second or two. He would have to be careful in what, when and how he let the information slip and most importantly it had to be plausible.

The cell door opened, and two guards entered. Christian steeled himself for another trip to the room with the bright light. His body was a single mass of pain, it was impossible for Christian to differentiate between where on his body the pain started and finished.

The guards hauled him to his feet, almost carried him down the corridor, his flying boots dragging behind him. His eyes rolling in his head, Christian was unable to comprehend direction. His senses, some still functioning were alerted. He felt cold air on his face, dim light appeared through his swollen half-closed eyes. He heard the clunk of a car door opening and was lifted into a confined space. The smell and touch of leather was cooling to his grazed and battered skin, then motion followed, if only he could sleep.

Freddie Moreland was pacing up and down in the confined space of the radio operator's room at RAF Northolt. Christian should have landed over an hour ago, and he was worried. Freddie battled with himself, what should he do next? Give Christian more time, inform Commander Brethwell? No, no not yet, could be engine trouble, weather, a hundred different reasons for Christian's delay. He'd wait; give him another 30 minutes or so. If he hadn't heard anything by then he would act, but only then.

Yvette Granville from her concealed vantage point saw the staff car start, move forward and park outside the side entrance of the building on Rue du Nord. Yvette saw the battered young pilot being manhandled into the back of the car. An SS Oberstleutnant sat in the front seat alongside the driver, the staff car pulled away heading she assumed in the direction of the airfield. Yvette returned to where she had left her bicycle, mounted the saddle and began pedalling in the direction the car had taken.

Steiner stood by the truck that was turned 180 degrees to the road as if in a roadblock. The marine corporal, his machine pistol slung across his chest, stood two paces to his left, three paces behind the Officer. Both men stood silently, alert, waiting.

Steiner saw the car, only a black dot in the early morning light crest a hill on the horizon before beginning its descent amidst the patchwork of small fields and hedgerows of the undulating French countryside. Steiner knew it would disappear shortly only to rise again into the shady tree lined crest of the hill upon which he stopped the truck.

When the car disappeared from sight as predicted, Steiner unfastened the cover on his officer's holster, withdrew the Luger, fitted the silencer before putting the weapon in the belt of his trousers. The two marines that had travelled in the back of the truck did the same from their positions of concealment on either side of the road. The staff car came into view a few yards in front of Steiner, the driver of the car reacted quickly to the situation braking hard managing to stop a few feet in front of the officer standing in the middle of the road.

Steiner had held his arm in the air signalling the car to stop. The front two seats of the Mercedes were open to the air, the soft-top being pushed back, Steiner approached the staff car, its engine still running.

"What's the matter?" The Officer in the front passenger seat demanded.

"Sorry, Oberstleutnant." Steiner smiled, took out the pistol and shot the officer from slightly above, the bullet making a small hole in his head. The back of the skull smashed, particles of brain and blood splattered the soldier in the back seat directly behind the SS officer. The bullet, which had killed Oberstleutnant Carl Metzer, entered the soldier's groin. In a half second Steiner had shot the other soldier, killing him instantly. The two marines had sprung from their hiding places, one shooting the driver who tried desperately to drive away, at the same time reaching for his weapon. He succeeded in neither. The other marine put the splattered, groin shot soldier out of his misery, his eyes wide and staring, shock, disbelief still evident in death.

Christian was aware of something happening but neither his mind nor his eyes could comprehend.

"It's ok, Flight Lieutenant, you're safe for the time being." Steiner's voice was low, calm, concerned, almost sympathetic. "Those bastards won't hurt you anymore."

As Yvette pushed her cycle over the crest of the hill she saw the German staff car stopped in the middle of the road. Yvette hesitated, had they spotted her in Rennes or perhaps in the woods when the aircraft had landed? She thought about turning, making her escape. Options, options, but which one Yvette? They must surely have noticed her following. Seen her descend the hill into the dip in the countryside. Known she would not be able to cycle up the hill to where she stood now. Yvette's body started to react, the reaction of fear.

After weighing the options, she knew her only hope was to continue, act innocently, bluff her way past the stationery car. Yvette approached the staff car cautiously, just a local girl on some errand she had decided. Something, something wasn't right but what was it?

Yvette Her training, years of uncertainty, danger, mistrust, came to her. Something was odd about the car's position. It was awkwardly parked, as if the driver was in a hurry, surprised by something that made him stop sharply. She was close enough now to see the four Germans she had seen get into the car outside the barrack block in Rennes. Alarm spread within, but where is the pilot? The Polish airman. Where was Christian Kowalski?

Still no movement, Yvette was about three paces from the car when she realised, they're dead...but who? She laid the bike on the roadside quickly checking the immediate area for eyes, nothing. She scanned the road in front, behind, nothing. Yvette opened the basket seated on the handlebars of the bicycle, took out the linen bundle, carefully unwrapping the cloth to expose the Walther. She pulled back on the weapon hearing, feeling the bullet slip into the chamber. Slowly she approached the stationary vehicle. The Walther held with both hands in front of her moving slowly from head to head. The sight that met her eyes brought the nausea to her mouth, German or not, the scene that confronted her was horrific, brutal.

Regaining some semblance of composure, Yvette examined each corpse, the Oberstleutnant in the front had been shot, executed from close range, and each of the four Germans had a neat hole in their foreheads. The man seated behind the officer had been shot twice. She assumed the second bullet's entrance was in the centre of the rust coloured patch that stained his trousers. On closer scrutiny Yvette realised the bullet had come out of the brain of the officer.

Yvette studied the scene, as a policeman would do, there was no sign of panic; no guns had been drawn yet each man carried a machine pistol. She checked, none had been fired. There were no bullet holes in the vehicle. 'My God,' she thought, whoever had done this must have been known to the SS officers.' Kawolski, where was Christian Kawolski? Who had taken him, where to and why?

The truck had driven back to the Chateau at Vitre, Kawolski had been taken to a large room where a nurse did all she could to treat the young man's battered body. Although still unconscious, Christian was given a mild sedative to help him rest, allow nature to begin its own healing process. He lay on the large four-poster bed the barred windows obscured by the heavy curtains.

Steiner reported to Mosel.

"Hans. How did it go?"

"No problem sir, thirty, forty seconds at the most, caught them totally by surprise."

"No witnesses?"

"No sir," Steiner was very matter of fact.

"Kawolski? How is he?"

"Bit battered and bruised, sir, He'll live."

"Where is he now, Hans?"

"The nurse attended to him, gave him a mild sedative, should be out for the count."

"Good…Hans? Well done." Mosel was pleased with the young aide's actions, his professionalism.

Freddie Moreland conceded to the inevitable, Christian wasn't coming back. Not for sometime anyway. Freddie's face became pale, sad….perhaps never.

He knew what he had to do. Freddie called the emergency number for Commander Brethwell, after a few moments the phone was answered.

"Brethwell."

"Sir, it's Flight Lieutenant Moreland here, sir."

"What is it Freddie? Has Kawolski arrived back?"

"No sir…sir…I don't think he's coming back." Freddie's voice portraying his thoughts.

"What! Explain!" Brethwell was not a happy man.

Freddie told him everything.

Emily awoke early; she was excited. Today, this evening perhaps, she would be able to speak to Christian, hear his voice, see him maybe. She dressed for work quickly, she wanted to be early and use the office phone to speak to the base before her boss arrived. A last minute check in the wardrobe mirror then she was off, taking the stairs that led from her flat two at a time.

Harry Milburn telephoned Commander Peter Thompson at home.

"Hello, Harry, what's happened?"

"Its our boy, he's disappeared sir."

"Disappeared!"

"Yes sir, apparently he didn't make it back to Northolt. I've just come off the phone with Commander Brethwell, Freddie Moreland called him about twenty minutes ago, told him no sign of Kawolski, he suspects he's been captured or run into Jerry fighters. He contacted the coast guard, air sea rescue; they've heard nothing.

"What about Lucien?" Thompson knew what the answer would be.

"No sign either sir, We're a bit in the dark at the moment, perhaps we'll hear something soon." Harry tried to sound hopeful.

"What about Yvette?"

"Nothing yet sir..." he paused. "Sir, maybe Yvette's in the same boat as Kawolski, and Lucien."

"Yes, maybe you're right." Commander Peter Thompson was sure Yvette would not have shown herself. She would have waited, watched, found out where Kawolski had been taken, worked out all the possibilities before contacting London. Yvette Granville was a pro. Anybody who could survive and operate right under Himmler's nose, first in Warsaw, then Paris. Somebody who had out thought, outwitted the Germans for five long years was not going to risk her cover, easily.

"If Yvette makes contact or we hear anything, let me know immediately Harry."

"Yes sir, will do." The line went dead.

The Storch reconnaissance aircraft had searched the area from the Normandy coast south of Cherbourg to almost the estuary of the Gironde near Bordeaux. Low on fuel it had returned towards its base at the airfield outside Rennes. On its final approach the pilot had radioed the control tower to tell them that there was a fire, a large fire, in what appeared to be a clearing in the woods to the north of Rennes, close to the road from Vitre to Fougeres.

The controller in the tower had asked for confirmation that the fire the pilot had spotted was the wreckage of the missing Junkers 52. The pilot, honest in his assumption, confirmed that it could be an aircraft fire but he couldn't be certain. The controller accepted the pilots view telling him to proceed with his intended landing, that he would contact the army first thing so that they could properly access the reason for the fire, report any sign of aircraft wreckage.

The army following the co-ordinates given by the pilot of the Storch found the wreckage, reported to the Luftwaffe Commander at the airfield that the scene of the report was indeed a crash, aircraft wreckage was strewn all over the clearing in the woods. The fire, which had followed the downing of the plane, must have been intense, as no clear identification marks had been found.

Had the controller, tired after a long stretch in the tower, told the Army that a Junkers 52 was missing, they would have told him the wreckage was not that of a large three-engined plane but of a smaller single engined craft. To the Luftwaffe Junkers 52/3 call sign Phoenix no longer existed.

Book found Freddie in the tower still desperately searching the radar and the sky. Hoping Christian's plane would suddenly appear.

"What is it Birdy?" Freddie had noticed that Book was breathing heavily, "you'll have to give up the fags Birdy," he thought to himself.

"It's a young lady sir, Wants to speak to you . . . its about Mr Kawolski."

"What did you tell her Book?" Freddie's tone reverting to the formal.

"Nothing sir, told her a load of fibs, but she's persistent, wants to talk to you sir, won't take no for an answer."

"Ok Birdy, have her put through, will you."

"Already done that sir, she's on line two."

"Thanks Birdy, that will be all." Freddie hesitated before finally picking up the phone.

"Moreland…Hi Em, how are you?….Can't say anything, Emily, this is an open line, you understand. Yes…yes… of course I will…Emily it's just routine…No, Christian won't be able to…not today…Yes perhaps I might be able to get away later…look I'll meet you at that pub, the Plough? Yes that's it…ok….ok see you there…Bye, Em." Freddie Moreland's face said it all, just how was he going to tell her?

Major General Alexander Popowski was in the line with the two Polish divisions in Italy, a short distance from monastery hill. The American attack in the west was in full swing. US General Clark's force was predominately American with a smattering of British units for support.

The British had mounted a localised offensive to distract the German defenders to the East, on the banks of the Rapido River. The centre, Cassino Town itself and the monastery, like some gladiatorial sentry guarding the entrance to the valleys and plains that led to the city of Rome, was relatively quiet. Monastery Hill, towering over the town, had been the focal point of the whole campaign, not so much for its strategic value, but for the symbolism of defiance. The kingpin upon which Kesselring's Gustav line psychologically depended.

If only the British and Americans would let him devise a plan or put one of the many he had submitted to action, Popowski was convinced the brave Poles would take the monastery. However, that was not to be, political pressure upon Alexander had forced the issue. The Americans under the vain, conceited Clark would have the first crack. Alexander weighed down by the diplomatic niceties of the sometimes-fragile alliance between American and British political ambitions, as opposed to strategic actions to win the campaign, was forced to sit and wait. If the Americans failed, he knew exactly what he would do, the Poles playing a most significant part.

Popowski, disheartened by the lack of activity, was at least grateful on a personal basis to be at the front. Opposite the Poles were some of the most determined and professional soldiers available to the Axis forces, Fallschirmjager, the German paratroops. The Poles would have preferred the Nazis, SS battalions, Hitler Youth, but a dead German was a good German. The Poles would take anything, providing they could be used as Polish forces, not fed piecemeal into the fight in other unit activities. For this purpose Popowski had badgered Alexander into allowing the Poles to fly their own flag.

To the German defenders, the audacity displayed by the openly flying of Polish flags along the length of the line, therefore breaching the security of British troop dispositions, was matched only in the knowledge that the soldiers in front of them were fired by patriotic fervour, interspersed with hatred. That would make the Poles determined in assault, liberal in casualties, ferocious in battle, a foe to be reckoned with.

The Poles themselves, fired with anticipation, knew the battle when it came would be costly in terms of human suffering and sacrifice. The monastery on top to the rugged mountain stood as a symbol of everything Nazi. They would attack it when the time came, with the same tenacity as they would if it were the Reichstag itself. Major General Alexander Popowski was determined to be there when it happened.

His courteous admonishment from Alexander had strengthened his resolve to play a decisive part in the final conduct of the European war. If he could prove his abilities, not just in planning and liaison but in battle itself, there was no way Eisenhower could ignore him or his beloved Poles. He would have to be recalled, put together again with the practical Montgomery, ready to play a major role in the invasion of occupied France. If Popowski had known then just how much of an important role he would play in the invasion of occupied Europe he would have been less enthusiastic.

Emily had asked her boss if it would be OK to take a later lunch so as to fit in with Freddie's time scales. He agreed, as she knew he would.

Emily was seated in the garden outside the public house, in the same seat as when she had met Christian. Emily sipped on her lemonade its bubbles exploding in the liquid; the oxygen expanding in its desperate journey to the top of the glass was exactly how her tummy felt. The fear, excitement, stimulating gastric reaction.

She saw Freddie's car as it crested the top of Ducks Hill, the shiny little red roadster, reminding her of the day she had spent with Christian by the river, their tender lovemaking that night. The night before his first Lysander operation. She watched as Freddie drove into the car park of the Plough.

When she saw him, panic set in. Freddie's face was concentrated, nervous tension showing in his furrowed brow, sadness in his eyes.

"No Freddie, no…it can't be; not Christian, not my Christian." Emily's whole body began to shake in fear and trepidation. Her eyes became moist, her throat dry, her hands fidgeted. "No please God not my Christian."

Freddie could see Emily's hurt. He cursed himself for appearing obvious. Emily said nothing; she just ran to Freddie and threw her arms around him for comfort, her head on his neck. He could feel the wetness of her tears, the heaving of her shoulders. He held her tightly as a father might do with a tearful daughter, firm, reassuring but caring.

Emily sobbed, her heart heavy, her mind in constant indecision as to Christian's fate.

"Is he…is he.." Emily could not bring herself to say the word.

"We don't know yet, Emily…we've heard nothing." Freddie searched his vocabulary for the right phrase; something that would bring hope to the suffering Emily was experiencing.

"No news is good news." God that's wrong, trite, thought Freddie.

"What I mean, Em, is the longer we go without news, generally means he's ok. Means he may be free…a prisoner at worst."

Emily raised her head to look into Freddie's eyes, She saw his hurt, and felt selfish in her actions. Freddie loved him too, the way a man would love another man, not the same love as a woman for her man, but love all the same. Emily squeezed Freddie tightly, holding him as he held her, saw the tears begin to fall embarrassingly from Freddie's eyes; Emily was now the protective one. "I know, I know, Freddie…you're right of course, the longer the better." Freddie started to tremble Emily held him firmer, the two friends their hearts torn by the same loss, stood silently together, not speaking, just holding each other.

Kawolski came to consciousness aware only of the pain others had caused to his battered limbs. Christian was unaware of the pain being felt by others faraway. Just opening his eyes took all the strength he could summon, the blurriness of his limited vision causing him distress.

Things came momentarily to view before fading into obscurity. He sensed, rather than felt, himself to be on a soft linnened bed, a canopy like a cloud above him. Light from a window punished his swollen pupils. A face…a face he knew . . . Emily? Monica? Monica, no, no, it couldn't be. What tricks were being played on him? The unfairness of it all, the face again, Monica. Two darker shapes holding her back, a voice, Monica's voice a language he knew, a name he knew – Christian – his name. He begged for it not to come, pleaded with all his determination, but the darkness still came.

Steiner came into the dark panelled library of the chateau at Vitre; Mosel was drinking coffee from an ornate cup. "Hans, how is he?"

"He came round for a moment sir, He's taken quite a beating. It will take time, I think."

"Keep me informed, Thank you, Hans."

Emily and Freddie had consoled each other, fortified with a brandy each. The sharp tasting alcohol allowed some relief to their tortured stomachs. Emily was calmer, more positive now. She and Freddie had discussed the possibilities of Christian's safety in detail, neither venturing into fateful conclusions.

Freddie looked at Emily, but what he saw was not the chirpy confident barmaid he had assumed she was, this was the real Emily, the Emily Christian had exposed, a beautiful, loving, caring sensitive young woman. Her overall aura portraying strength of mind; tenderness of love. Freddie knew why Christian had fallen in love with the girl, Emily was the sort of girl every man wanted to fall in love with.

They parted company a short time later, each promising the other that Christian would be Ok. Freddie promising Emily he would contact her the moment he knew anything. Emily promising Freddie that she would keep the faith, keep her chin up. Emily returned to work, unable to concentrate – Freddie returned to the airfield, his belief in Christian Kawolski's ability renewed.

The call Commander Peter Thompson had been waiting for, regarding the young Polish pilot came through.

"What is it, Harry?"

"It's Yvette sir, We've got some news regarding our young friend." Harry Milburn related the whole story as set out in Yvette's communiqué. When he had finished, he waited for his master's response.

"Tell Yvette to keep tabs. Try and find out what's happened to Kawolski, see if she can find out where they've taken him. And another thing, Harry." He added. "Find out what's happened to that bastard Lucien."

"Will do sir," was the only response, before the line disengaged.

Henri Dacourt, 'Lucien' his deceit having enabled him another day in his life as a collaborator, made his way to the prearranged meeting at the Chateau. He was pleased with himself. The smirk of satisfaction was evident in the dark eyes set within the swarthy complexion. Like a Judas of old, the thirty pieces of silver lay without guilt in the pocket of his persona.

Henri Dacourt's whole life had been based upon deceit. He had learned to connive his way in life as a child, an extra piece of bread here, a friend's stolen possession there, only his avarice had grown in stature. He no longer required the basics of life, but the objects of a man possessed by his own grandeur. His own self styled depravity.

The lives of the men and women he had betrayed were of no consequence to him. The rewards, the praises of his adopted German masters, were an ally to his cravings for material gain. 'What gaineth the man who inherits the whole world only to lose his soul?' the scriptures of his Catholic upbringing had said. To hell with his soul, he wanted to gain everything he could, no matter who was hurt in the process. His soul was already on its journey to its obvious end.

Mosel greeted Lucien in the library feigning pleasure at his arrival. Mosel after all was a soldier and a human being. He detested the conceited little traitor, tolerated his presence only in the knowledge that he was using Lucien to his own ends.

It was a fine spring day; the sun shone brightly in the deep blue sky a single small cloud interrupting the completeness, like a zeppelin gently cruising across the horizon. Mosel decided they would take their refreshments on the garden terrace, the library having been putrefied by the traitor's conceitedness. He opened the huge glass double doors, ushering his guest to the terrace.

"My dear Henri." The words almost stuck in Mosel's throat.

The two men were opposites in stature, and in integrity. They made strained conversation before getting to the point of the meeting.

"Herr Mosel, from your manner I can only assume all went well with the Polish pilot."

"Yes, my dear Henri, exactly as planned, anything to report from your side? Any reaction from London?"

"None as yet, mind you I have made myself evaporate so to speak, the English fools no doubt worrying about my demise – Let them, the pigs." Lucien spat out the words.

"You, Herr Mosel, will no doubt be pleased with my hypothetical death, this could allow me to be of use to my German friends, within another network."

"Oh, yes I have plans for you Henri." The smile disguised Mosel's contempt, "but first security, have the British put a watcher on the ground?"

"No Herr Mosel, I would have known, the fools still trust me." Lucien lied.

"I am convinced they have." It was almost an accusation to Lucien's ears, if he thought that, then he was right. Lucien hesitated before replying, trying to sound casual, unconcerned.

"Oh, there is a girl, no importance really just…" Lucien was cut off in mid sentence.

"What girl?" demanded Mosel impatience had turned to authority.

"She's a non entity from another network. Visiting a sick relation."

"I should have been informed immediately!" stormed Mosel.

"I…I…didn't want to upset your plans Herr Mosel. I…I just thought I would deal with her later…in my own way…you must believe me Herr Mosel, I was…" Lucien was grovelling now, infuriating the angry German naval officer.

"Her name?"

"Yvette, yes that's it, Yvette."

"Surname?"

"I don't…I don't know yet, please Herr…"

"You fool, If my mission is compromised by your stupidity…your head, my dear Henri, will fall! Do you understand?" Mosel's rage was evident on his purpling face.

"Herr Mosel, I promise you on my life that I will find the girl and dispose of her."

"No!" snarled Mosel, "no" his voice softening. "No Henri, you will find her and you will bring her to me, unharmed. Do you understand?"

"Yes Herr Mosel, trust me."

Trust was the last thing Ernst Mosel would do with Henri Dacourt. He dismissed the pathetic little excuse of a human being the way somebody might dismiss an annoying insect, with a simple wave of his hand.

Harry Milburn spoke yet again to Commander Thompson.

"What is it, Harry, have you heard from Yvette?"

"No not yet, it's something else sir, Kawolski, you remember you asked me to find out about his background."

"Yes." Thompson remembered.

"Well, it seem he has a wife…" Harry let it sink in before continuing. "And two young daughters sir, Anna and Maria."

"Have you checked on them?' Thompson's voice becoming alarmed.

"Yes sir, nobody at home."

"What about parents?"

"Our people in Poland have been busy on this sir. Kawolski's parents were killed during the bombing of Warsaw at the start of the war."

"Her parents?" Thompson quickly responded.

"I was just coming to that sir, our people checked on that also, seems she was there but she's gone…the children too, sir."

"Bugger."

"Well, not too bad, sir. The parents were also missing but here's where we've had a bit of luck. Seems the Poles have nosey neighbours as well, sir. Apparently a dark car, with a driver and two men came to the house early in the morning and took the woman and two children away."

"Mosel or Gestapo?"

"Mosel, I think, sir, apparently the elderly couple were picked up later, that was Gestapo, I reckon."

"You think Mosel's going to use the wife and children?"

"Yes sir, that's exactly what I think."

Cavenaugh was keeping a low profile after the beating he had received from Duffy. His nose was still badly swollen, the plaster an affront to his dignity. More importantly, his standing within his peer group and his vision of himself as the gangster leader, surrounded by his loyal mobsters, had been seriously damaged. He saw Duffy in his own mind's adventure as the FED, himself naturally, as heading the most wanted list. Just as in those American films, Cavenaugh was plotting his revenge.

Cavenaugh had to find Duffy's weak spot. He had to take him out of the frame without upsetting the boys in Dublin. If Dublin could point the finger of Duffy's demise firmly at Cavenaugh, especially now that the merchandise was beginning to flow again, Cavenaugh's life would not be worth living. He had to find a way of ridding himself of Sean Duffy without Dublin being suspicious, but how?

An evil smirk began to spread across his face; the dark rimmed swollen eyes betraying his devious mind. The girl, that little whore Emily, that was Duffy's weakness, he was protective of the little bitch. The bitch that had embarrassed him at the Litten Hotel back in 1942. She had nearly destroyed Cavenaugh's standing within the organisation; she had put a stain on his file. A stain that was permanent. If he could get to the girl, Duffy would be sure to come to her rescue, making him a target, a legitimate target, Cavenaugh thought.

Duffy had telephoned Emily at her place of work. He had found out from Freddie Moreland about Kawolski's situation by chance. They had bumped into each other in Ruislip Manor. Freddie was obviously concerned for Emily, knowing Duffy had affection for the girl. He was sure Duffy would be of some assistance in helping to console poor Emily. Duffy had naturally agreed, assuring Freddie of his intentions towards the girl.

"Hi Emily, it's Sean." He said when he was put though.

"Oh hello, Sean." Emily was being brave, trying to concentrate on her work, but her thoughts kept turning to Christian.

"Listen girl, I bumped into Freddie in the Manor, he told me about Christian. I'm sorry, Emily, I think I know how you feel."

Nobody knew how she felt, but she appreciated Duffy's concern.

"Thanks, Sean."

"Listen, Emily, I know I'm not the most ideal person to advise you on Christian, bearing in mind our history. But...but I am a good listener. If you need someone to talk to I am here. I promise I won't butt in with I told you so or the like. Perhaps we could meet, neutral ground perhaps?" Duffy's tone was sincere. Whatever had happened between her and Christian he accepted, he was just being Duffy, a caring shoulder to cry on, and a friend in need.

"OK Sean, maybe, perhaps tomorrow."

"Lunchtime?"

"No, no Sean, tomorrow evening, is that ok?"

"Fine, I'll pick you up about 8 o'clock. If that's ok with you Emily."

"No Sean, I'll meet you somewhere else, somewhere more discreet." Emily racked her brain.

"How about the Queens Head in Pinner? I've got to deliver some invoices over to Pinner tomorrow, I could scrounge a lift with one of the boys on site."

"Ok Emily, what time."

"Would six be ok Sean?"

"That's fine, Emily, I'll see you there, bye for now girl."

"Bye Sean, and Sean..." the line had gone dead, "thanks." Emily whispered.

Christian came round, his vision became clearer. This time it remained clear. Whatever had happened to him, his beatings, his short period of wakefulness followed by the inevitable blackouts, nature was doing its job. His body, mindful of the need for sleep, was repairing the damage done in its own inimitable way.

Christian stared at his surroundings. He was in a large decorative bedroom, high ceilinged, a chandelier evident. He lay on a four-poster bed with soft linen; heavy curtains covered the windows.

Wherever he was, it was clean, and comfortable. His senses all began to come into their own, the smell of the wooden panels, the clean air aroma of the bedding, a smell, a smell of...what, Christian think, a smell of....that was it! He was pleased with himself, like a child who had put a right shaped object into an equal space of shape and size, the smell was the smell of history. Christian knew he must be a very large country house or estate; there was no noise of town or city – only birdsong. He must be in a rural setting, but where?

Steiner reported to Mosel on Kawolski's progress. He had informed the nurse that the Polish pilot was awake; ordered her to attend to his wounds, make sure he received a nourishing meal. Most importantly, he had reminded the woman not to speak or portray any gestures that might lead the pilot to establish her identity or her country of origin. Mosel had made it clear that Kawolski was not to know where he was or who was in control. That would made the Pole uncertain, and give him less time to prepare his mental defence.

Mosel had also informed his trusty aide of the context of his meeting with Lucien, and told him to keep an eye on the detestable little Frenchman. Also he had told Steiner about Yvette. Mosel knew Yvette would try and find out about the airman, in order to report his whereabouts to her controllers in London. That would make her stand out, make it obvious to the locals, her inquisitiveness confirming her as an outsider.

Christian ate the meal the nurse had brought greedily; despite his condition – he was ravenous. For all he knew it was the first food he had eaten since Sunday, and how long ago Sunday was he didn't know. He had tried to engage the nurse in conversation, but she had simply ignored him. Whoever she was, whomever she was working for, she was keeping to herself. Whoever was keeping him, and attending to his needs, wanted something from Christian. What exactly, Christian had no idea, "I don't really know anything of importance, I'm just a pilot that's all."

When the nurse had left the room, Christian tired to get up. He needed to find out where he was, without that basic information he would be vulnerable, unable to plan his response. He tried desperately to raise himself from the bed, but the physical exertion had worn him out. The excruciating pain of his now useless right knee, its old wound having been compounded by the beatings, brought bravado to heel. He was just too weak, he'd have to rest, let his tortured body heal a bit more before trying again.

Yvette knew Kawolski was no longer in Rennes. The staff car, its corpses now devoid of their souls, had been heading to the airfield, she was sure. Whoever was responsible for the carnage she had found must be headed north towards the crossroads she had seen the night the pilot was captured.

To the North of the crossroads were the woods; no houses or farms inhabited the area for some miles distant. Therefore, the perpetrators of the massacre must have headed east or west. They would not have been able to go far due to the condition of the pilot. His treatment by the SS evident. He would need urgent medical attention and not in a public place, there would be too many eyes.

Fougeres to the east was a larger town, probably garrisoned, thickly populated. To the West was the small hamlet of Vitre with its impressive chateau – the château; it would be ideal! Thought Yvette. Whoever had taken Kawolski must have been well organised, the planning, the obvious inside information. The fact that the SS soldiers had not been surprised by the ambush meant that the instigator of Kawolski's temporary escape was somebody of authority and German.

Yvette pedalled towards Vitre confident that she was making the right decision. If Kowalski were being held in the chateau it would be obvious to someone of her training. Once she had confirmed her suspicions she would inform London, let them decide what she must do next.

SS Obergruppenfuehrer Manfred Von Ebstein was furious when he was told of the brutal slaying of his men in the countryside outside Rennes. The disappearance of the Polish pilot only compounded his anger. Whoever had committed this vile act would suffer the most horrible consequences and he Von Ebstein would be present at their humiliation, their deprivation. Von Ebstein screamed at his aide, he wanted an aircraft ready to fly to Rennes immediately, wanted a full report upon his arrival at the airfield outside Rennes as to exactly what had happened. More importantly he wanted someone to take the blame, somebody else to take the responsibility for the atrocity.

The call from Noel Riordan had brought Tommy Boyle's mind from the humdrum of police work, paperwork, mountains of the stuff.

"Hello Noel, this is a surprise. What can I do for you?"

"It's more like what I can do for you, Tommy, it's about your case, Duffy, the murders."

"I'm listening Noel, what is it?" Boyle's brain engaged.

"I've had a call out of the blue, this chap Phelan called, said he had some information about Duffy's whereabouts in 1939. Says he's got a witness who can prove Duffy's complicity."

"Go on Noel."

"Well, It appears this witness Phelan has dug up was present at the murder scenes, particularly Dublin, says Duffy was the murderer of both the prostitutes."

"Can we trust his information, Noel?"

"I think so, he seems to have all the facts about the Dublin case, facts that we in Ireland didn't make public."

Boyle was desperately trying to conceal the excitement in his voice. He had to react like a policeman, not show any pre-conceived malice or condemnation of the suspect.

"Do you think he will talk to me, Noel, this Phelan? Or better, the witness himself?"

"Yes Tommy, I think so," Noel was silent for a moment, thoughtful, "He seems more interested in your murder in Hammersmith, Tommy."

"What's bothering you, Noel...I know you, remember."

" I don't know Tommy, It's just the copper in me, suspicious, you know."

"Yes Noel. You think it could be a set up?"

"Possibly Tommy, It's just a bit coincidental don't you think?"

"Maybe, Noel, maybe, but I must follow it up, when can I meet this Phelan. Will he come over here?"

"No Tommy, He's adamant. Says he could be in danger in the UK, wants you to come over here to meet him."

"Where?"

"Roscommon, Tommy, He knows it's our home town." Noel's voice was unable to hide his unease at the sudden interest in cases that happened over five years ago. Why didn't this witness come forward at the time and why did he urgently want to speak about it now.

Boyle noted Noel's concern, but had to meet the man. A man who might be able to solve his dilemma, prove once and for all that the man he had pursued relentlessly was in fact the man who had brutally taken the life of Molly Redburn. He had always thought that man was Sean Duffy, now he might get the proof.

"Tell him I'll come, Noel. I'll let you know the details later, and Noel…thanks."

Boyle put down the receiver, now he thought is the difficult part, how the hell am I going to get the Commander to let me go back to Ireland so soon – God, he thought, Mary will kill me.

Kawolski awoke, refreshed by nourishment and sleep. He could sense his body would now be more capable of movement. It was dark, silent; it must be in the middle of the night. Now was his opportunity, he must find out where he was and who was holding him. Christian swung his feet out of the bed, placed them both on the soft carpeting, testing his right knee first - it was painful but bearable. Pushing with both hands, he found himself upright. Christian felt the blood rush from his brain and began to lose balance. Steadying himself with his arms, his determination finally overcame his body's objections.

Christian hesitated, regaining as much strength as he could muster before attempting the arduous journey to the bedroom door. It was only a few paces but at that stage of his recuperation it was like a marathon to him. Slowly he put one foot in front of the other, trying to bridge the gap between the bedpost and his objective. At two paces away, he made a dash for the door handle, catching it almost in a lunge. It broke his fall, allowing some respite. Once he had caught his breath he tried the handle on the door, turning slowly, pulling it towards him. The door would not budge; it was locked.

Christian decided to make for the window, but not on his unsteady painful knee, He would sit on his backside and with a lift and pushing movement drag himself across the floor. This method took longer but used less of his precious reserve of strength allowing Christian enough energy to raise himself to the window level. Christian slowly parted the curtains, and his heart sank. The window was barred.

His eyes scanned the darkness, trying to identify the scope of his temporary imprisonment. In front and below was a courtyard, fairly large in area, edged by outbuildings, which huddled against the walls. The walls themselves rose to level with his window, mentally judging the height Christian assumed he was on the third floor. The tops of the wall interspersed with battlements. The main gate was bordered on each side by two huge round towers each windowed, probably inhabited when the house, chateau, castle whatever it was had been occupied before the war.

Christian heard footsteps, and waited, trying to determine their direction. He cursed - they were getting louder, coming towards the room. He made a desperate attempt to reach the safety of the bed and he was only a couple of paces away from discovery when he heard the key being inserted into the lock. 'Come on Christian, only a few metres, you can make it.' he told himself. He was at the bedside when the handle turned and the door began to open, light beginning to flood the darkness. 'Move, Christian, move.' He threw himself onto the bed yanking at the covers at the same time. It was too late; the door was fully open.

Christian was breathing heavily, his heart pounding, his knee in agony. The tall, dark figure of a uniformed man filled the doorway, his silhouette enhanced by the light coming from the hallway. He didn't speak; he just shook his head and closed the door, locking it from the outside.

Christian's eyes became heavy; the exertion of his recce around the bedroom had taken its toll. Drowsiness was coming to him. At least it would take away the pain from his knee. 'Yes, a brave man.' thought Steiner as he made his way back to his room. The pilot would be ready for Mosel's gentle persuasive interrogation tomorrow, definitely a brave man.

Yvette believed she had found what she was looking for in Vitre. The chateau standing above the small hamlet was guarded, not by low priority troops as expected but German naval marines that meant somebody of importance was in residence.

Acting the role of young woman visiting her sick aunt in Rennes, she had asked the locals as to the history of the chateau. Which family had owned the property before the occupation, why the German navy was in attendance? In most cases all she received for her endeavours was a raised eyebrow, a suspicious look or a total rebuff.

Yvette decided to take a drink at the local café. When she entered, some of the locals made a hasty retreat. The French population as a whole accepted the German occupation, provided they could tend their fields, protect their animals, then life would go on. Restricted, compared to before the war, but life nevertheless. Nobody wanted to upset the applecart, endanger the fragile existence. The pretence of normality hung over the proud peasant people like a plague. Like an illness or deformity in the family, nobody wanted to talk about it.

The serving girl behind the counter was about the same age as Yvette, young, the war had deprived her of her most formative feminine years. Attractive and most of all desperate for a conversation with a woman of her own age, Anne Marie chatted freely with Yvette, as two young women would do, the subject's universal, men, fashion, love, romance.

The conversation lasted for two full glasses of wine, before Yvette was able to bring up the subject of the chateau. Anne Marie confident in her new found friendship was generous with details. Anne Marie told Yvette that the chateau remained unoccupied most of the time. The staff remaining in attendance to serve any visiting German dignitaries when required. The latest guests had arrived on Sunday during which there had been a considerable amount of activity. Since then all had gone quiet.

Yvette probed Anne Marie for specifics as to the identity of the visitors. Anne Marie divulged all she knew. Two cars had arrived on Sunday from the airfield at Rennes. In one a staff car, were two high ranking German officers, in the second car rode a young blonde woman, German in appearance, there was also a driver and guard. Yvette had asked Anne Marie what made her think the man was a guard? Anne Marie explained the blonde woman's demeanour in detail, it was obvious she was reluctant to enter the chateau; she looked frightened. She was obviously not there of her own accord. Yvette made her farewells and promised to visit again soon, providing her sick aunt could spare her.

CHAPTER 10

Christian breakfasted well; his body had recovered sufficiently for him to be able to bathe. The warm water poured by the mute nurse refreshed his muscles easing the stiffness caused by the still evident bruising. When he had finished his bath he was allowed to shave and dress, his uniform, cleaned and pressed, lay on his bed. A comb, together with toothpaste and brush lay at his disposal. His knee was still painful but the simple routine of washing, feeling clean and being in uniform had invigorated his body, stimulating his mind.

A lieutenant had escorted Christian to the library in the chateau where he was given fresh coffee and cigarettes, English cigarettes! The lieutenant, tall and handsome, had a strong face, the blue eyes sharp, the mouth generous, his manner genial. He had left Christian alone in the room locking the door behind him.

Christian lit a cigarette, drawing deeply. The first intake of breath releasing the nicotine to his body caused slight dizziness, as the drug permeating throughout his body brought relief, a calmness of mind, clarity of thought, like an addict taking a long awaited fix. Christian moved towards the windows, as he did a guard appeared, his machine pistol slung across his chest. Christian made a hasty retreat to the comfort of the large sofa and sat, continuing to enjoy the inner strength the cigarette was providing.

Christian had smoked several Players, even picked up a book, written in English, about the DeMontford family. Apparently the DeMontford's had played a role in the history of the chateau, predominantly when it had been a keep, a resting-place between battles. How appropriate. Christian thought.

The time passed slowly. During the first hours, Christian had been relieved at the lack of attention with his body becoming more functional every minute. Boredom began to set in, and with boredom came indecisiveness, apathy – with apathy, came collaboration.

Christian knew he would have to concentrate, apply his mind as to why he was here? And for what reason? His circumstances had gone from deceit, to cruelty to care, finally culminating in congeniality. He had faced the whole spectrum of human emotions in the space of a moment. Some people could never have travelled such experience in a lifetime, let alone a few days, he thought.

Christian's thoughts were interrupted by the appearance of Ernst Mosel with the handsome lieutenant he had seen earlier.

"Good morning, Flight Lieutenant Kawolski, I hope you have recovered sufficiently from your wounds to be able to talk." The man reeked of authority. "My name is Mosel, Ernst Mosel, this…" he pointed towards his aide, "is Leutnant Steiner, I believe you and Hans have made an earlier acquaintance."

Christian made to stand in the presence of a senior officer.

"Please, remain seated, Herr Kawolski. Do not put pressure on your knee." He turned towards Steiner again, a broad smile on his face. "Hans would be most upset to see all his careful nursing suffer a setback." Steiner smiled accordingly. "Hans, some fresh coffee for our guest, please excuse my manners, lieutenant." Mosel's expression conveyed sincerity. Steiner rang the bell, and within seconds a servant appeared, recognised Mosel's stare at the single coffee pot and cup, nodded his understanding, and retired to provide fresh sustenance to his masters.

"First of all, let me apologise for the treatment you received from er, my countrymen, they're Nazis. I am not; to me you are a soldier fighting for your country, regardless of which uniform you wear. Therefore, you are entitled to be treated as a prisoner of war." Mosel hesitated before continuing. "Unfortunately for you the Nazis under the laws instigated by them on the Third Reich, see you as something different…a traitor."

"What? That's ridiculous." Kawolski could feel his anger raising.

"I would agree with you, Herr Kawolski, however, their view is that because Poland is a conquered nation, under the protection of the Third Reich, that its people's loyalty under law should be to the Fatherland, the greater Germany. Therefore your escape to England to fight with the RAF is considered to be treason."

"No court in the world would accept that." Kawolski was clearly agitated.

"You are, of course, right. However, a German court would find you guilty." Mosel let the statement sink in.

Mosel was displaying a subtle approach to the art of interrogation. Firstly, offer kindness, then upset, shock your suspect, unbalance him, before coming to his aid with a solution, which allows him to do as you wish. This would allow him some semblance of pride or conviction – simply a get out.

"Those persons who captured you are a little out of sorts due to our illegal intervention on your behalf. Quite simply, Flight Lieutenant, they want you back, and they will stop at nothing to ensure your recapture."

The coffee arrived at the perfect moment for Mosel. Kawolski was still recovering from his treatment by the SS and was at a low point in his ability to think clearly. Mosel forced Kawolski down a path whereby there would only be two options available to him. His instinct for survival was already close to its maximum, and would opt for preservation, provided that some form of integrity could be maintained.

"You see, my dear Kawolski, if we were to hand you over to the Wermacht, it would not be long before the SS or the Gestapo found you. They, of course, are embarrassed by you. Firstly you blow up your aeroplane in front of them, then you have the audacity to escape. My worry, Flight Lieutenant, is that when and it is a case of when, they recapture you, is that the authorities, the powers that be, will simply execute you. After they have had their revenge of course, they will simply say you were shot trying to escape." Mosel's voice portrayed no malice, only a certainty of his convictions.

Kawolski was confused. His mind was still struggling with the pain his body had received, and was now confronted with the realisation of what Mosel had said. The SS would, he knew extract revenge on his body and mind, culminating in his certain death. The glib excuse of being shot whilst trying to escape was plausible in time of war, as so many souls departed could vouch for. Kawolski knew he had two choices, escape or death, the former a distant hope, the latter a certainty.

Christian looked at the eyes of his gentle tormentor. For although Mosel's kindness and sincerity were evident to Christian, his rationale was not so forthcoming.

"So why did you bring me here?" Christian's voice betrayed his fear.

"I am a German and a soldier, I have my duty, however, I am still a human being, I cannot simply stand by and watch a brave man be lost to the ugliness of revenge. On the other hand, I can't just let you go, so you see, my dear Kawolski, I have somewhat of a dilemma – duty over conscience." Mosel was a master in the art of subterfuge. His cunning camouflaged to the point of obscurity. His manner that of a father to a long lost son.

"You must have had an ulterior motive for freeing me from the SS." Christian's mind was desperately searching for a third option, an option however vague that could allow an honourable way out.

"No, not really," Mosel was expertly moving the interrogation to its next level. "However, you may be of some service to us."

"I'm no traitor." Christian's integrity was still in one piece.

"No of course, I would never ask you to betray your principles, nor your country." Christian believed he had upset the gentleman, he saw the hurt in his eyes.

"No, I would never ask that of you, Flight Lieutenant, more importantly, I would never expect you to agree…no…but if there is another way… perhaps…"

"What other way?" Christian was annoyed with himself; his mind's desperation to find an acceptable solution was clouding his resilience. Leapfrogging over his logic of thought, betraying his resistance, allowing himself to be manipulated into choosing the correct course of action.

"If we were able to provide you with a believable method of escape, allowing you to complete your mission, to bring back to England the traitor Lucien."

"You know my mission? But how?" interrupted Kawolski.

"Of course we know your mission, Lucien has been working for us for sometime. You didn't know, Herr Kawolski?"

"No, I didn't." Christian was feeling even more miserable. No wonder the SS had been waiting for him. It wasn't coincidental, nor the fact that Lucien had been captured, tortured, made to confess, he'd simply walked into a trap.

"But London . . ." Christian asked.

"London have suspected Lucien for some time my dear Kawolski, They…they simply had to prove his treason." Mosel could see the realisation hit Kawolski like a punch.

"You mean they knew, knew what would happen?" Christian felt sick, the nausea attacking his throat.

"Of course they knew…I'm afraid you were expendable Herr Kawolski." Mosel was assured of Christian's realisation that London had set him up – betrayed him.

"I am sorry…you didn't know?" Mosel was compounding his victory, ready for the final kill, but not yet, not just yet. He still had his ace to play, an ace that would make his victory total.

"My dear Herr Kawolski, I can see you are very upset. Hans, we should leave our guest for a moment to consider what he has just heard, leave him to come to terms with the magnitude of his discovery. Come Hans, let us leave this young man with his thoughts."

Mosel and Steiner left Christian alone in the library. Christian's attitude was not self pity, although anyone who had experienced the trials and tribulations he had been asked to deal with, could possibly have forgiven him if he allowed pity to raise its head. But it was not pity that Christian Kawolski felt at that moment; it was betrayal. Was Freddie involved? No, not Freddie, Freddie was just like Christian, a pawn, a small cog in the greater mechanism of deceit. It was S.O.E. and MI6 that were the perpetrators. They and they alone had put him in this situation, a situation that had forced him to decide between co-operation and certain death, a no way out scenario.

Christian's eyes filled with tears, the tears of a condemned man knowing his innocence. Christian's disgust with the conduct of his English masters was allowed to fester just long enough for his brain to decide a form of retribution.

Mosel the skilful interrogator was sure the next instrument of coercion, his ace, would totally destroy any patriotic fervour or sense of commitment the young Pole had left. Mosel was satisfied with his performance so far as he took a short walk in the gardens of the chateau. His eyes may have taken in the beautifully tendered lawns, the spectrum of colour provided by the spring flowers, but his mind was firmly on the matter in hand. Kawolski, worn down by the SS with their special brand of brutality, had been further debilitated by Mosel's skilful yet more subtle persuasion.

Steiner joined his superior in the gardens.

"Hans, you have news?"

"Yes sir, its about the French girl, Yvette, seems she's in Vitre. She's been asking questions. I think the young girl in the local café has told her of our presence, should I arrange to pick her up, sir?"

Mosel thought for a moment. "No Hans, she could be useful to us, she will be able to confirm our intentions with London."

"Do you think the Polish airman will break sir?"

"Yes, Hans, it's only a matter of time . . . and I think now is the time."

If Christian thought he had seen everything he was in for a shock. Mosel's next move would throw his mind into the abyss.

Mosel entered the library, confidence oozing from every pore of his body.

"Herr Kawolski, I have a little surprise for you, a pleasant one I trust." Mosel glanced over his shoulder towards the open doors. "Hans, our other guest if you please."

Christian Kawolski was totally dumbfounded by the sight that met his eyes.

"Monica...Monica but...but how?" Christian's heart was in his mouth.

"Christian, Oh Christian!" Monica rushed to Kawolski throwing her arms around his neck. "Oh Christian, I never thought I would see you again." The tears were exploding from her eyes.

"Monica how did...the girls...Monica the girls are they . . . ?"

"They're safe, for the time being darling, Oh Christian. I never thought I would see you again." Monica was sobbing, her shoulders heaving.

Mosel interrupted the reunion.

"I shall leave you alone with your wife, Herr Kawolski. Lunch will be served at 1.30 sharp; Hans will call you when it is ready. In the meantime enjoy your re-acquaintance. Mrs Kawolski." With that Mosel left the room, a courteous nod towards Monica.

Christian could still not believe what was happening to him, his guilt at not being able to visualise Monica or the girls clearly in his dreams, Monica her looks, her touch a distant memory, a faint recollection.

It had been five long years since he had seen, touched her. His emotions were in turmoil. His memory of her in some dark recess of his mind was somehow following a pinprick of light and recognition. Christian, unable to comprehend his feelings, just held her, held her tightly.

Monica looked into the handsome face of her husband, the passing of time had not altered his features, age had been kind to him, and the boyish looks were still intact. It was his eyes, those beautiful eyes that had changed. They were somehow distant. Monica knew at that moment that she had come close to losing Christian forever. Woman's intuition telling her what no other human mind could.

"Christian hold me close, please."

Christian did as she asked, the tears rolling down his face. She knew…she knew… he had failed… betrayed her. Monica consoled her husband, as only she knew how. A mental understanding came to both of them. The years of separation had taken their toll. Only the inner strength of their knowledge of love past could rekindle the love between them now. Like a perennial flower dormant for the winter, its life suspended, only awaiting spring to unfurl, to flower, once again becoming strong and beautiful.

Steiner entered the library on cue.

"Herr Mosel's compliments, Herr Kawolski, Frau Kawolska. Lunch will be in ten minutes. We will take our aperitifs on the lawn, since it is such a fine spring day." Steiner nodded to the guard who unlocked the double French doors leading to the terrace and the lawn beyond.

"If you would follow me." Steiner ushered the way.

Mosel was waiting by the rose garden.

"Ah, Hans, I see you have brought the Kowalski's. Champagne, Hans, I think."

"I took the liberty, sir." Steiner smiled.

"Excellent my dear Hans, excellent."

Commander Peter Thompson met Harry Milburn at the tearooms close to his Baker Street offices.

"What is it, Harry?" Thompson had waited until Harry sat down.

"We've heard from Yvette sir, seems she's located our lost pigeon." Harry was stirring his tea vigorously, the spoon clanking against the china cup much to Thompson's annoyance. "It's a bit vague, but apparently the SS picked our chap up." Harry looked around checking for ears. The teashop was empty save for an old lady of perhaps 70, whose hearing, Harry guessed, had departed long ago.

"Then the funny thing, sir."

"Carry on," Thompson was sipping the foul tasting brew.

"Seems he gets rescued. Taken to some chateau in Vitre, that's fairly close to Rennes sir, he's been held there since Monday we believe."

"Mosel?"

"That's what we reckon sir."

"He's in the bag then, what about Lucien?"

"No sign as yet sir…but Yvette seems to think he's still about."

"Why?"

"Well, she got to know this local girl who works in a café. She reckons someone answering Lucien's description went to the chateau…"

"And…?"

"Came back out again, cool as you like, sir."

"Thanks, Harry," Thompson got to his feet. "Let me know if you hear anything else."

"What about Yvette, sir?"

"Tell her to stay loose, see what happens, ok, Harry?"

"Right, sir,"

With that Commander Peter Thompson left. Harry finished his tea stood and walked towards the door.

"Oy, you," A plump lady behind the counter shouted. "That will be four pence for two teas."

"Typical." Thought Harry, he paid the plump woman.

The lunch provided by Mosel's staff was superb, medallions of beef, served with an excellent Chateau Margaux. Christian and Monica's minds, although fortified by the meal, were on other things.

When lunch was finished Mosel led Kawolski to the library, apologising to Monica for taking her husband away after so short a reconciliation. When they were both seated in the privacy of the large, airy room, Mosel waited for Christian to speak.

"What is it you want from me, Captain Mosel? If it's to betray my friends or country then forget it, I want no part." Christian was determined, resolute.

"My dear Kawolski, I would never dream of such, knowing you as I do, and I do know you Flight Lieutenant, I know you would never agree to something so crude."

"Then what's this all about?" Why did you rescue me from the SS, unless you had an ulterior motive."

Mosel smiled. "Yes, of course, you are right to an extent, Flight Lieutenant, let me explain. Should you return to England safely, your honour intact, your reputation as a hero enhanced by some remarkable escape, you will be chosen by SIS to undertake a special mission…we want you to accept."

"But why?" Christian's voice portraying his confusion.

"Because, Flight Lieutenant, the mission SIS is planning will provide us with an opportunity for the German people to rid themselves of Hitler." Mosel let the statement sink in. He was lying, of course, but he knew Kawolski would never agree to undertake any form of treason or anything that could be considered as treason.

"Hitler! You want to get rid of Hitler?" Christian could not believe what he had heard.

"Exactly Flight Lieutenant, the German people know the war is lost, we knew in 1942, but the Nazis were too powerful, however we believe now is the right moment. If we can make peace with the British and Americans, we can remove our troops from the Western front and attack the Bolsheviks en masse." This statement was not entirely a falsehood.

The German high command, the WEHRMACHT and ABWEHR (German Intelligence) in particular, did indeed have plans to remove Hitler, and conjecture put Rommel himself amongst the high-ranking German officers committed to the scheme. Admiral Canaris, Head of the ABWEHR, had made clandestine overtures to the Allies, but Himmler, distrustful of Canaris, had Hitler replace him. He was dismissed in February 1944. It all seemed logical.

"So where do I come in?" Christian, had he been fully in command of his faculties would have seen through Mosel's explanation but the combination of the betrayal by S.O.E., the beatings received from the SS, the kindness shown by Mosel and most importantly, the reunion with Monica had clouded his vision. Mosel was delighted with the way the plan had gone.

"We want you to obey your orders to the letter – with one small exception." Mosel proceeded to tell Christian in detail the events; circumstances and probable results of the S.O.E./SIS planned operation. When he had finished he waited for Christian's response.

"So I just follow orders as you have explained?" Mosel's appreciation of the planned operation together with the conduct of the war so far, seemed logical and entirely plausible to Christian. "What about my wife and children?"

"As soon as your mission is completed, your family will be moved from their temporary accommodation and flown on my personal aircraft to neutral Sweden and safety."

"And if I don't go along with your plan?" The question had to be asked.

"Then I will do all I can for your family…but the SS, the Gestapo…they will do everything and anything to punish you and your family for the embarrassment you have caused. SS Obergruppenfuehrer Frieherr Von Ebstein, of the German security service, is in charge of French operations; it was his men that were assassinated during your escape. He flies here today from Paris."

Christian did not need further explanation.

"And what of Monica, my wife?"

"She will be flown out of here to the safe house to rejoin your children in one hour. Steiner is packing her things at this moment. You will make your escape this evening, with our assistance of course." Mosel smiled.

"I have no choice do I?" Christian was being realistic.

"I'm sorry, not really, Flight Lieutenant." Mosel was honest.

"Is Lucien still alive?"

Mosel was slightly taken aback.

"Yes, he's still alive."

"Then I want to take the bastard back with me." Christian's face displayed his hatred.

"Yes, yes of course, he has fulfilled his use, you may have him…if you wish."

"Yes I do wish…now Herr Mosel, if you don't mind I would like sometime with my wife." Christian felt strong again.

"Yes, yes of course…I will see to it immediately." Mosel turned and left the library, leaving Christian alone with his thoughts.

Christian and Monica hugged each other tightly; Monica's tears cascading down her cheeks. Christian remained strong, manly on the outside, a little boy inside. He had told Monica she would be safe, Mosel had given his word as an officer and gentleman. Christian believed the man's sincerity. They had talked about the children, the girls growing up strong and confident, despite the upheavals of their short lives. Christian told Monica to kiss the girls, "Tell them Daddy was safe and that he loved them very much."

Steiner entered the library.

"Herr Kawolski, mein Frau." He nodded courteously at Monica, "It is time." Steiner stepped outside the door as a mark of respect, waiting patiently. Christian took Monica's face in his hands; he tidied a strand of blonde hair from her cheek and wiped away the tears gently from her eyes.

"I do love you, Monica…you…you do know that?"

"Yes, Christian, I know." The tears were forming again.

He pulled her close to him, his mouth on hers; they kissed long and deeply. Christian pulled away to look at her face; she kissed him softly on her forehead.

"Goodbye, my darling husband."

Monica pulled away, overcome with emotion, and almost ran towards the waiting Steiner. Her shoulders were pumping as she cried, her heart heavy, her mind in turmoil. Steiner opened the back door of the waiting car for her. Christian stood by the doorway and watched as the car pulled away across the courtyard and out of the main entrance to the chateau. Monica did not look back.

Whilst Christian and Monica were saying their sad farewells, Mosel had met with Lucien. He told Lucien to plan a mock rescue of Kawolski, take him to the Junkers 52, which was hidden in the woods to the north. There, Mosel's men would surprise Kawolski, killing him whilst he attempted to escape. Lucien, naturally presumed dead, would be given a new identity together with a small fortune, payment for his deceit, then provided with transport and false documents he would be able to make his way to neutral Spain.

Mosel was adamant that the French girl, Yvette, should witness the whole event, allowing her to report to London the brave action taken by Lucien and its unfortunate results. The operation was to be mounted at 11pm that night. The cunning of Mosel's plan appealed to the swarthy Frenchman. He would be exonerated by London, even praised, whilst collecting a considerable fortune from his German masters.

Lucien shook hands with Mosel promising a theatrical event that evening. When he had gone, Mosel washed his hands, not like Pontius Pilate but simply because he wanted to remove the stain of Lucien's grubby deceit from his skin.

Mosel's personal Junkers 52 had landed and refuelled at the airfield outside Rennes that afternoon. Once Monica and her ever-present guard had boarded the plane, the pilot taxied ready for take off.

Hans Steiner watched as the heavy craft took off, banking slightly to the right before levelling out, then continuing its climb. The emotional state of the beautiful young Polish woman sat heavily on Steiner's conscience. He shrugged his shoulders, got back into the waiting car and headed back towards the chateau at Vitre.

As Steiner's car left the airport perimeter a Storch light aircraft made its final descent towards the runway. On board the aircraft was SS Obergruppenfurher Von Ebstein.

Having completed her duties in Pinner, Emily made for the Queens Head public house in the High Street where, as pre-arranged, she would meet Sean Duffy. The warm late spring sunshine bathed the cottage style little shops and houses of the High Street. Each huddled against the next, trying to keep their balance on the precarious incline reaching to the church that stood like a shepherd on the hill watching over its flock. The Queens Head stood out from the other buildings, its long black and white frontage greedily stealing the eye.

Emily entered the door to the saloon bar; It's dark wooden rafters supporting the nicotined ceiling. Sean was seated on a stool at the bar, the obligatory dark stout matching the timber framing. He smiled as he watched Emily enter, the momentarily open door allowing the light to flood the dark interior exposing nameless faces in framed photographs, and silhouetting Emily's outline. The shape of her legs clearly visible beneath the cotton print dress, her hair golden with the sun, like firelight on a winter's night.

"Emily, you look radiant this fine evening, girl. What would you like to drink?"

"A gin and tonic please, Sean. Have you been waiting long?" Emily's smile pleased him.

"No I've just arrived, this is the first of the day." Duffy glanced at the almost full glass beside him.

Emily stood next to Sean, one foot resting on a brickwork plinth seated at the base of the bar. Duffy looked along the corridor between the counter and the back wall towards the raised public bar, trying to get the attention of the innkeeper. The landlord trundled down the length of the bar descending the two steps into the serenity of the saloon. He was a huge man built like a tramp steamer, the thick black beard giving the appearance of a sea captain or some character from a Dickensian novel.

"Gin and tonic for the lady please, James." Without speaking the huge man poured the colourless mixtures into a small stubby glass. Duffy paid him. Without speaking he took the two glasses, leading Emily to a quiet corner table by a window.

Emily sat crossed legged, the material of the cotton dress riding up exposing her bare legs, small, dainty little blonde hairs reflecting in the permitted light. As Emily noticed Sean's stare, she gently eased the material back over the exposed skin, admonishing him with her eyes, forgiving him with her smile. Duffy noted the look, returned the smile, before becoming serious again.

"Any news of Christian yet?"

"No, no I've heard nothing, they won't tell me anything, it's not fair, Sean."

Duffy took her hand in his. "I know, Emily, I know." He patted her hand.

"Why Christian? Why now....? We've only just met, only just...." a tear formed in her eye.

"You're in love with him, aren't you?" it almost came as a statement. Duffy was annoyed at the lack of sympathy in his words; he hadn't meant it to come out the way it sounded.

"Yes, Sean...I do. I love him very much." Emily looked into Duffy's eyes and saw the hurt. "I'm sorry Sean, I know you have feelings for me, and you have been so kind and we were good for each other for a time, but..."

"But?"

"But...but I don't love you Sean, I never have, not in the way you would want me to, the way...the way I love Christian." Emily started to cry.

Duffy took out a clean white handkerchief; he mopped the tears away from her sweet face.

"There, there girl, I know...I've always known, but...but I guess I just hoped..."

"I'm so sorry, Sean, can you ever forgive me?"

I already have," Duffy's smile, his grin, told her what she wanted to hear.

"Oh, Sean." Emily threw her arms around his neck, her tears making his hair damp.

Duffy held her tight, the swell of her gently heaving breasts against his chest, the smell of her golden hair on his cheek. He wanted her more than anything at that moment, but knew his chance had passed; he'd lost her forever. Duffy eased Emily's face from his neck; he held her face in both hands, staring deep into her eyes.

"Listen girl, I love you...but...I do understand, I've seen the look in your eyes." Duffy smiled at Emily. "This Christian feller is a lucky man. A very lucky man not only is he coming back, he's coming back to you."

"Do you really believe that Sean?" a glimmer of hope in Emily's voice.

"I don't need to believe, Emily, I know girl." Duffy kissed her gently on the cheek. Duffy knew Christian would come back.

Emily wiped her eyes.

Yvette Granville was chatting with Anne Marie, the young French girl in the small café in Vitre. The waitress full of girlie small talk. The café was empty except for Yvette and the younger girl, the normal patrons still busy at their work in the fields or small shops. Anne Marie was in mid conversation when she stopped, her face betraying a mixture of fear and disgust, Yvette followed the girl's eyes to a small figure of a man stood by the door, his silhouette masked by the sheer size of the brute that stood behind him.

The small swarthy man approached the two girls, while his minder locked the door, standing guard. The nastiness of his stare was enough to make Anne Marie realise her presence was no longer required. She made a hasty retreat to the other end of the café.

"You are Yvette?" the small man questioned.

"Who are you?" Yvette's voice strong, unperturbed.

"Forgive me, mademoiselle, I am Lucien, you perhaps have heard of me?" He attempted a smile the yellow teeth exposed by the parting of the thin lips.

"Should I have?" Yvette's return was sharp.

"There is no need for that tone, Granville, I am Henri Dacourt, Head of the Lucien circuit as you well know." The little man glanced at the ape guarding the door. Yvette followed his gaze.

"What do you want with me? Monsieur Dacourt."

"As you are well aware a Polish pilot is being held at the chateau on the hill."

"I am aware of his presence." Yvette, unlike most people in the area, was not intimidated by Lucien.

"I propose to break him out, provide a method for his escape, a return to England."

"On whose authority?" demanded Yvette; she could see the annoyance in Lucien's face.

"On my authority." Lucien screamed. He realised the girl was winning the battle of nerves, he lowered his tone, his voice softer, less agitated. "As I was saying, I shall make his escape at 11pm tonight. Your duty Yvette will be to observe and to inform London of his escape, is that possible within your busy schedule?" Lucien's sneer was compounded by his look towards Anne Marie before returning his gaze to Yvette.

"I will be available, now if you don't mind, I have something to do before tonight."

Lucien found his anger hard to hide; he stood up stormed towards the door, not giving the ape enough time to unlock it. Lucien stamped impatiently until the door was opened, before sliding sulkily into the street.

Anne Marie approached Yvette, nervously checking to make sure that Lucien had gone.

"You were very brave, Yvette, he is a very bad man, he has hurt many people."

"Don't worry, I can handle Monsieur Dacourt, Anne Marie. I need a cognac, I have a bad taste in my mouth."

By the time Sean and Emily left the Queens Head it was dark, with a chill in the air. Duffy put his jacket over Emily's shoulders, his arm around the girl in a protective manner. Emily had been cheered by Duffy's humour mixed together with his natural charm had halted her sadness. She had also become slightly drunk, the lack of food allowing the alcohol to take command.

"I'm starving, Sean, what about you?"

"Yes, I haven't eaten yet. How about some fish and chips for supper?"

"Lovely, Sean, with lots of salt and vinegar, yummy." Emily was like a child on an outing, happy and contented. They entered the warmth of the chip shop, the steam fogging the windows. The aroma stimulating the taste buds. They ordered the piping hot chips together with the battered fish, the whole meal wrapped in newspaper like a parcel.

The couple made their way to where Sean had parked the car, and once inside Duffy took a picnic blanket from the back of the van, putting it over Emily to keep her warm. Then he started to unwrap the good smelling bundle.

"Wait, Sean. We can eat them when we get to my flat."

"I'm starving, Emily girl, just a couple to start with." Duffy picked up a handful of scalding chips, blew on them trying to cool the heat, and put a couple in his mouth, tumbling them over his tongue trying to avoid burning the sides of his mouth.

"You bad man, Sean Duffy. Give me some." Emily giggled. "Now wrap the rest up and wait until we get home." Duffy smiled, the hot food spread warmth throughout his stomach as he started the car and drove off into the night.

The dark figures skulked from one piece of concealment to the next, the moonlight silhouetting their objective. They were dressed totally in black, their faces camouflaged so that nothing could be seen. Each carried a machine pistol. The lone sentry at the gate was making his round of the castles approaches, his movements in typical German fashion, precise and on time. The guard stopped for a cigarette; he was two hours into his duty, with another two to go. Boredom, the bane of a soldier's life, had set in.

The sentry cupped his hands to shield the light from the match, illuminating him for a moment. That was all one of the dark figures needed. He ran silently through the grass to the other side of the main gate, the recess in the chateau walls providing cover and an opportunity to control his breathing.

The sentry slung his rifle over his shoulder, and continued on his repetitive journey, as he passed the main gate his body slumped to the floor, the cigarette still smouldering on the path beside him. Having struck the German on the back of the neck with his machine pistol butt, the figure that was hidden in the shadows by the main gate, dragged the unconscious soldier out of sight before throwing the man's weapon into the bushes.

Upon seeing the demise of the sentry, four figures sprang from their positions, running fast and silently they reached the main gate without incident. The inset door within the huge frame of the main entrance was opened slowly, stealthily. A small metallic sound resonated as the metal lever passed over metal. The dark figures hesitated, trying to perceive each deceptive sound. A footfall, a human voice, the bolt of a rifle supplying the chamber – but all was silent except for the sound of their breathing and the croaking of a toad as it stood its nightly vigil. The first figure entered into the chateau courtyard utilising the shadows cast by the wall, with a signal of his hand the others followed one by one.

It was still early so the lights on the chateau were still on, casting a faint yellowy glow on the lawn by the terrace, which rose from the garden to the double doors of a large room. The man who had despatched the sentry scrambled across the courtyard to the safety of the terrace wall, his rubber soled boots betraying no sound on the cobbled surface. Checking that all was clear, he mounted the steps of the terrace holding his machine pistol at the ready.

Once at the double glassed doors, he peered through the opened curtaining for any sign of life. All was still. Seeing that their comrade had made it to the large room on the terrace, two men rushed silently to his side. The other two having found suitable defensive positions, were ready to provide covering fire should a quick retreat become necessary.

Whilst his colleagues had made their sprint to his position, the first man had expertly forced the bar that held the double doors shut. Slowly the three men entered the room, which served as a library. The gold embossed titles of the book covers glinting in the moonlight. The library door was gently opened a few inches, the light from the main hallway flooding the once darkened room outlining the three figures that waited within its mahogany confines.

The tones of Lily Marlene filtered through to their ears from a gramophone some distance away. One of the men passed through the door, his back finding a wall to brace himself upon, his machine pistol following his eyes as he searched the hallway and stairs for any sign of life. Seeing all was clear, the other two members of the team, a small dark man and a huge figure, sprang across the hallway mounting silently the steps of the large winding staircase two at a time.

Once they had reached the top they paused – reconnoitring the passageway that led to the rear of the chateau, its deep carpeting pointing towards a parallel passageway. Stealthily the two men made their way along the passage passing closed doors dispersed evenly along both sides.

When they had reached the junction where the two passageways intersected, they paused again checking for the signs of human activity, none was apparent. The smaller man approached the first door on the right. As he drew level with it his heart stopped, the door behind him was opening. . . instinctively he pulled himself to one side.

A figure in white appeared from the now open doorway, a female nurse. From the corner of her eye the nurse saw something lurking against the wall, her head turned, her eyes panicking, her mouth opening in alarm. The small man reacted quickly, his pistol butt slamming into the woman's jaw. Blood from her cracked teeth and torn gums filled her mouth. Her body tried desperately to compensate for the sudden impact, but lost its battle and gave way.

The noise of the woman's body as it hit the floor, although softened by the thick carpeting was like a crescendo to the man's ears. He looked towards the large man, who had traversed his pistol ready to dispatch anyone who might respond to the sound of the nurse's collapse. All remained silent, except for the noise from the distant gramophone.

With a sigh of relief the small man turned the handle of the door in front of him. The door opened slowly, the man increased the pressure on the finger coiled round the pistol's trigger. The small man's eyes focussed on the handsome young pilot's face. He smiled at the uniformed man, noting the wings on his breast pocket, the Polish insignia on his arm. The small man loosened his grip on the trigger. Stretching his arm towards the Polish pilot.

"Flight Lieutenant Kawolski, I'm Lucien, pleased to meet you."

Christian had regained his composure after the initial shock. "Lucien, you are a little late." His voice slightly sarcastic.

The little Frenchman shrugged his shoulders in acceptance, before speaking again.

"Come, monsieur, time is short, we must make your escape, we have a car waiting in the copse outside the main gate." With that Lucien turned and disappeared out of the doorway, Christian followed.

Tommy Boyle answered the phone at his home in Ruislip. He wondered who could be calling at past ten o'clock.

"Hello, Boyle."

"Boyle, this is regional headquarters, your application to travel to Ireland has been approved, the papers will be at your station at nine tomorrow morning, you and your wife will catch the 2.30 train to Liverpool…"

"That's marvellous," Tommy responded but the line was already dead.

He could not believe his luck; he'd thought his application for travel would be turned down considering he had returned from a trip to Ireland so recently. Even better his wife, Mary, could travel with him. Mary had sulked and pleaded with him not to leave her alone again. Tommy had explained the difficulty in applying for his own papers and that the chance of getting Mary included was going to be impossible. Mary had been adamant.

He could now fulfil his task; he could meet the witness, the man that might solve the Hammersmith case at last! 'Who knows,' he thought, 'perhaps me and Mary might have a bit of time to do some sightseeing, visit some old friends, purchase a bottle of Bushmills even'. Tommy decided he would tell Mary the good news in the morning, otherwise she would be up all night packing and Boyle needed to sleep.

Duffy and Emily pulled up outside the young girl's flat. The mixture of alcohol and lack of food had passed them both into the land of merriment, each giggling in turn like school children on the verge of some pre-arranged prank. Duffy parked the van askew; he'd stalled the van.

"Heavens, Sean! A woman could have parked better." Emily's comment would have caused provocation from the male orientated character of Sean Duffy at any other time. However, the alcohol had caused Sean to giggle at the girl's observation of his driving skills.

"Jesus girl, I got you home didn't I…and more over, supper is still warm." Duffy looked towards the parcel of fish and chips placed upon Emily's lap. "And I'll guess that's not the only think that's been kept warm." A sexy glint in his eye.

"Sean Duffy behave yourself. I'm not that sort of girl." Emily was gorgeous in her look and demeanour; she just oozed sexuality. Emily, her beauty having attracted his mind, could secure his heart in a moment.

Emily saw the look in Sean's eyes.

"Come on, Sean, let's eat, I'm starving. You make the coffee, I'll warm the oven . . . and forget any randy thoughts you may have, Sean Duffy. There will be no buns in my oven tonight!" She giggled.

"I bags the cod." He said laughing openly.

The pair left the car, moving towards Emily's front door, neither noticed the three men seated in the dark saloon some distance away.

Frankie Cavenaugh was still seething, his bruised and battered nose a testament to the pain he felt inside. "So you're still seeing the little whore while the pilot's away? That girl will be the undoing of you Sean Duffy" Cavenaugh said through gritted teeth. "Well enjoy yourself for the time being, both you and the little bitch will not be on the earth for long. Nobody does what you have done to Frankie Cavenaugh and lives." Cavenaugh, spurred by his thoughts of revenge, sat back in the leather of the car. "Drive on, Porrick, I've seen enough for tonight."

Christian, Lucien and his men had slipped silently out of the house and grounds of the chateau. When they reached the car that was hidden in a clump of trees, Christian got into the back, Lucien and the huge man in the front. The other three men had melted into the night. The huge man fired the engine, drove the car out of its concealment and headed east towards Fugeres.

They took a back road to avoid the centre of Vitre rejoining the main road about a mile east of the small town. After perhaps two miles the car turned left on to a smaller road that twisted and turned as it navigated the gently rolling landscape. After five minutes the car turned right onto a small track that led through the woods, before stopping at a clearing. The three men sat in the car waiting, for what Christian didn't know, he decided to ask.

"What are we waiting for, why have we stopped?" Christian asked, his voice calm almost casual, but before any answer could be given Christian saw the car's headlights. The vehicle moved off in the direction of where they had seen the lights.

When they had reached the designated spot, they got out and approached the car. A dark figure stood in front of them, his clothes those of a French peasant, his face unrecognisable, hidden in the darkness of the trees. Lucien looked towards the huge man.

"George's," it was the first time Lucien used his name, "take the case back to the car." Lucien pointed to a briefcase that sat on the bonnet of the other car, Christian had not seen it before, but he did now, the moonlight illuminating the metal of the case. George's picked up the briefcase turned and walked back to where he had parked the car. Lucien watched him before returning his eyes to the dark figure in the shadows.

He was about to speak when both he and Christian heard a thud. They both turned towards the sound, and saw a large heap beside the car, with a figure standing over it. Lucien's face was covered in fear, he turned his head back towards the figure in the shadows, his mouth open, but no words came out.

The dark figure stepped out of the shadows, the moonlight unmasking his features; it was Mosel, his face smiling at the little Frenchman.

"Excess baggage, not necessary for this journey."

Lucien, having overcome his fear, felt logic returning slowly. He looked at the heap, which had once been his friend George's. A thin smile came to his lips.

"You're right of course, Herr Mosel, but it's a pity, he was a good man." Lucien was unperturbed by his friend's death, after all, he thought George's wouldn't need his cut of the money any longer, that meant more for him.

"Good evening, Flight Lieutenant, I hope you have had a pleasant evening, I am sorry for any inconvenience you may have suffered." Mosel's mood was that of a master magician having pulled off an illusion, the finale of his trade.

"I'm well, Captain Mosel and not at all surprised."

"Of course," Mosel accepted the praise, no matter how it was meant.

"Hans."

"Sir," the aide answered.

"Leave the body where it is, I want to show the Leutnant his means of escape, the second stage so to speak...Leutnant if you would kindly follow me."

Christian followed Mosel together with Lucien and Steiner to a recess in the canopy of trees. Christian was impressed.

"Your transport, Flight Lieutenant, a Junkers 52...can you handle her?" Mosel asked.

"I should think so, after all, it's just an aeroplane."

"Of course you can." Mosel admired the steadfastness of the young Pole. "She is fuelled and ready to fly, Flight Lieutenant, if you please." Mosel pointed to the aircraft. Steiner had come to the side of the party slightly behind Lucien, Mosel looked directly at Lucien, his eyes had become harder.

"You too, Monsieur Dacourt."

"What! What do you mean?" Alarm was written on Lucien's face. Mosel's authority had shaken the little Frenchman.

"Hans," The simple word was enough; Steiner brought the barrel of his pistol to Lucien's temple the cold hard object causing pain in the side of his head. The physical pain Lucien felt bore no comparison to the pain he felt inside. Why hadn't he brought the other men with him? Mosel could never have brought off his plan if he were outnumbered. He knew the answer: it was greed, since the other three men were patriots, and their endeavours had been for France, not financial gratification. Now it was too late, Lucien thought.

Christian wasted no time over Lucien's plight. He climbed into the aircraft, strapping himself into the pilot's seat. It only took a few minutes to understand the cockpit layout; the basic instruments of flight were the same in all aircraft, getting the craft into the air would be a different matter. Once airborne she should fly by instruments, probably a bit heavy, but an aeroplane all the same, and once he was airborne Christian would only face one major problem – landing.

Christian slid open the Perspex window of the pilot's left hand side. The magnetos fired, one by one the BMW radials spun into action. When he was happy with the idling speed, Christian signalled his readiness. Mosel seeing Christian's signal, moved quickly to the car. He took out a standard German infantry rifle raised it up, the barrel pointing directly at Christian's head. Christian did not move, his eyes locked onto Mosel and the rifle barrel. Mosel lifted his cheek from the cold metal, a smile on his face, his eyes returned to the sight.

Lucien stood watching the scene, his mouth open, Steiner's gun still firmly pressed against his forehead. Christian's stare was fixed, he saw Mosel's finger close on the trigger. Mosel fired five shots, each carefully aimed, and five holes appeared in the fuselage close to the pilot's seat, none had hit Christian, or any vital instruments. Mosel let the rifle drop to his side, before looking directly at Christian, his wry smile conveying its message to him.

The shots close to the cockpit were a testament to his escape. If he had stolen the plane, naturally it would be acceptable for some shots to be fired; the last shot had been uncomfortably close to Christian's head. Christian was convinced that one was a warning to him. Lucien watched the display with incredulity. Mosel turned to Steiner

"Hans, please escort our passenger to his seat."

"What? No...no you can't . . . I can't go back with him. The English will shoot me...Please, Herr Mosel, I beg of you." Lucien fell to his knees crying like a baby, like a coward.

"Please, Herr Mosel...I can still be of use to you.. I...I can. . . ."

"Wrong, Monsieur, on both counts, you are no longer of any use to me. The British know of your treachery, so I have decided to let them have you back, and secondly, they won't shoot you. They will probably hang you....Hans."

Steiner pulled the blubbering Lucien to his feet by his collar; the gun barrel pressed firmly in the back of his neck propelled him towards the waiting aircraft.

Lucien thought about making a run for it, taking a clean bullet, but he was too scared to die now, too much of a coward. Steiner forced the little man into the aircraft's co-pilot's seat, where he strapped the now highly pungent Lucien into his seat. Christian noticed the vile smell.

"Have I got to put up with that all the way back?"

The normally expressionless face of Steiner broke into a huge grin, he shrugged his shoulders, turned to walk back down the aircraft to the open door, stopped, before turning to look back at Christian, his face once again serious, but with a difference, the eyes were sincere almost compassionate.

"Good luck Flight Lieutenant."

Christian watched as Steiner left the aircraft.

Christian increased the throttle and the Junkers lurched forward. He turned the aircraft ready to taxi, his eyes catching Mosel's movement. As the aircraft turned the co-pilot's window became level with Mosel, he raised the rifle and fired a single shot. The bullet crashed through the Perspex window before entering Lucien's head. The little Frenchman died instantly.

Christian felt the anger and nausea rise at the same moment. His knuckles turned pure white, his grip like vice on the controls. He pushed hard on the throttle almost shoving the aircraft forward. He had to get away from Mosel as soon as possible, had to put out of his mind the execution he had just witnessed, had to concentrate on getting the Junkers airborne.

The bulky aircraft increased speed along the bumpy surface of the provisional runway. Christian's eyes were focussed on the ground speed, he felt the aeroplane ready for flight, hesitated for a moment gaining extra speed, just in case. At last he pulled back on the controls, the three BMW radials cutting through the air. The aircraft didn't respond immediately. "Come on girl, come on you heap of corrugated iron, fly." Christian swore at the machine. Almost as if hearing Christian's words the nose began to rise, the wheels left the ground. The big Junkers had sulkily left mother earth.

Christian banked the aircraft in a climbing turn; retracting the wheels the moment the aircraft had left the ground, his wingtip almost seeming to touch the dark canopy of the woods. At 1500 feet the throttle was eased back allowing the Junkers to continue its climb in a more leisurely fashion.

CHAPTER 11

Yvette was waiting in the woods at the arranged meeting place, her bicycle hidden in the undergrowth. Yvette was pensive, she didn't trust the little Frenchman one bit, and with every moment that passed she became more worried. After twenty-five minutes, Yvette decided that something was desperately wrong. Had the plan failed? Had Lucien double-crossed everybody again? Had the Germans discovered his plans?

She had decided to give him another five minutes when she heard a distant sound, audibly low, but a sound she recognised. The sound of engines, aircraft engines. Yvette became annoyed, had she gone to the right rendezvous? Had there been a change of plan? Her thoughts were interrupted by the distinct noise of rifle fire, five quick shots. An ambush? What? What was going on?

Yvette decided whatever the reason she was in the wrong place, she extracted the bicycle from its hiding place, pushed it through the trees to the track which led out of the woods, mounted and pedalled towards where she thought the gunfire had come from.

As she approached the scene, Yvette heard the sound of a single shot, she turned into another track that led to the road. When she had reached the road she cycled faster, the smoother surface less strain on her calves, the wheels gaining speed. Yvette suddenly braked, stopped in the middle of the road, something in the distance had alerted her, lights, moving lights. She waited in anticipation…it could only have been a few seconds, yet it seemed longer.

Yvette's mind played games with her, her heart was pounding, her legs unsteady, but still she waited. Yvette then saw it again. There was no mistaking this time, two sets of headlights, the second set slightly higher than the first, crested the brow of the small hill in the foreground, moving at speed.

Yvette moved quickly, almost throwing the cycle into a deep ditch at the side of the road, she followed behind, attempting to make herself as small and inconspicuous as possible. When the vehicles, a staff car and lorry, were about 300 yards away, Yvette's ears were filled with the rushing sound of air and the straining noise of engines. She looked up at the sky, a dark shape of a large aircraft passed a few feet or so it seemed, above the treetops. The noise deafened her. Yvette's eyes watched the departing aircraft for a second before returning her gaze towards the two vehicles, which had stopped about fifty yards from her concealed position.

She studied the vehicles. She could not identify how many bodies were in the car but she counted twelve helmets in the rear of the lorry. Their faces were illuminated in the moonlight as they had watched the aircraft pass overhead. The soldiers had not had time to focus their weapons as the aircraft had passed over them so quickly; all they could do was to watch as it climbed high and out of range.

The passenger in the front seat of the staff car, a junior officer, like the rest of them had watched in surprise as the aircraft passed overhead. His attention had been suspended during the unforeseen aerial display. Realising his commitments, he rushed to open the door for the senior officer seated at the rear of the car. The large man berated the junior for his lack of urgency as he climbed out of the rear seat, his face as yet in distinguishable in the shadows.

Yvette, concealed from view, tried to control her breathing. The large officer turned slowly towards the moonlight, highlighting his face. "My God," breathed

Yvette, "Von Ebstein." Revulsion permeated her body, the butcher, the beast of Paris was here…why?

Yvette wanted to shout, scream at the apparition before her. If she only had a gun, she thought, she could kill him, now instantly, ridding the world of one of Himmler's vermin, if only…Yvette recovered some composure, the hatred that burned within her like a volcanic explosion was flooding every atom of her body. Even if she'd had a pistol at her disposal, she would not have been able to proceed with the execution of the beast. Her mission must come first; London must know what had happened.

Her years of training, the years spent in the field, always in constant danger, knowing her life and those she served could end in a moment, came like a blanket to a fire: her objective must come first. Von Ebstein, like all the others, watched until the aircraft had disappeared from sight.

"Come, schnell, hurry!" He screamed. "We still have time to capture the French bitch." He returned to the confines of his vehicle, a sadistic smile on his face. He would enjoy displaying his very special art upon the body of his captive.

Christian had levelled the aircraft so as to identify any idiosyncrasies the Junkers 52 may have had. She was heavy but fairly easy to fly, so he now focussed his mind on the lesser of two evils. At what height would he make the journey back to England? If he took the Junkers to its ceiling height of 16,000 feet the trip would be faster whilst allowing the ability to dive quickly should fighters attack. The alternative would be to fly at wave height, a bumpier slower ride, but out of normal sight or radar of night fighters. Christian decided to wave hop. The longer he was invisible to radar, the more opportunity he would have of reaching Northolt on radio. There was only one problem with wave hopping, if he made a mistake, it would be his last.

Christian allowed the converted bomber to lose height. When he finally decided to level her out, he was glad he had chosen to fly at that level. At 16,000 feet it would have been extremely cold, and Mosel's personal air conditioning would probably have frozen him to death. At least at this height he thought that the bullet hole in the canopy at least allowed some escape from the smell of Lucien's corpse.

Mosel returned to the chateau at Vitre together with Steiner. The guard on the gate was unhappy with the treatment he had received from Lucien's party, but a day's leave would compensate him. The nurse, however, was not so lucky. The vicious blow she had received from the butt of Lucien's machine pistol had broken her jaw, displaced four teeth and left the previously attractive woman with a disfigurement that would last for the rest of her life.

Mosel although tired after the day's events, decided to take a nightcap. He asked Steiner to join him in a good Napoleon before they retired for the night. Standing in front of the unlit fireplace like a country gentleman, Mosel raised his glass towards Steiner, "Hans, a good day, yes?"

"Yes sir, a good day in many ways." Steiner was glad Lucien was dead, he was a traitor and traitors played no part in Steiner's worldview.

"The pigeon has flown the coup." Mosel smiled at his witticism

"Operation Golden Egg."

"Operation Golden Egg!" Steiner replied.

The weather had been fine and clear for the flight and Christian was enjoying the thrill of flying again. He had taken a similar route to the one he had taken on his way out, only this time it was in reverse. He used the moonlight to identify the body of water below his wings. Glistening on the surface, it had allowed him to fly with a margin of safety as the weather was fine and the sea was calm, with no white breakers to give away its surface.

The aircraft had buzzed several small ships no doubt alarming her crews but with its German insignia it had not been fired upon which suited Christian. When he got to the English coast it would be a different matter. Many friendly aircraft had been shot down by over zealous gunners even though they had displayed the distinguishable RAF roundels.

Christian decided to gain some height once he had cleared the English coastline. Hopefully his speed and low angle would not allow any trigger-happy gunner enough time to traverse his weapon. It was a new form of tactic to Christian; in his Spitfire he'd had the advantage of speed, turn and height. Now, he was flying a slow, cumbersome, unarmed passenger plane, the hunter had become the hunted. A smile came to Christian's face: if only he had kept the brandy Freddie had given him.

SS Obergruppenfurher Von Ebstein was not a happy man; he had lost the pilot and four of his men, including the Oberleutnant, together with the Frenchman Henri Dacourt and the girl Yvette. Add to this that Mosel, his opposite number at the ABWEHR, was in residence in the area at the chateau, while he, Von Ebstein, had to contend with a Major's quarters at the barracks in Rennes.

It was not only the humiliation he was suffering, nor the embarrassment that Mosel's presence would cause, but also the fact that Mosel was in residence at the Chateau where he should have been. The chateau was fitting for his station, not only in military or security terms, but also because it would be ideal location for his other, more perverse activities.

Von Ebstein was sulking like a child by the time he settled in the uncomfortable bed, the thoughts of what he would do with the girl Yvette when he caught her; his only solace.

Christian peered into the darkness through the Junkers' windshield. He was close to the coastline of England by his reckoning, if he was right the Isle of Wight and Southampton water would be to his right.

Christian decided it was time to alert Northolt of his arrival - radar undoubtedly having warned the coastal defences of his approach. He switched on the German radio system, adjusting the set to a frequency he knew.

"Hello, this is 'Patriot', can anybody hear me?" The only noise was the interference coming through his headphones. He tried another pre-arranged setting.

"Hello, this is 'Patriot', I am a friendly, please respond." Christian waited, but no reply was forthcoming. He could feel the frustration build, and realised he would have to try another setting. He peered again through the darkness. There in the foreground directly in front of him was the outline of the coast of England, the white beaches lit by the moonlight like a welcoming mat.

"Hello this is 'Patriot', do you receive me?" Christian knew time was running out, the anti aircraft batteries already informed of his approach would be ready to intercept the unidentified aircraft.

Again he tried. "Hello, this is 'Patriot' do you receive me?" An edge had crept into Christian's voice.

"Hello, Patriot. Please identify yourself."

"Hello this is 'Patriot', I am Flight Lieutenant Christian Kawolski, Polish Squadron RAF Northolt, do you read?"

"Hello Patriot, we receive you loud and clear."

"Can you patch me in to Flight Lieutenant Freddie Moreland at Northolt, over." Christian awaited the response.

"Hello 'Patriot' Flight Lieutenant Moreland is waiting to receive." Freddie had been awoken by Birdy with the news of Christian's return. He had rushed, dressing at a run, towards the radio room.

"Hello 'Patriot' switching you through now." There was a pause, then Freddie's voice came through Christian's headset.

"Hello 'Patriot'...this is Northolt...Is that you, Christian?"

"Hello Northolt, this is 'Patriot'...yes Freddie, it's me!" Neither of the two friends could control their excitement.

"Christian, are you ok? What happened? How did you....?"

Christian interrupted. "I'll tell you all about it when I get back. Listen Freddie I'm flying a converted Junkers 52, three engine job, in German livery."

"Christ," Freddie said.

" Freddie, I'm approaching the Isle of Wight, can you get me in? Let the ack ack boys know, stop them from taking a pop at me?"

"Hello, 'Patriot' will do....Right Christian, fly towards the left of the Isle of Wight. That should bring you over Milford on Sea. Fly over the new forest to Basingstoke before turning 85 degrees to port. I will give you all the vectors in due course, is there anything else you need in the meantime, over."

"Hello Northolt. Is Emily OK, Freddie?"

"She's fine, Christian, missing you like crazy...she's been a very brave girl."

"Good Freddie, thanks for that...Freddie by the way, all your brandy's gone." Christian smiled.

Freddie Moreland gave Christian the co-ordinates he would need in order to make his homeward flight before rushing to the tower to watch his friend's arrival. Once in the tower he informed S.O.E. of Christian's imminent return.

The phone rang in the bedroom of Commander Peter Thompson's home in Ealing. Thompson reached a pyjama'd arm out of the bedclothes and picked up the phone. His wife, used to the numerous nightly intrusions, slept soundly.

"Thompson," he answered, "Hello, Harry, what is it?"

Harry Milburn informed Thompson what Freddie Moreland had told.

"Ok Harry, we had better get over to Northolt tonight, get to Kawolski whilst he's still tired." Thompson consulted his watch. "Pick me up in ten minutes, Harry."

"Ok sir, see you outside in ten."

Thompson put the phone down and sat thoughtfully for a moment before climbing out of his bed to ready himself for Harry's arrival.

Christian made his final approach towards Northolt, skimming over the rooftops of Ickenham. The aeroplane's flaps were fully down, slowing the Junkers whilst at the same time losing height. The gear was lowered, increasing drag; the wheels ready to touch the smooth surface of the runway. At the last moment Christian pulled the nose of the aircraft up, allowing the wheels to take the weight of the Junkers, applied the brakes, allowing the converted bomber to slow to a taxi speed. Christian turned the Junkers onto the taxiway and proceeded to a main hangar, guided by an aircraftsman. The German craft entered the huge doors and came to a stop.

Christian cut the three engines, unstrapped himself from the seat, stood up and stretched his legs. The long flight had taken its toll on his still recovering body, his right knee stiff and painful. Christian took a last look at the crumpled stiffened body of the French traitor. His mouth open as if trying to catch a last breath of air before his life was taken from him, his eyes still displaying shock. The hole in Lucien's head had emptied blood all over the seat and floor of the co-pilot's bay. The crusted stain of its flow identifying the path it had taken, while the smell of excrement was nauseating.

Christian could not sympathise with the demise of Lucien, he had been a traitor, had betrayed countless numbers of his own countryman as well as the brave agents sent by S.O.E. Christian made his way to the main door in the aircraft fuselage. Climbing down, he stood on the tarmac, his lungs greedily sucking in the cool fresh air, his feet back on friendly English soil.

Freddie appeared, he shook hands with Christian.

"Christian, I'm so pleased you're back. How was it?" Freddie noticed the exhaustion in Christian's face, he was obviously worn out.

"Not now, Freddie, later perhaps." Christian's reserve of strength was waning.

"Of course, old chap. Later will do fine, get some rest now."

"Thanks Freddie." Christian's words almost falling away.

"Christian, one last thing….Lucien?"

Christian's eyes moved towards the flight deck.

"He's in there," Christian didn't wait for Freddie's words, he moved towards the jeep that had arrived to take him and Freddie to the main admin. Block.

Freddie surveyed the bullet holes that spread like a map towards the final hole, which had pierced the Perspex canopy. Its blood-splashed surface telling Freddie that Lucien had not made his latest trip to England alive. Freddie ordered a corporal to remove Lucien's body, telling him to take it to a temporary morgue in the main admin Block before joining Christian in the waiting jeep.

Commander Peter Thompson and Harry Milburn had watched from the window of the Adjutant's office as the Junkers touched down at Northolt. They had arrived about five minutes beforehand. The journey through west London in the early hours of the morning was fast and efficient, the only conversation related to the tabs Harry's men had put on their related suspects. Commander Thompson had fired the first shot.

"How are your boys doing on the surveillance, Harry?"

"Nothing on the main one sir, fairly routine, nothing of interest."

"What about the other?"

"Now that's where it gets peculiar sir. The second one seems to be following the first. With our man following him, it's a bit like a daisy chain, sir." Harry paused at his remark. Thompson wasn't amused.

"Do you want me to do anything, sir?" asked Harry.

Thompson paused. "No, leave it as it is, but keep me informed. If anything happens we can't let our main man be compromised…not now."

Thompson made towards the weary eyed adjutant. His sleep, like most, disturbed by Kawolski's unannounced arrival.

"Will they bring Flight Lieutenant Kawolski here?" Thompson enquired.

"No sir, de-brief room across the parade ground." The adjutant responded.

"Ok, we'll make our way over." Thompson paused, turned back to face the sleepy officer.

"We will need coffee, lots of black coffee."

"I'll see to it straightaway, sir."

"Thank you." Was all Thompson said. He and Harry left the adjutants office and made their way to the de-briefing room. It was the same room they had met Kawolski in last Sunday, a lot had happened since then, and Commander Peter Thompson R.N. S.I.S. wanted to know everything.

Thompson and Milburn had reached the de-briefing room just prior to the arrival of Christian and Freddie. Thompson rearranged the furniture; he did not wish the scene that met Kawolski to appear threatening, that would only spur the Flight Lieutenant's resolve. No, a simple, more understanding, compassionate environment would make the returning hero more communicative, more unguarded. Christian entered the room, with Freddie a pace behind. Kawolski looked tired, abused. The beating he had obviously received was still apparent, the tiredness, a combination of stress and endurance.

When Christian saw the smiling face of Commander Thompson, his hand outstretched in recognition of something achieved, his eyes became more focussed, more concentrated.

"Flight Lieutenant Kawolski, congratulations upon your safe return." Thompson's voice had an edge to his pleasantries, Christian thought. He offered his hand but remained silent.

"This is my colleague, Harry Milburn." Thompson moved his hand to Harry who stood silently behind him. Harry nodded at his inclusion. Christian stared at the figure of Milburn a moment before returning his gaze to Thompson.

"I assume you want some details of my exploits, Commander?" Christian's voice resolute.

"If you would be so kind Flight Lieutenant, some coffee is on the way, would you care to start now?...or would you prefer to wait until the refreshments arrive?" Consideration was next to exploitation. Christian thought. Thompson was good, but compared with Mosel's gentle manipulation he was an amateur.

"What do you wish to know Commander?"

"Everything." Thompson said.

They had consumed the fish supper, Emily having warmed it in the oven and washed it down with beer from a quart bottle. They had both been giggly, messing about, the alcohol they had both drunk since 6.30 was having its carefree effect. Duffy pinched some of Emily's chips while she turned up the big band music pumping from the wireless. When Emily turned and caught Duffy in the act she rushed to him in an attempt to steal some back, a mock fight ensued. Both Emily and Duffy rolling around on the sofa.

They were both laughing aloud, Emily trying to shush Duffy. "The neighbours." She kept telling him between girlish laughter. His fingers tickling her. Suddenly Emily stopped laughing, she became sad, her eyes moist as she turned towards the wireless. It was playing Lavender Blue, the song she had danced to with Christian. Their song.

Emily stood and walked to the wireless, turning the volume up. She put her arms around her waist, started to move slowly as if in an imaginary dance, remembering her first dance with a Christian. She continued her private fantasy, a tear rolling down her cheek, a slight smile on her lips. Her body moved rhythmically, sensually to the sweet music. Duffy lit a cigarette, blew the smoke hard as if to provide a veil between him and Emily, a veil that would hide the hurt he felt inside.

When the tune had finished, Emily stood still, silent, her thoughts only on Christian. She turned towards the window, imagined Christian's face. The patterns on the curtains played tricks on her mind. Emily didn't see Duffy get up, but she heard the front door of her flat close. Emily turned, called out Duffy's name but he had gone. She felt guilty over her treatment of Sean Duffy, he was a good man, he didn't deserve the neglect she had imposed upon him, she had been selfish whilst Duffy had been anything but. Emily would not sleep well that night, nor was she the only one.

Christian had told Commander Thompson everything that had happened since Sunday night, except the detail of his meeting with Mosel and the agreement that had been reached. Thompson had gone over various segments of Kawolski's statement again and again. Each time he tried to draw more information from Christian. Continuity was paramount, any deviation in Christian's recitals led to doubt, to further questions, to suspicion. Thompson kept jumping from one section of the escape to another, trying to unbalance Christian - and succeeding.

"These men that extracted you from the clutches of the SS, no names were mentioned?"

"No, as I have already told you, no names were mentioned, just rank." Christian, his tiredness beyond comprehension was becoming not unnaturally agitated.

"What rank?"

"A captain, naval uniform, he was the older man. The younger man was a lieutenant."

"The Lieutenant, Naval or Army?"

"Army – God I've told you ten times already." Christian did not know how much longer he could go on, at least with the beatings there had been periods of unconsciousness.

"The captain," Thompson continued, "describe his features again."

Christian went into memory mode again, reiterated his previous description of Mosel, most of it fairly accurate. In order for deception to work, there had to be an element of truth, how much truth was critical, too much invited additional interrogation, while too little would encourage doubt.

"So this Mosel chap, the captain." Thompson interrupted.

"I did not know his name." Christian emphasised.

"But I'm sure you did, Flight Lieutenant, Harry, your notes." Thompson turned to Harry Milburn who was seated at his right.
Harry flicked through the hand written notes, feigning an attention to detail.

"Sorry sir, no name mentioned."

"Ah, I could have sworn you did. Sorry Flight Lieutenant, my mistake, I do apologise." Thompson's voice lacked contrition.

"Perhaps you too are tired, unable to concentrate Commander" Christian's words hit Thompson like a hammer on a thumb, sharp, intense.

"Perhaps you're right, Flight Lieutenant, perhaps we should continue this later in the day….2pm in here, is that ok with you, Flight Lieutenant?"

"Whatever you say." Christian responded, the words almost falling from his mouth. "Just as long as I can get some sleep."

"Of course, right Harry, we need to get some sleep also." Thompson had turned to face Milburn; He turned back towards the shattered Kawolski. "Right, gentlemen, we will re-convene tomorrow. Thank you Flight Lieutenant Kawolski, Moreland." Thompson nodded towards the silent Freddie.

Freddie and Christian rose to their feet, turned and walked towards the door.

"One last thing, Flight Lieutenant." Thompson asked.

Christian turned half way out of the door to face Thompson.

"Mosel's age?"

"About 50, I guess." Said Christian. "I could be wrong."

"Thank you Flight Lieutenant." Thompson nodded, convinced Kawolski wasn't telling him the whole story.

Christian made his way across the parade ground with Freddie in tow, towards their sleeping quarters. The sun was up, illuminating the huge hangar, which contained the stolen Junkers 52.

Thompson was deep in thought. Kawolski had made an error, an important error. Harry had noticed the casual slip also.

"Thought you let him off lightly, sir."

"What, sorry, Harry." Thompson turned to his junior.

"He obviously knows it was Mosel, he's just as good as admitted it, sir. Thought you might have picked him up on that, that's all."

"Yes, you're right, Harry, but he didn't seem to realise what he'd said. I think with a little rest he may compound the transgression....and if he does, we've got something."

"What sir?"

"I don't know, Harry, I just don't know...but he's hiding something, that I do know. If you were Mosel, Harry, and you knew we were suspicious of Lucien, what would you do?"

"Take him out, sir."

"Yes, maybe, but if you did 'take him out'. as you put it, it would prove you had been using him. You would be assuming that we knew all about Lucien." Thompson pointed out.

"Sorry sir, I might be losing you."

Thompson continued, "If Mosel disposed of Lucien outright he would be letting us know that Lucien had been rumbled, but if he let Lucien continue, he would not be able to trust the information Lucien was passing to him, therefore, Lucien is obsolete which ever way you look at it.

"Yes sir, I see what you're getting at, but which way would you turn." Harry put the question back to Thompson, knowing the Commander had already formulated his response.

"Well, if I were Mosel, Harry, I'd make Lucien appear treacherous at first, spread doubt, then I'd turn him into a hero, that would cause the opposition to ponder, to delay."

"Then sir, once the other side know of his heroics their only choice is to believe he's been ok all along, perhaps somebody else within the organisation is at fault."

"Exactly Harry, but you're missing one very important point." Thompson's eyes were wide.

"Sir!"

"You need a witness to his heroics."

"The Polish pilot, sir." Harry followed Thompson's logic.

"Exactly, Harry, you arrange a witness to the whole procedure, someone who can verify the circumstances."

"Someone you can trust sir." Interjected Harry.

"Someone who's above suspicion, Harry, what better than an innocent, an innocent who is also a hero?"

"Yes I do see, sir, Kawolski is the perfect solution."

"So he is, and now all you have to do is take Lucien out, and murder him as part of the escape."

A huge sense of achievement was written on Thompson's face. Harry scratched his balls; he always did that at times like these. It was his way of expressing his agreement with what had been said, it also acted as a spur to his counterpart in the discussion to get a move on, pull your finger out. Thompson saw Harry's movement. "Patience," He said. "I'm coming to the point now. We come back to Kawolski, Harry,"

"So you believe him sir, believe what he's told us is the truth."

"Ninety-eight per cent, yes Harry. But, but let's just say he's not exonerated yet. There's still something he's not telling us, and we need to know what, Harry. We need to know."

Christian closed his eyes immediately once his head had touched the pillow. His body and mind had been persecuted over the last few days. 'Is that all it was, a few days?' It had seemed like an eternity. He was desperate to sleep but sleep would not come.

Christian could not empty his mind. The debrief had brought back the whole host of experiences he had felt during his time in France. He tried to think of something different but his mind would only give him two options, the last week or Monica. When he thought about Monica and the girls, Emily's face would appear as Monica's. It was too much for his tortured mind to contemplate; guilt riddled everything.

Christian decided to have a cigarette. He parted the blackout curtains carefully, making sure the sunlight did not disturb Freddie's slumbers. He opened the window so that his smoke would not stifle the precious balance within their shared quarters. Smoking helped Christian to rationalise. "Bugger!" he exclaimed, the smoke billowing from his mouth. 'Mosel! His age!' Christian had virtually admitted he knew the captain's name.

Christian thought hard and deep, Thompson was bound to bring the subject up again at the next meeting. Christian would have to come up with a rational explanation for his familiarity with the name Mosel. He lay on his bed again, and this time sleep came. His mind now aware of the transgression that had kept him awake until his powers of thought could process the loose thread.

Commander Peter Thompson and Harry Milburn walked across the parade ground as the sun became prominent in the sky.

"Anything from Yvette yet, Harry?" Thompson asked conversationally.

"Not that I know of, sir, but if there is anything, centre will probably have it in de code."

"Check it out will you?"

Harry stopped in his stride, "now sir?"

"Yes Harry, now!" Thompson did not stop or turn towards the now stationary Milburn, but continued to walk towards the main building where temporary accommodation had been provided for the two intelligence officers.

"Yes Commander, right away," Harry peeled off towards the communication room knowing he would not sleep for a while yet. "A nice cup of tea is what you need Harry. Let's see if you can scrounge some off the radio operators." With that Harry disappeared into the complex.

CHAPTER 12

Tommy Boyle was awoken early with a cup of tea that Mary had brought to his bedside.

"So are you off to Ireland today then Tommy?" A slight look of disappointment in her eyes.

"Yes, Mary, I catch the 2.30pm to Liverpool then a boat to Belfast, from there a train to the Republic, providing there's one available, if not, then I'll stay in Belfast overnight."

"How long will you be away?" asked Mary.

"Not long enough for you to miss me Mary dear." Tommy was playing with the woman's emotions.

"And who says I'll miss you? Anyway, Thomas Boyle, you're not around enough to miss."

"Well I know you won't miss me on this trip, Mary Boyle!" A huge grin on Tommy's face. "Because… you're coming with me."

"What!" Mary's face was caught between excitement and mistrust.

Tommy burst out laughing, inadvertently spilling some tea in the saucer.

"Is it true? I'm coming with you?" Mary's face a picture of happiness.

"Yes my dear, it's true. I don't know how I managed it but yes, travel papers for Mr & Mrs Thomas Boyle, return Sunday." Tommy poured the spilt liquid from the saucer back into the cup.

Mary put her arms around her husband and kissed him loudly on the cheek.

"When did you find out Tommy?"

"Oh, last night." Tommy admitted.

"Last night, last night, why didn't you tell me, Tommy? There's so much to do, packing, my hair what am I to do with my hair? The milkman, cancel the milk and there's…"

Tommy cut her short. "This is why I didn't tell you last night, Mary, Panic. You would have had us both up all night with your fussing. We both needed a good night's sleep, we probably won't get much on the journey."

Mary hit Tommy with a pillow playfully, spilling more tea into the cup, a huge smile on her face.

"And you can get out of that bed, Tommy Boyle, there's a lot to do, I had better have a list." Mary had changed her expression to one of determination. She rushed from the bedroom, woman's work on her mind.

Tommy smiled to himself for a moment, before draining the tea and rising from his bed.

Emily also woke early that morning her fitful periods of sleep disturbed by her guilt for the way she had upset Sean Duffy the night before. She wondered how she could have been so insensitive.

To distract her mind from her behaviour of the night before, she ran a bath. When the steaming liquid had reached an acceptable level, she let the dressing gown slip to a huddle at her feet.

From the corner of her eye she caught the reflection of her naked body in the large bathroom mirror. She turned to study her form, her eyes following her figure down the length of her body. The breasts firm with youth, her nipples upright and swollen by the change in temperature. Her stomach flat and hard, devoid of the problematic strains of childbirth. She turned slightly, her head over one shoulder to admire her bottom. She was proud of her curvy backside, heart shaped, full, firm and sexy. She smacked her bottom cheek with the palm of her hand quite hard. The sound echoed in the enclosed space, and a pinkish imprint of her hand appeared on the creamy mound.

"That's for being a bad girl to Sean." She told herself with a little giggle.

Emily slipped beneath the surface of the bubbly water, feeling the exhilaration and relief before her mind returned to Christian. 'Oh Christian, where are you? Please come back to me. Please God, I'll do anything, give my life, but please bring Christian back to me.' Had Emily known then that Christian was indeed back safely, she would not have been so liberal with her pact with the almighty?

Mosel had breakfasted on the terrace of the chateau at Vitre; the sun was warm, the late spring weather allowing natures blossoms to bloom. Mosel stood sipping his coffee, admiring the view. His thoughts were interrupted by the arrival of Steiner.

"A fine morning, Hans." Mosel's eyes still on the scenery in front of him.

"Indeed it is sir, it reminds me of the Rhineland, my home." Steiner too became lost in thought for a moment, remembering the small farm, his parents, the brother he had lost in North Africa. Mosel interrupted Steiner's kaleidoscope of memories.

"Hans, we will probably have a guest for lunch, Von Ebstein will be sure to grace us with his presence." The name Von Ebstein was pronounced with contempt. "Please inform the kitchen staff so that they may prepare a fine lunch."

"Yes sir, I will see to it straightaway." Steiner turned to walk away.

"And Hans, the best wine, the Thirty six I think," Mosel added.

Steiner did not question his officer's orders, he simply continued about his duty.

Yvette had cycled to Rennes after the near miss with Von Ebstein. It was not only dangerous being outside during curfew, but also because Von Ebstein was residing in Rennes. Yvette was determined to let London know all that had happened. She took farm tracks to avoid the main roads; her circuitous route took nearly an hour to reach the house of Rene Discart.

Rene had been sent to this area by S.I.S. as a back up to the Lucien network. His real name was Philip Descan; he had been a lieutenant with the Free French in North Africa before being recruited by S.I.S.

Yvette wrote out the information that would be required by London. Philip had promised Yvette that the message would be sent at the earliest opportunity, and had also tried to get Yvette to rest, but the girl had too much to do. Also, she did not wish to stay in Rennes, in so close a proximity to the man she feared the most, the beast, Von Ebstein.

Yvette took a different route back to Vitre, and by the time she reached the café she almost fell into the arms of Anne Marie. Shattered beyond her level of endurance. Yvette was shown to a bunk in the small room towards the rear of the small café. She was asleep before Anne Marie pulled the cover over her shoulders.

Mosel was reading a report when Von Ebstein's car entered the main gate of the chateau. Its long black shape navigated the curved carriageway before coming to a halt at the main door.

Mosel folded his papers and put them in his briefcase, he then entered the library via the two large glazed doors from the terrace, just as Steiner was showing Von Ebstein into the comfortable room.

"SS Obergruppenfuhrer Von Ebstein, sir" Stiener announced.

"Thank you lieutenant." Mosel handed his briefcase to Steiner, before turning his attention to his uninvited but expected guest.

"My dear Manfred, how are you?"

"My dear Ernst, thank you for receiving me." Von Ebstein forced a smile.

"A drink before lunch, a cognac, a very good year?" Mosel paused. "Forgive me, Manfred, I did not ask. You will stay for lunch, I hope?"

"At such short notice…yes, yes I will, if it will not cause you or your staff any inconvenience." Von Ebstein's smile snaked across his fat lips.

"Not at all, my dear Manfred." Mosel put his hand on the fat man's shoulder and led him to the doors. "Let us drink on the terrace." Mosel led the SS man outside. "And how is Berlin?" Steiner, amazed at the spectacle, shrugged his shoulders at the small talk between the deadly enemies, then turned to arrange the details for lunch.

The lunch was excellent, sea bass with wild mushrooms, followed by braised calves liver in burgundy, all washed down with an excellent range of wines. Cognac was taken on the terrace with fine cigars.

"An excellent lunch Ernst, you have treated me with the utmost courtesy." Ebstein puffed, the fat fingers clamping the cigar like a vice.

"A pleasure, my dear Manfred." Mosel lied.

Von Ebstein surveyed the view, the courtyard, the well-tended lawns, the rose garden not yet in full bloom, the castle ramparts and the gently rolling patchwork of fields beyond.

"A beautiful chateau don't you think?" Von Ebstein was coming to the end of the small talk, he was moving slyly to the purpose of his visit.

"Yes, excellent for my purposes." Mosel would lead him on; take control of the conversation. Keep one step ahead of the nasty excuse for a human being, fouling what otherwise would have been a perfect vista.

"And what purpose would that be?" enquired Von Ebstein.

"Why of course, the war games in Bordeaux this weekend, you haven't forgotten Manfred." A wry grin on Mosel's face.

"No, no of course not…but why did you arrive so early? A full week ahead. And why are you staying at the chateau? There are some excellent hotels provided for our use in Bordeaux."

"It is simple, Manfred." Mosel was enjoying the other man's discomfort. He knew the SS man wanted the chateau for himself; it suited his pompous nature as well as his other less discerning activities. "A hotel would not suit my requirements nor that of my guests."

"Guests?" Von Ebstein raised his eyebrow. "What guests?"

"Why my guests for the war games. As you know I am on Field Marshal Rommel's side, we are the German defenders who oppose the Allied invasion according to the rules of the game scenario."

"Rommel, is he your guest?" Von Ebstein was jealous.

"Amongst others." Mosel's grin widened.

"Others, what others?" Demanded the SS man.

"Von Rundstedt. Model…." The names of some of the most distinguished figures in the German high command casually rolling off Mosel's silvery tongue. "And possibly Heinrich."

"Heinrich!" Exclaimed Von Ebstein. The name put fear into the eyes of the SS man.

"Possibly, I am waiting for confirmation." Mosel let the name sit with Von Ebstein for a moment before continuing. "My dear Manfred, but of course, I know you admire the Chateau. I should invite you…but whom would I have to disappoint? And you are the enemy of the Reich." Mosel watched as the fat SS man squirmed. Hatred in his eyes.

"What me? An enemy of Reich?" Von Ebstein's face took on the appearance of a ripe plum. The perplexed features narrowed the beady eyes.

"For the purpose of the war games, you are on the enemy side. The Allies…My dear Manfred, I hope you did not think….think that I would…." Mosel's face feigned apology.

"No, No. of course not. No, no I did not presume such a thing." Von Ebstein was embarrassed by his outburst. "In any case I have very suitable apartments in Rennes which I will use until I depart for Bordeaux tomorrow. I have an aircraft at my disposal on the airfield close to Rennes." Von Ebstein was closing the verbal exchange and he knew it, he would have to deflect the conversation, try to gain the upper hand with the slippery Mosel.

"Ah, that is good then. More cognac, Manfred?" Mosel held the decanter towards Von Ebstein's fat hand.

"Yes, if you would be so kind, Ernst."

Mosel filled the brandy glass, dwarfed by the fat flesh of Von Ebstein's fist.

"You also have a plane do you not? Or am I mistaken Ernst?" Von Ebstein changed tack.

"I have my own personal transport yes, it will arrive with my guest tonight."

"Tonight? But I thought your aircraft had been lost." Von Ebstein hoped to see panic in Mosel's eyes but none appeared.

"My aircraft lost? No, my dear Manfred, my aircraft is in Berlin."

"But, but the Junkers 52 that was lost. Call sign Phoenix, that was your plane I heard."

The SS man's face was regaining some of its composure.

"No, my dear Manfred, that was not my aircraft, that was one that I utilised, my aircraft was due for service, I merely used an available alternative."

"But it was lost." Compounded Von Ebstein.

"Yes so I hear, but not my aircraft, although it is the one I travelled in. The pilot was testing his instruments so I believe; he had complained on the journey that he was having trouble with the altimeter? I do not know about aircraft, I am a sea captain – seems he wanted to test the machine before making his way back to Germany – a sea mist, I understand, a tragedy," Mosel looked disconsolate.

"But I saw a Junkers flying extremely low yesterday nigh,." a smirk of satisfaction on Von Ebstein's face. "And it was in the same locality that the first Junkers apparently disappeared."

"Ah, Yes that must have been my aircraft. It left yesterday for Bordeaux before returning to the area later last night on its way back to Germany." The statement was true; the aircraft had been diverted to Bordeaux with Monica still on board. It was to fly close to the region on its return to Germany that night.

"But why was it flying so low then?" Von Ebstein was rising to the task.

"Probably checking instruments…after the loss of the other Junkers and bearing in mind my guests for this evening. I would imagine the pilot was just being cautious." Mosel hesitated for a moment; he could see Von Ebstein was weighing up the possibilities of Mosel's explanation.

"The other Junkers, Manfred, was discovered in the woods not far from here. A tragic accident, wreckage strewn everywhere, a fire on impact, I believe." Mosel's factual account adding credence to his earlier rationale.

"It was troops under your temporary command that reported the wreckage, was it not, my dear friend?" Mosel saw the nod of acceptance, it was time to end the conversation, he had won.

"My dear Manfred." A smile spread across Mosel's face "I know its call sign was Phoenix…but….but you really did not think it rose from the ashes?"

"No, no of course not." Von Ebstein conceded.

Mosel smiled in victory. "Would you care to take some more coffee or do you have any other business to attend to?"

"Er, yes, yes I must be on my way, thank you, Herr Mosel, for your company and the fine lunch, but I must go, important matters to see to, you understand?" Von Ebstein was totally deflated.

"Not at all, I will get Hans to show you to your car."

Manfred Von Ebstein, Obergrupperfuhrer SD, was not a happy man. The meeting with Mosel had gone badly, his carefully laid plan had borne no fruit; instead he had been humiliated.

Von Ebstein spoke to his driver. "Sigmund, there is a small café in the village, stop there, I need a drink."

Steiner joined Mosel on the terrace.

"How did it go, sir?" he asked.

"Fine Hans, the pig has returned to his sty. Now what of our guests, is everything ready for their arrival?"

"Yes sir, the aircraft should arrive about six, the cars will be waiting."

"Good, Hans," Mosel offered his aide a glass of cognac, Steiner politely refused. "And by the way, Hans."

"Sir."

"The girl, Yvette? Any news?" Mosel's voice had become more serious.

"No sir, no sign as yet." Steiner responded.

"Find her, Hans, find her before Von Ebstein does or he could ruin our gains so far."

"Yes, right away sir." Steiner left his officer alone to study his thoughts.

Thompson had finished the meagre lunch provided for him and Harry Milburn in the officer's dining area at Northolt airfield.

"Any news from Yvette yet?"

"Yes sir, it's still in decode, should get the clear in about half an hour sir, direct on the Teletype." Harry was trying to dislodge some of the meat from the awful stew that had got stuck in his teeth. Thompson looked in disgust at Harry's less than polite table manners.

"I want it ready for the meeting, see to it, Harry."

"Sir." Mumbled Harry half a fist is his mouth.

Thompson went to the hangar where the Junkers 52 was encased. He wanted to look over the aircraft, try to understand its very recent history, in the way a police inspector needs to see the crime scene. A mechanic was working on the engine, partly through interest, partly because it was his function to maintain the machine in working order.

"Hello Corporal. Commander Thompson."

"Sir," The man saluted to the title as Thompson was in civilian clothes.

"What's she like?" Thompson's eyes scanned the aircraft.

"Good engine sir, but slow compared to the newer stuff, fairly reliable I would imagine sir."

"These bullet holes, are they close to anything vital?" Thompson pointed to the five holes in the fuselage.

"Not really sir, fairly superficial except this one." The Corporal pointed to one particular hole. "That one's close to the main hydraulics."

"Is that important then?" asked Thompson genuinely.

"Yes sir, it controls all the moving bits, sir." The corporal could see the lack of understanding in the Commanders face. "It's the system that's responsible for rudder, flaps, wheels the lot sir, basically if the system goes sir, the aircraft won't fly, no control sir." The corporal made a diving movement with his hand, which was self-explanatory.

"So you couldn't take off?" asked Thompson.

"You can take off sir, but she might stall early, and if you did get her up, you wouldn't be able to turn, descend, well, not without a tremendous skill and a lot of luck sir."

"Oh I see." Thompson could picture the nightmare in his mind.

"Good job she was stationary."

"Stationary? Why do you think the aircraft was stationary?"

"Well, sir, look at the holes, if she was moving there would be more of an angle on each hole, these holes are fairly straight and the distance between holes is uneven, so it's rifle fire, probably about 15 paces away, due to the up angle."

"Rifle fire? What makes you so sure?" Thompson was fascinated by the man's thoughts.

"Well sir, a machine gun or pistol fires at a steady rate, now if you know the rate of fire, the bullet holes would be fairly evenly spread. The distance between holes would then give you the speed of the aircraft at the time of firing sir. Mathematically speaking."

"Anything else about the holes, Corporal?"

"No, not really sir, lucky bloke Mister Kawolski, sir."

"What do you mean, lucky?"

"Well, Jerry must have been a lousy shot sir, five bullets miss a stationary or near stationary aircraft from about fifteen paces."

The corporal was unaware of what he had just said but Commander Thompson was not. "Lucky indeed." He thought. Thompson looked throughout the aircraft, the corporal by his side, but no other startling facts came to light.

The scene in the cockpit with the dried blood and excrement stains together with the lingering odour had nearly brought the lamb stew back up. Thompson was glad to be back in the fresh air. He thanked the corporal and made his way across the concrete to the debriefing room.

When Thompson entered the room Harry was already seated, the transcript of Yvette's message in his hand. He passed the Teletype print out to Thompson who read the document.

When he had finished he looked towards Harry Milburn.

"What do you think Harry?"

"Seems to bear out what Kawolski had told us sir."

"Yes maybe, Harry, maybe." Thompson wasn't so sure.

Christian and the ever-present Freddie entered the debriefing room - it was two o'clock.

"Thank you, gentlemen for being so prompt, however, the meeting has been suspended. You may both leave, carry on with normal duties."

If Christian and Freddie's faces both displayed surprise at the statement, Harry Milburn's held a look of complete incomprehension.

"Sorry to have delayed you, Flight Lieutenant, congratulations on your amazing escape, no doubt you are in need of some much deserved rest." Thompson smiled approvingly.

"So that's all?" asked Christian his voice uncertain.

"Yes, Flight Lieutenant, Thank you."

"Sir." Both Christian and Freddie saluted, turned and made to leave.

"Just one thing." Thompson said as Christian turned.

"Yes?"

"When the aircraft was shot at during your escape were you moving or still?"

"Taxi-ing I believe, ready to take off." Christian answered honestly.

"Thank you that will be all, Good day gentlemen." Thompson began to re-read Yvette's signal, conveying to Christian and all present that the meeting was over.

Christian and Freddie crossed the parade ground, Freddie exuberant.

"Well Christian, thank God that's all over."

"Not yet Freddie," Christian's mood was rehabilitating itself, his mind had gone through the barometer of emotions, it now lay firmly in the uncertain.

"What do you mean, Christian?"

"I don't think Commander Thompson believes me."

"But he's just called off any further debriefs."

"For the time being Freddie, for the time being."

Harry Milburn, like Christian Kawolski, was perplexed at his boss's change of direction. Just when Harry believed Thompson had caught Kawolski out; he had let him go. Like an angler baiting trout, pulling them in, letting them struggle and wear themselves out, then letting them go, easing the line – before reeling them in again for the final kill.

Harry knew something was troubling his controller but if he had decided to pull back then there was a reason, a bigger picture than the one Harry had perceived. Harry shrugged his shoulders; it would be a quiet journey back to the office.

SS Obergruppenfurher Von Ebstein seated himself at a table in the small café in Vitre. The one or two patrons that had been in the café when he had arrived had melted into the background. The SS insignia on his shoulders had convinced the locals that more important tasks were at hand.

When no staff member had arrived, Von Ebstein displayed his mood to the meagre audience by banging his fat fist on the table. Anne Marie came from the back of the café. She had been checking on Yvette, the banging alerting her to her duties, waking Yvette in the process.

When Anne Marie saw the fat SS officer she almost froze, fear, trepidation flowed through her body. She took a deep breath to compose herself before approaching the unwelcome customer, a false smile upon her lips.

"Monsieur, I apologise for keeping you waiting, what can I do for you?"
On catching sight of the girl, his earlier tantrum dissipated as his eyes took in her form.

Anne Marie was eighteen years old; her body was going through a transformation, the process from adolescence to womanhood. Her hair black and shiny as a midnight sea, lay on her shoulders emphasising the swell of her breasts within the white blouse she wore. Her eyes blue and mysterious, her face full of colour, the necessary smile.

"Ah, Mademoiselle." Von Ebstein licked his lips, "a cognac if you please, bring the bottle and make sure it is your finest."

"Yes Monsieur." Anne Marie almost curtseyed before turning to fetch the order. Nausea caused by fear palpitating within the pit of her stomach.

Von Ebstein's eyes went to the swell of her rear, the full curves evident within the black material of her skirt, her legs long and tanned from the spring sunshine. He licked his lips again, the saliva resting in the corners of his mouth.

Yvette, awakened by the banging, had risen from her brief slumber; she took a drink of cold water and splashed some of the refreshing liquid over her face. When she had prepared herself with a modicum of self-respect, she stood by the door, which was slightly open, that led to the confines of the café. As she was about to enter the bar, a voice, a voice she knew, invaded her senses. She hesitated to listen again, her head close to the gap in the door.

Anne Marie had returned with the drinks to the table where Von Ebstein sat. With the tray in one hand, she leant over the table, placing the cognac bottle and the single glass with the other hand onto the flat surface.

"And what's a pretty young thing like you doing working in a place like this?" Von Ebstein's hand had gone to Anne Marie's waist.

"It's my uncle's café, sir, I work here during the day." Anne Marie said as she bent over the table to serve the alcohol.

Von Ebstein's hand followed her movement, the fat fingers sliding over the girl's backside, lingering. The girl stood up, her face flushed with humiliation.

"I need a waitress to serve my guests at my quarters this evening, perhaps you would wish to be of service to me?" Von Ebstein's hand squeezed Anne Marie's bottom cheek. "I of course, will make sure you are well compensated for your presence." A trickle of saliva ran from the corner of his mouth.

"I am sorry, sir, but I have been told I am working at the chateau tonight, many important people are arriving...."

"What?" Von Ebstein's tempestuous nature was rising again. He tore his hand from the girl's skirt. "Mosel, Herr Mosel, is he your paymaster tonight?"

"I do not know the officers name sir, I was just told to report,." stammered Anne Marie, her earlier composure deserting her.

"That is correct, sir."

Both Anne Marie and Von Ebstein turned towards the voice.
Hans Steiner, tall handsome and resplendent in uniform, stood holding open the door at the front of the café.

"You have made all the arrangements for tonight, Mademoiselle?" His voice strong yet courteous.

"Yes sir," Anne Marie smiled, noticing the look in Steiner's eyes.

"Good, then I need to talk to you," Steiner looked directly at Von Ebstein. Although junior in rank to the SS man, Steiner's voice was full of authority and purpose.

"If you would excuse us for a moment, sir." Steiner took the girl lightly by the arm leading her towards the private quarters at the rear of the café.

Yvette had witnessed the whole event, seeing Steiner and Anne Marie approach; she slipped back into the room leaving the door slightly ajar so that she could listen.

Steiner and Anne Marie stood by Yvette's door.

"I apologise for that officer's behaviour, Mademoiselle." The word officer was almost spat out.

"Thank you, Lieutenant." Anne Marie noticed Steiner's rank, amongst other things, "your timing was perfect." She smiled.

"Actually I do have a favour to ask of you, Er…"

"Anne Marie."

"Anne Marie, a beautiful name for a beautiful girl." Steiner smiled warmly, his eyes telling the girl that this was indeed a pleasurable experience for the young man.

"Thank you." Anne Marie responded, captivated by the lieutenant's good looks and manners.

"Actually, we do need some assistance at the chateau tonight. Perhaps you…and maybe a friend could be of assistance to me…I assure you those present are fine officers and gentlemen." Steiner added.

"And what about you, Lieutenant?" The cheeky smile Anne Marie gave the young man brought a huge warm smile to Steiner's face.

"I will try, Mademoiselle, I will try."

"Please Anne Marie, say yes," Yvette pleaded from the other side of the door. Her prayers were answered.

"Yes I would be delighted, Lieutenant…Er…"

"Steiner, Hans Steiner…about eight o'clock would that suit?"

"Yes Lieutenant Steiner, we shall be there." Anne Marie smiled back at the handsome man. Steiner took her hand and kissed it gently.

"Until tonight, Anne Marie."

"Until tonight." Whispered the girl, flattered.

Steiner left saluting the SS Officer as he did so.

Yvette opened the door, Anne Marie's face was like a girl asked to her first dance."

Oh, Yvette are you ok now? I have just been talking to…"

"I heard." Yvette cut in.

"Have I done wrong?" Anne Marie stammered.

"No you have done right." Yvette softened her voice, "your timing is excellent, well, in one area at least." She smiled knowingly at the girl. Von Ebstein's banging brought both girls back to reality.

"You had better see to him." Yvette nodded towards the café. "And Anne Marie,"

"Yes?"

"Be careful, he is an evil man, don't cross him…put up with certain things, if you know what I mean. Your life could depend upon it."

"I know what to do, Yvette, but I won't enjoy it."

"I don't expect you will." Said Yvette.

"The things we do for France, eh! Yvette." With that Anne Marie returned to the repugnant German's attention.

"The things we do for France, how right you are, Anne Marie."

CHAPTER 13

Major General Alexander Popowski was a frustrated man. The Polish divisions had been rotated through the line but as yet had seen no offensive action. General Clark's battle in the west was not going according to plan. The Americans had been fed into the mincing machine, the bodies thick on approaches, resembling the bloody slaughter of a First World War battle. The Texas division alone reported seventeen hundred dead.

The British in the east did not fare any better. New Zealanders, Ghurkhas, French Moroccans and Indians had all been pushed back, Castle Hill and the ridge, remained firmly in German hands. The Poles, with 50,000 men, had been kept in reserve, their willingness to fight overlooked.

Popowski complained to Alexander but to no avail, the genial Commander was unable to usurp his American subordinate due to political pressure. Popowski then fell back into his old ways, letters were sent to his father, to senators and even Eisenhower himself. A myriad of ciphers to influential figures left the Polish signals unit on an ever increasing basis, somebody, somewhere would have to take notice. Somebody did. His name was Ernst Mosel.

Commander Thompson sat across the desk from Sir Stewart Menzies at S.I.S. headquarters. His report contained his findings on what now was called the Polish question. C looked up from the papers, "You believe this to be true, Commander?"

"Yes sir."

"If you're right all our plans regarding Fortitude maybe to no avail."

"I understand sir."

"Winston needs to be informed." C picked up the phone, "Winston, now please." was all he said. "Ah, Prime Minister, I have Commander Thompson's report…I think we need to talk sir….Yes he's here with me now….yes sir we'll leave now…" C put the phone down. "God help you if you're wrong Commander." He said gravely.

"God help us if I'm right sir."

Eisenhower was in a meeting with Montgomery and Air Chief Marshal Sir Arthur Tedder when an aide delivered a folder of Teletype transcripts, relating to Popowski's ciphers. As Eisenhower read the documents his face became flushed with rage. Montgomery noticed the supreme commander's consternation.

"Troubles General?"

"You could say that, first Patton and now Popowski."

Montgomery raised an eyebrow. "Popeye? What's he been up to?"

"See for yourself," Eisenhower pushed the folder towards Montgomery who read the details, his facial expressions highlighting his thoughts. When he had finished he looked up, his eyes firmly on those of his superior officer.

"Well?" Asked Eisenhower.

"Frustration, bordering upon insubordination, I would say, General."

"Exactly, you know him better than I do Monty, what do you think?"

Eisenhower's flexibility of command, his ability to co-ordinate, include his junior officers from a host of nationalities and characters, into a functional command structure was coming to the fore.

"Well he has the confidence of his own convictions, coupled with an animosity towards those who do not countenance his views, arrogant, brash, typical of the new army. Yet a passionate staff officer with an almost fanatical attention to detail."

"So you rate him?" asked Eisenhower dismissive of Montgomery's eloquence.

"Yes General, I do." confirmed Monty. "Unlike certain Americans, your good self not included, I find him dedicated and forthright."

"Patton, you mean?"

"Yes sir, now you come to mention it."

"Patton's my problem, Monty," Eisenhower's voice was authoritative. "Anyway, George is doing his penance at FUSAG". First United States Army Group was a fictitious army corps based in East Anglia to confuse the Germans as part of Operation Fortitude. "Popowski's your problem," stated Eisenhower.

"I beg your pardon, sir," It was Montgomery's turn to feel flushed.

"Bring him back Monty, use his knowledge in the planning for 'Overlord'."

"But sir…"

Eisenhower ignored Montgomery's protests by turning to Tedder. "Air Chief Marshal, your special ops boys can bring him back?" Tedder nodded, not wishing to upset the American. "OK, I'll let George in on our discussion."

"Right let's get Bradley in here and continue, gentlemen." Eisenhower's authority ended any further discussion on the subject.

In his subterranean office in Whitehall, Winston Churchill read the document 'C' had put before him. The old man unclamped the cigar from his teeth, put his hands upon the table in front of him and spoke.

"If your suppositions are correct we have a problem of the utmost gravity and magnitude. A problem that would cast a shadow of much grievousness upon our forthcoming actions. A problem that, unless given the proper considerations, could lead to folly." Winston paused to draw on his cigar. "A problem of time. Should we have to postpone our endeavours to rid the world of Hitler and his felonious crew, a time in which he may draw upon his munificence to breed further malignity. This does not sit comfortably with our expectations."

Winston drew long and hard on the fat Havana, thought processes permeating his mind as the smoke did within the confines of the room.

"Let us fox Herr Hitler with deceit, a good fellow in times."

"Yes sir, so you agree with my plan."

"This Mosel," Winston said. "Let him come like a fly to our web, be immersed in an irretrievable belief in his folly and be subjugated to our greater will."

"Sir," C said, "I need you to speak to Eisenhower and if need be to the president himself."

"Roosevelt?" Winston said, "Is a man of great vision, a man who has the heart and grace of a nation committed to our cause, yet has the strength of purpose combined with a cunning, yet subliminal process of thought. He will adhere to my terms, his support never wanes."

"Thank you sir," C said, "now if you please forgive myself and Commander Thompson, we have much work to do."

Sir Stewart Menzies and Commander Peter Thompson thanked the great man for his attendance at such short notice, and made ready to leave.

"The British people, this proud nation, their hopes raised in the final victory, are at your mercy, gentlemen. Do not let them down, for there is little time left." Winston's parting words lay heavily upon Thompson's shoulders.

General George Patton was looking out of the window of his office, staring at the vast array of tanks, artillery, transport, administrative and communications buildings. All the mass of ordnance necessary to launch a massive army group across the channel to invade occupied Europe.

The American 1st Army corp., FUSAG, together with British and Canadian Army corps directly under Patton's command, was in fact a deception. A highly sophisticated and meticulously planned ruse to fool the Germans. Thousands of dummy tanks, transport, air support together with extensive radio traffic had been set up all over Essex and East Anglia, under the codename Operation Quicksilver II, as a part of Operation Fortitude, to make the Germans believe that the invasion would be led by Patton on the Pas de Calais.

Patton remonstrated with himself. "God damn, George, you're in charge of a plywood and cardboard army, is this how you are going to end the war?" A flock of ducks took off from a nearby waterway. "Just a God damn decoy! That's all you've come to, George." He said aloud.

"Sir are you OK, sir?"

Patton had not seen the aide nor heard him come in, his thoughts clearly on his own predicament.

"Sorry Frank, I didn't see you there, any news from Ike?"

"No sir, usual excuse. He's in a meeting, can't be disturbed, I've got those reports you asked for sir." The aide looked at the dejected General. He'd been with Patton since North Africa seen his brilliance, seen his madness, an almost compulsive tendency to put his foot in it just when everybody was about to praise him, and Patton needed praise.

"I slap one lousy coward and they stick me in this God damn awful place, where the hell are we anyway, Frank?"

"Norfolk, British East Anglia sir."

"Might as well be Norfolk Virginia for all the good I'm doing, one lousy slap."

Patton was referring to the incident in which he had slapped a Private across the face, in a hospital bed, accusing the man of being a coward. The Press was present; the world's media had a field day with Patton. His esteem in the public's eye falling to its lowest point in Patton's whole career. Patton was forced by Eisenhower to make a public apology to the soldier, who had been suffering from shell shock, via the world's media.

"Ike could have sent you home, sir."

"Yes, He could have, instead he sent me here, Jesus it's so flat, Frank. Haven't the Limeys got any goddamn mountains? It ain't nothing like Virginia."

"Yes sir, they have as a matter of fact in Scotland and Wales, I believe sir." The aide was trying to be helpful.

"Typical." Was all Patton said, he moved away from the window to a large map of Europe. The aide followed with his eyes.

"North Africa," Patton prodded a finger at the map. "I took North Africa."

"General Montgomery, sir?" The aide said impartially.

"What! Ok, Monty was there too," Patton conceded. He prodded the map again.

"Sicily!" A smirk spread across Patton's face.

"Monty sir," pointed out the aide.

"Are you trying to rile me, Frank."

"No sir, I just pointed out…" The aide waited, not wishing to antagonise his general anymore than was absolutely necessary.

"Ok Monty was in god damn Sicily too, happy Frank?" His look admonished his junior.

"Look Frank," Patton continued, "I'm the best guy for the job, we're about to mount the greatest invasion the world has ever seen and Eisenhower puts me in god damn Norfolk with no god damn mountains!" Patton was now strutting about the office, his thoughts only on his own situation. "Ok they've got Bradley, good guy, Brad, and they got that pompous ass Monty, but they're not up to the job Frank." Patton had turned to face the aide.

"Sir," was Frank's only reply.

"Brad's too easy going. Monty's too slow, too pragmatic, what they need is someone to kick Von Rundstedt's ass, me, Frank – instead Ike's playing politics sucking up to that cripple Roosevelt." Patton's anger had erupted; his ability to self-destruct was surfacing once more.

His aide, through his long association with Patton, knew how to handle him in such situations, knew Patton had not meant what he said about the President and Eisenhower.

"What?" Patton tried to bring his mood back to a level plain.

"Well, Ike, as I said sir, could have replaced you, as could the president, but…but they didn't, did they." The aide let the statement bite. Once Patton had cooled a little, he continued. "Instead they put you here for a reason. Let me put it this way, General, the krauts like Von Rundstedt know you're the best field Commander we've got, sir."

"Carry on, Frank," Patton liked that statement.

"Well sir, if you're here and don't move when we hit the beaches, the krauts will think…"

Patton interrupted. "They'll think it's a feint, they'll think Bradley and Monty are running the side show."

"Exactly sir," the aide breathed with relief.

"Then, then Frank, when Brad and Monty are stuck on the beach with their feet still wet, they'll call for George to wade in and show them the way to Berlin."

"Exactly sir, I couldn't have put it better." The aide was sure he could but he didn't want to allow Patton to fall back into his tantrum.

"Hey Frank?" Ike's not such an ass after all." Patton was triumphant; his aide had vindicated in Patton's mind all that had gone before.

"Nor the President sir," the aide added.

"Yes, him too…Jesus, but Frank," Patton's demeanour had hit a bump, "Frank, they're giving a job to a Polack, a god damn Staffer, Jesus, Frank, I could lead the Poles in, I don't need to speak Polish, I just point and say 'that's the way to Warsaw boys.'"

"Sir!"

"Sorry Frank, yes you're right, wait my time, let Monty and Brad screw up, then Ike will give me the call eh? Frank."

"Right sir," the aide was almost worn out by the confrontation – every discussion with the egotistical general was a confrontation. Patton returned to the window, his pride restored.

“Ok Frank, what’s on for today?” Patton’s hands were clasped behind his back, the interlocked fingers flexing.

The aide consulted his notes, “a visit to the Women’s Institute.”

“Not more old limey broads and tea?”

“Yes sir, and after a review of the local defence force…”

“Jesus, Frank, old guys with incontinence.”

“Sir!” The aide’s voice was firm and positive.

“Ok Frank, ok, I get the message, I got to play the part.

“Yes sir,”

“Frank, what would I do without you?” Patton said, almost condescendingly. The aide knew, but he wasn’t going to say.

Friday afternoon in Ruislip was bright and sunny with a comforting breeze. Emily sat in the garden of the Plough public house in the company of her workmates. Their everyday chit chat oblivious to her. Freddie had phoned saying that he had some information regarding Christian. She had begged him to say more but Freddie refused to speak openly on the phone, his assurances that Christian would be ok fell on Emily’s already heavy heart.

Emily had not been in the best of spirits, even her boss had commented upon Emily’s lack of attention. She had apologised for her indifference, trying desperately to join in the joviality, but her thoughts kept returning to Christian. Emily glanced at her watch. Where the hell was Freddie? He was late, he had promised to meet Emily at two o’clock and it was now half past. Emily’s colleagues wished her a good weekend as they made their goodbyes before returning to work at the Builders merchants. Emily having taken half a day’s holiday now sat alone.

The barman appeared. Emily thought he’d come over to remove the clutter. Instead he placed a bottle of champagne and two glasses on the table.

“What, I didn’t order anything…you must have made a mistake.” Emily exclaimed.

“No mistake, madam, courtesy of the gentleman in the lounge bar.”

“Well you can take it back.”

“I’m sorry, madam,” apologised the barman, “but the gentleman was insistent.”

“What…right I’ll show him.” Emily’s anger was rising; she picked up the bottle of champagne and its two glasses. “Show me who this gentleman is.” She demanded.

“He’s the only gentleman in the lounge madam.”

“Right, I’ll show him what he can do with his champagne.” Emily stormed into the lounge bar, her face flushed with rage, her small delicate fingers clamped around the bottle and glasses.

The door to the lounge bar clashed loudly against its restraints, Emily’s temper was now in full swing, though she had not intended to be so heavy handed.

“What the bloody…” Emily stopped dead in her tracks, her body began to shake, gone was the temper, and in its place, incomprehension mixed with excitement. Her eyes began to moisten, her lips quivered.

“Christian,” the name almost a whisper.

“Hello Em,”

“Oh Christian.” Emily rushed to his arms.

Christian, slightly off balance, had to adjust his body in order to catch Emily as the girl almost jumped into his arms.

"Oh Christian, I…I…I thought." Emily was sobbing now, her tears of joy dampening his neck.

"I'm ok, Em." Christian held her tightly – the mere feeling of her body next to his causing Christian's normal functions to disappear, to be invaded by his need to smother her with affection. Christian kissed her hard on the neck, his mouth moving to her face, their lips met, the kissing became intense. Only lack of air forced their mouths to part.

Christian gently let Emily's body gain contact with the ground, her feet once again touching the surface of the carpet. Having gained her steadiness Emily parted from Christian's clutches, her eyes still on his, she took a step back, disbelief in his safety still playing upon her senses.

"You bastard," she said with meaning, followed by the most beautiful smile Christian had ever seen.

"Sorry, Em," Was all Christian could say. "Champagne?" his voice tentative.

"Too bloody right." She said, a giggle lighting up her face.

"What would I do without that giggle, what would I do without you, Emily?" It was Christian's time to become emotional. "I love you, Emily Cassidy." He said.

"And I love you, Christian Kawolski." Emily's voice petered out as her lips met his.

When both Emily and Christian had gained some sense of normality their conversation became more subdued and rational.

"What happened over there, Christian? Were you badly hurt? Oh God, please say you weren't…"

"Now, now Emily, later." Christian said, not wishing to spoil the reunion, his heart was not ready to disclose the inner turmoil his guilt was causing. "Later Em, Please later."

"Ok, I'll wait darling, but I know something's troubling you and I …I want to help."

"I know Em, but let's just enjoy the moment please."

Something beyond Emily's comprehension was hurting Christian, spoiling the moment; something that would fester within unless allowed to be brought into the open. It would worry Emily for sometime to come.

Mosel was pleased with the information Steiner had given him; Berlin had forwarded the de-coded American cipher direct to the Teletype printer at the Chateau.

"This is excellent news, Hans, the Allies are bringing our goose home to roost."

"Just as you said they would, sir. They are playing the game exactly as planned."

"How is Schloss doing with the preparations?"

"Very well sir, much better than I would have expected."

"But is he ready, Hans?"

"He will be, sir."

"Good, when we have finished our duties here we must return, probably Sunday night to headquarters, we have much to do in so short a time." Mosel paced around the library - it always helped him to think, to put things into perspective.

"Hans."

"Sir?"

"Our man in England, he must keep careful watch on our Polish friend, especially now."

"I took the liberty of informing Dublin via our Rudy network sir. They should be able to pass the information to London tonight, tomorrow at the latest."

"Hans, as usual you are in complete harmony with my thoughts." Mosel's smile conveyed his regard to his trusty aide. "Is everything ready for tonight?" Mosel changed the subject. The arrival of his guests prior to the war-games now paramount in his mind.

"The cars left for the airfield five minutes ago sir, the weather is fine over the flight path, we do not expect any delays sir."

"Excellent, Hans, now we must prepare ourselves for our guests."

Mosel left the library together with Steiner; their conversation now centred on the evenings events.

Christian and Emily made love in the bedroom of her small flat in Ruislip. Not a raucous passionate romp, but a slow, tender, affectionate mingling of body and mind. They lay body to body on the surface of the sheet, the bedclothes having been removed lay in a heap on the floor. The perspiration from their endeavours mingled, their breathing was slow and gentle.

Emily relaxed in a soft sleep, her head on Christian's chest. Her hair like a golden shawl on his skin, her breast heaved with each breath. Christian looked at Emily as only a lover can do; she had the face of an angel and the body of a goddess. Her features were soft and feminine; her smell sent little shock waves of delight to every nerve in his body.

Each thought of Emily brought a clash of conscience, love versus guilt. How could he tell her about Monica, the proposition Mosel had made and his intended betrayal of all that was sacred to him? Emily and honour on one side, Monica and the girls with betrayal on the other. Whichever way he looked at the mess that had been created, deceit and disloyalty were the only victors.

General Popowski was delighted with the news he had received via the cipher, no less than Eisenhower himself was to send for him. He would return to England to work with Montgomery again. His reason for recall must be to do with the invasion plans. They needed his skills, his attention to detail and no doubt his special relationship with the fifty thousand Polish troops stationed in Italy, who would, he believed, be sent back to England to bolster the invasion forces.

They had come to their senses at last, Popowski thought. His role in the forthcoming D.Day operations would only enhance his position. He would achieve the notoriety and respect, so long delayed, that was his destiny.

CHAPTER 14

Yvette arrived at the chateau together with Anne Marie, their crisp white blouses and black skirts informing all of their function in the evening's proceedings.

Both girls were shown the serving areas and introduced to the kitchen manager by Steiner.

"Herr Goefeld, this is Anne Marie and…."

"Margot," Yvette interrupted.

"Margot, so pleased to meet you. My name is Steiner, Herr Geofeld will inform you of your duties in the kitchen area. But first, I will show you the dining room together with the great hall, which is where our guests will be taking pre-dinner drinks.

"If you would follow me." Steiner waved his hand to allow the girls to walk in front of him. He smiled courteously at Yvette, his smile lingering longer on Anne Marie. The girl noticed his intentions and returned the compliment.

When the party had reached the great hall Steiner gave them the full itinerary for the evening.

"The guests will be shown by the butler to this room and announced, champagne will be served prior to dinner which will be at 8.30. The wines have been pre-selected. Herr Goefield will show you which wines to serve with the courses, four in all." Steiner hesitated to see if the girls understood so far, both nodded accordingly. "After dinner, cognac will be served with cigars here in the great hall. Champagne will be served at 10.30 when a toast will be made by Von Rundstedt, after which, Schnapps will be available with coffee for those guests who wish to remain in conversation. Your duties will finish at 11.30. Any questions?" Steiner looked towards the girls.

"Typical German precision." thought Yvette.

Anne Marie's thoughts were only for the handsome lieutenant, hanging on every word he spoke, like a child enamoured with an adult's conversation.

"Does anybody speak French?" asked Yvette.

"Good question, Margot, yes, but all conversation will be in German. Do you speak or understand our language, Mademoiselle?"

"No sir, only my native French."

"And what of you Anne Marie?"

"Only French, but I understand some German." The girl answered honestly.

"That is no problem, now let me take you back to the kitchen, Herr Goefeld has much need of your assistance, report back to the great hall at 7.45…Ladies." Steiner held the door for the girls.

As the threesome headed towards the kitchen Steiner held Anne Marie back for a moment.

"Mademoiselle, a moment if you please. Margot you may proceed to the kitchen." Yvette nodded leaving the two others behind. She worried about Anne Marie's ability to keep her mind on the discussion Yvette had with her before they had arrived. "Keep to our story. Do not let your affections for the young man allow your mind to wander."

"Anne Marie, you look so pretty tonight."

"Thank you, Lieutenant Steiner." Anne Marie's smile adding to her prettiness.

"Your friend…." Steiner's voice more formal.

"Margot?"

"Yes, yes Margot, you have known her long, she is your friend?"

"No, she is my cousin from Paris, but also a friend." Anne Marie added.

"I do not see any family resemblance." Steiner told her.

"Cousins rarely do…Is there a problem sir?" Anne Marie's flirtatious smile seemed to soften Steiner's line of thought.

"No of course, no, don't worry. Perhaps after my duties have finished tonight we could get to know each other a little better. If that would be acceptable to you, Anne Marie?"

"That would be lovely, Hans." Anne Marie's smile oozed possibilities, which brought feelings so long forgotten by Steiner to the surface.

"Until later then, Anne Marie." Steiner kissed the young girls hand.

"Until later, Hans." She giggled, before turning to follow Yvette's path, her femininity working overtime to show her willingness to please the handsome young lieutenant.

Christian leant over the naked body of Emily and kissed her gently on the forehead, the touch bringing the girl slowly from her sleep. Her arms snaking slowly around his neck pulled him gently to her.

"Christian." She almost sighed as she kissed him gently, her lips warm, tenderness in her touch.

"I've got to go, Em." Christian was already dressed ready to leave.

"No, Christian, come back to bed. Make love to me." Emily gripped Christian's neck tightly.

"No! I said No." Christian pulled her arms away, his voice betraying his mood.

Emily looked upset, the little girl pout on her lips. She turned onto her tummy burying her head in the pillow. Christian slapped her exposed bottom.

"Don't sulk Emily, I really do have to go." Emily turned at the impact, her eyes annoyed, wakefulness coming instantly.

"Go then! If you don't love me then go!"

"I do love you Emily." Christian's voice became normal again. "I do love you but I must go." His face saddened, the little boy look dissolving Emily's previous anger.

"I know Christian, I'm sorry it's just…"

"I know, lovely," He said, leaning over to kiss her deeply. "I will see you in the pub later."

Christian felt guilty for letting his inner turmoil show; it wasn't Emily's fault. He was wrong to take it out on her, she was young and very caring, she hadn't deserved to bear the brunt of his frustration. She deserved better than that.

"I'm so sorry for being naughty. I'm acting like a silly schoolgirl. I…" Christian put his finger on her lips.

"It's not you darling, it's me…still a bit stressed out, I need…"

"Oh no, Christian!" Emily bounded onto her knees, her arms around his neck again. Her eyes close to tears, her hair falling over her bare flesh. "It's me, I'm so silly…I just can't help it…I'm so in love with you. Please forgive me."

Christian held her tight her body warm, smelling sweetly. He hugged her as if never to let her go, gaining strength from her. Dissipating his feelings of hurt, of guilt.

"I love you, Emily."

"And I love you too, Christian."

With that the two bodies parted slowly in unison. Christian kissed her again on the forehead before leaving. His smile a reconciliation, hers, a commitment.

When Christian had gone Emily lay for a moment. Her thoughts on their first little tiff. Their lovemaking, their making up. She smiled contentedly to herself. He did love her.

Emily brought her senses back to reality as the clock chimed six o'clock. "God" she cried, "I'll be late for work." She jumped out of bed and, still naked, she skipped into the bathroom and ran the tap to fill her bath. When the water was ready, she slipped beneath its comforting surface wallowing in its luxuriousness, her mind as ever on Christian.

Tommy Boyle and Mary reached the dockside area of Liverpool in time to catch their passage to Belfast. The train journey had been long, the frustration with the continual stops, had almost threatened to spoil their plans. The last thing Tommy needed was to spend a night in Liverpool, with the added haste of trying to find another ship the next day.

All the traffic had been heading south, locomotives moving ordnance, tanks, guns, and all the paraphernalia of war. The ships too were heading in the same direction. The only reason for all this commotion pointed to one thing – invasion. Everybody sensed something would happen soon; the rumourmongers at full stretch each with his or her informed opinion, a brother in this, a mate in that.

The small convoy of ships going to Belfast would have a corvette as an escort to try and dissuade any U-boats. It was like using a puppy as a guard dog; instead of re-assurance, its presence would highlight the danger.

Tommy had been glad of Mary's company on the long train journey; the sandwiches and the flask of tea she made had brought welcome relief. Now fearful for her safety, he wished she had remained at home.

Yvette and Anne Marie had been kept busy; the guests numbering ten in all had arrived en masse. The five main guests with a senior aide each, three generals, one a Luftwaffe man, together with two field marshals, Von Rundstedt and Rommel.

Yvette almost had to kick herself; here she was in the company of some of the most senior officers in the Third Reich, officers and gentlemen not gutter scum or bullies like Von Ebstein. London would never believe her.

Yvette noticed that Rommel and Von Rundstedt although extremely courteous, kept to different sides of the reception room. The same scenario was played out at dinner, each occupying guest of honour status, one at each end of the magnificent dining table. It was as if they both had formed a different opinion of something, something important, something that alerted Yvette's intuition. She would have to discover why.

There was no opportunity to find out at dinner, she was kept constantly on the move by her labours. Yvette was unable to follow the private conversations in detail, her excellent German only acting as a disturbance to her serving. Whatever the rationale Mosel had for staging this evening, it was not apparent in what Yvette had heard so far.

The meal provided by Mosel was sumptuous; his guests savoured the delights of lobster, quails, ribbed beef with Pavlova to finish. An excellent vintage wine accompanied each course.

If the food and wine was magnificent then so was the setting. The thirty-foot solid mahogany table was filled with the finest crystal, the gold-rimmed plates matching the solid gold cutlery. Two Louis XIV chandeliers providing the light, which reflected in a myriad of colours. The carpeting with the heavy curtaining softening resonance, the paintings of heads of table long past, tight lipped in silent stares.

Emily arrived at the Plough ten minutes late, which did not best please the landlord George. His gruff reception informed the girl of his annoyance at her tardiness. Only Emily's physical appearance stopped George from berating the girl.

The pub was busy considering the time, the warm sunshine bringing out the trippers to the lake, as well as the casual drinkers. Emily set to work immediately, and her verbal skills together with her natural attributes soon cleared the backlog, each customer impressed with her dexterity.

When the bar was back to some semblance of normality Emily turned to George.

"Sorry about being late, but it was really important."

"Your young man?" George's earlier temper had dissipated as he saw the girl's attitude to her work.

"Yes, he escaped, he's back George and he loves me…I just had to see him." George could see the radiance just the mention of her young man had brought to Emily.

"I'm so pleased for you Emily, my dear." George gave the young girl a great big hug, his huge arms lifting Emily off the floor.

"Thanks George." Emily kissed the landlord on the cheek as he let her down. "Where's Tommy tonight?" Emily had noticed the empty seat by the door where Tommy always sat, every Friday night.

"I don't know, perhaps he's on a case."

"A case? What is he, a lawyer or something?"

"It's solicitor in this country, Emily." George tutted. "American films. Anyway he's not a solicitor or lawyer, he's a copper."

"A policeman?" Emily was startled.

"Yes, didn't you know?" George asked.

"No, no I didn't." Emily almost whispered. The mere mention of policemen brought bad memories flooding back.

Emily's thoughts were disturbed by the arrival of the mercurial Duffy.

"Hello, Emily. How are you girl?"

"Oh hi, Sean, Fine thanks and you?"

"Not too bad. A pint of Dublin's finest if you please."

"Sean." Emily came to where Duffy stood. She leaned over the till to speak quietly to him. Seeing her need for privacy Duffy leaned closer, the smell of honeysuckle in her hair filling his nostrils.

"I'm so sorry about the other night. It. . . It was very rude of me, especially as you have been so kind."

Duffy could see the remorse in the young woman's eyes. The emotional roller coaster she had recently travelled plain to see.

"It's ok, Em. I still love you." Duffy's manner assumed the role of the jovial patriarch although the words he had said were the truth.

"Sean Duffy, you're the best friend a girl could ever have." Emily kissed Sean on the lips. Duffy was surprised by the affection, and not knowing which way to interpret the moment, he remained passive.

He wondered whether Emily still cared for him, or if she was just telling him that it was ok for him to be around, so long as he doesn't touch? Duffy felt like a kid in a sweet shop with no money in his pockets. So much wanting to savour, but with no opportunity to purchase. Almost compelled to say something, Duffy found the words that came out were not the ones he would have chosen had he been more in command of his faculties.

"So, how is Christian? Have you heard anything?" 'Dumb question, Sean.' He told himself. Why mention his adversary at this juncture. Duffy knew all thoughts of him would evaporate from Emily's mind at the mention of Christian's name. The look on Emily's face confirmed his fear.

"Oh, Sean. He's back and he's safe. I saw him today…I'm so happy, Sean."

Duffy was jealous of her reaction to his question; Duffy saw love, true love, almost devotion in her eyes. The look that tells a man that the object of his desires is not available to him. Duffy tried to smile enthusiastically, his eyes telling everyone that the smile was a falsehood.

"I'm so pleased for you Emily." He half lied.

"He's coming down later, probably with Freddie. He'll tell you everything then, isn't it great, Sean?" she beamed.

"Yes, really great, Emily."

"Sorry Sean…your pint." Emily floated to the other end of the bar to pour the liquid.

Duffy watched her movements, every action of her body stimulating his desire. He decided to change the subject.

"Yer man who sits in the corner, not in today?"

"No apparently he's on a case." Emily's casual remark disguising what she had learnt from George.

"A case?" Duffy raised an eyebrow.

"Yes, he's a copper." Emily's concentration on the head of beer.

Duffy's thoughts of Emily disappeared, his thoughts only on the words she had said. 'A copper.' Duffy became paranoid, his brain travelling backwards to a darker memory contained within the recesses of his mind.

Emily looked at Duffy's face as she brought the beer to him.

"That was my reaction as well, Sean." She put the drink down in front of him. "You know how I feel about policemen."

"Not too dissimilar to my own feelings. girl." Duffy mumbled.

"What is it about policemen that makes you always feel guilty?"

"I know what you mean, Emily, I feel the same way." Duffy took a sip of beer.

"That's on me, Sean. A thank you for all you have done for me." Emily said turning to take some change from her handbag, which was behind the counter on the far wall.

Duffy, deep in thought, missed Emily's gesture, his concentration registering a flicker of recognition, his brain searching through the minds filing system, stopped at a name, a place of importance.

"Hammersmith!" He exclaimed aloud.

"Sorry, Hammersmith? What about Hammersmith?" Emily had heard Sean utter the name.

"What, oh…nothing Em, I…I just remembered something to do with work." Duffy lied. Molly…it was to do with Molly…her murder in Hammersmith... that was it! Inspector Boyle…he was the copper involved with Molly's death…now he was here…every Friday night…Every time Duffy was there.

"This copper, Emily, the one that sits in the corner, what days does he come in?"

"Only Fridays, so George said."

Duffy only came in on Fridays – the man must be watching him, yes he did watch him, him and Emily – why Emily? Duffy's mind was confused. Then it came to him like a fist. Him and Molly, him and Emily, he was a suspect, yes that's it! The copper was following him, waiting for the repeat of what happened in Hammersmith all those years ago back in 1939.

Emily's touch brought Duffy back to reality as she laid her hand on his.

"Are you ok Sean? You look so pale, so distant." Her concern was honest.

"Yes, yes fine Emily girl. Just a problem at work, nothing I can't handle." Duffy lied again.

"Drat!" Emily exclaimed.

"What?" Asked Duffy surprised at her remark.

"I just caught my thigh on something." Emily looked towards her right leg. "I bet it's torn my stocking." Emily pulled up the hem of her black skirt exposing the damaged stocking, the suspender, the creamy flesh of her thigh.

"Blast, I thought so."

"Now that I'd like to handle." Duffy, eyes on the little blonde hairs that stood on the bare flesh of her beautifully formed thigh.

Emily giggled, slapping Sean playfully on his hand.

"You naughty boy, behave yourself, Sean Duffy."

"I'm trying girl, I'm trying." The familiar grin back on his face.

After dinner Mosel, ushered his guests once again into the great hall at the chateau, where Yvette with Anne Marie served cognac and cigars, combined with subtle femininity.

Yvette had watched Steiner during dinner, the handsome young aide's eyes had followed every movement Anne Marie had made, his thoughts only interrupted by cordiality towards his master's guests. Yvette's assessment of the young man's loyalty exposed his weakness – Anne Marie. If Mosel, as she guessed he would, made his move towards more private explicit conversation with any of the dignitaries, then Steiner would have to be distracted.

Yvette stood by Anne Marie's side and whispered to the young girl.

"Listen Anne Marie, if Mosel should leave the present gathering with one or more of the guests, I will have to follow him, find out what his intentions are."

"Why?" asked the young girl.

"For France, Anne Marie. I can't explain now, but it's very important, do you understand?"

"Yes Yvette, what do you want me to do?"

"The young officer," Yvette's eyes went to Steiner, Anne Marie's followed her gaze. "You like him?"

"Yes." Anne Marie answered, guilt visible in her eyes. "I know I shouldn't but…"

"If Mosel makes a move, distract the lieutenant, keep him busy."

"But how?"

Yvette looked at the young girl, a knowing smile on her lips.

"You are a woman, Anne Marie, and a Frenchwoman."

Anne Marie returned the smile, a sexy feminine glint in her eye.

"I will do as you say Yvette – for France."

"Watch me and wait for my signal, till then, carry on with your duties, ok?"

"Yes Yvette."

The two girls parted to circulate amongst the guests.

Christian, with Freddie and Cathy in tow, entered the Six Bells from the car park entrance. Emily almost ran down the length of the bar when she saw Christian, leaning over the counter, her arms went to his neck, her mouth to his. Christian, slightly embarrassed, returned the greeting. Emily's eyes were wild with excitement, her smile luscious. She greeted Freddie and Cathy with a similar exuberance.

Duffy, slightly off balance by the obvious affection displayed by the girl, made his greeting to the new arrivals in a more cordial, but equally warm way.

"Sean, good to see you again." Christian shook Duffy's hand.

"You too Christian. Hi Freddie." Duffy's eyes moved to the young English officer, before fixing on Cathy. "And good evening to you, Cathy dear." Duffy took her hand, kissed it gently, his eyes never leaving hers, his huge grin displaying his trademark Irish charm. Cathy curtsied in jest, her pleasure at the attention evident in her pretty face.

"Right! Whose for a drink then?" Sean asked.

Emily busied herself with the order, her eyes searching for Christian's at every opportunity. When the drinks arrived, Sean made a toast.

"The returning hero."

"I'm no hero." Christian felt the guilt, "but I'm glad to be home, amongst friends again."

"Christian," they all chorused. The chink of glasses filled the air. Emily leaned over the counter again to kiss him, this time with more subtlety.

"You're still my hero." She whispered.

The men deciding the time was right to discuss the adventurous side of Christian's adventure. Cathy, noticing their need, moved closer to Emily, for a feminine conversation.

The champagne was served for a toast to the Fatherland as planned. Von Rundstedt made his apologies to all present for his early retirement to bed, the old man looked tired, weighed down by his responsibilities.

When Von Rundstedt left, the great hall, Schnapps was provided for the younger men. The girls, Yvette and Anne Marie busying themselves with the constant refilling of glasses.

Mosel saw his opportunity, and signalled to Steiner to entertain his other guests as he made conversation with the lone standing figure of Rommel.

"Herr Field Marshal."

"Ah Ernst, an excellent meal and an excellent venue." Rommel surveyed the great hall.

"Thank you, Herr Field Marshal, the chateau has an excellent library, perhaps you wish to see it?"

"Yes, I would like that very much." Rommel responded.

Yvette had seen Mosel's movement towards the Field Marshal so she positioned herself within earshot.

"Gentlemen, more schnapps?"

"Thank you my dear, but we will be visiting the library. Tell the leutnant to send my special decanter along with two fresh glasses."

"Certainly sir, as you request." Yvette saw her opportunity; the two men were finally making contact and the object of Mosel's preparations was about to be fulfilled.

The two officers left the room in conversation.

"There are some great works of history in the library, I understand you are an avid scholar."

"Only a layman unfortunately, Ernst, but a great admirer…" The door closed, obscuring the remainder of the conversation.

Yvette approached Steiner and informed him of his master's request. Steiner made to go towards the door; Yvette put her hand on his breast pocket lightly, stopping Steiner's movements as she did so.

"The captain and the Field Marshall have asked me to take the decanter to the library. Herr Mosel asked me to tell you to entertain his remaining guests whilst he is in conversation." Steiner looked slightly put out, and after a moment's thought he was about to verify what the girl had said, when Anne Marie came to his side.

"Margot, you are hogging the lieutenant's precious time, I will see to his wishes." Anne Marie's beautiful smile halted the young man's thoughts. He shrugged his shoulders.

"See Herr Goefeld, he will decant the Schnapps in the cellar for you, Margot." Steiner's orders having been given, he turned his attention to Anne Marie.

Yvette left the great hall pleased with Anne Marie's timely interjection. "I'll make an agent of Anne Marie yet," she said to herself.

Yvette almost ran to Herr Goefeld to procure the decanter. Time was of the essence. She needed to know what Mosel was up to. When she had the Schnapps with two clean glasses ready, she ran back to the main area of the chateau pausing only to catch her breath before approaching the door to the library, where she would wait and listen.

Mosel continued the polite conversation with Rommel for a while before the Field Marshal turned to speak.

"Ernst, I feel you did not bring me in here to discuss history."

"No sir, not past times, but the present."

"The present! What exactly in the present."

"The Allied invasion."

"The invasion, yes…well I'm sure all that can be discussed at the war games tomorrow Ernst,"

"Yes, I know sir…but…how can I put it…"

"Simply, Ernst."

"Yourself and Von Rundstedt seemed very distant tonight. I can't help but assume you have a difference, a difference which I believe concerns the proposed location of the invasion…I would not normally seek clarification of this point, but I am working on a plan, which if successful, will provide us with a clear intention of where and when the invasion will take place."

"I see, yes, I see." responded Rommel, now deep in thought. "Von Rundstedt is adamant that the Allies will land in the Pas de Calais, I am not so sure."

"Your alternative?"

"If I were the Allies, I would not land in the Pas de Calais, It's too obvious. I would prefer Normandy and soon."

"My thoughts exactly, Herr Field Marshal, their Dieppe raid was a fiasco, there is no reason to assume that Calais would be any different."

"Normandy is our weakest spot," continued Rommel, "It is yet to be as comprehensive in defence as other parts of The Atlantic Wall. The country is too broken for our Panzers to move in, react quickly to any landing. It would give the Allies time to get enough materials ashore to build up a beachhead. From there they would be able to breakout with Paris as their objective.

"I agree entirely with your views, Field Marshal, but…." Mosel hesitated.

"But what? Ernst."

"A port sir… Normandy would not have an effective port for the unloading of supplies."

"What of Cherbourg?" Asked Rommel.

"Not enough practical sized beaches, the beachhead would be too far from the point of supply, their communications stretched, vulnerable, and that's assuming they take Cherbourg in time. A risky venture."

"So you feel Calais is their only practical target?"

"No sir, I believe it will be Normandy."

Rommel raised his eyebrows.

"But what of a port…as you so rightly said…they can't exactly bring one with them can they?" Rommel's mind could not correctly interpret Mosel's line of thought.

"No sir, I don't suppose they could…but something keeps telling me that Normandy is the correct site for such an undertaking."

"What of Patton? He will lead the assault."

"Yes, Field Marshal, perhaps…he is located in English East Anglia with the 1st Army group. We have been receiving a lot of signal traffic from their US 3103RD signals regiment, our aerial photographs also show a massive amount of ordnance…"

"Well, I suppose that confirms Von Rundstedt's argument. The Allies' positioning of this army, FUSAG I believe it's called, can only point to Calais."

Mosel still wasn't convinced.

"I suppose so sir, unless…"

"Unless?" Rommel was interested again.

"Unless it's a huge deception Field Marshal, and Normandy is the target."

Yvette had listened to the whole conversation, she should have arrived with the drinks by now, Mosel would become suspicious . . . just a moment longer, she told herself.

"A deception?" asked Rommel.

"Yes sir."

"Could you prove it?"

"I have a man in London who's above suspicion, he has been told to investigate this FUSAG."

"Good Mosel, can he be trusted?"

"Yes sir, he can."

"So is this the plan you spoke of?"

"No sir, I have a plan which will provide us with the exact intention of the Allies, the dates, times, number of units. Everything we will need to know in order to push the Allies back into the sea, and most importantly, sir, its location."

Rommel was impressed, He knew Mosel was brilliant, but this…if this plan succeeded he would have surpassed even Rommel's expectations of the man.

"Tell me more Ernst."

"Well sir…."

The conversation ended abruptly as the sound of a glass falling from the other side of the door alerted both men.

Yvette listening intently at the door had not seen or heard Steiner approach, his hand touching her shoulder had made her jump, spilling the glass onto the floor.

"Margot, What are you doing?" demanded Steiner.

"Oh, oh sss...sorry Herr Lieutenant, you frightened me." Yvette stammered, her mind seeking an excuse for her presence at the library door.

"You were listening at the door as I approached, Mademoiselle?"

'That's it.' Yvette thought. "Yes sir, I...I was listening…I thought I could hear voices…I…I did not wish to disturb the gentlemen in mid conversation…that would be rude sir."

"So you thought you would wait and listen until they stopped." Steiner's voice conveyed his suspicions regarding Yvette's excuse.

"No sir, not until they finished just until they paused…sir."

"Hmm!"

Mosel halted Steiner's interrogation as he opened the double doors to the library.

"What is going on, Hans?"

"Nothing sir, the silly girl dropped a glass that's all. Margot, fetch a clean glass immediately." Yvette, thankful for the respite moved quickly to the kitchen.

"My apologies for disturbing you sir." Steiner entered the library and placed the decanter with the single glass on the table. Mosel looked at his aide, concern on his face, Steiner responded with a look that told Mosel not to worry, he had everything under control, Mosel's face relaxed.

Yvette almost ran into the room with the clean glass, trepidation still in her eyes.

"That will be all, Margot, return to your duties in the great hall." Said Steiner dismissing the girl with the curt remark. Yvette curtsied her apology to the three men before leaving as Steiner had ordered.

Steiner bowed. "Herr Field Marshal, sir." Nodding towards the two senior officers as he made a gracious exit.

Anne Marie could see the consternation on Yvette's face as she entered the great hall. She moved quickly to Yvette's side.

"Yvette what happened?"

"Steiner caught me listening at the door. He suspects me, you were supposed to warn me."

"I would have done, Yvette, but he asked me to fetch some more glasses. When I returned he was gone." Anne Marie's face displayed the hurt she felt at letting Yvette down.

"It's ok Anne Marie, I understand. It just caught me by surprise that's all. You had better move away. Steiner will be back any minute, I don't want you involved in his suspicions."

"I think I will be anyway, Yvette, he is an intelligent man, he will put two and two together."

"Yes, you're right, Anne Marie, now quickly go."

Steiner came back into the great hall, walked passed Yvette continued his function as temporary host, nothing was said, but for the rest of the evening his eyes constantly checked on Yvette's position. He did not believe her story and Yvette knew it.

As it neared closing time, the demand for Emily's services became intense, the ringing of the bell causing a stampede of western movie proportions. Emily expertly serviced the requirements of the mêlée. Once everyone was satisfied with their last gasp libations, and another round for her group upon Duffy's insistence.

Cathy lent a hand with the glass washing as Christian collected the empties with Freddie in tow. Duffy acted as doorman. When the pub was emptied the group sat quietly to finish their conversation over the drinks.

"Can you get some time off tomorrow?" Emily asked Christian.

"Yes, I don't officially report back until Sunday, why?"

"Can we go back to Engelfield?" The excitement in Emily's voice was obvious to all.

"Yes, I suppose so, if you want."

"Englefield, where's that?" interrupted Duffy.

"Oh Sean, it's wonderful there, the views, everything…"

"Englefield Green, on the surrey border, near old Windsor." Freddie explained, joining the conversation. "Jolly good pub too."

"Oh! Sean, you just have to see it." Emily's enthusiasm was catching. "Why don't we all go?'

"'Fraid I can't." Freddie said, "I'm on duty all weekend."

Cathy looked disappointed.

"Sean could take Cathy, he would be the perfect escort."

"If Cathy doesn't mind, nor will I." Freddie always the perfect gentleman allowed Emily to further her cause.

"Please Cathy, please Sean."

"Ok with me." Duffy said.

"Same here, as long as Freddie and Sean don't mind." It was Cathy's turn to join in.

"So what's so exciting about Englefield Green then, Emily?"

"There's a lane on top of the hill with a little whitewashed cottage covered in ivy and climbing roses, with clematis around the door, a lovely big garden and the most breathtaking views across the river with London beyond – a paradise."

"We could all fit in the Morris," added Christian, "maybe take a picnic, or we could go to one of the local pubs for lunch."

"Good idea," they all joined in. Only Freddie felt a little left out.

When the 11.30 deadline arrived, Steiner told the girls they could leave, their duties having been carried out to satisfaction, their presence was no longer required.

When they collected their belongings Anne Marie was a little annoyed at the lack of attention she had received from Steiner since the episode with Yvette. Yvette, on the other hand, was glad no mention of the incident had been made; she was relieved when she and Anne Marie reached the café. Her earlier doubts as to Steiner's possible reaction faded as they reached the dark interior of the small establishment. She needed a cognac, a large one.

Steiner entertained the last guests until they departed his bed and a good night's sleep beckoning, before knocking on the library door.

"Any further refreshments required sir?"

"No, we are fine Hans, unless the Field Marshal?"

"No, not for me Ernst, I need my sleep...thank you for a most entertaining evening...and Ernst, keep me informed of your ideas."

"Certainly Herr Field Marshal, Hans, will see you to your room...Hans."

"No need to worry the young man, I know the way, until tomorrow Ernst, Lieutenant, Goodnight, thank you once again for a most enjoyable and informative evening...Gentlemen."

With that Rommel took his leave.

"Did your discussions with the Field Marshal bear fruit, sir?"

"Yes, Hans, a whole orchard full." Mosel changed tack, the incident with the girl outside the door...a problem, Hans?"

"No sir, just a silly girl," Steiner lied. "I will double check tomorrow, just to make sure."

"Good Hans, now how about a last drink, I think we both deserve it."

"Yes please, sir, it's been a long evening."

Duffy agreed to give Cathy and Freddie a lift back to the airfield; Cathy sat on Freddie's knee as Duffy pushed the van over the hill towards Ruislip. Meanwhile, Christian helped Emily with the final clearing up before they left to make the short journey to Emily's home.

The night was warm and humid. Christian drew the curtains, opened the window of the bedroom, allowing what precious air there was to permeate through the room. The lights off, the blackout, an every night routine since the beginning of the Blitz in 1940, still observed by everyone.

Christian pulled the covers off the bed, undressed to lay naked on the cool surface. Emily was still in the bathroom, washing herself. Christian lay on his back, adjusting his eyes to the darkness. What light was available filtered through the opened window. He sensed rather than heard Emily enter the room. She moved to the window where he could identify her features, and see the plain white nightie she wore, its hemline about four inches above her knee.

She did not speak; she inserted a finger underneath the strap of her nightie, easing it over her shoulder letting it come to rest on her elbow. The swell of her breast was exposed. The nipple, hard and erect, tantalisingly remained covered. Emily repeated the process with the other strap, a little shake of her shoulders allowed the white material to slip gracefully, exposing her breasts, the flat tummy, halting briefly on her hips, the mound of her bottom holding the descent momentarily, until it continued its journey to her feet. The light perspiration on her body glinting in the gloom, her eyes wide, white, her mouth sensuous.

Christian opened his arms ready to accept her. Emily moved to the bed, took Christian's hands, pressing them overhead, holding them there with force. Christian, understanding her intentions, made no response. He lay there passive, allowing Emily the control she desired.

She began gently to kiss his face, his neck. Christian's mouth desperately trying to catch hers, but to no avail, She avoided him, her mouth following the contours of his body.

Emily on all fours having gently aroused his whole body with her kisses, sat across his hips, inserting him inside her as she did. Slowly her controlled rhythmic movements brought soft gasps and moans, their bodies moved in unison. Emily threw her head back, her hand throwing the hair from her face. Christian unable to contain his feelings moved to sit up, his hands going to her breasts, squeezing the nipples hard. His mouth on hers, their tongues intermingled. Her nipples, pink, erect, sensitive, responded to each contact, her sublimity arousing his very being. Christian met her every movement, each thrust caused her fingers to dig in his shoulders. The pain Christian felt compensated by his ecstasy.

She felt him ready, her determination shot, her body taking control no longer, she accepted the inevitable. Their orgasms burst upon each other like a sunrise in a desert. Their sweat soaked bodies fell upon each other, becoming one. Their hot panting, causing each to swallow, allowing regular breaths to form. In unison the palpitations simmered into soft sleep. They lay subdued, their foetal positions as twins in a womb. The collusion of body and mind enveloping them in a cocoon of love.

CHAPTER 15

Tommy ate the breakfast hungrily, with Mary by his side. They had arrived in Belfast late after a non-eventful crossing, Tommy's concern for Mary's safety only subsiding as the steamer entered port. They found an acceptable lodging at the Railway Hotel, a short walk from the main line to the Republic. They would take the train, changing once, hopefully arriving in Roscommon at midday.

Mary was in her element, her excitement at seeing her friends and relations in her hometown, to see the beauty of her home, unspoilt by the tide of war was tangible, and justified Tommy's inclusion of his wife on the trip. They had agreed to meet their pals for lunch at Sweeney's Restaurant in the Market Square. Mary already had decided on what she would do when Tommy had to go about his business, shop until she dropped.

The train pulled from the station. The great puffballs of smoke floated past the window, the rhythmic staccato of the engine gained speed, the slab grey buildings of Belfast becoming less huddled as they left the city. Small patches of green prepared the mind to be ready for the beauty to come. Tommy sat watching his wife's expressions, smiling at her observations, laughing with her anecdotes, his eyes never leaving her face.

Christian and Emily awoke late, their still naked bodies entwined for warmth in the cool, morning light. The bedclothes undisturbed on the floor. Christian made the tea whilst Emily ran a bath for them both. They would share the limited warm water, Christian shaving from the remnants of the kettle.

When they had finished they towelled each other's bodies before dressing. Emily wore yellow shorts, which fitted the contours of her like a second skin, a pretty white blouse tied about her waist exposed her midriff, white plimsolls completed her attire. Her hair the colour of the sun lay gently on her shoulders. Christian also wore shorts, navy blue, exposing his long athletic legs. He wore a short-sleeved loose fitting shirt and sandals. The tooting horn of Duffy's van alerted them to his and Cathy's arrival. Duffy having picked Cathy up from her home.

The four friends piled into Christian's Morris, the two girls chatting busily in the back. Emily's excitement bubbled over, her infectious giggles captivating everybody. Christian sat in the front with Duffy. They tried to assert their male dominance, failing miserably, their mouths moved but the ears strained to pick up the snippets of information emanating from the back seat. Eventually realising the lost cause, both men reverted to concentrating on the journey ahead. Christian's eyes lingering on the rear view mirror, his heart beating fast as Emily's beauty filled his vision.

By the time they arrived by the river they were hot and thirsty. Christian turned into the car park of the teashop at Runnemede, the same one he had visited last time with Emily. The four friends stretched their legs, grateful of the fresh air, and the sun beat down on them from a clear blue sky.

Cathy, also wearing shorts, beige with a crimson red top, took Emily by the arm, the two blondes walked together still chattering away. The men silently following behind watched the two pretty girls, arm in arm in front of them, their thoughts both similar in nature. Duffy was the first to speak.

"God was having a fine day when he made them two." The grin ever-present, widening.

Christian nodded in agreement, Duffy was right, the two girls were stunning, each complimenting the other, yet in his eyes Emily was the winner. Like two runners in a sprint, Emily just reaching the tape first, winning the medal of his affection. Emily turned her head towards the men.

"Come on you two, hurry up." Her eyes told Christian all he needed to know.

Hans Steiner entered the small café his mind concentrating on his duty, his heart expectant, waiting to see the vision of its desire, Anne Marie. He was disappointed. A large, unshaven, dark man, his black eyes cold, his manner un-cordial, stood behind the counter. A casual acknowledgement of Steiner's presence, not endearing the grey atmosphere.

Steiner regained his composure as he approached the counter.

"Where is Anne Marie?" his voice authoritative.

"I do not know, Monsieur." The dark man opened his arms in bewilderment. "You have business with the young lady, Herr Leutnant?"

"She is working today, is she not?"

"She is supposed to be working, Monsieur, but she is not here." The man's arms opened again in a gesture to show the emptiness of the café. "These young girls, so fickle, their heads full of nonsense, no respect for duty."

"Is her cousin Margot here then? I will speak to her for the time being."

"Margot, a cousin, you say....Anne Marie has no cousin called Margot, Monsieur."

"Are you sure?" Steiner's voice betrayed his suspicions.

"Of course I am sure, Herr Leutnant, I am Anne Marie's uncle, Bernard Foullier, she has no cousin Margot." The man looked confused, edgy. "I'm sorry Monsieur, perhaps the Lieutenant is mistaken?"

"Perhaps...yes, perhaps I am...If Anne Marie returns..."

"Yes Monsieur."

"No...no don't worry I will see her later...Good day to you Monsieur."

Steiner left the small café, walking the short distance to the main gate of the chateau, his thoughts on what the man had said. Anne Marie had lied to him, had she also lied in the affection she had shown him? Was it just a cover for some devious, callous reason? Steiner pictured Anne Marie in his mind, the smile, the eyes, no, he was wrong. Steiner was an expert at assessing people's conduct by their eyes. An experience he had gained long before working with Mosel. No, the eyes didn't lie, Anne Marie had shown genuine desire, affection. But what of her cousin? She had lied about Margot. If that was her name.

It came to Steiner in a moment. He wondered how he could have been so stupid. He now knew the real name of the other girl, of whom he'd had his suspicions before. The girl listening outside the door when Mosel had been entertaining the Field Marshal, her sudden appearance in Anne Marie's company. Steiner carefully sifted through events of the last few days. Anne Marie said Margot had been visiting a sick relative in the area. Lucien had also said a young woman was visiting a sick relative, that woman and Margot must be one and the same, Yvette!

Steiner was now faced with two problems, Anne Marie, was she working with Yvette, or was she an innocent caught up in Yvette's deception. The second problem was what was he going to tell Mosel.

By the time Steiner had reached the gate he had made up his mind. He saluted the sentry and traversed the courtyard, making his way to the main part of the house. Mosel was standing on the terrace outside the library a coffee cup in his hand. Having seen his aide approach, Mosel called to him. Steiner joined the senior officer on the terrace, mounting the steps purposefully.

"Hans, all is well?"

"Yes sir, fine, thank you."

"How did your investigations go?"

"The young ladies are not at the café, I spoke to the owner, an uncle I believe, both girls have gone to the country to visit the sick aunt. They will be back on Sunday."

"Good, everything else is in order I presume?"

"Yes sir, everything's packed, the car will take us to the airfield." Steiner glanced at his watch. "In about five minutes, sir."

"Good, then you have time to join me in a coffee, then you must tell me all about this French girl…what is her name…Ah, yes. Anne Marie." Mosel saw the young man blush.

"Hans, do not distress yourself, I too was once young." Mosel smiled but his eyes did not.

Cavenaugh had received the message sent by Dublin via courier; he had sent a runner to fetch Seamus and Porrick, told him to tell them to bring the car. When the two huge men arrived, Cavenaugh told them of his intentions. They were to take him to Duffy's place. He would then inform Duffy of Dublin's instructions whilst leaving him knowing in no uncertain terms who was the boss in the London battalion. Both Porrick and Seamus grinned slyly their thoughts on the possible brutality to come.

The four friends had finished their tea. Refreshed, they left the cool interior of the tearooms to expose their skin once again to the hot sun.

"Shall we go for a walk along the river?" Christian suggested.

"Oh no, Christian, let's go to see the cottage first." Emily pleaded.

"We can see the cottage later after lunch, Em."

"No, I want to see it now," Emily turned to Cathy for support. "Cathy, you have just got to see the cottage, it's so…so wonderful."

"I don't mind," said Cathy, "I'm easy, what does everybody else want to do." Cathy remained diplomatic as usual.

"Sean, you want to see the cottage, don't you?" Emily's pout as usual destroyed any resolve Duffy might have had. He shrugged his shoulders. "I'm easy."

"Right, we'll go for a walk along the river first, then see the cottage on our way to lunch." Christian had decided to take control. Emily folded her arms in defiance.

"Cottage."

"River, and don't give me that spoilt brat look, Emily Cassidy or we won't go at all."

Christian took her arm forcing his hand into hers, tugging her towards the river. Duffy broke the mood. "Let's race to the river, last one gets a soaking."

Emily pulled her hand free from Christian's pushing him over as he tried to step over the small kerbside ditch, which ran between the car park and the road. Christian tumbled backwards landing with a thump on his backside. Emily saw the anger in his face, screamed, turned to run away, her laughter loud and raucous.

"You little..." Christian pulled himself up chasing after the giggling Emily who together with Sean and Cathy were some distance ahead of him. Christian's powerful legs propelled him forward, his arms flaying, grasping at the air, pumping in motion. He almost dived in front of Duffy to claim first place. Duffy, the older man, was bent over in some discomfort, his hands on his knees, his breath coming in short sharp blasts.

"Jesus, I'm getting too old for this malarkey." He panted, the sweat pouring from his temples, forming rivulets to run down his cheeks. "If God had meant Irishmen to run he'd have put the toilets a hundred yards from the bar."

The two girls, following in their own race, ran up to the two men. Emily jumping into Christian's arms, her legs encircling his waist, her arms round his neck. Cathy instinctively sought the sanctuary of Duffy's arms, the hot breath of her giggles on his neck. Duffy grabbed at her to steady himself, and lifted the petite blonde, swinging her in an arc. His balance unable to maintain an upright position, the two fell in a heap, Cathy landing on Duffy. They both lay on the grass their eyes and mouths inches apart. The laughter stopped, the moment frozen. They both tried to ignore what they felt, their faces parting, the embarrassment obvious.

When they had recovered sufficiently, the four friends walked along the riverbank in pairs chatting openly. Christian holding Emily's hand, Duffy, his hands in his pockets, walked next to Cathy, his eyes avoiding contact where possible. They stopped to watch the waterside wildlife for a moment before continuing to walk towards the weir. The fast flowing waters capturing each person's thoughts, as they stood silently fascinated. A lone Spitfire flew overhead, its single Merlin engine disturbing their concentration. Each looked to the sky instinctively and watched as the small fighter slowly disappeared from view, its vapour trail the only sign of its passing.

Emily felt the tension in Christian's hand. Her only rival at that moment for Christian's affection, the Spitfire, had come and gone.

"Come on everybody, Let's go back to the car." Emily urged.

"I could murder a pint," quipped Duffy.

"Me too," Christian and Cathy replied simultaneously. The little group turned, and following a footpath close to the road they made their way back to where the Morris was parked.

Commander Thompson read 'C's communiqué together with the decoded message from S.H.A.E.F. Harry sat quietly opposite Thompson in his office overlooking Baker Street, waiting for his controller to speak first. Thompson put the documents onto the table in front of him and looked up at Harry.

"Harry, it's on. Eisenhower has spoken to Montgomery regarding the American General Popowski, who, as you know, is currently serving as liaison officer to the Poles in Italy under the command of General Alexander. They seem to think he will be of use to them in the final planning stages for the invasion in Europe. What information do we have on him at present?"

"Nothing more than we have on file sir, the latest episodes with the open ciphers are all there sir, Bletchley de-coded them all sir, plus there's one other snippet, came in this morning."

"I haven't seen anything new."

"No sir, I only got the clear just prior to our meeting."

"Well, Harry?" Milburn's matter of fact approach was beginning to grate on Thompson.

"Well, sir, we picked up a German Naval Intelligence enigma signal sent to the Rudy network in Dublin yesterday, sir."

"Mosel?"

"Yes sir, he, as we know from Yvette, is still at the chateau in Vitre, where he held our Polish airman chap."

"Kawolski."

"Yes sir, Kawolski, well as I was saying…" continued Harry, "Mosel's HQ passed on the following message to the Rudy network."

"What message, Harry?" The tone in Thompson's voice let Harry know he was becoming agitated with Harry's prolonged delivery.

"You had better read it yourself sir." Harry feigned his lack of comprehension, allowing Thompson to win the prize, like kids in a classroom he didn't want to be one to put his hand up when the teacher asked a question. He'd leave it to the brainy kid, in this instance that was Commander Peter Thompson.

Thompson took the document and began to read:

O.K.W. (Ober Komando West)
German Naval Intelligence
Time: 23.00 hours
Eagle to Emerald Eyes stop. Goose to leave the coop stop. Pigeon to guide it home to roost stop. Have Magpie watch and wait stop. End. Stop.

Thompson raised his eyes, a smirk of satisfaction on his face. He looked at Harry Milburn across the desk. "Do you understand the synopsis of this message Harry?"

"Sort of sir, we know Mosel is the Eagle, The Emerald Eyes, well that's our friend Rudy in Dublin sir, The Goose, that must be our American General Popowski. That all connects with the differences from Mosel to the general's open ciphers, the ones you allowed to be broadcast, as for the Magpie, well a magpie is a bird known for stealing, a thief, in this case sir. The Magpie is stealing information so that will be the IRA set up we've been watching in London."

"One for sorrow, two for joy." Thompson cut in, his smile overstated for his pun.

"Sir?"

"The nursery rhyme, Harry."

"Oh yes sir, I see, very good sir." Harry was taking great delight in acting the fool. "But who or what is the pigeon?"

"The pigeon is Flight Lieutenant Christian Kawolski, the goose, is as you correctly said, General Popowski. What do they have in common? They're both Polish Harry. Mosel has somehow persuaded Kawolski to bring General Popowski to him."

"To kill him, sir?"

"No, Harry, think back to nursery rhymes."

Harry pondered for a moment; he raised his eyebrow, comprehension flooding his brain.

"No sir, he won't kill him."

"Why, Harry?"

"You don't kill the goose that lay the golden egg sir."

"Exactly Harry, and what's the golden egg?"

"The details for the planning of the invasion, sir."

"Brilliant, Harry, that's exactly what Mosel's up to. He wants the details for Overlord. The exact time and places for the invasion of occupied Europe."

Thompson was pleased with the little game that had been played out. Harry's face, however, still looked concerned.

"What is it, Harry?"

"Ok, I can see the plan in Mosel's mind sir. But...but how is he going to get the information from Popowski...the American general sir?"

"That bit I don't know yet Harry, but as long as we know what his initial game plan is, bearing in mind we now know the objective. All we can do is watch, listen and wait."

"Yes, I see sir, waiting for Mosel's next move, that's all we can do."

"Right, Harry, anything else?" Thompson put his hands flat on his desk, the fingers extended.

"Yes sir, Yvette!"

"What about Yvette?"

'She failed to send in her routine signal sir...nobody's heard from her since.

"You think she might have been compromised?"

"It's possible sir, there's been a lot of activity in the region as you know. Kawolski, Lucien, Mosel, Von Ebstein. The war games for the German high command in Bordeaux this weekend, a lot of security about."

"Do you think she's ok?" Thompson was sincere in his question.

"I think so sir, She's one of our best, she's been in a tight corner before. If I know Yvette she'll lie low, wait until the heats off before surfacing again."

"When do you reckon that will be, Harry?"

"Tonight sir, all the heat will be in Bordeaux for the war games, sir." Harry's explanation was logical, delivered with a sensitive voice. Harry knew what it was like to operate in the field. He had worked with Yvette, knew the girl's capabilities.

"If we don't hear tonight?" Questioned Thompson.

"We won't panic, sir, we'll wait and see. If we haven't heard by Monday, we'll have to send somebody in to pick her up or find out what's happened."

"Ok Harry, I'll leave that up to you." Thompson seated himself back at his desk. "Any news from our man?"

"No sir, they're all still playing follow me leader. However, this communiqué from Dublin might force a bit of action. We, like all the rest, will have to wait."

"Ok Harry, let me know if anything develops." Thompson returned to the mass of papers on his desk. "Right, get in touch with Freddie Moreland at RAF Northolt, will you."

"Via S.O.E. Sir?"

"No Harry, direct – with 'C' approval we don't need to let them know – get Moreland to set up a briefing for Monday. Kawolski goes to Italy on Tuesday to pick up our American chap. Make sure Northolt gets that Jerry plane tidied up and ready to fly."

"Will do, sir, will that be all?" Harry made to move.

"One last thing, Harry." Thompson looked up from his papers, 'get me everything you can on Popowski. Not the American stuff, I've read that. I want the information relating to his family's time in Poland before they emigrated. Everything seems to revolve around Poles and Poland – it might, Harry, just let us know how Mosel plans to get the golden egg."

"I'll see to it right away sir." With that Harry turned and left Thompson's office. 'No chance of a Saturday night with the boys,' he thought as he made his way back to his office.

Tommy approached Sweeney's Restaurant hand in hand with Mary. He held the door open for the woman he loved. As they entered the door they were met by a throng of friends, pals, relations, people who remembered the couple, those who didn't know them. All met them with equal grace, in a typical Irish fashion. Drinks were ordered, toasts made, questions asked.

A wizened old lady held on to Mary's arm, part in greeting, part to steady herself. Her frail legs barely kept her up.

"Mary Moore, its great to see you. I'm your mother's cousin on your uncle Bertie's side of the family; sure I haven't seen you since Maguire's wake. A little thing you were at the time. I'm eighty four, you know?" The old woman beamed, the smile distorting the wrinkled face like a brick being thrown onto an unmade bed.

"Of course I remember you, and how are you? Eighty four, that's a grand age."

"Come on now Granny Rooney, don't be hogging Mary just now." Mary's brother Jack interjected as he led the old lady by the hand before sitting her down in a wicker wheelchair. The old woman's wrinkles contorted again to show her indignity.

Jack returned to his sister and putting his big arms round her with affection kissed her cheek.

"Mary, my love, It's so good to see you and Tommy again. How are you, darling Sister?"

"I'm well Jack, thanks, who's the old biddy?"

"The widow Rooney, she turned up at Mammy's funeral. We haven't been able to rid ourselves of the old bird since…still she's harmless…she's eighty four you know?"

"So I've heard, Jack…Let's join Tommy at the bar, He'll be missing me."

"That he will, girl, that he will." Jack brought Mary back into the heaving mass at the bar, where Tommy was engulfed in questions.

When the multitude of questions had been asked the repetitious answers given, and huge quantities of alcohol consumed, the party numbering twenty sat down at the table arranged for twelve. The restaurant proprietor greedily instructed his staff to provide additional tables and seating to accommodate the overflow.

After the initial bustling with the orders, the group settled down into broken, diverse conversations. Tommy sat next to Mary, his hand on hers, as he related the answers to whatever questions were put; Jack sat on Mary's other side proud of his sister and her man.

Steiner sat next to Mosel as the aircraft lifted into the clear blue sky. His thoughts still on Yvette and Anne Marie. Mosel was busy with the endless paperwork his position demanded, his concentration sidelined by the events of the week. His plan, its conception based on a simple divulgence of his overpowering father's guilt, was proceeding to a satisfactory conclusion. Its improbable birth was finally coming to fruition. Its result could define Mosel's destiny.

Steiner was a troubled young man, all his life he had been programmed to serve, duty was the only means of expressing whatever character had evolved. His parents, his tutor at school, his sergeant during basic training, Mosel. All had been mentors in Hans Steiner's regimented life. Dedication, his only solace. Now that brittle existence was being undermined. He had been conservative with the truth and had not told Mosel everything that he should have done.

For the first time in his life Hans Steiner seemed capable of individual thought, capable of emotion, capable of love. The object of his transformation to manhood, the spur that drove him to think independently of orders was the young French girl Anne Marie. The thought that she was somehow embroiled in Yvette's clandestine art was tearing him apart, his devotion to duty at odds with the desire to embrace Anne Marie's whole being.

His mind stumbled over Yvette; it was she that had caused the collision of responsibilities. How could he protect Anne Marie without protecting Yvette? Steiner bore the young woman no malice; she was brave beyond her age and physical form. Patriotic, all the things Steiner would admire in a man let alone a young woman, but she was the catalyst that could destroy his new found inner self, the real Hans Steiner, the man.

Mosel could feel the consternation the young man was experiencing. He knew Steiner had been economical with the truth regarding the whereabouts of the two young French women. At this juncture it caused him no alarm. Yvette had served her purpose; she had been the witness he had needed. The proof that London would demand. He would exert pressure on Yvette, forcing London to extract her from the area.

As for the younger girl, her significance in terms of security would diminish with the disappearance of Yvette; her brief excitement replaced with the normal domesticity conducive to the area. That would allow Steiner to complete the transformation to manhood without compromising the operation or himself. Mosel, his paternal instincts in full flow, would allow the young man his moment, he more than deserved it.

They had lunched at the Barley Mow, sipping warm beer between the overs of the cricket match being played on the green. Duffy tried to explain the rules to Christian, his endeavours in vain. Duffy had no time for the gentleman's game, rugby or a football match was more to his liking.

The four friends once again piled into the Morris heading for the cottage. Emily began, once again, to bubble over with excitement, now that she was finally getting her way. Christian pulled the car into a clearing and Emily sprang from the back before the Morris had come to a complete halt. She ran to where the cottage stood, jumping up and down like a schoolgirl, screaming for the others to follow. When they had caught up, Christian, who had seen the cottage on their last trip, stood to one side, allowing Cathy and Duffy an opportunity to view the cottage in full.

The whitewashed two-storey building stood amongst a pretty walled garden. Its brickwork festooned with ivy, climbing roses reaching for the roof. Clematis wound its way round the other plants for support, its bright flowers providing a kaleidoscope of colour. Rose cottage was beautiful in its simplicity. The leaded light windows reflecting the sparkling sunshine. Its slated roof at eye level gave it a picture postcard identity.

"Lets knock on the door, see if anybody's at home?" Emily beamed.

"We can't, Em, it would be impolite." Christian was slightly embarrassed by Emily's naivety of such basic manners.

"Oh yes we can." Emily, ignoring Christian, opened the wooden barred gate heading down the path towards the cottage; she turned, beckoning the others to follow, which they did, Christian reluctantly.

The little path wound its way through the neat manicured lawns, a miniature avenue of monkey puzzle trees guiding the way down the gentle incline until it reached a small brick wall. Here the path split, the right hand side continued to drop with the slope of the ground until it reached a plateau. From there it passed through a small wall before meandering to the rear of the building. The left-hand path led to a gap in the wall and round the front of the cottage.

Emily, still leading, decided to take the left-hand path. When the group reached the gap in the wall they all stood for a moment in awe. The small wall fell to a drop of twelve feet to the ground floor of the cottage forming a walled front garden area. A wrought iron staircase wound its way down between two large ponds, its green paintwork matching the olive green waters, before it settled on a flagstone patio. An oak door with bull's eye windows stood beneath the pretty tiled porch, pink roses encircling the frame.

"It's beautiful, Em." Cathy's eyes were wide with delight.

"Wow." was all Duffy could say.

"I told you, isn't it just wonderful?" Emily's smile subdued Christian's earlier embarrassment. She took his arm in hers before knocking on the door.

The group waited in anticipation for an answer, Duffy waiting for the bark of a dog. The others trying to discern what type of reception they would get when the door was eventually opened. When no response happened the group stood, hesitating, fidgety, not knowing what to do next. Emily knocked again.

"Can I help you?"

The friends turned at once to the voice, which had come from the walled garden to their right. There stood a little old lady with a walking stick, in her other hand, a strawberry basket filled with bright coloured flowers. The bonnet on her head masked her face in its shadow.

"I'm so sorry to bother you." Emily spoke first. "I came here with my young man sometime ago, we and our friends were visiting the area again and I just had to show them your beautiful cottage, I hope you don't mind."

The old lady lifted her head, her face no longer in shadow, was exposed. The green eyes stared at the group for a moment. She studied each face in turn, the two pretty girls, the two handsome men, one slightly older than the other. A black Labrador, old and overweight through years of overindulgence, made to growl, the phlegm deep in its throat beginning to reverberate.

"Silence, Rosie." the old woman commanded, the dog, not wishing to disobey its mistress sank onto all fours. Its head resting on its two front paws, its eyes like the old woman's scanning the four intruders.

The old woman focussed on Emily again, noticing the big smile, the innocence in her eyes, she too smiled. She held out her thin hand.

"I'm Mrs Hall, Patricia, Paddy to my friends."

"Hello Mrs Hall, I'm Emily, this..." said Emily pointing to Christian, "is my young man Christian, and..." Emily pointed to the others. "This is Sean," Duffy nodded. "...and Cathy." Cathy smiled back at the old lady.

"Pleased to meet you, would you like some tea? You must be parched."

"We don't want to put you to any trouble."

"No trouble, at all young man," she smiled at Christian.

"Can I help?" offered Duffy.

"Are your Irish?" The old lady asked, squinting up at Duffy from the corner of her eye.

"That I am, Patricia, or may I call you Paddy?" The grin was pure Sean.

"Yes and yes." Said the old woman, "Now take my arm. It's been a long time since I've had a handsome young Irish man at my side. Where do you come from, Sean?"

"The most beautiful village you have ever seen, Paddy." Duffy took the old woman by the arm, steadying her as she led the way, the others and the dog following sheepishly.

As they reached the rear of the cottage their appreciation of its beauty soared. The garden fell by a series of small walled terraces to a millpond surrounded by trees. Cherry, apple, birch and oak all added to the serenity. A willow drooped beside the water, its branches hovering above the glistening surface. Beyond the trees the ground fell dramatically before it levelled out, with the Thames cutting its way through the gentle pastures and London visible in the haze in the distance.

"Isn't this just the most beautiful cottage in the world?"

"Yes Em, it is."

When the lunch had finished and the festivities were over for the time being, alcohol having been consumed in great quantities, the parties began to drift away. Tommy Boyle, still next to Mary at the table, glanced at his watch. It was four thirty. He leaned towards his wife to whisper in her ear.

"Mary, my love, its time I was no longer here."

"Do you have to go already?"

"Yes, my love I do, after all the meeting I have is the main point of our visit here." Tommy looked at his wife's eyes. "Will you be alright on your own?" Mary smiled.

"Of course I will Tommy, Kate, Jack's wife, has agreed to come and do a bit of shopping with me. I'll be just fine." Mary tapped Tommy's hand with hers reassuringly.

"Well, if you're sure. Then I better get some coffee down me. Black and strong. I'll need my wits about me."

"Jack wants to come along with you."

Tommy raised his eyebrows. "You haven't said anything to him have you?"

"No Tommy, but Jack's not stupid. He knows that your not here for a holiday. He knows there's police business in the air. Everybody in Roscommon knows you're a copper. This man you're seeing knows it too. Jack won't interfere; he'll just act as back up, watch your back in case there's any trouble. He's also got a car."

Tommy thought for a moment, Mary was right. He didn't really know the people or the area well anymore. It had been a long time since he was in Roscommon and things did change. Jack would be a suitable ally. He was big, strong and could handle himself. If there was trouble, Tommy would have back up in such a circumstance back home, so Jack's presence would be appropriate, plus he had a car.

"Ok Mary you win, Jack comes."

Tommy stood up, kissed his wife's head, and signalled to Jack with his eyes. Jack stood up when he saw Tommy's look. Both men headed towards the now empty bar. Tommy ordered two strong, black coffees.

"Jack, I understand you want to come along to this little meeting of mine?" Tommy's voice was just above a whisper.

"It that's ok with you, Tommy? I thought I might be of use to you; sure I have nothing else to do that's important. Shopping with the girls does not appeal to me."

"What do you know of this Phelan feller?" Tommy scanned the room; nobody seemed to be interested in the two men's conversation at the bar. Jack's eyes hardened.

"Phelan himself is a wimp of a man, a nasty little piece of work, but no trouble on his own. Mary could take him out, but..." Jack hesitated, his face showing concern, "But he's mixed up with some nasty people."

"IRA?"

"Not Dublin's IRA, Tommy, no, a breakaway section, men of real violence, bombers, murderers, petty gangsters. There not interested in a united Ireland unless it's ruled by them. They would make the Dublin boys look like pacifists."

"You think they'll be present at this meeting?"

"I'm sure of it Tommy, Phelan wouldn't go anywhere on his own." Jack's look showed the contempt he felt. Tommy was glad Mary had persuaded him to include Jack.

"How long will it take to get to this place?"

"About twenty five minutes by car."

"Right, we'll leave at five. I want to reconnoitre the place before we go in. If it's a set up I'll know." Tommy was about to add something when the barman returned with the coffees. Jack made irrelevant conversation until the man returned to his duties out of earshot.

"I think I should go in first, do the reconnoitring for you, I'll be able to identify any faces that look odd. People who shouldn't or wouldn't be there."

Jack was right, Tommy would stick out like a sore thumb, or more importantly, like the copper he was. Tommy smiled.

"You're a good man Jack, a sensible one too, it will be a pleasure to have you with me." Jack beamed a great big smile back to Tommy. Pleased with his inclusion.

"I'll not let you down, Tommy."

"I know you won't Jack, I know."

The two men ordered more coffee before returning to the table. The diners that were left were making ready to leave, the kisses, goodbyes, good lucks were being exchanged.

Tommy shook hands with the guests promising to keep in touch, to visit again soon. When everybody had left he sat down with Mary, Jack and Kate to finish his now tepid coffee. At five minutes to five he and Jack stood up kissed the women goodbye and left the Sweeney's restaurant walking towards where Jack had parked the car.

The journey to the village of Glenamaddy did take twenty-five minutes. During the ride both men spoke little, they had their minds on the job ahead. Jack lit a cigarette puffing intermittently, as Tommy looked out of the window at the scenery but not taking it in until they crested the hill that led to Glenamaddy.

The village was set deep in the valley floor; there was only one road in, one road out. A perfect spot for a meeting, or an ambush. Any approach could be seen for miles. Tommy sank down in the passenger seat out of sight as the car made its way down the twisting road, which hugged the valley side. A small copse of trees, its dark shadows obscuring vision from the village would be the perfect spot for Tommy to alight.

When they reached the trees, Tommy got out whilst the car was still moving. Hiding in the shade, he watched as Jack's car approached the village before stopping outside Riley's bar.

When Jack had entered the public house, Tommy skirted the trees using whatever cover was available and made his way to the valley floor, and then on to the main road of the village, and down the street towards Riley's bar, trying to look as inconspicuous as possible.

Opposite the bar was a post office come general store, Tommy slipped into the interior of the shop. It was empty save for two children who stood admiring the vast array of sweets, unable to decide how to spend their meagre combined resources. The children bombarded the old lady behind the counter with questions as to how much this and that cost. Tommy busied himself by pretending to look at some postcards that were displayed in a rack; the usual mixture of uncommon blue sky looking down on small stone whitewashed cottages amidst a patchwork of coloured fields, quintessentially Ireland.

Tommy looked at the pictures, his eyes scanning the road with Riley's opposite. Jack appeared, a pint in his hand. He sat at an empty wooden table outside the bar, casually looking up and down for a sight of Tommy. Jack held his glass with three fingers showing. That was the pre-arranged signal they had decided upon on the journey. It meant Phelan was in the bar, together with two others.

Tommy left the shop without making a purchase, much to the old lady's annoyance, which she now vented on the quizzical children. He approached the main door of Riley's before opening it, entering into the cool dark interior, completely ignoring Jack's presence at the table outside.

As Tommy walked up to the bar he saw two men sitting at a table. One was thickset, red curly unkempt hair dominating his face. The other was small and skinny, with greying sandy hair, the jaw weak, the lips thin. This must be Phelan, the man fitted Jack's description. The two men looked up as Tommy entered, their faces grey. A third man seated at the end of the bar also noticed Tommy's entrance. Tall, wiry with a sallow complexion, he, Tommy decided, was the other man. Jack had signalled three. Two other men played dominoes and seemed oblivious to Tommy's presence. He would ignore them.

Tommy spoke to the barman ordering a Jamesons Irish whiskey. As he did Jack entered the bar with a newspaper under his arm. He selected a table by the door where he could watch the proceedings almost unnoticed. The red head approached Tommy.

"Mr. Boyle?"

Tommy nodded, "Yes."

"Mr Phelan is at that table." The red head pointed towards the slimy character with sandy hair. Tommy took his drink, sat at the table facing Jack, opposite Phelan. That way he could observe the whole bar whilst Jack with a similar view could watch the rear door to Tommy's back.

"Mr Boyle?" Phelan put out a bony arm.

"Mr Phelan," Tommy took the man's limp, wet handshake.

"Are you alone?" Phelan's eyes went to Jack then to the two domino players. The limited audience took no notice of his look.

"Yes I am, but you're not." Tommy saw the indignant look. "That fellow at the bar is with you."

Phelan smiled a greasy smile. "Yes, of course, you have already met Patsie."

Tommy leaned closer to Phelan. "You have some information for me Mr Phelan?" His voice curt.

"Regarding Mary McGrath…Yes, I do. Poor Mary, a sweet innocent child, led astray, brutally cut off in her prime by that bastard."

"Which bastard?" Tommy cut in.

"Before we go into that…there's a small thing we need to discuss…my compensation for the information. He's a bad man, I need to be sure you put him somewhere where he won't be able to get at me. Plus I want money, cash, Irish money."

"Or else?"

"Or else I will not divulge his name Mr Boyle." Phelan sat back pleased with himself.

"I already know his name…Sean Duffy." Tommy could see the surprise on Phelan's face. "I want proof, not for Mary's death, although I'll take any information you have. My interest, Mr Phelan." Tommy continued, "Is with regards to a murder that took place in Hammersmith in England the same year as Mary's death. The same circumstances. Probably the same man." Tommy hesitated then he began to stand up.

"I'm sorry, Mr Phelan, I think you have been misinformed. My interest is in the Hammersmith case only. I was told you could help…obviously my sources were wrong."

Phelan stretched out the bony arm again, his hand on Tommy's, his eyes staring into his.

"Please Mr Boyle." The red head looked up, thought about moving but remained. "Molly…Molly Redburn is that it?"

Tommy stopped, his face lowered towards Phelan. "What do you know about Molly?"

"Everything…Please sit down Mr Boyle. I can help you there too but the same rules apply."

"What rules?" Tommy sat down again. His arms folded to convey his lack of interest.

Phelan leaned closer to Tommy. "I know who did the Molly murder as well, Mr Boyle."

"So do I…Sean Duffy…I want proof." Tommy demanded, he made to get up again.

Phelan this time put both hands on Tommy's, his mind working overtime. "I have all the proof you need Mr Boyle, but first my needs." Phelan looked easier again. Tommy sat down again.

"Go on, Mr Phelan."

"Well, I'll need protection from your friends at the Garda."

"Go on." Tommy said.

"I will not travel to England…my presence there would cause concern."

"Why?" Tommy demanded.

"Let's just say British Intelligence would be overjoyed to see me on British soil."

"Because of your IRA connections?" Tommy could see the alarm spread on Phelan's face.

"No, no Mr Boyle. That was a long time ago. I have nothing to do with the IRA any longer; my service at the time was no different to any other Irishman. I did my duty as everybody else did at the time, It's…it's just the British are a vindictive race, they never forget. So as you can see Mr Boyle, it would be foolish of me to go to England."

"So what can you offer me, Phelan?" Tommy leaned closer his eyes only a few inches from Phelan's face. Phelan pulled back instinctively.

"I have the proof you seek. The weapon that was used very unusual, wasn't it?"

"What about it?" As hard as he tried Tommy's excitement was beginning to show.

"A double bladed knife, one side sharp and smooth, the other with jagged teeth for sawing or cutting through bone, the type the British commandos use."

"And?" Tommy let Phelan know of his impatience. "Anything unusual about it?"

"Yes Mr Boyle…It has three teeth missing, I'm sure your forensic fellers back at Scotland Yard already know about that. Am I correct Mr Boyle?"

"Go on." Tommy prompted.

"Well, we have possession of that knife."

"We?"

"Sorry?" Phelan looked perplexed.

"You said 'we'." Boyle pointed out.

"Ah yes, so I did." Phelan thought for a moment. "Let's just say the weapon is in safe keeping."

"What about prints?"

"Preserved, whatever prints are on the knife will identify the murderer."

"Duffy?"

"Exactly, Mr Boyle…as you know the weapon was the same one used in Mary's murder." The thin smile on Phelan's lips displayed the nicotine stained uneven teeth.

"How and when can I get this weapon, the knife?"

"That brings me to my other demands." Phelan leaned forward with both hands on the table. "Firstly, I want Special Branch off my back, my past, all the information they have on me, destroyed." Phelan watched Boyle's expression. Boyle thought long and hard.

"That's possible…you know I can't guarantee that but I'll certainly try, what else?"

"Five hundred pounds cash, in Irish notes."

Tommy raised his eyebrows, shook his head. "No way, Mr Phelan, they won't agree."

"The weapon, Mr Boyle." Phelan was about to play his trump card.

"What about it?"

"It belonged to Duffy's father. His name, his British army number, is on it."

Phelan sat back satisfied with his revelation. "There's one more thing, Mr Boyle."

"What?" asked Tommy.

"I also have a witness who could prove Duffy was involved with Mary's murder. He saw it all happen, now you know who killed Mary, using the knife we have in our possession, and if the knife is the same one used in Molly's murder in Hammersmith, then…then, Mr Boyle, you have a cast iron case."

"I see, Mr Phelan, you're right of course, but the Yard would not fund you five hundred pounds, the reward will only go to one hundred, that's based upon a conviction as well."

"Three hundred that's the least I can accept Mr Boyle."

"Two hundred, that's it, take it or leave it." Tommy stood to go.

"Two fifty." Phelan said aloud.

"Done." Said Tommy.

"You drive a hard bargain Mr Boyle, but two fifty it is." Phelan was not overjoyed.

"When do I get what I want?" Asked Tommy.

"You will be contacted in London by our associate in due course, Mr Boyle. You will bring a letter from Special Branch together with all the files they have on me. The letter will exonerate me from all investigations past and current. A pardon, in reality. The money must be exchanged at the same time."

"Agreed." Tommy nodded his approval. "I will be in touch Mr Phelan."
Tommy did not shake hands with the man; he simply left by the front door.

"That bastard copper!" exclaimed Phelan, his voice just carrying to Jack's ears.

The red head stood beside Phelan. Phelan looked up at the man as the other accomplice drew level at the table.

"You heard then?"

Both men nodded their heads. "Two fifty, the stingy bastard, still it's something. Patsie?"

"Yes, Mr Phelan?"

"You'll make the rendezvous with Boyle in London. "You, Donal," Phelan looked towards the tall thin man, "you Donal, will kill that bastard Boyle when Patsie has the money."

"It will be a pleasure, Mr Phelan." The evil grin spread across Donal's face.

Tommy took the same circuitous route he had taken on his arrival, stopping continuously to check if he was being followed, though nobody did. Feeling safe he returned to the darkness of the trees to await Jack's arrival with the car.

Jack's car appeared about five minutes later, Jack decreased speed; the door already swinging open-his eyes fixed on the rear view mirror. Tommy ran and jumped through the open door.

"Thanks Jack, everything all right?"

"If you mean were they suspicious, no, I don't believe so." Jack glanced again at the rear view mirror, "They're not following us either."

Jack had remained in the bar ordering another pint so as not to raise any suspicions.

"Jack, what's wrong? I can see the trouble in your eyes."

"I overhead something Phelan said, when you left."

"What Jack? Tell me."

"Tommy…."

"Yes Jack…"

"Tommy, Phelan gave an order to the tall feller, the one at the end of the bar."

"Yes, I noticed him, what did he say Jack?"

"He told him to kill you, Tommy." Jack's face showed the enormity of the statement.

"Oh…I see…" Tommy looked pale. "Thanks for letting me know, Jack."

Tommy sat back in his seat, his thoughts on what Jack had just said. Neither men spoke until they reached Roscommon town.

"I need a drink, Jack."

"Me too." replied Jack.

CHAPTER 16

The four friends, together with the old lady, the dog obediently at her side, sat in the garden of Rose Cottage. The tea had been finished. Duffy had done the washing up, and the five of them were enjoying the late afternoon sunshine.

"How long have you lived here, Patricia?" Emily asked.

"Twenty two years. My husband, Donald, and I bought the cottage in 1922, our children, two boys were killed at Passchendaele in 1917."

"Oh, I'm so sorry." Emily could see the hurt the memories were stirring in the old woman's mind.

"It's a long time ago now, but I still think about them. What they might have done if their young lives hadn't been taken so uselessly. Grandchildren, I would have liked grandchildren. I think I would have made a nice granny."

"You would have made a lovely Granny, Patricia."

"Ah well, it wasn't to be. Donald, my husband, died two years ago, so I'm on my own now. Just me and Rosie." The old lady reached out her thin arm to pat the old dog on the head. The dog, grateful for some attention, licked her hand in appreciation. "The cottage," continued the old lady. "is getting too much for me these days. I've been thinking of selling up, moving to the south coast. I have a sister, Maureen, who lives in a village by the sea. Milford on sea it's called, do you know it?"

"I do," Cathy, who had been listening to the old woman's story, cut in. "It's lovely, Milford, although you would be hard pressed to find a cottage as beautiful as this."

"Yes, I know, my dears, but I really can't manage on my own. Perhaps I should sell…still I have a bit of time yet."

"If it was my cottage, I would never leave it."

"Emily?"

"Yes, Patricia?"

"Your young man, Christian, what does he do?"

"He's a fighter pilot."

"He's a very handsome young man."

"Isn't he just."? Emily's eyes went to Christian. He and Sean were now standing by the terrace wall looking at the magnificent view.

"And you my dear, are a very pretty girl, you make a handsome couple."

"Thank you Patricia." 'If only' Emily thought.

"And you, Cathy," the old lady turned to face her. "Is Sean your young man?"

"No…no my young man is a pilot too…Sean…Sean's just a friend."

"Pity…you also make a pretty pair…if I was a few years younger." The old lady paused, a glint in her eye. "I would not let a feller like Duffy off the hook so easily."

Cathy blushed, her eyes looking towards the floor for a moment before seeking out the elusive Duffy.

The two men returned to the table.

"Come on girls." Christian said. "We've taken up a lot of Patricia's time, I think we should start heading back." Reluctantly they all agreed.

The party thanked the old lady for her kindness and hospitality, each kissing her in turn. The old lady with the dog in tow walked to the gate with the youngsters.

"Now you make sure whenever your in the area that you pop in to say hello."

"You have been so kind." Emily hugged her, kissing her cheek.

"Not at all, Emily dear, I have enjoyed your company." The old lady took Emily's face in her two veiny hands. "Such a pretty girl. You look after your young man…who knows…the cottage will still be here." Emily started to cry. "There, there, no tears now. You come back and see me…promise?"

"I promise." Emily spluttered, she turned to walk away; Christian took her hand to comfort her. Cathy made her goodbyes also hugging the old lady. Then it was Sean's turn.

"Duffy, you're a mighty handsome man, you have made an old lady happy. You can come anytime you like."

"You just try and stop me, Paddy." Sean blew a kiss from the gate, making the old lady blush.

Yvette cycled towards the café in Vitre, it had been a long ride from Philippe's' house on the edge of Rennes where she had stayed overnight. The message she had sent to London was plain, simple…get me out. Not wishing to compromise Philippe's position, she had left that morning to head back to Vitre; she thought everything should be quiet in the area for the time being. Von Ebstein and Mosel, her two main fears, had left the area temporarily for the war games in Bordeaux. They would not be back until late Sunday, so for the moment she would be safe.

The information Yvette had discovered whilst working at the chateau with Anne Marie was, she was convinced, of vital importance to London. If Mosel and Rommel were convinced that an invasion would take place in Normandy, they would take measures to ensure that the coastal defences were reinforced, probably moving Panzer divisions to the area. That would be a catastrophe for the men landing on the open beaches. It could also mean all the elements of Operation Fortitude would be to no avail.

The landings in turn might need to be postponed, allowing the Germans time to strengthen the whole Atlantic wall, whilst allowing them additional resources to bolster the tide of the Red Army surging forward in the east. Somehow, London would need to expand Fortitude to convince Mosel that the Pas de Calais was in fact the real site for the invasion. From what she had seen, Mosel was more than capable of convincing Rommel to his line of thought.

Philippe had promised to contact Yvette at the café with London's response. Her fears of Mosel's intentions were too critical to send by the normal channels, she would have to tell London in person.

Vitre was quiet; the temporary lack of activity at the chateau was being reflected in the small town, the pavements and shops seemed almost deserted.

Yvette parked her bike outside the small café before entering. Anne Marie was behind the counter; she had stayed at a friend's house the previous night on Yvette's insistence. She did not want the young woman's involvement to become permanent that would cause Yvette additional security problems, problems she could do without at the moment.

Anne Marie's face lit up when she saw Yvette, She rushed from behind the counter to embrace her, a childish excitement in her eyes.

"Yvette, it is so good to see you, I have been worried about you."

Yvette returned the greeting in traditional French fashion, kissing Anne Marie on both cheeks before taking both her hands in hers and looking deeply into the young girl's eyes. Looking for anything that may betray the girl's feelings.

"Is everything ok, Anne Marie, your friend?"

"No problem, Yvette, I told my friend that I had an argument with my uncle and that I did not wish to stay at the café that night."

"Did she believe you?" Yvette kept her eyes on Anne Marie's.

"Oh yes, completely, I often argue with my uncle, she knows this, I sometimes go to her when this happens. She is very sympathetic. I am a good actress don't you think?"

"Yes, yes…what of your uncle what did he say…he asked where you were?"

"Yes I told him I went to see Nicole, he believed me."

"Did anybody ask for you whilst you were away?"

"Yes, my uncle said somebody did ask for me."

"Who?"

"The handsome Leutnant Steiner, Hans." Anne Marie was so full of herself about the young German's obvious attraction to her that she couldn't see the danger that behind the young German soldier's eyes.

Yvette felt the alarm bells ring. She did not want to upset the young girl, or worry her unnecessarily, but she had to point out the possible dangers that her naivety in such matters could cause. Not only to herself, but also her uncle, this Nicole and, more importantly, Yvette herself. Under no circumstances would Yvette allow herself or her mission to be compromised. Her alternative would be to dispose of Anne Marie. This would be abhorrent to Yvette but she would do it if she had to.

Yvette decided that for the time being she would try to impress upon the girl the true nature of what she was caught up in. Try to instigate awareness in the girl, provide her with a sense of self-preservation.

"Anne Marie, this young Leutnant Steiner." Yvette paused allowing her face to take on a more considerate, understanding look. "Hans, he is very handsome, I know your feelings but he is a German, an enemy of France. If he knew of your involvement with me…then he would have to follow his conscience, disclose our activities to higher authorities…do you understand me, Anne Marie?"

Anne Marie's face saddened. "But he has been so kind…"

"I know," Yvette took the girl in her arms, giving her a sisterly hug. Yvette pulled back slightly from the girl, her eyes concentrating hard on Anne Marie's, which were beginning to well with tears. "Supposing," she said softly, "that out of duty alone, he did tell some higher authority, then Von Ebstein would get to hear of it."

Anne Marie pulled back in shock, her face showing the horror that Yvette's words had meant.

"He wouldn't."

"He might have no choice, Anne Marie." Yvette's concern shook the girl to her senses.

"Oh Yvette, I have been so silly, I didn't think…" Anne Marie burst into tears.

Yvette pulled her close, stroking the young girl's hair maternally.

"I know, I know, come child don't cry."

Yvette held Anne Marie, consoling the girl until her tears subsided. She poured a cognac for Anne Marie to ease the burden of guilt the young woman felt. When the girl had composed herself, Yvette asked her where her uncle was.

"Upstairs." The girl replied. Yvette knew she would have to speak to the uncle to find out exactly what had been said, until then, she would try to restore some self-esteem in the young girl.

It was sometime before the uncle appeared. Anne Marie had calmed down. Yvette offered to help out so that Anne Marie could lie down for a while. The uncle reluctantly agreed. The café devoid of customers could spare the girl until things started to get busy. When Anne Marie was safely asleep, in the small room at the rear of the café, Yvette made her move to discuss the possible situation that had arisen with the terse old man.

The uncle stood behind the counter polishing glasses with a towel as Yvette made her approach. Seeing Yvette's intention he looked up from his chore.

"You wish to speak with me, Mademoiselle?" The uncle continued to polish the glasses.

"Yes Monsieur, I believe you had a visitor yesterday whilst Anne Marie was at Nicole's."

"How do you know?"

"Anne Marie told me, Monsieur."

"She had no business, the silly girl is playing a dangerous game, getting mixed up with the likes of you." The uncle displayed his animosity towards Yvette. "You, Mademoiselle, also have no business."

"But I do, Monsieur, I am French. What the Boche are up to I have made my business. It should also be the business of every French person…are you French, Monsieur?"

Yvette's direct approach had shocked the uncle, he stopped wiping the glass, his eyes burning. He responded to Yvette's question.

"I am French, I fought at Verdun…I was part of that war."

"And you and I are part of this war, Monsieur…so is Anne Marie."

The uncle spread his arms, he was confused, he knew what he wanted to say, but the words would not come out…"It's…it's just that I feel for the girl, she lost her parents…she has been like a daughter to me…I…she's just eighteen, so young."

"Yes, she is young…I am not much older, Monsieur."

The uncle could see the strain in Yvette's eyes. He had seen that look before, long ago in the trenches at Verdun – he could see the girl was almost at the end of her tether. He put down the glass with the cloth, picked two fresh glasses and a bottle of cognac. He smiled, taking Yvette by the hand leading her to a table where he sat her down, pouring two large measures of the dark liquid.

"I apologise for my behaviour, Yvette. You are a very brave young woman, I had no right to treat you that way, I assure you it was based only upon my concern for Anne Marie."

"No need to apologise, you were, as you said, only protecting Anne Marie, I have similar feelings for the girl, but I must insist that you tell me everything that was said, everything, Monsieur."

The uncle began to relate the full extent of Steiner's brief visit to Yvette. When he had finished, Yvette began the questioning.

"So you told him that you did not know of Anne Marie's whereabouts?"

"Yes, I did not mention Nicole, I did not see any point in expanding the list of would be suspects."

"Good thinking, Monsieur, but Steiner, did mention me by name?"

"Yes he did…at first his interest was purely for Anne Marie, when I told him she had gone away to see a sick relative he asked about you."

"Did you mention the relative's name?"

"No Mademoiselle, this Steiner did not ask, he seemed more interested in you."

Yvette thought hard for a moment, it must have been when Steiner caught her at the door of the library. That had alerted his suspicions. Yvette thought she had just managed to convince Steiner of her innocence, but obviously she was wrong.

"Steiner, did he ask any further questions?" It was important for Yvette to know.

"No Mademoiselle, but . . '"

"But what?"

"When Steiner asked for Anne Marie, he also asked for Margot, her cousin…that I assume, is the name you must have used….I…I told him that Anne Marie did not have a cousin in the area…I'm sorry Yvette, I didn't mean to…"

Yvette saw the remorse in the old man's eyes. Unwittingly he had betrayed her, and she was in trouble, big trouble. Yvette patted the uncle's hand, trying to console his newfound guilt.

"Not to worry, Monsieur."

"Are you in serious trouble because of me?"

"I don't think so." Yvette lied.

"I am sorry, Mademoiselle." Yvette believed his sincerity. She thought about the circumstances. If Steiner was suspicious, why didn't he inform Mosel? Why wasn't she being hounded by German troops? Then it came to her, Anne Marie! Somehow Steiner was protecting Anne Marie. If this was true, then she would have to leave the area immediately or at least before Mosel and Steiner returned on Sunday evening. Until then, she was relatively safe. London, what the hell was London doing? They must have got her message hours ago.

The news in the paper was sombre; the Allies had again failed to capture Cassino. Anzio, the great move to outflank Kesselring's Gustav line was now pinned in its own perimeter, the American General having failed to capitalise on the out flanking movement. The landing was unopposed, the road to Rome clear, but he had waited in order to strengthen his beachhead. The Germans, reacting spontaneously, had sealed the gap. The opportunity had been lost, and the Allies now had to stiffen their resolve in order to maintain a foothold. Winston had summed it up succinctly.

"I thought we were launching a wild cat on the shores of Anzio, instead all we have is a great whale, lumbering upon the beach."

Commander Thompson's Saturday afternoon was disturbed by the arrival of Harry.

"What is it, Harry?"

"Yvette, Sir."

"What about her?"

"We got this message sir,"

"Read it, Harry."

"She wants out."

"Is that it?"

"Yes sir, Read it for yourself."

Thompson took the document; he read the brief message, his face for once betraying his concern.

"She sounds serious, could we get her out tonight?"

"I doubt it, sir, we could manage it this end, but by the time Yvette gets the de-code back…well, I doubt she would have time." Harry explained.

"Ok, tomorrow at the latest, who have we got available to do the fly in?"

"Only Kawolski and the instructor, Moreland, Flight Lieutenant Freddie Moreland."

"Then Moreland it is, let Northolt know will you, Harry."

"Yes sir," agreed the long-suffering Harry.

At that moment Thompson's wife Angela appeared with lunch and a cold bottle of white wine on a tray.

"Would you like to join us in a bit of lunch, Harry?" she asked politely.

"I'm afraid Harry is busy, dear." Thompson said to his wife before looking directly at Harry.

"Yes, Yes I am, Mrs Thompson, but thank you for the offer." Harry knew his company was no longer required. He stood up and wished Thompson and his wife a pleasant afternoon. "Bastard," he breathed as he left the garden.

Thompson continued to read his newspaper, ignoring his wife's look.

Cavenaugh had been trying to locate Duffy's whereabouts all day, with Porrick and Seamus in tow. They had eventually found his car outside Emily's place, however, when they knocked loudly on the door, no answer came. Instead, annoyed at the fuss they were creating the lady from downstairs spoke to them, informing Cavenaugh that Emily had left earlier that day with three friends. The three men canvassed the local pubs, even the lake, but no sign of Duffy or his entourage could be found. They decided to go back to Duffy's place and wait.

The four friends in the meantime had decided to stop off for a drink on the way back at the Plough. Oblivious to Cavanaugh's search, they entered the bar missing the three gangsters by a couple of minutes.

Freddie Moreland received Harry Milburn's call regarding the extraction of Yvette, planned for Sunday night. Normally Freddie would have been delighted to receive an operation such as this. The constant boredom of routine had taken the edge off his flying skills, but the thought that he would be operating in exactly the same territory as Christian had miraculously escaped from, filled him with trepidation. The area, alive with SS, Gestapo, so recently embarrassed by Christian's exploits would be fully alert, desperate to restore their reputation. Freddie would be flying into a recently disturbed hornets nest, his chances of success minimised, his chances of capture or worse, not in his favour.

Freddie Moreland was a pilot and an officer first, duty the creed by which he stood, it was an order and orders had to be obeyed. Reluctantly, Freddie set about collating the mass of material he would need for the briefing tomorrow, weather reports, flight plans, all the necessary details ready for the operation, code named Dentist.

Yvette got the call she had been waiting for later that evening; she agreed to meet Philippe at the crossroads on the Rennes road at nine o'clock. Yvette told Anne Marie's uncle she would have to go out. He asked no questions, he did not want to get involved anymore than he already had. He merely wished her luck, his sentiments honest.

Yvette set off at eight thirty, the air was cool, a front moving in on the area had lowered the temperature. Yvette, wearing a tight Mac, her long dark hair wrapped in a scarf, set off cycling casually. At this speed she would reach the rendezvous in plenty of time.

When she arrived at the designated point, Yvette hid her cycle behind some bushes, took off her coat, reversing it so that the black side was now visible, before putting it back on again. She had taken the revolver, concealed in the false bottom of the basket and put it in the pocket of her Mac. The coldness of the steel made her shiver, while the weight of the piece made her pocket sag.

There was a small shed close to the crossroads, which stored tools for the farmer. Yvette had agreed to meet Philippe there. She approached the small wooden structure from the rear, carefully placing her footfalls so as not to raise any alarm. She stealthily crept towards the shed.

When she had reached its back, Yvette paused to control her breathing, the revolver gripped tightly within the Mac pocket ready to be used. She peered into the dark interior through a knothole, listening intently for any sound. Hearing none, she slowly skirted the building until she came to the front of the shed with its door and window that overlooked the crossroads, both illuminated briefly by the fading light.

Yvette approached the door, stopped, listening again. All was silent; slowly she turned the handle on the door, the revolver drawn ready for action. Gently Yvette applied pressure on the door. Her eyes piercing the darkened interior, searching the gloom for any sign of ambush. Her heart was pumping, the adrenaline causing every bodily function to operate at once.

Something moved, a noise, a rustle. She raised the revolver, her finger beginning to apply pressure on the trigger. It moved again! Yvette was about to fire when the rat, frightened by her intrusion, made a final dart for freedom. Its thin fur brushing against her bare ankle as it passed in its desperate escape.

Yvette swallowed hard, then took a deep breath. When her breathing subsided into a normal rhythm she took out a handkerchief, wiped away the perspiration on her forehead, replaced the revolver back in her pocket and waited.

She heard the burp of the small motor scooter as it approached the crossroads. She watched as the scooter slowed at the junction before coming to a halt, the engine being cut. A dark figure of a man, as yet indiscernible in the darkness, dismounted the machine before guiding it to a small wall. The man lifted the scooter over the wall concealing its presence from any chance passer-by.

The man took off his gloves, exposing the white skin before walking towards the shed. Yvette held her revolver as she waited for the door to open. She heard footsteps as the figure approached the front door, suddenly they stopped. Yvette watched as the handle was turned, the door began to open. She raised the firearm to eye level, the barrel pointing towards the silhouetted figure that filled the doorway.

"Yvette?"

"Philippe?"

"Yes,"

Yvette lowered the revolver, breathed out again and saw the pale, shocked look on Philippe's' face. She smiled briefly, easing Philippe's tension.

"I'm sorry about the gun, but with everything that's happened recently, it's better to be safe than sorry."

"I understand, but I'm not so sure my bowels do." Philippe grinned.

When he had given in detail London's reply, Yvette felt easier. Just one more day. She kissed Philippe, thanking him for bringing her the good news.

Yvette retrieved her cycle, and waved goodbye to Philippe before making her way back to Vitre.

The four friends finished their drinks before returning to the car for the short drive to Emily's house. They said their goodbyes, then Duffy sped off with Cathy in the van, Christian waved as Emily opened the front door.

She mounted the stairs with Christian following close behind and switched the wireless on as she made her way to the small kitchenette to put the kettle on. Christian sat down to read the paper, after a few minutes the kettle began to boil, the whistle screeching.

"Em, kettle's boiling." When he didn't receive a reply he repeated himself.

"Emily, the kettle's boiling."

"So am I." Emily said sexily.

Christian looked up from his newspaper, the sight that met his eyes took his breath away. Emily stood in the doorway, her legs encased in black silk stockings tautly suspendered, the straps framing the bare flesh of her thighs before slipping under the black silk of her French knickers. From the waistband up, she was naked, her blonde hair resting on her shoulders, her breasts full, swollen. Her eyes portraying a wicked naughty glint.

"You naughty girl." Christian whispered.

"Not yet, but I'm going to be." She giggled.

Duffy dropped Cathy off at her house; neither spoke much on the relatively short journey, both still slightly embarrassed by each other's closeness. Cathy kissed Sean's cheek before getting out of the van. Duffy watched her as she walked to the door, opened it and disappeared from sight. She didn't look back.

When Duffy reached home, he parked the van outside and was about to get out when something caught his eye. He was sure the curtain in the downstairs front window moved. Duffy reached under his seat and felt the cold steel of the barrel. He unclipped the weapon from its restraint, checked to see if it was fully loaded before tucking it into this waistband.

He opened the door as normally as possible, once inside he removed the gun, switched on the hall light and opened the door to the front room, switching on that light as he did so. Duffy dived into the room in a low crouch, his back supported by the wall, his hands extended, and he swept the room with the weapon. The surprise on the three men's faces was complete.

"What the Feck are you doing in my house."

"Jesus Christ, Sean! put the fecking weapon down." Cavenaugh's face was terrified.

"Talk…and you two," Duffy swept the gun to cover Porrick and Seamus, "don't move." The two men did not need telling twice.

"Calm down, Sean, we let ourselves in by the back door, slipped the bolt; we've been looking for you all day. We couldn't just sit outside in the car, that would be too obvious." There was certain logic in Cavenaugh's explanation but Duffy still trained the weapon, moving from one to the other.

"Dublin sent a communiqué, it's urgent."

"I told you to call." Duffy reminded Cavenaugh.

"I couldn't on this occasion, there's too much to discuss on an open line. Here read it yourself." Cavenaugh had reached slowly into his inside pocket taking out a paper, which he passed to Duffy. Sean took it in his left hand, keeping an eye on the three men as he read the document. It was the same message as Harry Milburn had given to Commander Thompson. Duffy identified his German codename "Magpie."

He lowered the weapon, his point having been made. Everybody within the movement knew of Duffy's expertise with a handgun, the overstated rumour 'that he could shoot the bollocks off a fly at twenty paces,' made sure the three men made no sudden moves.

"There's more."

"What, Francis?"

"You're to keep a keen eye on your Polish friend, He's the pigeon."

"What else, Francis?"

"You're to go to Norfolk tomorrow."

"Norfolk?"

"Yes, it appears that's where Patton's army is based. Berlin wants to know if it's real!"

"What do you mean, 'if its real'? They could send a plane over, see for themselves."

"A plane wouldn't show whether the tanks were real or dummies, camouflaged, here's the map map, Jerry wants the answer by Monday." Cavenaugh passed the map to Duffy. Several areas of Norfolk, Suffolk and Essex were ringed in red ink.

"Jesus! They're not giving me much notice are they?" Sean's face showed his bewilderment.

"That's why we had to see you Sean, let ourselves in, so to speak." Cavenaugh's grin was present again, now that the adrenaline had ceased to pump.

"Right, now that you have delivered your message, I need to sleep, it will be a long journey, oh, and Francis?"

"Yes?"

"I'll need some more petrol coupons for the bike."

Reluctantly Cavenaugh passed a wedge of the scarce petrol coupons to Duffy who accepted them less than graciously before ushering Cavenaugh and the two gorillas out of the door. Cavenaugh once again allowing his anger to show, cursing Duffy as he walked towards the car. The two gorillas, Seamus and Porrick, followed obediently behind him.

Duffy thought for a moment, if he left his obligation until tomorrow, he would be late getting back on Monday. That meant he would be late for work. The old bag, Mrs Clack his secretary, no doubt informing head office of his latest transgression. Reluctantly, Duffy decided he would have to set off tonight. If he was lucky, he could be in a position to view the areas marked before daylight, allowing him ample time to return on Sunday. Duffy shrugged his shoulders, put the kettle on and waited for it to boil. He would need coffee, black and lots of it.

Christian slipped out of the flat, leaving Emily in a deep sleep. He had kissed her forehead gently before leaving. As he got into the car he felt the knee that had stirred from sublimity to pain, due to the rigorous demands of their lovemaking. His hands massaged the swollen knee gently, as soon as the pain began to dissipate, Christian started the motor and returned to the base.

When he reached the quarters he shared with Freddie he found Freddie awake, fully dressed and pacing nervously about the small cramped quarters.

"Hi, Christian, did you have a nice day?" Freddie asked politely.

"Yes thanks, Freddie." Christian responded looking closely at his friend before he continued. "What is it, Freddie?"

"Oh, it's nothing, Christian, honestly." Freddie's voice didn't fool Christian. He continued trying to put a brave face on the inner fear, which gripped his stomach.

"I've got an op, a little jaunt to France and back, nothing serious…just the usual taxi ride." Christian noticed the concern in Freddie's eyes.

"Where to Freddie?" he questioned.

"Rennes, same place as you went…I've got orders to pick up Yvette, she's in trouble. London want her out…Seems I'm the only one available."

"You can't! not so soon." Christian's thoughts returned to his nightmare trip, the capture, the torture – Mosel.

"Well they could hardly send you back, Christian." Freddie had a point. "And anyway…" he continued, "…they wouldn't expect another operation in the same area so soon after the last little show would they?"

Christian conceded to Freddie's excuse, he was right, but only to a point. The Germans and particularly the SS would be on full alert after the debacle with Christian and his escape. He tried to console Freddie's natural feelings.

"You're right, Freddie, they wouldn't expect lightning to strike twice – certainly not in such a short space of time." Freddie smiled thinly, attempting to reconcile his safety with Christian's words, but failing dismally. Christian patted Freddie on the back.

"If I can help in any way…." His words faded.

"Thanks, Christian, I appreciate it."

"When do you go Freddie?" Christian asked.

"Tomorrow night."

'Shit', Christian thought, but he said nothing.

CHAPTER 17

Duffy was ready to leave, pumped with black coffee but with an empty bladder - years of hiding and waiting for British patrols to pass had been good training, he could hold any calls of nature for twenty-four hours. Satisfied all was well, he pushed the bike towards the main road, before straddling it and kicking the engine into life. When the engine responded, Duffy flicked it into gear, let out the clutch and slowly let the bike ease him forward.

Duffy sat back in the saddle, he felt invigorated to be riding the bike once again, the air rushing to his face, his mouth grinning unseen behind the scarf that covered it. If Commander Thompson at S.I.S. knew what he was up to tonight, he'd have kittens, Duffy thought to himself. Now all he could do was to concentrate on the long arduous journey ahead. The journey would take about three hours; there would be no traffic just the possibility of unnecessary questions asked by bored, overzealous policemen.

Duffy was wrong about the traffic; it was constant, like a tapeworm it followed the contours of every road endlessly snaking southwards. Fortunately for Duffy his heading north allowed him time to wonder at the sheer mass of ordnance that passed. Trucks, tanks, low loaders with tanks aboard, jeeps darting in and out of columns of vehicles like wasps on a jam pot. The total endeavours of the free world forged into a single purpose, the destruction of Nazi Germany. The swathe of military hardware built by James Lowe IV of Iowa, or Gladys Potts from Mosside, all added up to one thing, everybody and everything possible would be ready for the liberation that surely must come.

Occasionally Duffy was held at roadblocks, to allow the constant stream of vehicles to pass. Only when a gap appeared could he let the throttle on the bike open fully. Fortunately for him, the MPs and local police were so busy with the traffic that a single rider on a motorcycle caused no alarm. Not wishing to delay his journey more than was necessary, Duffy decided to avoid the areas likely to cause congestion, towns, and major junctions –he skirted such possible bottlenecks by taking a series of back roads.

It was not until he moved from Hertfordshire towards Cambridge that the traffic seemed to evaporate, movement signs no longer pointed South, instead they gave new settings, everything started to inform the visitor of F.U.S.A.G. (First United States Army Group) Duffy travelled no more than three miles at a time in any direction before Army personal became visible, watchful, alert. Deciding that anything other than tracks or tiny lanes would prove awkward, Duffy criss-crossed the now flatter countryside never staying on the same compass setting for more than a mile at a time. His estimated time for arrival at his destination now seemed unattainable.

It was late when the war games ended, Field Marshal Rommel's team including Mosel, were declared the victors. Their surprise choice for the landing in Normandy had completely out-foxed the defenders, which included Von Ebstein. According to the game, the Allies had won the first battle; they had successfully landed on the supposedly impregnable Atlantic Wall with little or no opposition.

"A brilliant move, Herr Field Marshal," Model had conceded.

"Thank you, Model," Rommel replied, "a lesson to us all."

"What do you mean, Erwin?" Model asked.

"If I were Eisenhower that's exactly what I would do. In addition I would strike at southern France from the Mediterranean one week later, and advance north easterly up the Rhone valley."

Rommel went to the map of France, which adorned one wall. "Look Model, with the bay of the Seine on one side and Paris a short distance away, my right hand flank would move up the Rhone Valley." Rommel banged his finger on the map emphasising his point. My right flank is protected by the Alps and Switzerland, my left flank protected by the sea…in between…"

Model studied Rommel's train of thought.

"In between, no opportunity."

"Exactly Walter, the terrain is not conducive to freedom of use, therefore I have no flanks, just a wedge that would move in only one direction…Germany, Walter."

"My God, Rommel. It's so simple, it's brilliant."

"Except for one thing, Model."

"What?"

"The Allies would not have the foresight to do it…even if they could. Patton and Montgomery would fail, each would try to vie for the best positions…only a single aim, one objective, can win…that is why it will not happen."

"I hope to God you are right, Rommel," Model concluded.

Mosel was pleased with the result of the team's performance, it reminded him of the earlier, happy days. The German armies pushing all before them, like a tidal wave they had swept over Europe. Now the residue of that great flood of German expansion was slowly, but inevitably, being pushed back to its source. The appearance of Steiner interrupted Mosel's thoughts.

"An excellent victory, may I too congratulate you, sir?'

"Thank you, Hans." Mosel's tone was not that of a victor.

Steiner could see his captain deep in thought, the eyes normally bright with ideas looked saddened, almost lost. He tried to spur Mosel.

"The exercise was an outstanding success, sir."

"Yes Hans, almost too good."

"Sir?"

"Hans, what if the Allies do land at Normandy? It's not complete, our defences are weak, the bocage is a network of small fields and hedgerows, our Panzers would be useless in assault. The Allies would gain a foothold, a foothold that may become impossible to dislodge."

"Supply, sir," Steiner stated.

Mosel looked up at his aide; the young man was as resolute as usual. Mosel put his hand on Steiner's shoulder, thankful for his sensible support.

"As usual Hans, you are correct, the Allies need a deep water port, and none would be available in the initial stages. To land without such an important element would be suicidal. The whole invasion would be untenable, unless…"

"Sir?"

"I don't know, Hans, I just get the feeling we are missing something. I don't know what it is…but I do know it's important." Mosel returned to his earlier morbid state.

"Operation Golden Egg, sir."

"What about it, Hans?"

"In a few days we will know exactly where the Allies plan to land, and that will give us time to make all the necessary preparations." Steiner's tone was firm but polite.

"Yes, Operation Golden Egg is the key...Hans, we must return earlier than planned. The war games have served us well, but the plan is more important now than ever."

Mosel looked directly into Steiner's eyes, what he said next made a shiver run down the young lieutenant's back.

"If we fail, Hans....it will be the end of us....and Germany."

Sleep would not come to Yvette that night. She prayed to her God, a God who had served her well over the years, had kept her alive, if only just. The years of working in such close proximity to the Germans, every second waiting for the knock on the door, the knock that would end her life, had taken its toll.

In the early days it had been almost an adventure, exciting. Yvette had pitted her wits against the total resources of the German regime and had won. Now, alone in her bed, that fortitude and resilience had waned, eventually deserting her. She was at the end of her endurance, her bolt shot...and she was frightened.

Only Emily, wrapped in the softness of Christian's love, slept well that night. Duffy had decided to stow the bike and make the rest of the journey on foot. The security was almost suffocating; every corner seemed to be teeming with military personal. Whatever he was supposed to find was close, very close indeed. Duffy wheeled the motorcycle into a workman's shed on the edge of a large field of wheat, not yet ready for harvest. Duffy would have to return to the shed by dawn, the farmers would by that time be ready to work in the fields again.

Duffy pulled back the balaclava over his face, only the eyes showing. When he was ready, and his concealment complete, he made his way to the other side of the field via the tractor paths, making sure he didn't trample on the wheat, which in the daylight would show his passage.

When Duffy reached what appeared to be a small copse on the other side of the field he was disappointed. His circuitous route had taken too much time, on top of which the trees were not a copse but a windbreak built to protect the awaited harvest. Instead of sanctuary, Duffy found himself confronted by yet another field of grain. Once again he set out to navigate the field, this time taking a shorter route.

He was half way round the field when instinctively he slipped silently into what seemed to be some bushes. Something had alerted his senses, and his natural ability to survive, practised on numerous occasions in the bandit country of Eire's borders with the north, came to the fore.

Duffy lost his footing, stumbling into the ditch, which was full of nettles, the ditch acting as a breaker between the crops. He lay silently for a moment, the sharp irritating sting of the nettles burning all the exposed skin. The need to move filled his brain, but the need for silent observation made that impossible. He lay there passive, waiting.

Duffy heard the footfalls first; at least two men of heavy build were tramping the undergrowth close to the edge of the field. Duffy peered over the parapet of the ditch, above a yellow beam of light traversing lazily followed closely by the tramp of heavy boots. Two American GIs, their hamburger shaped helmets disclosing their identity, approached before stopping directly overhead.

"Jesus, George, this is the third time you stopped since we came on duty." A voice said in a cowboy drawl.

"It's this god damn British beer, warm crap it is, it goes through you like a cab on 42nd Street," the other, New York sounding voice responded.

Duffy turned his face to the undergrowth, praying to god. He heard the zip's metallic sound as it was quickly lowered, the fumbled murmuring of the New Yorker as he attempted to release his weapon from the mangled confines of his boxer shorts. Then it happened. The unmistakable sound of urine being released. Duffy tensed every sinew in his body awaiting the inevitable drenching of the foul smelling liquid. When he felt nothing he released the muscles in his chest, allowing himself to breathe again. Fortunately, the American GI pretending to be a gunner on a B17, sprayed his waste in a wide arc, imagining he was following the trail of a passing ME109.

When Duffy sensed that all the Messerschmitts had been downed, the spray subduing in to a trickle, the noise of the zip being reset, he slowly opened his eyes. Not daring to move until the departing voices of Americas finest had been lost to the night, Duffy refocused. Just a few inches from his eyes stood an indignant field mouse. Instinctively Duffy's eyes closed as the small rodent shook himself. "I know just how you feel, Mr Mouse, but what the hell are you going to tell the misses when you get back to the nest stinking of beer and urine. May God go with you, my furry friend."

The episode, amusing now it was over, had released the earlier stress Duffy had felt. More relaxed, Duffy set off to continue his journey. He extracted himself from the ditch, removing as many thorns as possible. When he finally reached the other side of the field, the ground began to fall gently towards the inky blackness of a river. Studying the scene in front of him, he saw that the river was fast flowing, deep and probably over thirty yards wide. Crossing would prove dangerous and uncomfortable, so Duffy decided to look for a boat.

After about five minutes careful reconnoitre of the bank, Duffy found what he was looking for. A small rowing boat complete with two oars was tied to a small jetty, which protruded, into the dark waters. Duffy untied the rope and stepped into the boat, his movement causing the craft to wobble slightly. Once aboard he pushed the boat from the jetty and sat down to row, slowly and purposefully, across the divide. The crossing proved to be easier than Duffy at first thought, and his presence was unnoticed by any watching eyes. Duffy hid the boat in an outcrop of bushes, which encroached the waterside, happy with the boat's temporary concealment Duffy set off across the open ground.

He did not expect the next obstacle so soon, but directly in front of him was a double barbed wire fence. Without wire cutters, Duffy would not be able to pass through the wire. Feeling slightly dejected he sat beside the fence and thought hard.

He finally decided that movement provided the best means of safety, he had covered some two hundred yards before he found what he was looking for, a tree close to the fence with an overhanging branch stretching into the no mans land between the wires. Duffy scaled the tree, crawled along the overhang before gently slipping to the ground.

He was about to spring towards the other wire when he heard a man's voice some distance away. The voice seemed to be talking to someone or something. The next sound was apparent, a command. "Sit, Brutus."

"Dogs! Shit." Duffy hissed. "I hate dogs." He laid prone, his body as close to the ground as possible. He licked his finger, slowly raising his hand, the coolness on his fingertip showing him the direction of any breeze. He was lucky, he was downwind of the animal, so providing the beast and its master remained a good distance away he would be safe.

Duffy lay in no mans land like a corpse for over ten minutes before the voice moved on. He searched for another tree, moving in the opposite direction from where the voice had come. Duffy travelled perhaps over a quarter of a mile, but no trees were in sight. He would have to climb the fence.

The climb proved long and painful, the noise of the straining wires seemed more like a cymbal being banged aggressively, causing Duffy's heart to stop on more than one occasion. Eventually, the sweat rolling off him, Duffy's feet touched the ground on the other side of the fence. He remained motionless allowing his body to recuperate from the stress.

When Duffy was satisfied, he made his way through the undergrowth to a clearing. The early signs of dawn were approaching fast. The birds began to stir, pumping their chests, ready for the morning chorus of song. The sight that appeared through the gathering light filled him with wonderment. Row upon row of Sherman tanks, trucks, personal carriers, half-tracks, artillery pieces and all the paraphernalia of merchandised warfare lay before him. Literally thousands of vehicles of every description were laid out as far as the eye could see.

Duffy knew he would have to take a closer look, so he inched his way on his stomach over the long grass for perhaps about thirty yards until he came to the bulk of a Sherman tank. Using the tank for cover, he leant against the surface to survey the mass in front of him. Duffy smiled to himself, the grin spreading all over his face. 'The cunning bastards," he mumbled under his breath.

Happy that he had seen all the information that he needed, he returned to the relative safety of the bushes. The sun had now appeared in the sky, the birds were in full voice, and there was no time for careful navigation of the obstacles. Duffy would have to take the risk. He scrambled over the two wire fences, tearing the material of his cycle suit as he did so. When he reached the river, still undetected, his heart pumping excitedly, his feeling of elation sank – the boat was gone.

Duffy made the only choice available, it wasn't palatable, but then again nor was the alternative, he stripped. Keeping only his underpants on Duffy wrapped his clothes in a bundle, which he fastened to a small branch from a tree. With goose pimples embossing his pale skin he eased himself into the cold black river.

The temperature of the water took his breath away, causing Duffy to shiver uncontrollably. Only when he was moving through the water, one hand above the surface to hold the pole with its bundle of dry clothes, the other paddling, with his legs providing propulsion did the numbness from the cold ease. The crossing was uninterrupted except for the quizzical attentions of two swans, which had landed close by, taking it in turns to investigate the phenomenon that navigated the channel, its pink skin like a plucked chicken.

When Duffy finally reached the other side he clambered up the bank, the silty black mud clinging to his hands and feet. He was cold, exhausted from the night's activities and numb. The dip between the riverbank and the tree line provided the ideal cover he needed. Duffy rubbed his arms and legs to raise his body temperature. Feeling close to normal, reasonably dry, he put his clothes back on. He washed his hands and feet in the river, before making his way back to the shed where he had left the bike.

“Thank you, God.” He said aloud, when he found the bike undisturbed. He eased it onto the road, mounted and kicked the engine into life. Now all he needed was a cigarette, a cup of tea, and a bit more luck.

It took Duffy forty-five minutes to clear the area; the traffic was light allowing him to make some distance once he reached the main road in Cambridge.

Tommy awoke early, the festivities of the previous day, together with the information he had obtained from Phelan, having cheered his soul. Phelan’s threat was put to one side. The morning was grey, overcast; the smell of rain was in the air. Tommy made his way downstairs to order breakfast. Mary was still readying herself after her bath, and would follow him when she was ready.

Realising that they would have to depart for the station at three o’clock, they had decided to get up early so as to savour as much of Ireland as they could during the short time they had left.

Christian, upset that S.O.E. were sending Freddie into the inferno in Rennes, stormed into the briefing room at RAF Northolt. Freddie, his face pale, his normal happy exuberance subdued, shot a worried glance as Christian entered. The pale stark faces of Commander Tim Brethwell and the station commander were not so placid. The look they gave Christian displayed their annoyance at the intrusion.

“Flight Lieutenant Kawolski, what is the meaning of this?” The Station Officer roared.

“Sir, you’ve got to stop this, what you’re doing is bordering on insane,” Christian screamed. “You’re sending Freddie on a mission that can’t succeed, it’s madness.”

“Control yourself, Flight Lieutenant,” ordered the CO.

“Wait a minute.” Brethwell said interrupting the CO’s tirade. “Let’s hear what the man has to say…take a seat, Flight Lieutenant.” Brethwell pointed to an empty chair.

“Thank you sir,” Christian sat down, tried to calm himself. When he felt more at ease, he looked closely at the other three men. Freddie sat almost as if in a trance, no emotions showed on his face.

The CO, still flushed with anger, sat on the edge of his seat, his body language telling Christian that he would be demanding a full explanation for Christian’s conduct. The S.O.E. officer, Brethwell, on the other hand, seemed more responsive to Christian’s point of view. Christian decided to face the S.O.E. man, put his argument to him directly.

“Sir, I apologise to everyone for disturbing this briefing.” Christian’s tone was relaxed, “But I could not sit back and say nothing…when I know this mission is doomed to failure.”

“What makes you so sure?” Asked Brethwell

“I’ve been there, sir, I know what it’s like…Freddie doesn’t stand a chance sir.”

The CO made to speak, but Brethwell raising his hand stopped him.

“Continue if you please, Flight Lieutenant.”

“Sir, when I landed the Germans were waiting for me, I was captured and tortured.” Christian’s mind went back to his time in Rennes. “It was a set up…I didn’t stand a chance. I was betrayed.”

“By Lucien?” Asked Brethwell.

"Yes sir." Christian answered.

"Lucien is dead!" The CO interrupted. "He's hardly in a position to influence this operation."

"He's dead, sir, but the point is, his legacy is still there. We can't trust the local's sir, If Lucien was working for the Germans then the whole network could have been jeopardised.

"What about Yvette Granville?" Brethwell asked sincerely.

"I don't know about Yvette sir, perhaps she's not involved in the treachery."

"She's not."

Everybody in the room jumped as the voice spoke.

"Sorry to interrupt your little soirée." Commander Thompson followed by the ever-present Harry Milburn said as he entered. "May I?" He pointed to an empty chair, without waiting for a reply he sat down. Milburn devoid of a seat stood awkwardly hovering behind his boss.

"Yvette Granville is totally safe." Thompson said, taking control. "Yvette is one of our most secure and best operatives in France, I know, I recruited her. She was sent to the Rennes area for the express purpose of flushing out Lucien, since we have had our suspicions about Henri Dacourt for some time. Sorry, Tim." Thompson shot a glance at Brethwell, whose turn it was now to look confused. "Yvette has information which is of the utmost importance to the war effort, it is essential that she is picked up now."

Thompson passed a buff folder marked 'Top Secret' to Brethwell. The S.O.E. man opened the file and read the letter stamped, 'action this day', its contents precise, the signatures of 'C' and the Prime Minister conclusive. Brethwell raised his eyebrows at the document, the CO nodded his acceptance. "So you see gentlemen, this operation must go ahead." Thompson said, his words final.

"Then let me go sir." Christian broke the silence. "I know the area, I've got a better chance of succeeding than anybody." He blurted.

"Out of the question, Flight Lieutenant."

"But why, sir?"

"I'm afraid you're going somewhere else. Harry. . ." Thompson turned to Milburn.

"Yes sir," Harry said passing another folder to the in control Thompson.

"This is your mission, Flight Lieutenant."

Duffy cleared the area, confident that he had put some distance between himself and what he had seen. He decided to stop at the roadside café; the endurance of the long night had made him hungry. Duffy ordered a sausage sandwich with a steaming mug of tea. The huge slabs of bread swamped the thin brown meat. As he ate, his mind went to what he had discovered the night before; he would have to go to Hanwell to see Cavenaugh, to make sure his information got to Dublin and then Mosel tonight.

When he had finished, Duffy sat on the bike, kicked it into life and pulled onto the main road ready for the long journey ahead.

The Junkers 52 lifted off the runaway, banked tightly then rose into the deep blue sky. Mosel sat next to Rommel, the two men talking quietly about their joint fears over the Allied invasion plans. The significance of the war games exercise troubled both men. If the Allies could somehow sustain their troops on the beaches, then Normandy would be an effective place to land. Rommel, more than anybody, knew Normandy was the least protected area in the Atlantic Wall, with inadequate defences. Since the bulk of the German army's best formations together with most of its armour, surrounded the Pas de Calais, any landing further south would be virtually unopposed. He decided some resources would have to be put into strengthening the area. He would have to talk to Von Rundstedt, probably on the second leg of the journey.

Mosel had decided to accompany the party to its final destination. Steiner would be dropped off at Rennes to complete their move from the chateau at Vitre before making his way back to Berlin a day later. The significance of Steiner's absence from Mosel's side was two-fold. Firstly, to hunt down Yvette, with SS assistance if necessary, and secondly, to eradicate whatever emotion he felt for the young French girl Anne Marie. Mosel, aware of the young man's distraction, could not allow Steiner's mind to be focussed anywhere but on the operation ahead. Golden Egg was entering its first critical stage.

Christian sat in another briefing room with Commander Thompson and Harry Milburn, dumbfounded by what Thompson had told him. The nightmare devised by Mosel back in the chateau in Vitre was now becoming a reality. British Intelligence were now playing directly into Mosel's hands, irrationally. They were now setting in motion a series of events that must end in tragedy, a tragedy that Christian would play a significant part. Christian Kawolski was being ordered to undertake a mission that would leave him with an inhuman choice, betray his country, or his wife and family.

The dilemma facing Christian had forced him to analyse the options, neither of which brought redemption to his inner torture. All he could do was to sit limply and listen as the nightmare unfolded.

The operation would be planned for Thursday that would allow Thompson to evaluate Yvette's information, providing that Moreland could bring her safely back to England. If Yvette's discoveries proved to be of significance, the mission would go ahead, if not, then a short delay might be necessary. Whatever happened, the mission would go ahead, Churchill's signature confirming its finality.

Christian went into shock, suddenly something frightened him. What if Yvette knew of Mosel's intentions? What if she knew of Christian's proposed involvement? He began to sweat profusely, his eyes staring at the horror his mind had evolved.

"Are you alright, Flight Lieutenant?" Thompson asked seeing Kawolski's demeanour.

"No...no I don't think so sir." Christian mumbled, his face grey.

"Would you like some water?"

"No, no thank you sir...but perhaps some fresh air."

"Yes, yes of course." Thompson said sympathetically. "We'll reconvene in about twenty minutes." He turned to Milburn. "Harry, see if you can rustle up some tea."

Christian rose unsteadily, his strength deserting him, his mind in turmoil. "Thank you sir," He said shakily as he made his way to the door.

When Christian was outside he sucked deeply at the air, filling his lungs with the much-needed oxygen. He lit a cigarette to try and calm his nerves. Should he tell Thompson about the deal he had made with Mosel? He shook his head, deciding that would only compound his position. He would have to go with the flow, see what happened and make a decision when he had to. Whatever decision he came to, hopefully things might have changed, perhaps something unexpected would occur, making his situation less painful.

Christian stubbed out the cigarette with his shoe, grinding the half finished Players into the ground, then returned to the briefing room. Outwardly he appeared more controlled, more assertive, inside the deceit strangled his emotions.

"Ah, Flight Lieutenant...you look better, are you ok to resume the briefing?" Thompson asked. "Harry a cup of tea for the Flight."

Christian took the hot brew from the cordial Milburn, and stirred the non-existent sugar out of habit before sitting down, his mind now centred on the practicality of the flight. Thompson watched Kawolski's reaction, his doubts multiplying. When Yvette was safely home, then he would make his move, until then he would continue acting as if all was well.

"Right, Flight Lieutenant, where were we? Ah Yes..." he continued the briefing.

Harry Milburn watched the two men with interest. Kawolski had recovered his composure, but Thompson seemed to revel in Kawolski's suffering, his sardonic look echoing the pleasure he was exacting.

The phone rang; Anne Marie answered the call. The male voice asked for Yvette. Anne Marie looked up, her eyes scanning the café. Yvette saw her nervous glance; saw her hold the phone up indicating the call was for her.

The Junkers had touched down then taxied towards the waiting fuel truck. Steiner left the aircraft and got into the waiting car, which sped off towards the main gate of the airfield. When it reached the main road, Steiner wound the window down to watch the Junkers hurtle down the runway.

"Stop the car," he said to the driver. Steiner followed the aircraft as it took off, heading into the dark grey clouds that had begun to form. When the aircraft disappeared, enveloped by the grey mass, Steiner tapped the driver on the shoulder. "Carry on." The driver glanced in his mirror, then began to accelerate away.

Philippe had watched the scene from a vantagepoint hidden from sight by the shade of the huge oak's canopy. He mounted the scooter, then rode to telephone Yvette from a small estaminet on the outskirts of Rennes.

Yvette took the phone from Anne Marie.

"Hello...Philippe." She whispered putting her hand over the phone to conceal the sound of her voice. Her eyes darted to and fro to check if anybody was listening, seeing only the nervousness in Anne Marie.

"Philippe, what is it?" she asked.

"It's Steiner, he's just landed. He's heading towards Vitre, a car picked him up...Yvette, a driver will pick you up to take you back to mother, make sure you are ready." Yvette understood the code; the Lysander would pick her up tonight.

"Ok Philippe, I understand, tell mother I will be home soon."

"Yvette."

"Yes, Philippe?"

"Steiner, I think he knows something, get out now."

Anne Marie saw the look on Yvette's face.

"What is it, Yvette?" She asked innocently.

"Anne Marie," Yvette took the young girl by the arm, leading her towards the door at the rear of the café. "Anne Marie, I must go now. The Germans are coming for me I'm sure." Yvette's hands began to tremble. "You, Anne Marie, must go to your friends now."

"But Yvette, the café, I can't just leave the customers…"

"Now, Anne Marie!" Yvette gripped the girls arm tightly. "You must go now, get your uncle up, tell him you have to go…promise me you will leave this instant."

"Yes Yvette, I will do as you say." Anne Marie was frightened by Yvette's manner; she pulled her arm away from Yvette's grip. "I promise!" She said.

Anne Marie's uncle was not pleased at being woken from his slumber, but the look in Anne Marie's eyes told him it was urgent. His manner changed from gruffness to paternal in an instant.

"Get some things together and go, my little one, I shall see to the café."

"Thank you, uncle."

"Anne Marie."

"Yes, uncle," she replied.

"Take care, my little one…You know I…"

"I know, uncle," she said standing on her tiptoes to kiss the unshaven rugged face. The uncle took the girl in his arms and hugged her tightly.

Anne Marie gathered some clothes, stuffing them into a small canvas bag, which she then slung over her shoulder. Not wishing to upset her uncle more than was necessary, she slipped out of the café by the rear door, and then went to the small outbuildings where she always left her cycle.

When she entered the building, panic set in, her cycle was gone. Suddenly a hand came to her mouth – she tried to scream. She could hear her own voice filling her ears, yet no sound past through the tightly gripped fingers that surrounded her mouth. She tried to kick but the grip tightened. She panicked, her mind unable to cope, her eyes bulging in their sockets, she passed out.

Yvette went out of the front door of the café to where she had parked her bicycle. Relieved to find it exactly where she had left it, she slipped into the saddle and pushed hard on the pedal.

"Halt!" The German voice was harsh and unforgiving.

Yvette's heart began to pound, turning her head; her eyes met the face with the voice. Obergruppenfuehrer Manfred Von Ebstein stood a few paces behind her, the cruel eyes piercing her. The thin lips in a cruel smirk, his Luger pistol in his right hand extended, pointing directly at Yvette.

She felt sick, the colour drained from her face, her hands shook uncontrollably on the handlebars of the cycle. She gripped the bar tightly, her knuckles pure white, but still the shaking would not stop. Von Ebstein saw the distressed look on the girl's face and he smiled, glancing at the gun in his hand then back to Yvette.

"Ah so, it is you, Mademoiselle, I thought that it was perhaps Anne Marie, the younger girl from the café, please accept my apologies." Von Ebstein said replacing the Luger in its holster. Yvette started to swoon, her head spinning, her knees weak.

"Margot!" A voice somewhere behind Von Ebstein spoke, Yvette tried to focus. Eventually the face of Lieutenant Steiner came to her, Von Ebstein turned to face him.

"Sir, my apologies." Steiner saluted the superior officer. "Margot," He said forcefully, "attend to your errand girl, now be off with you." Steiner turned to face Von Ebstein.

"These French girls," he smiled at the officer. "So casual, don't you think, sir? I send the girl on an errand for the Field Marshal and what happens…" Steiner looked at Yvette again, his eyes pleading with her, "… now be off with you before I take a stick to you girl." Steiner looked into Von Ebstein's eyes.

"It's the only way with these French girls, sir." Von Ebstein licked his lips.

Yvette somehow managed to get back on her bike and pedal away, the vomit still held in the back of her throat. Steiner watched as she slowly cycled out of sight.

"Sir," he said, turning once again to Von Ebstein, "Captain Mosel was so upset that you were unable to travel back with our party. He has asked me to provide you with a bottle of his favourite Schnapps; I took the liberty of bringing it to the café… Would you do me the honour, sir?"

Steiner guided the dumbfounded SS man towards the café, the thought of losing the opportunity that had been presented with Yvette now at the back of the SS man's mind. Now he was focussed on the Schnapps, and perhaps a chance to see the younger girl, Anne Marie, since he like them young.

When Yvette finally made it to the main crossroads, she dismounted the bicycle and pushed it into the shed in the farmer's field where she had met Philippe. She closed the door and sat down still shaking from the experience with the SS officer; Yvette finally broke, and began to sob uncontrollably.

Tired after the long journey, Duffy had parked the motorcycle once again in the shed at the rear of his bungalow in Ickenham. He washed, shaved and changed. Feeling more comfortable he decided to go for a drink, and shortly after he pulled up outside the Plough in his van.

When Duffy entered the bar he saw the troubled lonely figure of Christian leaning against one end of the bar, a solitary unfinished pint in front of him.

"Christian, how the devil are you?" Duffy said patting him on the back. Duffy looked round, "no Emily?" He asked expecting to see the girl appear at any moment.

"No, she'll be along soon, she's getting ready." Christian said quietly.

"What about Freddie and Cathy?"

"Freddie's on ops…he won't be coming…he may…" Christian's voice tailed off, the memories of the morning's briefings came once again to him. "I shouldn't be here either, Sean…I…I should go. I'm supposed to be back at the base. I've got ops. This week also…I should go." Duffy could see the pain in Christian's eyes.

"I'm sure the bloody RAF can do without you for an hour or so." Duffy put his arm around Christian. "Come on man, another pint, that one's stale." Duffy signalled to the bar man. "A pint of Guinness and a fresh bitter for my friend."

"I can't stay Sean," Christian said, "tell Emily I'm sorry…I'll make it up to her…I've got to go." Christian turned and left. Duffy watched as the young pilot left then turned his attention to the Guinness. He drank slowly his mind on Christian's words.

Commander Thompson stopped the Airman, recognising him.

"Book, isn't it?" he asked, "You're Flight Lieutenant Kawolski's orderly, aren't you?"

"Yes sir," Answered Book.

"Where is he?"

"He's just popped over to see…" Book hesitated.

"It's alright, Birdy," Christian said, as he approached un-noticed by the pair, "What can I do for you, Commander?"

Anne Marie began to wake. Her eyes slowly focussing on the distorted images which finally came into perspective. She was staring at the canopy of a four-poster bed.

"What, where am I." She started to panic, she made to get up. A soft hand stroked her forehead, Anne Marie turned to see the face of Steiner, he was smiling at her.

"What happened? Where am I?"

"You fainted, Anne Marie, rest, you're alright now…safe."

The memory came flooding back, Anne Marie shot bolt upright.

"Yvette," she shouted.

"She's safe." Steiner gently eased the girl's head back onto the pillow.

"But who…? A hand on my mouth…" Anne Marie exclaimed.

"I'm sorry, it was the only way."

"You…it was you?"

"Yes Anne Marie," Steiner said gently. Anne Marie shot up again.

"The café! My uncle!"

"It's fine, he's fine," Steiner whispered. "You can't go back to the café just yet, Von Ebstein is still there – drunk by now I would guess, so you must stay here until he leaves tonight – you can return to the café tomorrow."

"Where am I?"

"In the chateau, Anne Marie." Steiner gently held the girl.

"But why?" Anne Marie asked more softly.

"You don't know?" Steiner held her face in his hands, his eyes softly looking into hers.

"Oh Hans!" The two hugged each other, Anne Marie crying softly.

"Sean, where's Christian?" Emily said. Duffy hadn't seen her enter.

"He had to go back to the base…he asked me to tell you." Duffy could see the hurt in the girl's face, her lip quivering. He put his arm around the disconsolate girl.

"But…but he…" Emily mumbled.

"He had to go, Emily, orders, he shouldn't have come in the first place." Duffy kissed Emily gently on the forehead, the tingling inside him began. "What you need is a stiff drink, a gin and tonic please, landlord," he said, shooting a glance at the hovering barman.

He stood back and looked at her, the mouth pink and soft was in a hurt little pout, her blue eyes moist – the whites so bright. Her golden hair shrouded the soft pale skin of her face, a strand lying across one eye. She was beautiful, thought Duffy.

"Hey, listen, get that down you," he said, passing the drink to her. She took a sip and he watched her as she swallowed. "Come on there's a table over there." He picked up his pint and led her by the hand. They sat down. Emily put her head on his shoulder, and Duffy felt tenderness rise in him. "It's ok, listen, when we've finished I'll take you to the base to see him."

"Would you, Sean," Emily lifted her head from his shoulder and looked into his eyes.

"Yes of course I will," He said his hand gently guiding her head back to his shoulder. He wanted to scream 'I love you, Emily Cassidy!' yet no words came from his mouth.

Commander Thompson received a call from the stationmaster at Northolt. He had a request from Flight Lieutenant Kawolski asking if he could leave the base. Thompson thought for a while and then answered yes, providing that the officer was back on base by 23.00hrs.

Duffy dropped Emily off at the entrance to Northolt airfield. After some confusion Christian came to the main gate and took Emily with him. He thanked Duffy then turned to escort Emily to the adjutant's office. Duffy made his way to Hanwell to see Cavenaugh.

Although drinking up time had been called some hours ago, the pub was still serving alcohol to Cavenaugh's select crew of thugs. When Duffy entered, Cavenaugh, who was playing cards with a couple of his cronies, glanced up from his hand, a look of foreboding on his podgy face.

"Sean, what is it?"

"In private, Francis," Duffy scowled, nodding towards the back room.

Cavenaugh put his hand down. With a nod Seamus sat in his chair protecting the hand whilst Cavanaugh and Sean made their way to the back room. Cavenaugh shut the door and sat down.

"What is it, Sean?" he asked.

"That little trip I've been on…its real, big stuff, I need to let Dublin know. Also I've picked up something else today which is even more important."

"Tell me, Sean." Cavenaugh pointed to a seat.

"Sorry, Francis, this is too big…it's got to be done in person."

"I'm the Brigade Commander…the quartermaster in London!" Cavenaugh screamed. "And I'm your boss, Duffy don't forget that… Listen Sean…" Cavenaugh spoke in a more controlled voice, the outburst having had no effect.

"Sean how am I going to run things in your favour when you won't communicate with me properly. Now, I'm sure you're excited about this information that you have discovered, but we must observe the protocol. Things must be done through the proper channels…otherwise security may be compromised."

Cavenaugh sat back in the chair, his fingers interlocked, his hands resting on the swollen beer gut of his stomach, a big friendly smile on his face.

"Cut the bullshit, Francis," Duffy grinned before his face became more serious. He leaned forward banging his fist on the surface of the desk. Cavanaugh saw the intent, and shot forward in his chair, his relaxed smirk no longer visible.

"Tell Kilbride," Duffy said, "that he is to contact Mosel and get me a submarine, or a plane to Jersey or Sweden, I don't care, but I need to see Mosel immediately. Tell them to inform me through you if necessary." Duffy continued. "I need to go tomorrow night at the latest. Francis, contact Kilbride now, this afternoon. I will contact you tonight for confirmation, and Francis…. Don't mess with me on this one…or else you could find your balls in a sling." Duffy grinned wickedly again at the thought and before Cavenaugh could answer the door was shut-Duffy had gone.

Cavenaugh cursed Duffy under his breath for the outburst. With his dignity in tatters he tried to compose himself, before he called Seamus into the room.

When Duffy reached the house in Ickenham he noticed a lot of activity on the base at Northolt. He parked the van and then set across the fields to get a closer look. Strolling along the footpath close to the wire fence, appearing to the entire world as a walker out for some fresh air, Duffy was able to identify the reason for the commotion.

A Junker 52, obviously the one Kawolski had escaped in, was being towed from the huge hangar onto the tarmac on the approach to the taxi station. Duffy watched in awe as the three BMW radials were powered up individually. The roar of the engines would raise memories in those who had heard the distinctive sound during the earlier years of the prolonged blitz.

Duffy watched as the engines were put through their paces before he noticed something unfamiliar about the Junkers' shape. Underneath the main fuselage hung two large cylinders, painted in the same camouflage paint as the main hull, only just discernible in the fading light. "Long range tanks," he told himself. "They're fitting it with long range tanks." The only conclusion that could come to mind was that the Junkers was being prepared for a long-range mission, a mission that would take it over occupied territory...but where?

Duffy thought hard at the options. North Africa...no, it could land at Gibraltar to refuel. The US...no, there was no point; they could do that via Iceland, Greenland, Canada. Then where? It came to him a moment later...Italy.

What were the British doing flying to Italy directly over occupied territory. Kawolski! His mission. Duffy grinned almost in admiration. "Jesus, Christian, that's some fecking trip you're going on."

Christian and Emily stole a few precious hours together. Christian explained to Emily his fears over Freddie's op. His concerns were accepted with grace. Emily knew of his dedication for his friend. They made tender love together before bathing in a shallow bath of tepid water.

When he was dressed again, Christian made to move, it was only nine o'clock but he wanted to be there to see Freddie off and he needed to get a bottle of brandy from somewhere. The two lovers hugged and kissed and Christian promised to see her as soon as he could. What neither Christian or Emily knew was that, unbeknown to either of them, Emily now carried the seed that would develop into Christian's son.

Yvette woke up cold, frightened and alone. She had fallen into a deep sleep in the confines of the small labourer's shed. Her mind, devastated by the torturous endeavours of the last few days, had cut all its communications with the other resources in her body. With the resurgence of mind and body, she came too staring at her watch. It was only ten o'clock, plenty of time to make the rendezvous, she told her troubled mind.

In the corner of the shed lay two full sacks; hunger having set in, Yvette cut the bags open with a small penknife. Luck was once again with her; inside one sack were fresh green apples, in the other carrots. Yvette greedily filled the pangs that burned within her belly.

Christian saw Freddie through the last fretful minutes before he undertook the operation to fly to the hornet's nest that was Rennes, even strapping his friend into his seat ready for take off.

The engine fired into life, and then began to idle as Freddie adjusted the mixture. Christian tapped Freddie's helmet to gain his attention. Freddie looked at him, the noise covering any attempt at conversation, as Christian passed the bottle of brandy to him. Unable to speak, he gave Christian the traditional thumbs up. Christian pulled away the earpiece of the leather-flying helmet and shouted into Freddie's ear.

"Listen, Freddie, it there's anything you want to know about flying this Lysander, let me know."

"Bugger off, Kawolski." Freddie shouted, the words inaudible but the movement of the mouth, followed by the huge grin conveyed the meaning satisfactorily.

Christian smiled, before patting Freddie on the back. The canopy was closed, then Freddie began his taxi to the main runway.

Christian watched as the Lysander left the tarmac, climbed and disappeared into the blackness

CHAPTER 18

Mosel received the decoded message in the early hours of Monday morning. Without the resourceful Steiner, the message to the tower at the airfield in Rennes was delayed. Fulfilling the second part of the message, regarding the request from Dublin to send a method of transport to pick up Duffy, would be more involved but it would get through.

Anne Marie, still in the four-poster bed in the chateau at Vitre, slept easily that night. Next to her, his body still smelling sweetly from the culmination of their lovemaking, lay Lieutenant Hans Steiner. Anne Marie, her virginity lost forever, lay in a deep sleep of knowing tenderness and ecstasy. Everything she had ever hoped for was now a reality. The only problem yet to reach her conscious as she slept was that she as a French girl had just collaborated with the enemy. She had willingly given herself to a German.

The thought of the treasonable act had not escaped the young, handsome, lieutenant. Although dedicated to Germany's cause, and the fulfilment of the trust and honour Mosel had bestowed upon him, Hans Steiner now had a new priority, Anne Marie.

Freddie had been warned about the front that had come into the channel. The bad weather expected over the latter part of his flight, driven by strong, almost gale force winds, was closing in rapidly. Before he had left the shores of England he'd had to change altitude several times to avoid the buffeting turbulence that had enveloped the Lysander.

Yvette cycled to the new rendezvous that both she and Philippe had agreed upon. It was some distance from the area in which Christian had landed, and although the pilot would have to be over land for a few precious extra minutes, overall it was deemed to be a safer landing zone.

It took about twenty minutes of hard riding to make it to the edge of the woods. Unable to cycle any further, Yvette dismounted then pushed the cycle the remaining distance.

Philippe met Yvette on the edge of the landing strip; there was still a great deal of work to do in preparation. Philippe would set out the L shaped lights in a clearing about half a mile away, whilst Yvette set out the markers on the field herself. Antoine, one of the men who had been involved in the rescue of Christian at the chateau, would keep watch.

Antoine was a loyal Frenchman, he had joined the resistance in the first days of the network, and he was trusted. He slung the captured German machine pistol over his shoulder, wished Yvette good luck, kissing her on both cheeks, then set off. When everything had been done Yvette took the cycle and hid it in the undergrowth, all she could do now was to sit and wait.

Freddie had dropped the Lysander perilously close to the surface of the black bubbling waters of the Channel to establish a reference point. Satisfied that he was on course, he changed direction, heading towards the east of Cherbourg. This route would bring him over the Normandy peninsula; although that was dangerous due to the concentration of German ordnance, it would save time, and he was behind schedule. Freddie took a last glimpse at the approaching coastline before climbing steeply to hide the Lysander in the dark swirling clouds. The weather was beginning to deteriorate rapidly, huge swatches of black clouds filled his windshield. The rain, heavier now, made visual reckoning impossible. Freddie steeled himself for the battering to come.

Obergruppenfuehrer Manfred Von Ebstein still feeling the effects of the Schnapps he had consumed in copious amounts, swayed unsteadily on his feet in the torrential downpour as he made his way from the car to the main building of the tower at the airfield in Rennes.

His aeroplane had been fuelled and ready for take off for some time. The pilots, concerned about the weather, were in discussion with the flight controller in the tower. The consensus was that they would have to take off in the next hour or else the weather would close in, resulting in the cancellation of the flight. Reluctantly, the senior pilot would have to inform the overbearing Von Ebstein of their decision - either way, the fat SS man would not be pleased.

By now Freddie was passing due east of the Channel Islands on the last leg of the arduous journey. The storm was at its highest in the Bay of Biscay, the white caps of the boiling surf clearly visible on his last low level check. The buffeting had increased in its voracity, the turbulence throwing the Lysander all over the sky. Constant altitude flying was impossible, the aircraft plummeting then rising steeply according to the wind variations. Freddie certainly was having the ride of his life, an indefinite roller coaster experience over a prolonged period of time. He would be glad when he was on the ground; even a brief respite would be welcomed.

Finally, after a great deal of coercion, Von Ebstein was strapped in his seat. The thought of the delay, the lost time, time he could spend more comfortably in Paris with the obvious attractions, made his decision bearable.

The pilot completed his last checks as the converted Heinkel's engines beat out their steady rhythm. Happy with his finding the pilot began his taxi routine. The Heinkel's engines roared as the pilot increased the throttle. He looked at the runway in front of him, then turned to glance into the cabin at the fat nervous Von Ebstein, before observing the worried face of his co-pilot. Both men peered at the black sky through the rain soaked windshield, each silently in their own prayer.

The Heinkel thundered down the runway before lifting heavily off the tarmac, its wings desperately trying to keep level, its twin engines biting at the swirling air. The pilot retracted the wheels to avoid any unnecessary drag and climbed steeply.

At that same moment Freddie, approximately four miles off course, began a rapid descent in the Lysander, believing he was over Mont St. Michel.

Yvette sat under the umbrella of a tree, tired and soaked. The incessant rain pattered on the surface of her Mac and rivulets of cold water ran off her sodden beret, then down the back of her neck. Nervously she scanned her watch again,

As Freddie began his descent something began to meddle with his mind. He couldn't fathom what it was, an intuitive instinct or as a result of tension, he didn't know.

Something registered suddenly in his brain. Without checking, Freddie threw the stick forward and left. The Lysander banked in a steep dive, and just as the aircraft responded, a huge ear-splitting rushing sound came to Freddie's ears. Instinctively he ducked his head, the noise reaching a crescendo.

The aircraft was hurled through the blackness out of control, spinning wildly in the air. Freddie fought the controls, his head banging off the canopy, the seat restraints tearing at his body. A huge black shape closed in on his canopy as he blacked out.

It only took a couple of seconds for Freddie to regain consciousness. His hands grabbed the stick, as he fought the controls desperately. Eventually, after much exertion, the aircraft responded allowing some semblance of normal flight. Freddie, his whole body shaking, managed to prise the top off the brandy. He swallowed a huge gulp; the burning alcohol exploding in his stomach and dispelling the tingling nerve ends, as he slowly began to recover.

The German pilots had reacted as Freddie had done, and fortunately for all, they had also banked left, but had increased throttle to climb.

"My God, what was that?" exclaimed the pilot.

"Another aircraft," responded the co-pilot the fear still showing on his face.

"But...but there should be no other traffic in the area...where did he come from?" he said, still trying to bring the Heinkel level. When he had reached his cruising attitude the pilot relaxed some, he turned to the co-pilot and spoke.

"You had better check on our passenger."

"Ok." The co-pilot unbuckled his seat belt then moved unsteadily in the rocking confines of the cockpit to the main fuselage of the aircraft that housed the terrified Von Ebstein.

The sight that met his eyes almost made him smile. Von Ebstein's eyes were bulging in their sockets; tears were rolling down the fat cheeks. Spittle and small particles of vomit ran from the thin lips down his chin before dripping into the pool that had run down his tunic into his lap.

"Are you ok, sir?" he asked, Von Ebstein muttered something, the bubbles forming in his mouth disguising the actual words - but the meaning was not lost. The co-pilot searched for the orderly, who was beginning to recover from the obvious collision with part of the airframe, the blood seeping from an open wound in his forehead.

"I will see to the Obergruppenfuhrer, sir," the man said bravely, "I would be happier if you returned to the cockpit, you are needed there more than you are here."

"If you're sure," the co-pilot said, he then turned to make his way back to the cockpit, his body bouncing off the airframe as he did so. When the co-pilot had sat back in his seat, he contacted the tower at Rennes to report the near miss.

Yvette sat upright, as the noise of an aircraft engine came to her. She scanned the blackness, her ears straining, then it was gone. Yvette stood up, and then it came again, distinctive, lower than before, an aircraft. She ran towards the beacons, switching them on in turn, then hurried to the other end of the temporary airfield to light the others. Philippe and Antoine also heard the unmistakable sound, Philippe lighting his beacons, while Antoine pulled the bolt back on the machine pistol, the weapon now in the ready position, as his eyes scanned the blackness for any signs of intrusion.

The sharp lunge to the left had brought Freddie miraculously back onto the correct course, and flying at three hundred feet, he saw the beacons as they were lit one by one. He let out a huge sign of relief, then made preparations for his final descent.

Alerted by the tower at Rennes, impromptu parties of German soldiers were co-ordinated into a search and destroy pattern. As Freddie was making his final descent a truck bristling with German solders, accompanied by a small armoured car, approached the cross roads by the small shed where Yvette had slept

Freddie brought the Lysander in; the wheels banging into the soft soaked turf and momentarily lifting the aeroplane before gravity forced it back down. Freddie turned the aircraft round before taxi-ing back towards the waiting Yvette. When the aircraft had turned into the wind again, Yvette ran as best she could towards the waiting craft, her shoes clogged with mud, sank into the morass with every footstep.

Freddie unclipped his oxygen mask and welcomed the brave French girl; he pointed to the rear seat then smiled at the attractive passenger. A sudden staccato of a machine pistol fire burst into life. The German patrol, having heard the aircraft's final descent, followed the sounds of the engine. As they approached the edge of the woods, Antoine, who was hiding behind the trunk of a fallen tree, had let off a single burst, which had made the truck slew to an awkward stop. Agitated German soldiers jumped from the truck then began to take up firing positions in the drenched undergrowth.

The armoured car, alerted by the muzzle flashes, had peeled off to the left and was now covering Antoine's retreat. Philippe went to ground, having heard the burst of gunfire. Yvette turned towards Freddie both their faces registering the reason for the burst of fire.

"Get in!" Freddie screamed as he increased the throttle. Yvette climbed into the rear seat. The moment she sat down the aircraft began its forward motion. Craning her neck whilst buckling herself in, she tired desperately to find the direction from which the firing was coming.

She saw the searchlight from the armoured car as it moved erratically across the field, the deep rutted soil jolting it on its mounting as the armoured car raced towards them. Freddie gunned the throttle, and the Lysander began to gather speed, the engine screaming at the exertion it was being forced to endure.

A searchlight burst off the canopy of the Lysander, illuminating its precious cargo in an eerie, ghostly light. The flashes of the 30mm gun on the armoured car made both their body's rigid, red tracer like murderous balls of fire headed towards them. Terrified, but fascinated in a perverse way, Yvette watched as the bright red pieces of burning metal seemed to head directly towards her eyes.

Freddie pulled back hard on the stick, less gracefully than was normal, the Lysander begun to lift. The popping sound of the tracer as it entered the canopy alerted Freddie that something was wrong. A cold wet patch appeared on his thigh, instinctively his hand went to the area, and the dark stain on his hand confirmed that he had been hit.

The Lysander responded faster now, its frame skirted the treetops as it climbed away from the immediate danger. The red tracer thinned out, then was gone. They were up, flying away from the shocking intensity of the brief skirmish.

Antoine, still fighting desperately, heard the sound of the spring in the magazine as it extended, slamming into the lower guard of the breech. In horror his eyes went to the machine pistol, the magazine was empty.

"My God," he said, just as a bullet entered his brain.

The deathly silence that filled the air, now that the fierce little firefight was over, brought Philippe to the only logical conclusion, Antoine was dead. He lay silently in the undergrowth for a few moments before making his way stealthily back to where he had left the scooter.

Freddie climbed steeply until he brought the Lysander into level flight. He clicked on the mouthpiece in his helmet and spoke to Yvette in the back.

"Are you ok?" he asked.

"Yes," Yvette answered, her voice still trembling, "what about you?"

"I'm fine," Freddie lied; he looked down at the spreading stain. "Sorry about the take off, a bit bumpy…" He hesitated before continuing. "Yvette…?"

"Yes?" She answered.

"You had better strap in tightly, it's going to be a very bumpy flight."

Freddie managed, somehow, to free his belt from his trousers and wrap it tightly around his leg, making a tourniquet to try to stop the excessive flow of blood.

Steiner heard the Lysander as it flew over the chateau at Vitre, lying in the darkness next to the warm flesh of Anne Marie's body. He raised his eyes as if watching the aircraft pass over. He smiled, the white teeth showing in the darkness. "Good luck Yvette," he whispered, before turning to kiss Anne Marie softly and closing his eyes to sleep.

Mosel had returned to his office at the ABWEHR in Berlin. Field Marshal Rommel had decided upon his counter measures should a landing take place in Normandy. Vast areas inland would be flooded where possible, while those areas not affected would be covered in poles dug well into the ground to provide obstacles for glider-bourne troops. The artillery casements would be fitted with the most up to date artillery pieces, containing the latest endeavours of the Krupps' factory. Pointing skyward, these massive guns would be able to select their targets at random, blowing any ships the Allies could muster clean out of the water.

Mosel was exhausted after the events of the last week, but he still made time to check on the progress of Gunther Schloss. Seated in a small room off the main interrogation centre, Mosel relaxed in front of the two-way mirror, which afforded him a grandstand view of the proceedings.

Schloss, who had been kept awake for twenty-four hours, to acclimatise him to the rigours of the long journey ahead, was put through his paces by the skilful sadistic sergeant.

"Name."

"Alexander, Peter, Popowski."

"Rank?"

"Major General, United States Army."

"Father's name?"

"Peter," came the response, the brutal sergeant changed tack.

"Favourite pipe tobacco?"

"Old Virginie, Smokey." Schloss replied confidently.

"When can you smoke in Montgomery's company?"

"Never," Schloss replied, "Except..." he added. "When Ike was around, then for American officers it's almost mandatory...considering Monty hates it. Oh! and one other time?" he went on, "At tea in a general common room, although Monty still turns his nose up at it."

"Your aide in the Polish HQ?" The sergeant changed tack again, trying to unnerve the man.

"Oh, Thomas, you mean, Thomas Lomasny?"

"Well done, Herr Schloss." The sergeant said in German.

"Thank you," Schloss replied in the same tongue.

"Dumbkopf!" The sergeant exclaimed, his fist smashing into Herr Schloss' ribs, "do not speak in German at any stage."

Mosel was pleased with Schloss' development overall, the cruelty exercised by the sergeant was imperative if Schloss was going to undertake the mission, it might save his life. Mosel left the room, the small bunk in his office would have to suffice for the night, it would be a long one.

Freddie, relieved at the weather's decision to turn inland, now kept the Lysander at a fairly steady height. The loss of blood from the bullet wound had left him weak and nauseous. Freddie began to lose his faculties, one by one. Sheer intensity of thought was all that kept him awake, the desire to close his eyes was immense, if only he could sleep, he kept thinking . . .

Yvette, unaware of Freddie's injury, sat back in the seat, actually enjoying the freedom the aircraft brought to her. The tensions that had slowly suffocated her over the last few days began to dissipate, and now the weather had calmed she was actually enjoying the sensation of flying. She couldn't wait to get back to England, the thought of a comfortable bed, without the fear that her sleep had brought every night recently, filled her mind.

It wasn't until the coastline of England finally came into view that she actually smiled. Feeling safe for the first time in years, she looked forward in anticipation to a smooth landing on British soil. With this thought on her mind Yvette started to drift into sleep.

Christian Kawolski had drifted in and out of a fitful sleep, his mind still on the mission that Freddie Moreland was undertaking. Airman Book, on duty that night, had promised Christian that he would wake him with any news of his friend. It wasn't Book that woke Christian though, but the brightness of the sun filtering through a gap in the curtains. Christian sprang out of bed, washing and shaving quickly before making his way to the tower.

Yvette awoke not due to the brightness of the sunshine on the Lysanders canopy, but due to the sensation of losing height rapidly. Something was wrong; the rate of descent was too quick, the plane not in proper control. Her eyes went to Freddie in the front of the aircraft, then the shock hit her – Freddie was slumped over to one side. Was he asleep? No, he had passed out. Yvette screamed again and again into the mouthpiece. The sound of her voice eventually registered with Freddie. He came too quickly, his training instinctively coming to the fore; Freddie grabbed the controls, levelling the aircraft out, before climbing again to gain height.

Christian watched from the tower as Freddie made his approach. He could tell there was something wrong; the aircraft was flitting all over the sky.

"He's too low," he whispered to himself.

The controller in the tower was desperately trying to talk to Freddie via the VHF T2 1143 voice communications radio, but to no avail.

Yvette talked constantly to Freddie on the aircraft's communications, but Freddie kept lapsing into unconsciousness. As the aircraft came in it started to wander to the right, losing height. Freddie came too momentarily, he heard Yvette's anxious voice in his ears.

"Freddie too low! To the right!" She was screaming.

Freddie forced his eyes open, almost like an automaton he began to respond. The nose lifted then the Lysander came back towards it proper setting. But it was still too low.

The emergency vehicles rushed down the taxiways with their engines screaming, and took up their positions on the runway.

The onlookers watched as the aircraft dipped below the tree line, the impact surely only seconds away. Then, the Lysander rose hysterically over the treetops, its engines straining. Aircraft's men, officers, WAAFs, cleaners, nurses, clerks all watched silently, each praying for the popular young pilot's safety. Still the Lysander was too low.

"Come on Freddie, Come on Freddie." The same words came from perhaps a hundred mouths.

As the aircraft came in one of its wheels seemed to tear a gap in the hedge that skirted the perimeter, the Lysander slewed, rose about twenty feet in the air, then began to drop, its wheels crashing onto the apron of the runway at a perverse angle.

"Freddie!" Christian shouted his lungs at bursting point.

The aircraft bounced again, swivelled in the air, hit hard again. Like a screaming dervish, the engine gave one last deadly screech as the aircraft tore the turf from the ground at an impossible angle, its nose pointing downwards. The propeller blades tore at the ground like some demonic farm machine, before disintegrating in a shower of hot metal. Smoke began to seep from the wreckage, then a ball of flame engulfed the Lysander.

Christian ran as fast as he could towards the stricken aircraft, followed by hundreds of figures in RAF blue, like a pitch invasion at a cup final.

When Christian reached the aircraft, the tenders were already pumping chemicals into the fireball, while an aircraftsman with an axe smashed at the canopies, the flames licking at his coveralls. Yvette was dragged from the inferno still conscious, her face blackened, only the whites of her eyes showing. She refused assistance, running back towards the carnage. Two aircraftsmen grabbed her and pulled her back.

Christian rushed to the cockpit, the flames licking at his tunic, he could see part of Freddie as he was being dragged from the cockpit, then he was free. Christian took the limp, smouldering body with another helper, and laid him on the ground about twenty paces from the now fiercely burning wreck.

"Freddie, Freddie!" he kept calling. Two medics pushed him aside, checking Freddie's pulse, his heart. They nodded encouragingly towards the stretcher-bearers. Cathy, her eyes brimming with tears, rushed to Freddie's side. Christian saw her and stepped in between her and Freddie's prostrate body. He grabbed her, held her tight.

"No, Cathy, no," he said.

"Is he…?" she asked softly.

"No, he's alive."

Cathy buried her head in Christian's shoulder and began to sob.

Freddie was put in the back of an ambulance, its tinkling bell sounding as the vehicle rushed towards the medical centre.

A corporal helped Yvette to a second ambulance.

"Is he…the pilot…ok?" she asked, sombrely, the tears cutting channels through the grime as they rolled down her cheeks.

"Too early to say, but Freddie Moreland…well he's a good bloke, for an officer…all the boys are praying for him…he'll pull through." The corporal hesitated, then looked at the young woman's face.

"You alright, miss?" Yvette buried her head in his shoulder. Nervous and embarrassed, the Corporal put his arms around her, patting her back gently. The ambulance sped off to join the other at the improvised hospital.

Christian walked Cathy to a waiting jeep, once aboard; the jeep took them to the hospital where Freddie now lay.

The staff cut the smouldering clothes from Freddie's body. He lay naked and charred on the impromptu operating table. A drip was inserted into his shoulder, while a bag of blood seeped from another tube into Freddie's body. An oxygen mask covered his mouth. Feverishly the medics swarmed around his body like carrion to flesh. The doctor arrived and rushed to his side, he examined the burning bubbling flesh. With tears in his eyes, he shook his head. At once everybody in the room understood his body language.

Freddie tried to speak, desperately clinging to life. The bubbling sound of his voice was distorted by the mask.

"Pull that oxygen mask off nurse!" The doctor barked, "he's trying to say something and for God sake, somebody cover this man up, for Christ sake! Give him some dignity." The nurse did as she was commanded. The doctor leaned over the trembling body, his ear close to Freddie's mouth.

"What is it, Flight Lieutenant?" He asked gently.

"Cathy…Christian….Get Cath…."

A nurse hurriedly went to where Christian and Cathy stood.

"He's asking for you." Cathy made to move. "Both of you." The nurse prompted through her tears. Cathy gripped Christian's arm tightly. Gently he led her to Freddie's side. Cathy almost turned away at the sight that met her eyes, only Christian's strength made her go forward.

Freddie, his eyes now open, smiled at Cathy.

"Hello Cathy…sorry about this old girl…" Freddie's hand gingerly reached for Cathy's. She took his charred arm, kissing it softly, her tears cascading onto the blackened flesh before she moved to his lips, kissing them, her lips barely touching his.

"Be a brave girl for me…" Freddie mumbled. Cathy turned away, her shoulders heaving.

"Chris…."Freddie bubbled.

"I'm here, Freddie." Christian went to Freddie's side and leaned over to listen.

"Good mate…Christ…ian. look after Cathy…"

"I will, Freddie, now, come on mate…you'll pull through."

Freddie shook his head, and smiled at Christian.

"B…bl….blo…."

"What is it, Freddie?"

"B…bloo….bloody brandy….I for…got."

Freddie's body tensed, his chest rose, a huge gasp of air came from his mouth, the chest levelled, his eyes rolled then closed slowly.

Flight Lieutenant Freddie Moreland was pronounced dead.

Cathy screamed, and a nurse took hold of her gently but firmly she led the sobbing girl away.

Christian, his emotions torn apart, stormed from the room.

Once outside, he gulped the fresh air, filling his lungs almost to bursting point. Christian took out his cigarette case, his hands shaking uncontrollably as he desperately he tried to light the wavering cigarette.

"Put that bloody cigarette out," screamed a sergeant.

"Fuck off!" Christian yelled at him, his face determined.

The sergeant took one pace forward, saw Christian's expression, and decided to back down.

Duffy received word from Frankie Cavenaugh that morning; a sub would pick him up from Barafundle Bay in Pembrokeshire that night. Duffy packed a few basics into a rucksack and headed towards the shed where the motorbike was hidden. He wheeled the vehicle out, mounted the saddle kicking the machine into life. He headed towards the A40, turned right, and then accelerated away.

Duffy had heard rather than seen the carnage at Northolt. "Poor bastards," he muttered into the scarf that surrounded his mouth.

Yvette was treated for shock, then given a sedative to make her sleep. Miraculously she had walked away from the crash with a few cuts and bruises. She now slept peacefully in total safety, for the first time in two years.

Tommy Boyle slept deeply with Mary at his side; the long journey back from Ireland had worn them out. They were oblivious to the tragedy that had taken place a mile from where they slept. Tommy's mind only concentrated on one thing, the arrest, trial and official execution of Sean Duffy – vindication for Molly at last.

Christian made his way across the parade ground, not knowing where he was heading or why. The figures of Commander Thompson and Harry Milburn approached him. Christian saw the expression on Thompson's face, but not wishing to talk to anybody, he tried to pass them. He was halted by Thompson's outstretched arm…

"Flight Lieutenant Kawolski," Thompson said. "A word about your operation if I may."

"Not now, Commander," Christian said, trying to brush him aside.

"Yes, yes…I'm sorry about your friend," Thompson said matter of factly. "Still he did his duty and Yvette's safe."

"You bastard!" Christian screamed. He made to throw a punch at the stuffed shirted Thompson.

Harry Milburn reacted quickly, he placed his body in front of Thompson catching Christian's blow with his fist.

"Not now Flight Lieutenant, not now," Harry said.

Christian looked at the confused Thompson, then at the sincere Milburn. He pulled his arm away and stormed off still not knowing where he was going.

"Well!" Thompson said, dusting himself down from the blow that had not come.

"Shut it, sir," Milburn said through his teeth, "or I'll fucking deck you."

Thompson was about to say something, but changed his mind.

CHAPTER 19

The journey to Pembrokeshire would be long and tedious. It would have been quicker for Duffy to divert south of the A40 after Gloucester, but the mass of ordnance that was encamped all over the south coast - together with the obvious security - would bring problems of its own making. Wishing to remain as inconspicuous as possible, Duffy had decided to take the longer route. 'Anyway,' he told himself, 'it would be a pleasant trip through the Welsh countryside, providing the weather held and he did have plenty of time.'

The first leg to Gloucester had been fine. There were several stops to allow military traffic to pass, however Duffy was able to easily by pass most of the hold ups on the bike. Tired and somewhat saddle sore, he stopped at a little pub in a village in the midst of the Brecon Beacons.

Crickhowel was fairly typical of the villages that were dotted all over the beacons, cottages of flint and stone, grey, stark, like the Beacons themselves, huddled along the few man made thoroughfares that dissected the stunning landscape. Here the weather did not conform to the norm, one minute sunny, the next grey, dark, threatening. The mists that fell suddenly could confuse or distort the mind; landmarks that were seen and registered would disappear in a ghostly shroud in a matter of moments.

The pub was pleasant but deserted, the landlord, a thin man with a brush of sandy hair swept over one eye, seeming uninterested in his solitary trade. Duffy searched the pumps for the sign of the tell tale Guinness logo, he then did the same on the black bottles stacked to the rear of the bar, but finding no Guinness he settled for a pint of bitter.

The beer was yellowy in colour, warm and thin in taste, with all the flavour of rainwater. The landlord carried on with his mundane tasks, still not uttering a single word. Deciding conversation would not come easily, Duffy took the insipid pint outside, found a table and sat down.

Five minutes later, Duffy mounted the bike, kicked the machine into life then pulled away. The pint sat on the table alone, still half full, registering a sign that human life had once visited this remote planet.

Steiner dropped Anne Marie off at the café; out of uniform his appearance was less threatening to the locals who flitted about on their chores. Steiner entered the café first to check that no SS or Gestapo were concealed in its corners. Happy that all was well he approached the girl's uncle, who had seen his entrance. He stopped polishing the glass with a towel to stare hard at the young lieutenant.

"Where is Anne Marie?" he demanded.

"Outside, Don't worry, she is safe."

At that moment Anne Marie entered the café. Her uncle rushed from behind the bar to greet the girl, hugging her tightly.

"Anne Marie…when you…I didn't know, I . . . "

"It's alright uncle, I'm fine," Anne Marie smiled as she turned towards her lover, "Thanks to Lieutenant Steiner, I'm safe."

"Thank you, Monsieur." The man shook hands vigorously with the young German before turning his attention back to his niece. He looked at the girl, her eyes, then he knew. Anne Marie was no longer a child, something had happened, she had become a woman. Anne Marie's uncle pulled back from the embrace, his eyes telling his niece of his reservations regarding her newfound liberation. His eyes went to Steiner, and there was no hate in them, just a sad look that echoed his concerns for what might happen to the girl once the handsome lieutenant had left. Steiner saw the look, he moved forward.

"When this is over, I will come back for her." The older man shook hands once again with the young lieutenant.

"I know you will." With that Steiner turned and left.

Their goodbyes having been said several times that morning, Anne Marie moved closer to her uncle, the big man's arms surrounding her again. She did not turn to watch as Steiner left but held onto the security that her uncle was giving, a single tear rolling down her face.

Steiner was driven to the airfield at Rennes where a waiting Storch aircraft was being put through its final checks ready for the flight to Paris. Mosel had contacted Steiner that morning to tell him of Duffy's intended trip, and they would meet that evening in Paris, before flying to Brest where Duffy would come ashore.

General Alexander Popowski received the message he had been waiting for. The flimsy he held nervously in his hand instructed him as to all the details that were necessary for his flight back to England. He'd done it! They had finally taken notice, he was going to England to play a significant role in the overall planning for the greatest amphibious landing the world had ever seen, D.Day, the invasion of Northern Europe.

The Polish divisions in the front line south of Cassino were withdrawn. Rumours, prompted by radio traffic, had spread wildly throughout the ranks. They were being re-deployed. The mentions of convoys preparing to take them to a port of embarkation led many to the conclusion that they were going to England, and that could only mean one thing.

The radio traffic at Kesselring's Headquarters also buzzed frantically that day, as fifth columnists and Italian Fascists, those still loyal to Mussolini, bombarded the German headquarters with fantastic tales of a wholesale movement of British front line dispositions.

In a valley behind the German lines, close to the western seaboard of Italy, an airfield, similar in its physical characteristics to another on the Allied side of the lines, bristled with activity. Tents, vehicles, buildings, were all adapted to look like the airfield south of the line, even trees were moved added or taken down.

It was late in the afternoon when Duffy reached the small hamlet of Lamphey, situated close to the coastline of South Pembrokeshire. Tired, thirsty and hungry, he parked the bike outside a small village inn.

When Duffy entered the bar a pleasant man in his forties greeted the Irishman with a smile. He returned the compliment with a huge grin, the man stood directly behind a Guinness pump.

"Good evening," the landlord said. "What can I get you?"

"A pint of that delicious brew in front of you, if you please, landlord."

"Certainly sir, one Guinness coming up."

Duffy waited patiently until the creamy surface had settled then took a large gulp, swallowing half a pint. He wiped the foam from his lips, the huge grin returning as he placed the glass back on the bar.

"Do you have a room?" Duffy asked.

"Yes, you're lucky, just the one," replied the landlord. "I am afraid it's not in the main house, its over the storage cellar, but it's clean, comfortable with plenty of hot water."

"Sounds ideal," Duffy smiled, what time will you be serving dinner.

"From seven onwards, how long will you be staying Mr Er..."

"Duffy," Sean replied, "just the one night...I'll be leaving very early in the morning, what time are you up?"

"Six thirty normally...but I could . . ."

"Don't worry," Duffy smiled, "I'll be long gone before then."

"You here on business or pleasure?" The landlord enquired.

"Business," Duffy said, "Oil business at Pembroke, Milford Haven Refinery. It's a pleasure being in this part of the country, reminds me of home." Duffy said honestly.

"Ireland?"

"Yes...is it that obvious?"

"Well, I noticed the accent...also the Celtic mannerisms, the Guinness only compounded it," The landlord smiled.

"And an excellent pint it," Duffy picked up the pint draining it.

"Another?"

"No, no I daren't. I'd better pay you for room and board now, then if you don't mind I'll freshen up."

Duffy paid the man and then was shown to his room. Just as the landlord had said, the room was clean and comfortable. Duffy parted the delicate net curtains and looked out of the window. The room overlooked a section of the garden, which was surrounded by trees. The landlord returned to the unmanned bar, as Duffy continued his surveillance of the garden. The stairs that led from his room met the lawn, which was bordered by a wealth of colourful flowers. Just beyond the trees, Duffy could see the outline of a small wire fence, no problems there, he thought.

Happy that his departure would not be observed, he lay down to rest, he glanced at his watch, "One hour only, Sean." He said to himself before dropping off instantly to sleep.

Duffy woke; he looked at his watch, and saw that exactly one hour had passed. Duffy washed and shaved, and readied himself for food; his hunger had risen again.

Both Yvette and Cathy, heavily sedated, slept in the rooms off the main medical building at Northolt Airfield. Christian, torn by the events of the morning, longed for Emily's touch, the re-assurance that her body would bring. He decided to buttonhole the adjutant, and try to get his permission to leave the base and see Emily. The adjutant agreed, irrespective of what Commander Thompson might say. He knew of Christian's friendship with the amiable Freddie, knew the pain that existed inside him, understood the loss.

When Christian arrived, Emily was in the bath relaxing from the rigours of the day. She opened the door, a long white towel wrapped around her to protect her modesty. The bare shoulders and legs glistened with small drops of water; her golden hair lay on her shoulders, the ends damp from the bathwater.

“Christian!” She exclaimed not expecting him, her excited smile disappeared as she looked into her man’s eyes. “Christian, what is it? What’s wrong?”

“It’s Freddie, he didn’t make it…he’s dead, Em.” Christian began to shake. Emily reached for him, hugging him tightly, her arms bringing the needed strength.

“Poor Freddie…poor Cathy. Oh, Christian, I’m so sorry.”

When Duffy was ready he made his way to the main building of the inn, the bar now with a few customers dotted around looked welcoming. A pretty girl stood behind the counter, her pink lips parting into a wide generous smile as Duffy approached.

“Good evening.” She said in a lovely soft Welsh accent. “What can I get you sir?”

“A pint of Guinness and a menu please…Er?”

“Mary,” The girl answered with a smile, as she poured the pint. When the stout had been fully topped up she laid it in front of Duffy, turned then went to the back of the bar to collect a menu. Duffy watched her, she had a small pert backside with elegant tanned legs that were covered in a light print skirt.

The girl Looked in the mirror on the back wall, and noticed Duffy’s interest. She smiled as she handed the menu to Duffy, her hands flicking at the dark hair, the green eyes signalling her availability.

“Anything you fancy?” She asked before Duffy had read the selection of fare.

“Behave yourself.” Duffy grinned.

The girl was about to say something when the landlord appeared.

“Mary, help Gweneth in the kitchen for an hour would you.”

The girl pouted before making to leave, then Spoke softly to Duffy.

“And what if I don’t, Mr…?”

“Duffy, Sean Duffy, then you might be made to stay in the kitchen all night.”

Mary smiled then strutted towards the kitchen.

“Everything alright, Mr Duffy?” The landlord asked.

“Perfect.” Duffy replied. “Just perfect.”

Duffy ordered the house special of the day, Bubble and squeak, potatoes mixed with cabbage then fried with onion gravy, with two sausages completing the feast. When he had finished his meal he ordered a coffee, which he took back to the bar. Mary was chatting to some local lads, so Sean selected a bar stool in the corner, where he could observe her antics more openly. Every few minutes the girl would look at him, flick her hair with her long nails and then continue the hard to get approach with the boys.

When Duffy had finished his coffee, he made to go to his room. The girl, annoyed that he was leaving, spoiling the game she had been playing, gave it her best shot. She walked along the other side of the bar following Duffy’s movements. At the L shape where he would have to exit, she stopped and leaned over the counter provocatively, her backside rounded, her breasts exposed by the buttons that had been undone on her blouse, a come and get me look in her eye. As he passed she looked up at him.

“Goodnight, Sean.” She said a wicked smile on her lips.

“Goodnight, Mary.’

‘Would you like me to tuck you in?’ Mary giggled.

‘Behave yourself!’ Duffy smiled.

‘And what if I don’t want too?’

‘Then you’ll feel my hand across your backside girl!’ Duffy said firmly.

‘Ooh! That sounds nice,’ Mary pouted seductively.

Duffy grinned, then left the bar. He made his way to his room, it was ten o'clock, three hours sleep then he'd be off. Duffy lay back on the bed, his hands behind his head. He thought about Mary, smiled to himself and fell asleep.

Christian woke, and found Emily naked, curled in a foetal position next to him. The towel she had worn was discarded on the floor. He slipped out of the bed; dressed then covered the sleeping Emily with a sheet, kissed her gently, then left the room.

When he sat in the car, he lit a cigarette, took a deep breath then started the engine.

Steiner was greeted at the airport by the smiling Mosel.

"Hans, a good trip?" He asked as they both got into the back of the waiting car.

"Yes sir, fine. How was Berlin?"

"Busy, a lots been happening since you've been away. Duffy will be here by morning; Schloss is at the airport in Brest awaiting our return. The Goose has received his movement orders, he's leaving Friday, oh, and the Allies have withdrawn two Polish divisions from the front at Cassino."

"Is that all, sir?" Steiner smiled, the sarcasm evident in his voice.

Mosel smiled before answering.

"No, not quite, Lieutenant."

"What else sir?" Steiner became more official, noting his superior's tone.

"Our man has found out some information regarding Patton."

"What sir?"

"We don't know yet, Hans, It was too important to send, that's why he's coming in person." The car pulled up at the door of Mosel's waiting Junkers 52.

Two men boarded the Liverpool bound freighter at Belfast, their false passports and identities gaining swift access to the waiting steamer. As they stood on the ships deck by the railings, the tall thin man spoke to the red haired man in a Belfast accent.

"How are you feeling, Patsie?"

"I'll be a lot better when this heap of shit gets to the other side," The thick set, red haired man answered.

Duffy awoke instantly, his hand going to the Walther under his pillow. His eyes adjusted to the light in a moment, he levelled the pistol at the door as the handle turned. Slowly Duffy's finger increased pressure on the trigger.

"Sean…Sean are you awake?"

"Feck." Duffy whispered to himself as the Walther was lowered slowly to the floor beside the bed.

"Sean, it's Mary," the voice whispered nervously as the door opened fully, exposing the silhouette of the young barmaid in the moonlight.

"Mary, what the hell are you doing, girl?"

"I just came to see if you're alright," she giggled as she closed the door.

"I'm fine…now it's time you were in bed, young lady," Duffy said to the blackness, his eyes not yet catching up with the quick change of light.

"I know," she giggled as she stood by the bed.

Duffy's eyes finally adjusted again, the girl Mary stood completely naked in front of him, the next thing she was lying on top of him, her mouth searching for his.

"What the hell…why not." Duffy said to himself.

Commander Thompson answered the phone in the drawing room of his house.

"What is it, Harry?"

"Our man has done a bunk, sir."

"What? Why wasn't I told of this?"

"We've only just found out sir."

"Keep looking Harry, find him."

"Sir." Milburn said as he put the phone down.

Thompson went to the drinks tray on the sideboard, poured a malt whisky into a crystal glass, than drank the mellow blend in one. A smile came to his mouth.

Silently Duffy changed into clothes more suitable for the task ahead. When he had finished dressing he put his other clothes, the ones he'd worn earlier, neatly into the rucksack. Dressed in a thick woollen roll necked jumper, dark corduroy trousers and black rubber boots he left the room, kissing the naked Mary as he did so.

Once outside, Duffy like a cat, moved swiftly across the lawn, into the trees and over the small wire fence, before circling back to where he had parked the bike. Gently he eased the machine off its stand, then began to walk the vehicle to the edge of the village, heading for Freshwater East.

When he had reached the top of the hill that led down to the beach, he mounted the bike, freewheeling down the one in five hill until he reached the edge of the sand. Duffy stood for a moment to listen for any noise; there was none except for the rhythmical crash of the surf on the beach. He wheeled the bike through the sand, his arm muscles straining to push the machine on the difficult terrain. When he reached the beach huts, he went to number seven, his lucky number, and undid the padlock. He pushed the bike into the hut, put the haversack minus his cigarettes on the saddle then locked the door again.

Duffy began the long climb that led to the bay. He had selected this area because no roads ran to the small indentation on the south Pembrokeshire coast. It was two miles either way over rough cliff paths to the nearest access. When he finally made it to the dunes that sat behind the beach, he glanced at his watch. It was ten past two, thirty minutes before he was to signal. Duffy sat and waited.

Christian sat smoking on his bed in the quarters he had shared with Freddie, unable to sleep. Freddie's bedclothes, his personal effects and his uniform had been cleared and taken away. Christian stared at the empty side of the room; it was as if Freddie had never existed. When he had finished the cigarette, Christian picked up the photo, the one of Freddie, with his arm around Cathy. It was the one he had looked at the first day he arrived back at Northolt, the first day he had met Freddie.

He lit another cigarette, his mind on that day, the day the MO had passed him fit for flying again and the day he had met Emily. It seemed like years ago, yet so much had happened since that day.

Duffy glanced at his watch again; it was two forty, time to make the signal. He took the pencil torch out of his pocket and flashed the name 'pigeon' seawards in Morse code. He waited for a response, but none came, only the blackness of the sea stared back at him. He put the torch back in his pocket; he'd wait another ten minutes then signal again.

When the ten minutes were up, Duffy signalled again. Still no response. Then it came, a light, far out to sea signalled back. Duffy stood up, the torch in his hand sending back the acknowledgement.

After a short while he saw the rubber boat as it edged towards the beach. Checking around all the time, Duffy ran to the shore. A submariner jumped out of the rubber boat.

"This way, sir," he said, helping Duffy into the rocky little craft. "Hurry please," the sailor said nervously, as he pushed the boat into the surf, jumping on board as soon as the dinghy was clear of the sand.

The two submariners paddled the small, rubber boat against the incessant swells of the incoming surf. The moon had hidden the silhouette of the U boat, but it was now shrouded in cloud, so it wasn't until Duffy was almost alongside that he could see the distinctive black hull of the submarine.

As soon as Duffy clambered aboard, the U boat began to submerge, sliding down the hatch of the conning tower he was met by a bearded man with a kindly smile.

"Captain Wilhelm List at your service, "the bearded man saluted, "welcome aboard, sir."

"Thank you, Captain." Duffy returned the salute. The two men who had been in the rubber boat, slid down the ladder closing the hatch behind them. Duffy looked at the bearded man, he was dressed in similar garb to Duffy, only the captain's badge on the epaulets of his jumper distinguished him from the others. 'He can't be more than twenty-two,' thought Duffy although the dark rims around his eyes made him look older.

Duffy was shown to an officers quarters where he would sleep for a couple of hours, the officer whose bunk it was would be on duty until then. Duffy lay down; the smell of diesel and stale human sweat came to him, before he closed his eyes to sleep.

CHAPTER 20

Corporal Tom Riley made his way south; so far the going was ok. His escape from the POW camp had been a textbook operation. The Italian camp, north of Rome, had been better than some of the detention centres he had been in since his capture in North Africa in 1943. However, with the imminent arrival of the Germans to the camp, Riley had decided to make his escape earlier than planned.

Riley had been a member of David Stirling's elite S.A.S. Captured on the raid at Bardia; he had spent months in various transit camps before arriving at his last destination in January 1944.

Riley had two options for escape, north to the border with Switzerland or south to meet the forward positions of the advancing Allied armies. He had elected to go south for what seemed logical reasons. The Italians had surrendered with the invasion, therefore Riley assumed they would be more willing to assist in his repatriation, and that part was true.

Secondly, he believed the going would be easier in the south, added to the fact that the Allies would advance so quickly his journey should be shorter. On both those counts, he was wrong; the Allies became bogged down at Cassino on the Gustav line, which meant that instead of swarms of Germans retreating north, what he saw was a steady flow of men and ordnance heading in the opposite direction.

It had taken Riley six weeks of arduous travelling to make it to his present position south of Rome. Walking by night, remaining concealed and resting by day, the journey had been a marathon of endurance and mental stress, only his training which had been put to the test in Stirling's desert raids kept him going.

Duffy was woken with a cup of the bitter tasting Ersatz coffee, which a submariner had brought to his bunk. Duffy had slept longer than he had planned; the last couple of days' journey's taking their toll. He sipped the coffee sitting on the edge of the bunk and looked at the little parcel that had been left for him. It contained clean socks, a razor with a brush, soap and a little toothbrush.

When Duffy had washed and changed, he made his way along the narrow passageway of the boat, climbed a ladder then entered the main hive of activity in the conning tower. Captain List, his beard seeming fuller than the night before, greeted him cordially, the blue eyes more relaxed.

Duffy searched the faces of the other crewmembers, and saw the same story, every man looked less tense. They must be close to their base at Brest, and unless there was an unexpected act of God they would be safe.

The journey the U boat had undertaken was fraught with danger, the mass of Allied shipping all along the south coast of England, protected by destroyers, frigates and a mass of other smaller hunter killers, had made the passage a frightening undertaking. Like swimming in a shark-infested pool, the crew had expected at any moment to be discovered and consumed. It was nothing short of a miracle that the U-boat had got in and out undetected.

Duffy looked at the young captain. "I bet you played your part too Willy." He thought to himself.

"How long till we dock, Captain?" Duffy asked.

"About two hours," the Captain replied.

"Jesus, that long!" Duffy's face Looked downcast for a moment, his nostrils taking in the pungent range of smells, his ears the orchestra of sounds, his eyes the sheer intensity of human endurance.

The Captain saw Duffy's look. All landsmen were the same, he thought.

"Don't worry, sir, we'll go up top for the last hour, some fresh air would be welcome, yes?"

"Too right, Captain." Duffy gazed in admiration at the man. He couldn't understand what would make a human being risk the most awful ranges of death inside a travelling coffin, Submariners were a different breed,' he thought.

The aircraft touched down on the airfield just outside Brest. Mosel and Steiner had seated themselves in the waiting car, before it sped off towards the U-boat base at Brest. At the base, both were re-united with the waiting Schloss, now totally in character for his forthcoming role, Mosel went over the final details before Duffy's arrival.

Yvette came too in the small room just off the main medical centre at RAF Northolt. She felt relaxed and safe, emotions she hadn't felt for years. She began to weep softly, the tears not just for the brave pilot who had given up his life to bring her home, but for herself also.

A nurse had seen Yvette's sorrowful tears, but deciding it was to be expected, she left the girl alone. Instead she went to order her breakfast, a nice cup of tea would do Yvette the world of good, she thought to herself.

Cathy in the room opposite, had no tears for herself. She had hardly touched her food, but the full ashtray beside her was evidence of the present state of her nerves. Christian had popped in to see her earlier, his strength a welcome relief for the sympathy that had been bombarded at her, his regard for Freddie similar to hers but in a manly way.

Christian had told Cathy that the CO had agreed to let her stay with Emily for a while, providing that she was well enough. Cathy's condition had nothing to do with medicine, the type of treatment she would need could only come from the heart, and perhaps the soul. Emily would be good for her, Cathy thought, not only was she a friend, but she was also the lover of a pilot, she knew the emotions, she had been there with Cathy before.

Yvette accepted the tea the nurse had brought, cupping the warm mug with both hands brought comfort to her. The tears had subsided now, the distinctive taste of tea telling her that she really was home.

Commander Thompson and Harry Milburn made their way to the base at Northolt. Thompson's mind was buzzing with the possible answers he would receive to the vast array of questions he needed to ask. He was at a crossroads, only Yvette's first hand information could allow him to select the right choice, the proper road to develop the plan that overrode all other thoughts.

The U-boat surfaced in the grey early morning mist like a whale, its black shape pushing through the gathering surf. Duffy smelt the air the moment the hatch had been opened. Following the Captain, he scaled the ladder to the observation post on the top of the tower. Duffy took a huge breath, filling his lungs with the sweet fresh air.

"God, I don't know how you do it." He said to the Captain, "Weeks locked in this sardine tin, expecting to die at any moment, and for what?"

"This," The captain breathed in, "Freedom – safety, it's exhilarating don't you think?"

"Yes, yes it is." Duffy said understanding.

Duffy looked at the prow of the boat as it plunged in and out of the swell, performing like a real boat, the spray invigorating him. In the distance he could see the grey outline of the coast of France growing with every desperate movement of the boat. He offered a cigarette to the captain, then took one himself. He ducked below the rail, lit his, then passed it to the captain who lit his own. Both men took a long draw.

"English cigarettes…excellent." Willy said.

"Better than that Russian crap you boys get" Duffy grinned.

Christian drove Cathy to Emily's home. Awkwardly he carried her small vanity case to the door. The two girls held each other, as if communicating in some fantastic body language not understood by mere man.

Christian realised he was out of his depth, and he made to leave. Emily was wonderful; everything she said and did seemed to have a positive, effect on Cathy.

Christian held Cathy's hand, then kissed Emily on the cheek, her eyes telling him it would be ok now, she could handle it from now on. With that, Christian left, promising to return as soon as he could.

Expertly the Captain eased the boat into its mooring. The submariners not directly involved in the manoeuvre lined the hull of the U-boat, the welcoming shore party less audible, less triumphant these days.

When the boat finally came to rest, Duffy shook hands with the captain, praising him for the lack of excitement on his voyage. As Duffy strode down the ramp to land. Mosel stood waiting to receive him, with Steiner at his side, a black saloon in the background with its engine running,

"A pleasant trip, Sean, I hope?" Mosel asked.

"No, but a quiet one." Duffy grinned as he shook hands with the German officer.

"Good to see you, Ernst."

"You too Sean." Mosel shook Duffy's hand with genuine friendship and admiration. He turned towards Steiner, "may I introduce you to my aide, Leutnant Hans Steiner."

"Pleased to meet you Herr Major." Steiner said.

"Less of the formality, Hans," Duffy smiled. "I'm an Irishman first."

Steiner instantly took a shine to Duffy. "Gentlemen, the car is waiting," he said, adopting Duffy's express command.

The journey through Brest brought home to Duffy the revenge the Allies had taken. The town was shattered, full of broken buildings. Torn roads hastily filled in, littered the area of the docks and in particular the area around the submarine pens. The brave French residents seemed to accept the necessity for the nightly devastation the RAF had enacted upon their native soil. Spurred on, rather than dejected, they waited for the day when liberation would come.

Yvette had bathed then breakfasted well. She knew Thompson would come today, ready with a barrage of questions, questions that would bring back the memories, but at least she would be safe; after all it was her duty to report everything. Yvette steeled herself for the verbal and mental onslaught, just one more day she told herself.

Mary's arms searched the empty pillow for Duffy. Realising he was gone, she shot up in the bed, her naked body still smelling of him.

"Bastard," she said under her breath. Then a small wicked grin appeared on her face. Mary jumped out of the bed, gathered her nightie, which lay on the floor from the night before, then she made her way quietly to her own room in the main house.

Duffy was shown into a room within the Naval Intelligence building that, due to the RAF's visits, was now located on the outskirts of town. The sight that met Duffy's eyes impressed him; the man seated behind the desk was an exact replica.

"Excellent, you have done well, Ernst." Duffy said.

"Let me introduce you," Mosel said pleased with Duffy's compliment.

Duffy was introduced to Gunther Schloss, although that was not what Mosel had called him.

"Thank you for agreeing to see us so soon." Thompson said to the nervous Yvette, "I appreciate your courage. If you are sure you can handle things I'd like to make a start straightaway."

"Where would you like me to start, Commander?"

"At the beginning if you would please." Thompson smiled, "let's start with Lucien, before Kawolski went to France."

Yvette took a deep breath, then began to tell Thompson her thoughts. During the first part of the interrogation, Thompson interrupted when, and only when, he sought clarification on a certain point Yvette had mentioned.

"So you believe George's was involved right from the start?"

"Yes, he and Lucien," Yvette almost seemed to spit the traitor's name, "were always together, neither would speak to me in front of the others."

"Were the other members of the group suspicious?"

"Yes," Yvette answered, "especially Antoine and Philippe." A look of sudden horror came to Yvette's face. "My friends," she said, "did they make it away from the drop zone?"

"Philippe is ok, he contacted us today.... Antoine, I'm afraid...."

"Is he dead?" Yvette asked.

"Yes."

"Poor Antoine." Yvette looked away, sadness in her eyes.

"Ok, let's leave that for the moment." Thompson did not want to lose Yvette so early in the de brief. "Who knew about Kawolski's operation?"

"I did, naturally, but the others were not aware."

"Are you sure?" Thompson enquired.

"Positive," Yvette answered. "Only Lucien and George's knew, it was they that orchestrated Kawolski's capture."

"Let's move on to that for a moment, Kawolski's escape from the SS." Thompson paused to allow Yvette to speak freely.

"I knew something was wrong when I reached the scene of the massacre. The vehicles weren't dispersed, they were in single file, and!" Yvette paused, "none of the German weapons had been discharged."

"Perhaps they were taken by complete surprise."

"Impossible," Yvette said. "None of use were involved, and there's no way Lucien and George's, operating alone, could have taken them all out. Anyway, they were all shot from extremely close range, there were no skid marks."

"So what are you saying?" Thompson was leading the conversation.

"Whoever killed all those men was not a threat to the SS men, they had stopped quite normally, they were not in any way feeling threatened. In short, Commander, it was Germans who stopped the little convoy, Germans that they recognised." Yvette said with conviction.

"Mosel?"

"No, Commander, probably not in person, but his men…there were some marines at the chateau, it was probably Steiner who led them."

"Steiner?"

"Mosel's aide…Leutnant Hans Steiner," Yvette said, her face relaxing as she thought about the young lieutenant.

"Carry on." Thompson said noticing Yvette's facial change, the sudden softness in her voice when she had mentioned Steiner's name – he would come back to that later.

"Well as we know," Yvette continued, "Kawolski was taken to the chateau in Vitre, where he must have been well looked after, he had a miraculous recovery considering he was still in German captivity."

"Agreed."

"Then Lucien, with the help of most of the men in the circuit, miraculously breaks into the well guarded chateau, complete with Kriegsmarines and extracts Kawolski from Mosel's grasp."

"Magnificence or a simple cover up?" Thompson asked.

"The latter," Yvette said. "Then Kawolski escapes in a Junkers! Which had been commandeered by Mosel personally! Then somehow lost!" Yvette raised her eyebrows showing her disbelief.

Thompson nodded at the incredulity of it all.

"Why do you think Kawolski would be involved? You do think he's involved, don't you?" Thompson asked.

"Yes…yes, but I think there's something else."

"What, Yvette? What would make a hero like Kawolski, a Pole, a man who hates the Germans, betray all that he stands for?"

Yvette thought hard before she answered. "His family…perhaps….Perhaps Mosel might have a hold on him."

"Maybe." Thompson now knew the reason; Yvette had confirmed his suspicions, suspicions that had been backed by circumstances. Suspicions that were now clearly a fact.

"Let's move to Lucien, Herr Dacourt – was he killed in the escape?"

"No! He was executed!"

"By Mosel?"

"Yes, I think he had fulfilled his usefulness, Mosel would be unable to let him go free….he knew too much!"

Duffy was impressed with the performance he had witnessed. According to the information he had, Schloss had performed like a Shakespearean actor of note on opening night. If Schloss could be as convincing to those who knew his character, in a real life situation, then possibly Mosel's plan would work.

"What do you think Sean?" Mosel had asked when they were alone.

"Very good, Ernst, I'm impressed...but it's not me he'll have to convince."

Cathy had bathed, Emily never leaving her alone for long, just long enough for the small fragments of reality to form, which with Emily's help would complete the jigsaw of the healing process.

The girls, their legs underneath them, sat talking on the sofa in Emily's front room. A cup of scalding, healing tea in both their hands. Like a glass of cold water in the desert, Emily's quiet concern brought Cathy's body and mind onto a level plain, brought her something which so far that day seemed impossible, happy memories and most importantly a belief, a belief that life could go on.

Having paused for a cup of tea, Thompson pressed on with the debrief, he was happy with what he had learnt so far.

"Your night at the chateau, working with the French girl...err..."

"Anne Marie," Yvette prompted.

"Yes, Anne Marie, you mentioned you heard...or overheard something?"

"Yes," Yvette answered, "Mosel and the Field Marshal...."

"Rommel?" Thompson interjected.

"Yes, Field Marshal Rommel, he was the guest of honour, so to speak, at the chateau. He and Mosel left the main party after dinner, they went to the library. When I could get away, I was able to listen at the door for a short while."

"What did they say?" Thompson moved closer to Yvette.

"Well, I missed the first part, but I overhead them discussing plans for the war games."

"Oh!" Thompson said, looking less excited.

"Then they discussed the actual invasion itself."

Thompson moved closer again. "Carry on, Yvette."

"They discussed the probabilities, and came to the same conclusion – Normandy."

"My God!" Thompson exclaimed. Yvette continued.

"Both Mosel and Rommel opted for Normandy, Rommel even stating that if he were Allied Commander that's where he would land, followed a week later by an invasion in the south of France."

"If this is true, Yvette, then everything we've done...has been a waste of time."

"Rommel had one reservation."

"What?"

"The lack of a suitable deep water port – he said Cherbourg would be difficult to take, firstly, because there are no proper beaches large enough in close proximity. Two, the Allies could be bottled in on the peninsula. Three, Cherbourg even if it could be captured on the day, it wouldn't have the facilities to house the mass of ordnance necessary to sustain the beachhead."

"Well," Thompson exclaimed, "at least they don't know about P.L.U.T.O. or the Mulberries?"

"Well," Yvette continued, "he did say something on those lines."

"What?" asked Thompson, "Yvette, I need the exact words he used." Thompson tried to remain calm, but his mind was working overtime. Yvette took a deep breath to steady herself.

"Rommel said the only way the Allies could sustain an invasion in the Normandy area would be if they could bring their own harbours with them."

Thompson shook his head in disbelief. Did Rommel actually know the Allied plans? But how? How had he found out? Only those right at the top from Monty to Eisenhower, Churchill. In S.I.S. only he and 'C' knew and possibly a few in the other intelligence agencies – S.O.E.? Had the leak come from S.O.E? Was there a mole?

Yvette added, "My estimation sir, was that it was a joke on the part of the Field Marshall…or at least that's the way it seemed."

"The mere mention of the fact is cause for concern, the fact they mentioned it at all means that they will now investigate it as a possibility."

"I see sir." Yvette said.

"What happened next?" Thompson asked.

"I don't know," Yvette said. "Steiner caught me at the door, I was so busy listening…I didn't hear him approach…I dropped the tray of drinks."

"Did Steiner suspect you?"

"Yes…definitely."

"What did he do?" Thompson asked.

"Nothing…" Yvette answered honestly. "He covered up for me with Mosel."

"Why?"

"I don't know, sir."

Thompson sat back in his chair and both hands, the fingers extended, went to his mouth. He blew between his hands like a child would do whilst trying to imitate an owl's call, but no sound came. Thompson thought hard about what Yvette had just said.

"Unless…" he said at last. "Unless he wanted you to hear."

"But he was not present at the discussion, sir. How could he know what I heard?"

"Hmm…" Thompson knew Yvette was right, but something still niggled him. Steiner! He'd remembered something Yvette had said earlier. "Steiner! Mosel's aide, what's your estimation of him. This girl Anne Marie, is there a connection?"

Yvette chose her words carefully. She did not want to hide the truth, but she also wanted to protect Anne Marie and Steiner. She spoke slowly and confidently.

"I think there was a mutual attraction, they are both young. If Steiner did anything…I think it was more to protect Anne Marie."

"Ok, sounds feasible." Thompson said, "anything else about this Steiner?"

"Yes," Yvette told Thompson about the incident with Von Ebstein.

"Do you think he knows who…what you are?" Thompson asked when Yvette finished.

"Yes."

"Then why didn't he expose you?"

"I think it's because of Anne Marie." Yvette answered. She swallowed deeply before continuing. "If he had informed on me…Anne Marie would be complicit in the whole thing."

"Lucky you came across this Anne Marie." Thompson said without malice or intent.

"Yes sir, I think you're right." Yvette felt the relief, it was all out in the open now, it was over. She felt like a weigh had been lifted from her shoulders, she was safe now.

Duffy sat down with Mosel in the room. They were alone, not even Steiner was present. Mosel opened the conversation.

"What have you got for me, Sean?"

"Firstly," Duffy started. "Firstly, Kawolski's got a new mission, he goes Thursday," Duffy grinned. "And he's going in the plane you lent him."

"Do you know where?" Mosel asked.

"Italy." Duffy explained the logic.

"So it's Popowski?"

"Yes…although you probably know that already."

Mosel smiled. "We do have some other resources, Sean."

"How are you going to get him to do it?"

"Fear, Sean, the use of fear."

Duffy sat back in the chair, the grin widening. "Listen, Ernst, Kawolski, I know him, he's not your every day traitor…He's no Lucien…What have you got on him?"

"His family, a wife and two small girls." Mosel's expression showed his disgust at what he had done, even though it was a necessity. He didn't like it; it went against everything he believed in, a moral code, an Officer's code.

"You evil old bastard," Duffy grinned, then he hesitated. "You wouldn't…Ernst?"

"I have no choice Sean, things are different now…Canaris has gone…so has reason. If I had not acted, the Gestapo would have taken them…they tried, fortunately, they were too late, but they did take the woman's parents. They are in Dachau."

"I see…sorry Ernst…I didn't realise…of course you had no option." Duffy hesitated. "You will free them if Kawolski does his part… that's the agreement?"

"Yes…I gave my word." Mosel looked hurt.

"Ok, Point two. F.U.S.A.G. First United States Army group." Duffy said the words aloud.

"What about it?" Mosel now leaned forward.

"It's real, and Patton's leading it,"

"How do you know…for sure?" Mosel asked.

"I've been there…I've seen it."

Mosel looked surprised, his mouth open, yet no words came. Duffy continued.

"Thousands of tanks, planes, artillery, everything. Probably two hundred thousand men."

"My God, where? Where do you think they will strike?" Mosel asked.

"Well, they're in Norfolk, Suffolk, Cambridge, Essex, the Thames estuary…only one logical choice, geographically."

"The Pas de Calais?" Mosel interrupted.

"Only choice." Duffy confirmed.

"But what about the build up on the south coast…Montgomery…Patton, his disgrace."

"A dud, Ernst, a deception, a con. The allies…this is my estimation, Ernst… the Allies will make a feint, an attack south of the Seine as a diversion…"

"Where?" Mosel asked.

"I don't know. Bordeaux possibly. "This thing with Patton." He continued, "That's the con, a put up job. Patton is the best they have. It will be him that leads the invasion, politically the Americans would demand it."

"I see…yes it makes sense…my God." Mosel exclaimed, "The Poles."

"What about them?" Duffy asked.

"We just heard today, the Poles have just been taken out of the line at Cassino. Rumours are they are being sent back to England....50,000 men, fresh experienced troops."

"Then there's the British tenth army, under Dempsey I believe, and lets not forget the Canadian 15th Army…all…all, Ernst, in the same area as F.U.S.A.G."

"Yes, I know, we have been monitoring the radio traffic…so we were wrong!" Mosel said dejectedly.

"Who was wrong?" Duffy asked.

"Myself and Rommel…we thought Normandy."

"Ernst, I think you need a rest my friend. How…how could they land in Normandy? There's no port…and Cherbourg…"

"I know Sean, I know… but Rommel, we were convinced…" Mosel looked as if the world, his world had just fallen into the abyss..It had! The abyss of doubt.

"Anyway, Ernst, if this plan you're hatching, whatever it is…" Duffy was probing for some snippet of information, "succeeds then it won't matter or will it?"

"No, Operation Golden Egg will tell us exactly what we need to know." Mosel's confidence regained its earlier composure. "I would like to tell you everything, Sean, but not even Himmler knows of our plan."

"I think I've got most of it, Ernst." Duffy smiled at the German officer before continuing. "I want to go on the trip you're planning."

"What trip?" Mosel replied.

"The one to Italy…The one Herr Schloss is going on."

Mosel was adamant, he'd already told Duffy more than was absolutely necessary. However, the argument Duffy put forward would convince him that the Irishman could play a significant role.

Yvette, having been dismissed by Thompson, made her way to the barrack room in the WAAF's quarters, where she would stay for the time being.

Thompson made a call to 'C' and confirmation of the appointment was given. Thompson and Harry made their way to the car, stopping briefly to talk to Christian, who was heading their way.

"Ah, Flight Lieutenant. I'm glad I bumped into you." Thompson said.

"What is it, Commander?" Christian said coldly.

"You go to Italy on Thursday. Briefing 06.00 hours."

Thompson carried on his way to the car, leaving Christian with his dilemma. The fear, the turmoil returned to the surface. Christian, his face pale reached for his cigarette case.

CHAPTER 21

Thompson sat across the table from 'C', his verbal report having been given. 'C's reaction wasn't long in coming.

"If what you say is right Peter, then everything we've done, Fortitude, everything, has just gone out the window."

"Well, maybe not, sir." Thompson moved to the edge of his chair leaning forward. "I've had an idea. It's in its infancy at the moment, but with the right circumstances and backing it just might work."

"Let's have it, Commander."

Thompson spent the next twenty minutes explaining his idea to 'C'. The head of SIS moved constantly as Thompson spoke, his body language becoming more and more animated. When Thompson had finished explaining his plan, it was 'C' who was on the edge of his seat.

"Brilliant, Peter," 'C' said. "Do you think we can pull it off?"

"Yes sir,...of course, we'll need the backing of all the most senior members of the Allied Command....and Patton."

"Leave that to me. I'll get straight on to Winston, as for Patton, I'm sure he'll do it...He needs to show willing after his recent behaviour."

"There's something else sir." Thompson hesitated.

"What, Peter?" 'C' looked questioningly at Thompson.

"In order for this to work, sir, it's got to be fool proof."

"Agreed."

"The Germans," Thompson continued, "will need additional evidence."

"Fortitude."

"Yes, that's fine sir, but...but we'll need something else, something they will believe without question."

"I'm not sure I'm going to like this, Peter," 'C' said, his face grave. He had intercepted Thompson's look, he was right, it would be a decision that would haunt him.

"Live proof...an agent, sir...." Thompson didn't finish his sentence. He didn't need to, what he was suggesting was as obvious as it was abhorrent. Send an agent to France convinced that the knowledge he had was true, let him be captured, tortured, made eventually to talk.

'C's face showed the enormity of what Thompson was asking him to do. Sanction the certain death of a brave man or woman!

"Is there no other way, Peter?"

"Well, I've got a couple of ideas...but they would not probably be sufficient on their own, sir."

"I see, Peter...My God I see." 'C's face showed what he was thinking. No brave words or speeches, such as 'one mans life, to save thousands, probably tens of thousands,' came to him. Only one certainty emerged, he was going to authorise the sending of a human being to certain death, as good as executing the person himself.
"I'll speak to S.O.E., set it up right away...If we can come up with something else..."

"I doubt if we can...not as convincing anyway..." Thompson sat back in the chair.

The two men, one with red hair, the other tall and thin by his side, got off the train at Ealing Broadway Station. They had travelled all night on the steamer, then caught the train to London, from there they took the push and pull to Ealing.

The tall man was out of breath; the run to catch the bus had strained him. As he sat down on the seat on the upper deck next to the other man, he pulled out a packet of Black Cat cigarettes and lit one. Coughing whilst still wheezing, he took a long draw on the cat before flooding the immediate vicinity with blue smoke.

"Those bloody things will kill you," the red haired man said, fanning the smoke away with his hands.

Tommy Boyle sat at his desk at Ruislip police station, the file on Molly Redburn once again in front of him. His excitement over what he had heard on his trip to Ireland filled his mind. Boyle took out the black and white photograph of the young girl; Molly had been a pretty girl with long blonde hair. Her features were small, neat, childlike, only her eyes seemed larger than life.

Tommy stared hard at the photograph he had seen a hundred times before. His eye caught something, something he had seen before but now suddenly it became relevant. Calling himself all the names under the sun, Boyle took the photograph to forensics.

"Charlie," He said to the white-coated man. "I need a favour."

"What is it Tommy?"

"This photograph, can you blow it up for me?"

"Sure Tommy, any particular part?"

"Yes this bit," Boyle pointed to the area on the photograph.

"No problem, Tommy…it might be a bit grainy though."

"Thanks Charlie." Boyle almost ran upstairs to his office. Once at his desk he phoned Dublin. His fingers tapping excitedly as he waited for an answer.

"Inspector Noel Riordan please…yes I'll hold….Noel, it's Tommy…yes I'm fine. Listen Noel, Mary McGrath…have you got a photo? Good, get it blown up. look at the neck section, tell me what you see…Thanks Noel."

The two men entered the bar in Hanwell; they approached the barman asking for Cavenaugh. A few minutes had passed since the barman went into the back room before the door opened. Cavanaugh's face lit up at what he saw.

"Patsie! Donal! How are you?" He beamed.

"Fine, Francis, fine," the two men answered in chorus.

"Porrick, drinks for my friends, what will you have boys?"

"Guinness," the men said in unison.

"How did the meeting go?" Cavenaugh asked.

"Like clockwork," Donal said.

"Phelan's struck a bargain," said Patsie.

"How much?" asked Cavenaugh.

"Two hundred and fifty," Donal replied.

Duffy was given a complete set of clothes for his journey; the ones he had worn on the trip were laundered then neatly pressed. He waved goodbye to Mosel on the tarmac, then climbed the three steps into the waiting Junkers. As soon as he had sat down, the pilot started the engines. Nervously, Duffy strapped himself in, "first submarines now bloody aircraft, Duffy cursed"

The Junkers taxied then turned sharply onto the runway. The engines at full strain rattled the corrugated steel frame as the Junkers began to move. The roar of the BMW radials filled Duffy's ears, his eyes closed as he gripped the arm rests, his knuckles bone white. A sudden thump as the wheels left the ground made Duffy's eyes open, and a feeling of insecurity, of helplessness, filled his mind as the Junkers took to the air.

The aircraft banged and jumped as they passed through the clouds. Duffy breathed in and out slowly to try to steady the nerves, then the engines eased. Duffy forced himself to look out of the window below him the black clouds had given way to clear blue sky, the sun shining brightly.

"Is everything ok, Major?" One of the Junkers three-man crew asked.

"Yes, I'm fine." Duffy breathed. "Shouldn't you be doing something?"

"I'm the navigator sir, don't worry, they won't need me for a while." The man smiled.

"Fine, in that case, any chance of a drink?" Duffy grinned.

Christian, with some time on his hands, had met Emily and Cathy at the Plough. Cathy was still in the early stages of mourning, and low on conversation. Emily, however, as soothing as fire on a cold night, kept the occasion as bright as possible. Her chatting, the way she touched Cathy, the way she accepted the pain Cathy was going through, without offering condescending sympathy, was having a remarkable effect on the pretty young WAAF.

Christian was quiet, his admiration and love for Emily only surpassed by his feelings of inadequacy regarding Cathy's hurt. There was so much he wanted to say but couldn't.

Emily brought Christian out of his thoughts, "has anybody seen Sean?"

"No, not for some time." Christian answered.

"That's unusual, I wonder what he's up to?" Emily said.

Duffy was at that moment flying at 18,000 feet, the Junkers top cruising altitude. His earlier foreboding had turned into quizzical wonderment. He hated flying, but was always fascinated at the same time. What would man invent next he thought.

The weather for the first part of the trip was good, the flight comfortable. The navigator had brought some coffee and sandwiches, and Duffy had decided to fill his empty stomach. As soon as the coffee was poured, the sandwich half in his mouth, the Junkers hit turbulence. With his face pale and his hands trembling, Duffy sat back in his seat, praying to God.

Fortunately, the turbulence didn't last long,

"It's because they were flying over the Alps." The navigator had told Duffy. It had not made Duffy any the happier knowing there were mountains so close. His thoughts were interrupted by the presence of Schloss at his side.

"Fascinating, isn't it?" Schloss had said whilst leaning over Duffy to look out of the window.

"Yes, fascinating," Duffy had mumbled in reply, a sarcastic edge to his voice.

"You know," Schloss continued, "if you get up and walkabout, the sensation becomes easier. Flying, it seems to disturb you Mr Duffy?" Schloss seemed to refuse to recognise Duffy's rank. He considered him to be an outsider, not worthy of such acclaim.

"Is it now." Duffy replied, "and by the way it's Major Duffy."

"But you are not an officer of the Reich, Mr Duffy, you are an Irishman."

"I'm Irish, true, but this uniform says I'm a Major."

"Then in that case Mr Duffy, I am a General." Schloss said triumphantly.

"Point taken, Gunther," Duffy grinned. "Take a seat." Duffy patted the chair next to him.

"Thank you, Mr Duffy." Schloss sat down.

"So what made you get mixed up in this little pantomime Mosel's arranged for you, Gunther?"

"For the Fatherland, Herr Duffy." The Herr was Schloss's way of accepting Duffy finally. "What about you?"

"For the Motherland, Herr Schloss, for Ireland, Gunther," Duffy replied.

Schloss smiled to himself, perhaps this Duffy would be a good person to have around, he thought.

Christian had offered to drive the girls back to Emily's flat but they had decided to walk the short distance home. Christian kissed both girls on the cheek before making his way back to the base. When he arrived back at Northolt, he was stopped by the Station Commander.

"Christian, how are you feeling?" He asked informally.

"Fine sir, thank you."

"The CO took Christian by the arm as if wishing to speak privately.

"Listen Christian…I'm sorry about Freddie…Good chap….I know you and he were close."

"Thanks sir, and yes we were."

"Quite." The CO said nervously before changing tack. "Listen I've got all the details, flight plans, for Thursday's jolly for you. The long-range forecasts will be with me this evening…Perhaps you could pick up all the gen later. Stop by the office about six…will that be OK?"

"Yes, sir, that's fine." Christian made to leave.

"Oh, by the way, The Junkers is being pulled out for another engine test…you may want to start her up, see how she feels, familiarise yourself."

"Yes, sir, I'll pop over and see the sergeant now…will that be all, sir?"

"Yes, yes fine…" The officer mumbled.

Christian saluted sharply turned then headed for the hangar that housed the Junkers 52.

Duffy was beginning to enjoy the flight now; the simple expedient of talking to another human being had eased his previous tension. Schloss, he had decided, wasn't such a bad sort. He was still stuck up his own arse, Duffy thought, but there was a side to him that Duffy admired. After all, he was a true patriot, and not unlike Duffy in some circumstances. Both had been deceived by their parents, both their fathers had left them alone as babies, yet for vastly different reasons. All in all, some of the mutual feelings of abandonment had brought them together.

"Gentlemen," The navigator had interrupted, "we are now flying over the Italian Alps."

Both men instinctively looked out of the window, they both wondered what would happen once they landed on Italian soil. There was no going back now.

In the south of that country, to the rear of the line at Cassino, Major General Alexander Popowski was readying himself for his proposed departure that Friday.

"Thomas, make sure you pack my dinner suit, I'll be needing that in London. Oh, an don't forget those gold arm things."

"Cufflinks sir," Thomas, Popowski's Polish aide answered. "It's all done, sir."

"Good, what time am I due at Alexander's for dinner."

"Seven thirty sir, at the castle."

"Good, make sure my uniforms laid out and don't forget the...."

"The car is arranged, sir, and your uniform's being pressed...everything is in hand sir."

"Sorry Thomas, you must think I'm a real pain in the arse." Popowski said.

"Of course not sir." The aide lied.

Christian sat in the left hand seat of the Junkers. The cockpit had been scrubbed and scrubbed again, yet the smell still remained in Christian's mind. It had only been a few days since he had flown the Junkers in his orchestrated escape from France, yet it seemed an eternity. Only in his imagination, did Christian begin to remember the atrocity that Mosel had enacted. Christian stared at the right hand seat, the bullet holes in the cockpit canopy had been filled in, but in the seat normally occupied by the co-pilot, he could still see, smell, the decaying corpse of the traitorous Henri Dacourt – Lucien.

The imaginary thirty pieces of silver littered on the floor of the cockpit. It was he, Christian Kawolski, a Pole, a fighter pilot, a hero of the battle of Britain, who was now to follow in Lucien's footsteps, become a traitor! He shivered at the thought, arguments that he had only succumbed due to the natural instincts of any man to protect his family somehow didn't stack up. He just couldn't do it. He'd have to think of another way, but what?

It didn't take Christian long to make his mind up. He decided he must make a call.

The sergeant mechanic broke Christian's inner turmoil.

"Excuse me, Flight Lieutenant."

"What...sorry," Christian answered.

"She's ready sir, give her a spin."

"Yes, yes of course. Stand clear below." Christian shouted out of the window, his mind now back on the job in hand.

'C' sat opposite Winston Churchill, in the subterranean office in Whitehall. He had informed the Prime Minister of the discussions he'd had with Commander Thompson and the conclusions they had come to.

"Don't worry dear friend." The Prime Minister had said. "I will talk to Ike, Bedell and Monty and, as for the presumptuous Patton, he will no doubt fall in line. As for the other matter..." Winston paused to take off his glasses, before sitting back in his chair. "Do you have anybody in mind."

"Yes sir...." C paused as Winston re-lit his cigar. "Yes sir, I do," he said his voice distorted in his anguish.

"Who?" Winston said, sucking on the cigar, the smoke balls lifting into the confines of the room, like a steam engine ready to roll.

"Yvette Granville, sir." 'C' said finally.

Winston looked up, the eyes searching 'C's face, the cigar held firmly between the huge fingers. "The girl who has just come back from Mosel's web?" He asked.

"Yes sir,"

Winston rubbed his eyes, put his glasses back on again, staring hard at 'C's face, looking for any sign of doubt.

"Don't you think she's been through enough, C?" Winston asked.

"Yes sir, but…it….it would be believable sir….Mosel would…."

"Yes, yes…of course, you are right C," Winston said, his voice as heavy as his heart felt. "See to it, C." With that the great man took a pile of paperwork and began to read, ignoring C's reaction. Knowing his time was up Menzies made to move, but as he reached the door, Winston spoke again.

"Will she break, 'C?"

"Yes sir….but not easily." 'C' said, his voice for once letting him down in the growing nausea that filled the whole of his being.

Winston just nodded, then returned to his paperwork.

When Sir Stewart Menzies left the Prime Minister's war room, he stopped at the first lavatory he came to. Washing his hands, he stared at his reflection in the mirror. What he saw did not make him feel any better.

That evening, Christian made the phone call, a call that he had to make.

"Sir, it's…it's Flight Lieutenant Kawolski…I need to see you right away… Yes…I'll wait."

Christian put the phone back on its hook, 'Monica, forgive me,' he said.

The Junkers touched down briefly in Northern Italy to refuel, before taking off once again into a dark sky. The weather had turned again, rain was in the air. More coffee and sandwiches were served to the two men for the final leg of the journey. Duffy found Schloss interesting, the man's life had been anything but dull, only his bachelor status seemed to bring melancholy to his voice.

This proud, patriotic man would end his life the way it had started, in deceit. Duffy felt for Schloss, a simple twist of fate had brought him to the pinnacle of his existence; the next two weeks would decide his role in history.

When the Junkers 52 finally touched down on the prepared field to the north of the Gustav line, it was late evening. The battle for Cassino had stalled for the time being, the failure of the attack by Clark in the west had left both sides exhausted, and so a lull now existed, both sides resting while preparations for the next bloody onslaught were made. For Mosel's plan to work effectively, there had to be a cessation of hostilities at least until Friday evening.

Duffy was shown to a comfortable billet, where he slept peacefully. Schloss on the other hand, was once again put through a fusillade of questions regarding the identity he was to assume.

Christian kept his meeting with the man he had spoken to on the phone. Ashamedly, he disclosed the full details of his enforced complicity in the deceit. The coercion and the blackmail were all laid on the table. Regardless of what fate awaited him, Christian, honour bound, confessed openly. After his avowal, Christian awaited the response. His confessor leaned forward to speak; his words brought a glimmer of hope to Christian.

His spirits refreshed by the meeting, Christian made his way to Emily's house. It would be the last time that he could see her before the mission. They made love on the sofa, while Cathy slept in Emily's bedroom. Had Christian known then the tragedy that was about to unfold, he would never have left the sleeping Emily that night.

Tommy Boyle still in his office late that night received the blown up photograph of Molly. Using a magnifying glass, he saw clearly what he had hoped for, on Molly's neck hung a gold heart shaped pendant.

In a comfortable bed in General Alexander's' head quarters, Major General Alexander Popowski dreamed of the forthcoming invasion, and the part he would play in its success.

CHAPTER 22

Boyle had received the phone call he had been waiting for; Noel Riordan in Dublin had confirmed that Mary McGrath had also worn a heart shaped pendant. Boyle now had another clue to add to the others, all circumstantial he admitted, but they all pointed to his chief suspect – Sean Duffy. If Boyle could get hold of the murder weapon, with its prints still intact, he could finally lay to rest the tragic deaths of Molly and Mary.

The phone rang, "Boyle," Tommy answered.

"Mr Boyle, Phelan sends his regards. If you want the weapon that was used in the murder of Molly Redburn meet me at the Greenford Hotel, next to the iron bridge on Sunday night at one o'clock.

"Will you bring the evidence with you?" Tommy asked.

"One o'clock and bring the money." The voice said, then the line went dead.

Tommy sat back in his chair, at last, he said to himself. If things went to plan, Tommy thought, by next Monday morning he would have all the evidence he needed to arrest Sean Duffy for the murders.

Christian attended the briefing. The flight plan, fuel consumption, departure and ETA times had all been worked out. Providing the weather remained fairly stable, the fuel provided, with the additional load carried in the specially fitted drop tanks, should be sufficient for the journey. The long-range forecast had suggested that the weather should remain fairly clement for the next twenty-four hours, providing that the threatened front did not move too quickly.

Once out of the meeting, Christian checked with the mechanics as to the airworthiness of the Junkers. According to the chief mechanic, a dour Scots sergeant, all should be fine, although he had hesitated when discussing the range. Christian despondent with the lack of activity, combined with the mental frustration it caused, longed to be flying again, even if it was only in a converted passenger plane.

Unable to leave the base for security reasons, Christian had to console himself with the sound of Emily's voice. He phoned her at her office.

"Hello, Bryants Builders, how may I help you?" Her sweet voice had answered.

"Emily, it's Christian," he said, the excitement in his voice at hearing her showing.

"Christian, where are you?"

"I'm phoning from the base."

"Can you come and see me?" Emily's voice betrayed the emotions she was feeling.

"Sorry Em….I can't…I'm not allowed off the base." The silence that followed made his heart sink.

"Oh." Was all she said, her voice close to tears. Christian pictured her in his mind, the eyes sad, the mouth in that little girl pout that she always displayed when she could not get her own way, although this time it would not be from selfishness.

"Come on Em…you know the rules…I'm not allowed to…"

"Christian," She whispered into the phone. "Please take care…I…I couldn't ".

He interrupted her.

"Of course I will, Em, listen I'll be back on Friday...I'll see you Saturday...Emily..."

"Yes?" She said lamely

"I love you, Emily."

"I love you, too, Christian," Emily started to cry. "Come back to me." She said through the tears, then the line went dead.

His heart and soul in turmoil, Christian replaced the receiver. Whatever happened in the next forty-eight hours, Christian knew he had to get back; he had to be with Emily, hold her in his arms once more.

Christian's take off time was set for one o'clock. Escorted by a Spitfire, he would make the approach towards the French coast under the cover of darkness. At that point the escort would peel away to return home. Christian would complete the journey totally alone, hoping to make his destination in the early hours of the morning.

He tried desperately to sleep, but the thoughts of the undertaking now complicated after the meeting he'd had together with his guilt over his love for Emily, made restful sleep impossible. Lying on his bunk in the room he had shared with Freddie, his mind in purgatory. Christian counted the hours and minutes.

In the war room in Whitehall, Winston Churchill met Eisenhower and Montgomery; also present were Bedell Smith, Air Marshal Tedder and General Dempsey.

Churchill spoke in a controlled voice, but the enormity of what he told the assembled Allied High Command was not lost on them, their faces ashen. Not one of them daring to speak until the Prime Minister had finished. When Churchill had completed the summary of his earlier conversation with 'C,' he laid both his hands on the table, his eyes interrogating each face that sat around the table. Montgomery was the first to speak.

"Well, Prime Minister, it seems we have no other option, but will it work?"

"Truth and deceit are good allies when put together," Winston said.

"Quite, but will Patton do it?" Montgomery asked.

"George will do what he's told," Eisenhower interrupted. "And as it so happens, Monty, I think he'll do a good job, the son of a bitch can be fairly persuasive when he wants to be."

"It's agreed then." Churchill stated, his eyes receiving a nod from every face around the table in turn.

"Good, thank you gentlemen."

As the Supreme Allied Command stood to leave, Churchill beckoned to Eisenhower.

"Ike, a word if I may."

As the others left only Monty seemed to be troubled, indignant not because of the enormity of the undertaking, but due to the simple fact that the Prime Minister had not wished to discuss his concerns directly with him in person.

Christian strode across the tarmac to the waiting Junkers 52; the aircraftsmen had towed the aircraft out of the hanger ready for take off. The Junkers stood like some medieval beast, its dark paint symbolising the role it had been chosen for. Christian routinely checked the aircraft, not that the sergeant mechanic, the dour Scot, would have let her out of the hanger unless she was in perfect condition, but it helped Christian focus on the job in hand.

Satisfied with the inspection, Christian climbed aboard, passed through the cabin to take his seat on the left hand side of the cockpit. He would make the long journey to Italy alone, it had been decided. Mainly due to reasons of security, also with increased activity due to the impending invasion, most of the experienced crew had been seconded for other duties. Normally the Junkers would carry a crew of three when on passenger duty, so Christian would have his work cut out on the journey ahead. More importantly, it had been decided the fewer people who knew about the operation the better.

One by one the three BMW radials were fired into action. Slowly the dark shape of the Junkers began to move and taxi to the now empty runway.

Commander Thompson watched from the tower as the dark machine rolled down the runway. Just as it passed him the wheels left the ground, the Junkers was airborne, Kawolski was on his way. Thompson watched until the dark shape disappeared into the clouds, before turning to Harry Milburn.

"Come on, Harry, we had better see how Yvette is, then it's back to the office. We've got a lot to do in the next forty eight hours."

Harry said nothing; he just turned and followed Thompson out of the tower.

Yvette had watched the take off from the window of her room, she could fully understand the emotional strain that Kawolski would be going through, but she was glad that it wasn't her; she'd done her bit.

Christian took the Junkers to sixteen thousand feet that would be the operational ceiling for the rest of the journey. The aircraft settled into steady flight. Although heavy in take off due to the extra fuel load, the Junkers was fairly easy to fly. Christian sat back in his seat, once airborne he was always contented.

As he passed over the South Downs, he was joined by a Spitfire from Eleven Group. It would be his escort until they reached the coast of France. Enviously, Christian stared at the fighter, her elegant shape silhouetted against the moonlight. "Lucky sod," Christian thought to himself, what he wouldn't give to be back in Spits. When they reached the outline of the coast of France after an event-free flight, the pilot of the Spitfire wished Christian good luck, then peeled away to make his trip home. Christian was now totally alone.

It was Emily's turn now to be comforted. Cathy knew all too well what she was going through, and she held Emily tightly as both girls settled down to sleep. Their earlier girlish giggles over half a bottle of Ruby wine had subsided. Both young women's minds, intensified by the alcohol, drifted towards the faces of their lovers.

Freddie would be up there in the sky looking over Christian's safety, Cathy had assured her. Emily, feeling selfish, had opened her heart to Cathy. The two young women, one consumed with grief, the other consumed by the fear of grief to come, were mutually beneficial to each other. Taking it almost in turns to reassure each other, their natural feminine survival instincts coming to the fore.

The hairs on the back of Christian's neck stood up, his palms heavy with sweat, gripped the controls so tightly the veins in his arms began to ripple the skin. Instinctively, he knew he was passing over the area of Rennes far below him. The anxiety caused by the mind's ability to gain its own perception brought the memories flooding back. Inadvertently Christian swallowed, his mouth dry, his hands going to his mouth to wipe away some imaginary taste.

It was not until the aircraft had passed over the area that normality returned - like a driver approaching a notorious bend in the road, it was not until the expectancy of danger had passed that the barometer of trepidation fell. Now Christian eased the pressure on his body and mind and relaxed, allowing his flying instincts to take over.

Mosel received the call he had been waiting for; the tower at Rennes had reported the radar blip of an unidentified aircraft passing through their area of operation. Kawolski was on his way, the Allies, totally wrapped up in their conceit, were acting according to plan. Operation Golden Egg, having been fertilised, was now in its embryonic stage. Within a few short weeks, the egg would be delivered.

"Good news sir?" Steiner asked, seeing the smile spread across Mosel's face.

"Yes, Hans, very good news…its on."

"Congratulations, sir."

"Not yet, Hans," Mosel smiled, putting his hand flat out in front of him, his head moving from side to side, "Not yet. But soon Hans…soon."

"A Schnapps might be appropriate though, sir, I mean a toast might be in order?"

"Yes, Hans, yes why not." Mosel conceded.

As the Junkers passed over the Alps the cockpit was lit in a half-light. The moonlight complimented by the glow of the snow capped mountains, gave a cold reflective appearance similar to the start of a frosty dawn.

It was bitterly cold in the cockpit, too, Christian having to flex his toes and blow down his gloves to warm his extremities. His passage over occupied France had been uneventful, even mundane. The weather had been good all the way, the promised front having assisted in adding to the excellent time Christian had made. The only problem that came to mind was the possibility of flack from any nervous ack ack gunners, but so far nobody had bothered the lone Junkers on its journey. At this rate Christian was confident that he could reach his destination just before first light.

Corporal Tom Riley had started his nightly trek southwards at ten o'clock. So far he had made only five miles as the crow flies. The country in which Riley travelled was high, cut with deep valleys crossed by fast flowing rivers. The going was tough, the broken hillsides causing strain on the corporal's thighs and calves. Riley kept to the tracks just below the crest of the hills when he could.

The valley floors swarmed with German troops coming and going from the front, meaning that they were no go areas. Although travelling along the valley floors would have been easier, the chance of capture would have been too great, and the last thing Riley needed was to be compromised now, especially as he was so close to the Allied line.

Riley told himself if he could make another five miles or so that night, he would only be about six, possibly seven, miles away from the Allied positions to the west of Cassino and freedom. Due to the heavy concentration of enemy positions, Riley would have to give himself at least an hours grace in order to find a suitable place to lie up for the day.

Riley plodded on, his throat dry from lack of water, his stomach empty of food, his muscles sore and stiff. Only the thought of rejoining his own side kept the corporal going that cold wet night.

Christian had made excellent time. The weather had deteriorated as he flew down the spine of Italy, the clear sky having given way to cloud and rain squalls. Dawn was now approaching fast as Christian having skirted the defences around Rome made his way south. Another thirty minutes he reckoned, then he would bank right towards the coast, past the lines about three miles off shore then turn inland to make his final approach. Christian took the Junkers to its cruise ceiling of eighteen thousand feet, here the air was clean, the early morning sun bright.

He started making his routine checks ready for the descent, everything seemed fine, and the fuel, which was his greatest concern, was still showing a reasonable load. With luck Christian would land with fuel to spare, mainly due to the tail winds and the clement weather. If he met a head wind, or the weather for the return trip became heavy, then the margin of fuel available would become critical. Christian decided to worry about that when and if it happened. For now Christian concentrated on the job in hand, getting the Junkers safely on the field south of the Cassino line.

Riley had found his temporary billet for the long day's evasion. It was a small hollow created by an outcrop of rock, just big enough for him to slide into and lay almost fully stretched out. He gathered some bushes to help to conceal the entrance, then filled his bottle with some rainwater that had collected in the small indentations of the rock. He collected some dryish turfs from under the shade of a small tree before laying them down on the floor to the hollow to provide some comfort for the sleep to come.

Having made his temporary home as comfortable as possible, Riley was ready to enter his secluded hide when he heard the distinctive noise of aircraft engines far above him in the grey cloudy sky. Riley pinned his ears back, his eyes wider, his brain on full alert trying to recognise the increasing drone of the aircraft as it headed towards him. He'd identified the aircraft as a Junkers, too big to be looking for him he decided. They wouldn't use a single craft for bombing or re-supply, so it was probably carrying passengers. Whatever was the role of the Junkers it was preparing to make its descent. The drone of the engines had begun to soften; it was coming down, but where?

Riley thought hard, if the Junkers were beginning its descent, probably from about eight to ten thousand feet now, it would be probably about ten minutes before it landed. Riley's face became depressed, if that was the case, then he was further from the front than he had first thought. He had estimated it would take another day, perhaps two to reach the Allied lines, but he could now be facing three or four days of hard travel.

With his mind tormented Riley lay down to sleep, his heart at its lowest ebb since his escape.

Christian banked right and took the aircraft in a wide sweeping arc out to sea. When he was confident that he was well south of the front line, he communicated via the VHF set to the tower at the US air base.

"Hello Bonfire, Hello Bonfire, this is Crackerjack, do you receive me, over?" It only took a few seconds before the crackling sound of an American voice speaking with a heavy southern drawl, came back into Christian's ear piece.

"Hello Crackerjack, This is Bonfire, receiving you loud and clear Mac. We have a Mustang in your vector, will inform him to guide you in, welcome to Italy Mac. The weather here's like Georgia in the fall…crap." It ended abruptly.

Christian scanned the horizon, then he saw it, the Mustang levelling out and coming alongside. The pilot, a huge grin on his face, beckoned Christian to follow him.

Christian made the final approach, breaking the low cloud base at two thousand feet; ahead of him still, was the Mustang just visible in the lashing rain that spread across the cockpit screen. “Welcome to sunny Italy,” Christian mused sardonically as he lowered the bumpy craft.

The Mustang circling above watched as Christian brought the Junkers in with a textbook landing. Exhausted yet thrilled, Christian taxied the aircraft to a halt inside an improvised camouflaged hangar. With the props winding down, Christian unbuckled himself from his seat and made to exit the aircraft.

He was greeted by a small, smiling air mechanic wearing a T-shirt, slacks and sneakers topped off with a light visored forest cap.

“Welcome to Italy and especially Cassino, the permanent address of the US Army Air Force in this goddamned country, sir.”

“Thank you, Private,” Christian smiled noticing the chirpy New Yorker’s rank.

He was shown to a mess hall, still busy with its US officers. As Christian sat down an attractive US WAAF equivalent placed a huge plate of steak and eggs in front of him, accompanied by a steaming mug of real coffee.

“New York tenderloin,” The girl smiled. “I didn’t know how you like it cooked, Lieutenant, so I done it medium for you, is that ok?”

Christian stared at the feast in front of him.

“Looks like I joined the wrong air force,” he smiled, looking straight into the girl’s eyes Christian watched as she moved to a counter then stood awaiting any command he might have, her well tailored uniform displaying the full shape of her body. The girl noticing Christian’s stare smiled warmly back at the handsome young pilot.

When Christian had finished scraping the plate, he was shown to a comfortable bed.

“I’ll give you a wake up call at 16.00 hours, sleep well, Lieutenant.” The girl said as she departed. It took Christian only minutes to fall fast asleep, his mind now on Emily and Monica.

CHAPTER 23

The nervous tension that accompanies excitement was evident at the headquarters of the Polish army in Italy that day. General Alexander Popowski, US Liaison officer with General Alexander's forces, was displaying all the calmness of a child about to visit the seaside for the first time. The repetitive questions were beginning to grate on all those around him, no one more so than his aide Thomas.

"Thomas, what time's the car due to take me to the airfield?" He asked for the tenth time.

"Still 16.00 hours sir."

"Good, what time is the officers meeting?"

"14.00 hrs sir, and General Alexander will see you at 13.00 hours." His aide answered knowing what the next question would be.

"Sorry Thomas, you must think I'm a real pain in the arse." Popowski grinned at the patient Thomas.

"Not at all sir, if you were, Eisenhower wouldn't be sending for you, he's got enough trouble with Patton, sir." The aide lied.

"Patton…yes…it will be good to work with George again." Popowski hadn't seen Patton since North Africa. He'd been in Sicily at the same time, but for some reason their paths had not crossed. "What time do I take off?"

"19.00 hours." The aide answered, wishing today would end.

Duffy had breakfasted alone at the airfield north of the Gustav line. His companion for the trip, Gunther Schloss, was nowhere to be seen. Duffy decided to take a stroll; the early morning downpour had faded with time, and a brilliant sun now shone down on the valleys of southern Italy. Small clouds of hazy vapour rose slowly from the sodden ground.

Duffy lit a cigarette, his eyes scanning the view; the transformation that had taken place was remarkable. German troops, in co-ordinated working parties, had completely altered the appearance of the airfield. What had once been a local supply base, full of Luftwaffe personal, now took on the appearance of a busy front line US air force base, complete with MPs and all the paraphernalia of the USAF at war.

Dummy silhouettes of Mustangs, complete with a captured Dakota in full US livery only added to the illusion: jeeps, half tracks and Chevrolet trucks littered the field, replica administrative buildings completed the deception.

"Not as good as the FUSAG in East Anglia, certainly not on the same scale, but a pretty good effort all the same," Duffy mused to himself.

When Duffy had finished his cigarette, he ground the butt with his boot; it was almost symbolic of what would happen later that day. A bright light, extinguished by a German jackboot. Duffy strolled back towards his temporary billet; it was going to be a long day's night.

It was Bedell Smith, Eisenhower's Chief of Staff, who visited the fictitious US First Army Group based on England's east coast that day. Eisenhower, having decided his presence would probably only antagonise the dispirited Patton, had sent the pragmatic Bedell in his place.

"Bedell, it's good to see you." Patton put his arm around the senior officer in a show of over familiar camaraderie. "Come sit down." Patton said, the big toothy smile on display for all to see.

Bedell Smith sat down, fully knowing what would come next.

"So Ike's finally seen sense, what do I get Bedell, Normandy? Overall Command?"

Patton's grin lit up his whole face, like a child when he had misbehaved. He saw Bedell Smith's presence as a sign that he could now return to the fold, his earlier transgressions having been swept away by the embarrassment of punishment. "Listen, Bedell," Patton continued in his exuberance. "Monty's got it all wrong, now if I was leading the invasion…"

Bedell Smith shook his head in dismay at Patton's pre-emptive display.

"George, for God's sake, when are you ever going to learn to shut that mouth of yours. You've got a command, FUSAG! And it's important, do you understand?"

Patton, ever the optimist, looked downcast for a moment. He turned to stare out of the window, his thoughts processing all the evidence of Bedell Smith's sudden appearance, confident in his assessment of the situation. Patton now took a new tack. He turned once again to face Bedell, this time more respectfully.

"Listen Bedell, I know I'm an egotistical son of a bitch, I can't help it. It's just…just, I have a conviction about this war. I know I've got a part to play, and I'll do anything, anything to get back into action." The grin now came back to his face. "You know me Bedell, I'm a hot mouth, but I'm a damn good field officer."

"Everybody knows that, George." Bedell Smith conceded his manner more relaxed. "You're on probation George, you do exactly, and I mean exactly, what Ike demands, and he'll get you back in this war, but only then."

"Ok," Patton said as he sat down. "What do you want me to do?"

Bedell Smith explained.

Emily had gone to work that day making Cathy promise to call her at the office if she felt down, or needed her in anyway. It had taken Cathy an age of agreements to get Emily to leave and, when she finally did, Cathy was relieved. Deciding that she needed to face reality head on, she returned to the base at Northolt. Although officially still on leave, Cathy needed to surround herself with the familiarity of her grief.

When she arrived at the base, the adjutant called her to his office before closing the door, his face contorted in the awkwardness of the undertaking. The adjutant sat opposite the pretty WAAF, on the desk in front of him was a small parcel wrapped in brown paper and string containing the personal effects of Flight Lieutenant Freddie Moreland. Embarrassed by the lack of adequate words, the adjutant pushed the parcel towards the silent tearful girl.

"I guess Freddie would have liked you to have these," he mumbled.

"Thank you," Cathy said in barely a whisper.

Noticing her wishes, the adjutant made an excuse to leave. She stared at the meagre bundle. Not much for a hero, she thought, but appropriate for a young man of only twenty-three years of age. Slowly she untied the string unwrapping the brown paper as she did so. The routines of life were all there, his razor, some cufflinks, a badly charred watch, identify papers, ration card. Cathy stared at the papers the brutality of a clerk's simple stamp brought the grief rushing to the surface on each paper a read stain of a word – DECEASED.

Fighting back the tears Cathy put the papers to one side, and as she did so her eyes, wet with the clouding of tears, saw something shiny. Cathy pushed aside the contents of the package to investigate, there it was, a small gold heart shaped pendant on a gold neck chain.

Cathy stared at the pendant for a moment before gently placing it around her neck, once on she gently brought the pendant to her lips and kissed it. With her emotions at the pinnacle of endurance, she began to weep softly.

Commander Thompson had delayed speaking to Yvette about the proposed operation, deciding that the agent was not yet mentally strong enough. Reluctantly, he would have to put off the dreaded moment. His thoughts were interrupted by the presence of Harry Milburn.

"What is it, Harry?" he said annoyed by the intrusion.

"Something's come up sir." Harry said taking an un-offered seat. "Our Irish friend, seems he's got some visitors."

Thompson sat back in his chair, his eyes now fully focussed on the excited Harry.

"Who?" he asked simply.

"We don't know the names yet sir, but there's two of them, and according to our information they're from Roscommon in the Republic."

"Phelan?" exclaimed Thompson sitting forward.

"Yes sir, that's what we reckon, Cavanaugh seems pretty pally with them."

"But why are they here? And why now? Harry, do you think its something to do with our man?"

"Yes sir, but I don't know in what context…there's not a lot of love between them." Harry added.

"Ok, follow them, see what they get up to…and Harry, see what our man does."

"That's a bit of a problem sir…"

"What?" Thompson asked purposefully.

"Our man…He's done a bunk…no sign of him sir."

Christian awoke at four o'clock, the brilliance of the sun passing over his tired face. It took Christian a few moments to realise where he was, but when he had reassured his mind of his location, he made to ready himself. Having completed his shaving routine, he stripped to the waist and stood before the small circular mirror, his body muscled and taut gleamed in the afternoon sunshine.

A knock at the door brought Christian's thoughts back.

"Come in," he said casually.

The door opened to reveal the pretty young American girl.

"Oh, you're awake already, Flight Lieutenant," she said softly, her eyes scanning the exposed parts of his body.

"Yes, yes thank you," Christian said with boyish embarrassment.

"Commander O'Hare wants to see you," she said in her sweet tantalising accent. "I could wait…show you the way if you wish."

"No that won't be necessary…I'll find it thanks, Lieutenant," he added.

"As you wish." She smiled again before closing the door slowly.

Christian made his way to the base commander's office passing the Junkers complete with new drop tanks. The grey and black marked Junkers standing like an eagle in its profanity -The vehicle of deceit.

Commander O'Hare was a huge Texan, his lean six foot six frame towering over Christian's six foot.

"Lieutenant Kawolski. Good to see ya." The Commander pumped Christian's hand. "Welcome to Cassino."

"Thank you sir," Christian replied easing his hand from the huge fist.

"Your bird's ready to fly," the commander said as they both sat down. "Your passenger is due here at eighteen hundred, take off one hour later, ok?"

"Yes sir, that's fine."

"So how's things back in England? I ain't been there since forty two."

"Much the same sir, although Jerry doesn't come over very often anymore."

"Yep, you gave those smart assed Luftwaffe boys a bloody nose, were you in Spitfires?"

"Yes sir." Christian answered.

"You gotta try the Mustang, same Merlin engine, but a lot faster."

"Yes, so I've heard sir, perhaps I'll get a chance once this op's over."

"Right, your mission. I've got all the gen you need right here." The commander leaned over to collect some papers that he now put in front of the young pilot.

"I hope everything's there."

"Thank you sir." Christian said as he began to read the flight data.

General Popowski's car was ready on time. Popowski made his emotional farewell to his aide Thomas, promising he would do all he could to bring the Poles into action as an independent force as soon as he could get to England.

"Listen Thomas, we'll be reunited soon, In the meantime, you look after yourself, son."

"Thank you sir, you too," Thomas replied as the General got into the jeep. He watched as the jeep taking Popowski to the airfield disappeared from sight. For all his vainglory, Popowski was a dedicated professional soldier, a brilliant planner and overall a pretty good man. His heart was in the right place, even if at times his mouth wasn't. It would sure be quiet without the demanding American around. Thomas smiled at the thought, then made his way to the mess.

As Popowski drove through the valley past the great ordinance of war, his admiration for the brave Poles escalated. He knew the capability of these young men, knew given half a chance, they would prove themselves without any doubt on the field of battle. Popowski wished he could stay with the boys, lead them to Valhalla! But Ike needed him more, his destiny greater than the simple duty of command.

The stern Major was putting Gunther Schloss through his paces. Confident now some of the earlier arrogance had returned to the loyal German. Full of self-importance, compounded by the gravity of the role that had been bestowed upon him, he strutted about the confines of the room, his swagger exaggerated by the importance he now felt.

Duffy had also made his preparations for the journey, the uniform of a Major visible under the flight smock.

Commander O'Hare had formally introduced Christian to the nervously excited General. The formalities over, he had made his farewell to the huge Texan and the pretty WUSAAF girl, her smile conveying regret at the shortness of their acquaintance. Now with his passenger strapped in within the cabin of the aircraft, Christian increased the throttle allowing the Junkers to roll.

The sun, lower in the sky, forced the watching Americans to cover their eyes as the Junkers lifted slowly into the azure blue of the evening.

At fifteen hundred feet, Christian eased the nose of the aircraft into a gentle pitch, the ascent milder. The Junkers climbed to six thousand feet before levelling out.

Christian peered over his shoulder at the smiling general seated within the fuselage behind him, Popowski seemed happy and content. In a few minutes he would make the manoeuvre that would alter Major General Alexander Popowski's pre-conceived ideas of his destiny, irrevocably changed forever.

Corporal Riley, disturbed by his thirst, awoke in the cramped hide under the outcrop of rock on the valley side. The stiffness in his body forced him to stretch as best he could. Gingerly Riley peeled back the bushes that had obscured him from the sight of any overzealous patrols. Confident his enforced billet had not been discovered, he crawled out into the blue sunshine of the Italian sky.

As he crept stealthily towards the slight incline created by the rock outcrop, Riley's eyes fixed on the activity below. Unable to comprehend at first, Riley rubbed his eyes, desperately trying to awake his senses, what he saw made his heart soar.

There before him was a US Army Air Force base complete with personnel and hardware. Riley's heart soared. He had done it; somehow, after all the tortuous nights of evasion, he had stumbled through the lines. He was safe.

Instead of reacting to his heart's wishes, though, he listened to his mind's fears. Working with David Stirling's fledgling SAS in the Western Desert had taught Riley to re-evaluate all the circumstances. Something was wrong, his mind told him, luck was only a friend to good planning, and according to Riley's planning he was still some distance from the front line. Caution, the trademark of an operative working behind the lines, came to the fore. Regardless of what his heart wanted him to hear, caution and training would prevail. He was resigned to just wait and see just what would happen.

Christian cut the fuel to the number three engine on the starboard side of the aircraft. Within a couple of seconds the Junkers began to lurch to one side. General Popowski felt the sudden change in pitch, his hands going to the arm rests of his seat, gripping them tightly. He leaned against the pitch as if trying to compensate for the sudden adverse angle. His eyes wide, Popowski watched as the prop decreased in rotation, finally coming to a complete stop. He began to breath heavily, his voice praying to his God in an unfamiliar tongue. Polish!

"Are you ok back there, sir?" Christian responded in his native tongue also.

"What, what the hell happened?" Popowski now reverted to his more accustomed language.

"Problem with number three engine, she's feathered out…possible fuel starvation…maybe a blockage…" Christian shouted over his shoulder.

"What…what…are we going to do?" Popowski stuttered still gripped by fear.

"We'll be ok sir," Christian said in truth, "but we'd better turn back just in case…we can fly on two…but it's better to have all three props in order."

"Will we be ok?" Popowski answered in between the Hail Mary's he had been repeating under his breath.

"Fine sir." Christian replied over the noise of the two remaining engines. Easing the throttles to compensate, Christian had brought the aircraft back into a less drunken attitude. He could have brought the Junkers back to level flight but decided not too. The slight pitch angle with trim of drag and yaw would make the problem seem more realistic. Christian banked the now lumbering Junkers in a tight turn, making Popowski's hand grip all the tighter. His Hail Mary's were now audible.

"Do you want to come up front, sir?"

"No, no I'm fine here son, you just get this heap of shit back on terra firma."

Christian smiled to himself. "God help him if this was a Spit," he said quietly.

'Why are we flying in this Nazi crap anyway?' Popowski asked.

'We're going back the shortest route sir, right through enemy held territory.'

'But why?'

'Orders, sir!'

To all intents and purposes Christian was back on course for the base commanded by O'Hare. But there would be no O'Hare or pretty lieutenant to greet them when they touched down.

Confident that the General had no conception of his actual destination, Christian applied the flaps, using a couple of degrees heavy just for effect. The Junkers now began to loose height rapidly.

Corporal Riley heard the distorted sound of the rapidly descending Junkers. Down below him in the valley the airfield suddenly burst into life, Chevrolet fire tenders, and an ambulance in USAAF blue and several jeeps burst upon the fringes of the main runway. USAAF personal sprinted to their stations.

Instinctively, Riley's eyes went back to the sky. He could see it now, a Junkers 52 in full Luftwaffe livery. Its wings at an adverse angle, its nose depressed and its starboard engine lifeless.

Fascinated by the possibility of carnage to come, like passers by at an accident, Riley's eyes stayed glued to the trauma that was being enacted at two thousand feet. Questions flashed through his mind, his brain unable to answer the tirade of demands. What was a Junkers doing landing at a USAAF base? Was the pilot aware? Did he have a choice? Why had the US base not fired upon the Junkers? How come the accident vehicles had been scrambled so quickly? Almost ghoulishly, Riley watched the possible tragedy unfold.

Christian brought the machine down, 1,000, 800...500 feet. At the last possible moment, Christian brought her level, touching down in a perfect landing.

General Popowski sat glued to his seat, even when the aircraft came to a complete stop. His fingers still held firmly on the arm rests, the sweat caused by fear, tension and the muscular strain soaked his body, rivulets running down his temples.

Duffy had watched the whole drama from the window of the reception room located under the improvised tower.

"You bastard, Christian. The Yank must have prayed to every god in the universe," he said aloud. The huge grin spread right across his face. The emergency vehicles having found their services were not required, retired. In their place came two jeeps, a mechanic truck and a fuel truck.

Corporal Riley jumped up at the excitement caused by the drama, only the instinctive training born of hard lessons learnt with the SAS, stopping him from screeching out his compliments to the pilot. Now in complete control, he snaked closer to the unfolding scene, doubt and questions once again filling his mind.

"Are you ok, Sir?" Christian asked genuinely.

"I'm fine, son. You did a good job," the General said, the barometer of his fear having subsided to an almost acceptable level. "You did good, boy!" he continued, trying to make his knees accept the weight of his torso. "Will this heap of Bavarian shit be ok?" he asked.

"Yes sir, no problem...probably a bit of dirt in the fuel line...It must have been the downpour...she'll be fine I know it." Christian said confidently.

Riley was standing in his cover, now located much closer to the airfield, like a cinema go-er watching the climax of some popular movie, his concentration intensified, lest he miss something.

Out of the wounded Junkers appeared an American General in full regalia, followed closely by an RAF pilot. Their welcoming committee were two senior USAAF officers and two MPs, the latter's white helmets glistening in the fading light. The two jeeps carried the party, except for the pilot, to a building complete with an improvised honour guard, under the tower. The General and the two senior officers then went inside.

Riley, now almost certain he was on home ground, made to move when an alarm trigger when off in the recesses of his mind. Cautiously he remained.

The confidence of rank, and the mere presence of subordinates, filled General Popowski with importance, his earlier fears now dissipated as they now returned to normal. His grounding as an officer came to the fore. Purposefully he strode into the building, the swagger returning.

When he entered a small anti room, he stopped dead. The eyes wide with disbelief, the face drained of blood, the lips unable to mouth the words that would not come. Popowski was now in a frozen state, staring at the vision in front of him – there, like a mirror image, stood a complete reflection, an exact replica of himself.

"What the f...." He tried to say, his throat dry. His tongue obscuring sound.

"Major General Alexander Popowski, Let me introduce you to...Major General Alexander Popowski," smiled a fair-haired man in the uniform of Wehrmacht Major. "Or should I say..."

The replica saluted the General, and almost instinctively, Popowski went to return the salute stopping just short of his temple, his mouth aghast as if frozen in time. The replica staring back at him – a smile on his face – Popowski's face. Comprehension would not come, his mind raced, the reality of the horror was too much to be taken in.

"Or should I say," Continued the Major, "Herr Gunther Schloss."

Schloss smiled at the American, the deceit he decided complete.

"Well..." Continued the Major. "...Actually Gunther Popowski, your twin brother."

Both men shot a glance at Duffy, their eyes wide.

"Sorry Gunther....you didn't know?" Duffy grinned.

"It was Schloss' turn to look exasperated.

"W...What?" He mumbled in unison with his brother.

“Shit, you really didn’t know.” Duffy said in surprise.

“My God.” Schloss exclaimed. “But…but . . .”

“What the god damn hell is going on here?” screamed Popowski, regaining some composure.

“You, General, are a prisoner of the German Army, ” Duffy smiled, before his face grew serious once again. “Leutnant Shlitz.” he commanded.

Popowski’s eyes narrowed as he stared at the barrel of the Luger as it was held two inches in front of his eyes.

“Hands up,” screamed the officious Leutnant.

“You bastard,” Popowski spat at Duffy.

Duffy just grinned, removed the Luger from his holster, stared down Major General Popowski – the American, before pointing the Luger at Schloss, the barrel digging into the German’s side. “You, General Popowski, will now complete your mission. Move!” The force of the Luger barrel shoved Schloss into movement. As Duffy and the bewildered Schloss reached the door, Duffy turned and grinned once again. “Sorry to break up the family reunion boys.” Duffy prodded the silent Schloss again with the Luger as they made to leave.

“You bastard! As long as I live, I’m going to hound you, boy.” General Popowski screamed as the gun dug further into his forehead. The pain he felt from the pistol not registering – the pain he felt inside threatening to swamp him.

Christian greeted Schloss as he entered the aircraft.

“Everything’s ok now, General, strap yourself in, take off in about two…Sean! What the….” Christian gasped as he saw Duffy follow the General into the Junkers cabin.

“Hello Christian….Everything ready?” Duffy grinned.

“But…but…” Christian’s eyes went to the uniform, a German Major’s uniform, as he did so his eyes caught sight of the luger pointed at the ribs of Herr Schloss.

“What’s happening Sean…why are you here?” Christian demanded.

“Just to make sure your package gets delivered.” Duffy prodded Schloss again with the Luger. Schloss understood the reason for the prompt; silently he sat down in the seat that a few moments ago had held his brother. A brother he had never known, a brother he’d probably never see again. Once he was seated Schloss strapped himself in.

Christian’s mind was trying to understand just which side was Duffy on, as was Schloss. The German uniform, his presence here, but why? It came to him in a moment, Mosel! How else could Duffy know, he was working for Mosel! Christian felt sick. Duffy was supposed to be a friend. Christian’s face turned to one of hatred. Emily! Duffy had compromised Emily, she knew too much. Duffy could not leave Emily out of the equation. The sudden awareness filled Christian with anger; Duffy was going to kill Emily.

Duffy was ready for Christian’s reaction, he saw the fist clench, the eyes harden. Instantly the Luger was brought into the firing position, the barrel pointing directly at Christian’s eyes.

“You bastard,” Christian spat.

“Sit down and fly, Flight Lieutenant! Don’t accuse me, you self-righteous prick, you’re not exactly clean yourself.” Duffy’s voice was firm, threatening. Christian hesitated, taken back by the reality of the truth. The moment lost, he sat in the pilot’s seat, resigned to carry out his duty. He had no choice.

“Good thinking, Christian.” Duffy grinned, seeing the temporary retreat.

Christian started the engines, adjusted the mixture, this time to all three engines then began his taxi run.

Duffy quickly checked on Schloss, quietly he leaned towards Schloss' ear.

"Sorry about that Gunther, I hope you're ok? Sorry but it had to look realistic."

Still confused, but feeling slightly easier after Duffy's explanation, Schloss sat back in his seat ready for take off. Duffy scrambled to the cockpit in the shaking fuselage of the Junkers as it rolled down the runway at speed.

Corporal Riley watched as the Junkers took to the sky. Still hidden from sight, Riley was entertained to an exhibition of military precision accompanied by organised discipline. The airfield which a few moments before had resembled a front line US Base, was now returned to its former appearance. The dummy fighters were packed away, the pre-fabricated buildings, their frontage the only reality, disappeared. Like the closing down of a movie set, the whole deception was packed away.

Now more than ever, Riley knew he would have to make it back to his own lines, whatever had just happened, the High Command would have to know about it. Slowly, Riley crawled on his stomach back to his hide under the rock outcrop. He would wait until dark, then make the long night's journey. Each step would bring him closer to safety.

Christian took the Junkers up to eighteen thousand feet. His flight plan for the return trip taking him up the Western coast of Italy. Duffy sat appropriately, Christian decided, in the co-pilot's seat. The very one the traitorous Lucien had occupied. Duffy noticed Christian's stare, and somehow the putrid smell of the previous occupier of the seat came to his nostrils. Duffy swallowed hard, the simple action stemming the rise of nausea. He was still affected by the sensation of flying, which was now compounded by the nausea, as he sent the signal via the VHF radio set.

Mosel looked up as Steiner entered the room, his face bathed in a huge smile, the normal military etiquette absent.

"What is it, Hans?" Steiner asked.

"The message, sir, It's just come through. The Goose has flown." Steiner beamed as Mosel sat back in his chair, his finger tips together in prayer. He smiled.

"Good, Hans…very good."

One hour later Commander Peter Thompson RN received the same de-coded message.

CHAPTER 24

By the time Emily got home from work Cathy had also returned. Cathy put the kettle on for tea whilst Emily made her preparations for her work at the Plough that night. Once the bath had been poured Emily slipped beneath the water, its warmth bringing her release from the tiredness of the day.

Her thoughts were broken as Cathy brought the tea to her.

"Sorry Cathy, I was just dreaming." Emily said accepting the hot mug of tea.

"Only good things, I hope." Cathy asked.

"Yes…very good things Cathy" Emily sat up in the bath noticing the slight look of hurt appear on Cathy's face. "Sorry, Cathy." She apologised as sincerely as she could, ashamed of her selfishness. "How was your day," she asked brightly.
Cathy turned her eyes away.

"What is it, Cathy?" Emily asked softly.

"I…I…just picked up Freddie's things today." She said, her lip quivering.

Emily's hand came out of the water, its warm dampness touching Cathy's arm.

"I'm so sorry." Emily said, her voice compassionate.

"It's ok, Em. I'm fine now, look what I found." Cathy's face brightened bravely.

Her fingers going to her neck pulling out the gold heart shaped pendant from its hiding place under her sweater.

Emily stared in disbelief. "But…but."

"What is it, Em?" Cathy asked seeing Emily's reaction.

"Where did you get it?" Emily asked softly.

"It was in Freddie's things." Cathy replied. "He must have bought it especially for me."

"Yes, yes of course he did," Emily lied, knowing where and how it had come into Freddie's possession.

"Don't you like it?" Cathy asked, her newfound security fading.

"It's lovely Cathy…really lovely." Emily whispered.

Duffy reappeared in the cockpit, strapping himself back into the co-pilot's seat. He had been to see Herr Schloss in the cabin of the Junkers on one of his regular visits to the German. He had brought Schloss some hot coffee. Now seated again, he poured the mud coloured liquid into a mug and offered it to Christian.

"No thanks," Christian said curtly as the coffee was offered.

"Come on Christian…it won't harm you," Duffy grinned.

Christian took the drink, "what's going on, Sean?" he asked.

"It's best if you don't know everything at this stage, Christian. Just follow your orders. Your job is to get Schloss back to England, my job…" Duffy hesitated, "is to get both of you back."

"Whose side are you on?" Christian demanded.

"Mine," Duffy grinned.

"What about Emily?" Christian's mouth fumbled her name.

"What about her?" Duffy looked serious.

"Are…are you going to kill her?" Christian said tentatively.

"What?" It was Duffy's turn to look shocked. "I have no more intention to hurt Emily than I do to hurt myself. Jesus, what made you think that?"

"Well, she knows too much." Christian stammered.

"Emily knows about as much as you do. And that's not even the half of it," Duffy said almost sarcastically. "Emily's in no danger from me, Christian."

"Are you sure?" He asked.

"I'm sure," Duffy smiled. "Now, you just concentrate on getting this heap back to England. Where are we now, by the way?" Duffy asked.

"Just approaching the foothills of the Italian Alps." Christian answered.

"How's the fuel going?" Duffy looked pensive for a moment.

"Fine at the moment, should be ok."

"Good," Duffy said. "Let me know when we're over France, we need to make a little detour."

"Where?" Christian stared at Duffy.

"I'll let you know nearer the time," Duffy said.

Realising that was the end of the conversation as far as Duffy was concerned, Christian sipped the warm drink, his mind trying to fathom out exactly what Sean Duffy's role was in this whole nightmare.

Outwardly, Emily's appearance was bright and lovely, but inside her emotions were in turmoil. Missing Christian figured heavily in the tension she felt inside, the episode with Cathy and the pendant only compounded her troubles.

Although the pub was busy, it seemed empty without Christian and Sean. Where is Sean? Emily said to herself time and time again. Her eyes inadvertently stared at the clock as the hours passed. Something must be wrong, Emily thought, Duffy never missed their Friday nights together. Chief Inspector Tommy Boyle in his usual seat by the front door, had the same thoughts.

The weather deteriorated once the Junkers was over the Alps. The front promised for the day before now grew in strength bringing inclement weather to the whole of Western Europe. The weather didn't bother an experienced pilot like Christian Kawolski, but the rising head wind did. If it grew any more in intensity if would have serious effects on the Junkers fuel consumption.

As the weather deepened so did the tension in Sean Duffy. His hands now gripped the co-pilot's seat, his face was pale. Instinctively Duffy tightened the seat restraints, his head daring to occasionally look over his shoulder at the man in the uniform of a US General, seated unperturbed in the body of the Junkers.

"Is there any way we can avoid this lot?" Duffy asked hopefully.

"No, not really Sean, we are at maximum height, most of the worst weather is still just below us."

"What about trying to get below it?"

"Yes… that's if you fancy mountain hopping." Christian grinned.

"No thanks," Duffy replied trying to return the grin.

Christian looked at Duffy and saw the fear. Sean might have the gun, but up here he was in control.

Schloss seated within the belly of the Junkers concentrated his mind on the job to come. Thinking in an American voice helped Schloss in his preparations. His earlier confusion and discomfort had subsided, and now, in complete control of his faculties, he was determined to press ahead with his mission. His meeting with the American general he was now to impersonate, the shock of the statement regarding his links to the man had been filed away in the depths of his mind.

It was impossible, he told himself, his parents, his doting mother, somebody would have told him if it were true. No it was a ruse, a test, probably invented by Mosel to unbalance the American. After all Mosel could have used it to force him to comply with his plans, but that wasn't necessary since Schloss had virtually volunteered for such a mission. No…no when he looked at all the circumstances Schloss was convinced it was nothing more than a cruel joke. The real cruelty was that it was not a joke; Alexander Popowski was the elder brother of Gunther Schloss.

With the dark night still ahead of them, the three men in the Junkers concentrated their own thoughts as the aircraft fought its way through the deteriorating weather.

Surprised by Duffy's absence, and intrigued by the possible reason, Tommy Boyle left the Plough at the usual time, the slice of gammon that Mary had got for his supper now uppermost in his mind.

Cathy had promised Emily that she would come to be pub later on. Now, as the time passed, Emily became concerned for the girl's mental state.

The turbulence had increased in intensity and, like a stone skimmed across the surface of the water, the Junkers bounced violently against the gathering storm. Duffy said nothing. He didn't need to, his face, the strain of his arm muscles as he gripped his seat ever tighter, told the story of his fear.

Christian, unable to do anything about the comfort of the ride, concentrated on keeping the aircraft in trim, his eyes darting to the fuel gauge constantly. The veins bubbling to the surface on his arms and wrists, showing the firmness of his grip on the controls.

Captain Ernst Mosel stood facing the large map of Western Europe.

"Where are they now, Hans?" He asked the attentive Steiner who sat opposite the desk in Mosel's office.

"Nothing definite so far sir, but Luftwaffe control would put them about here." Steiner said as he stood up, pointing to a spot on the huge wall map.

"When will we be able to get a proper fix?"

"Not for some time sir, our radar is useless in this weather. Also we have been unable to put any fighter intercepts up for the same reason, sir."

"My God, Hans, after everything we've done…it would be a travesty if we should lose everything because of the weather."

The weather began to ease, the head wind dropped. According to Christian's calculations, he was somewhere just north of the town of St. Rochel on the coast of occupied France. He put the Junkers into a dive to lose height rapidly.

"What's happening?" Duffy said as he scrambled to the cockpit.

"I think we're over the water," Christian said calmly. "I need to take her down to get a reckoning."

Duffy sat in the co-pilot's seat strapped in tightly. He watched Christian as the pilot put the aircraft through its paces. His eyes concentrated, his hands only just touching the controls, feeling his way.

Duffy was impressed by the coolness of the pilot. Fascinated, he followed Christian's every movement especially the eyes which darted to and fro from the array of instruments. Duffy noticed the main concern that Christian had been the altimeter, which spun at an alarming rate anti-clockwise. As they lost height Christian eased the rate of descent almost levelling the aircraft.

At eighteen hundred feet they finally broke the cloud surface, there below them was the French coastline and the sea, only just visible. Christian levelled the aircraft, before banking slightly to a new course setting, then sitting easier in his seat.

"How long now?" Duffy asked.

"Not long, Sean, not long."

Duffy pleased that he could at least see something relaxed. He took out a map from the breast pocket of the tunic and spread it open.

"Right, Christian, I need you to drop me here for my little diversion." He pointed to the map.

"Why there?" Christian asked.

"That's where I'm getting off." Duffy grinned.

"I've got no co-ordinates for that Sean, at best it would only be guesswork. You could end up anywhere, the sea even."

"I'll trust you…you've done pretty well so far."

Christian looked at the map. "This things too big to put in a field." Christian said gazing directly at Duffy.

"You don't need to land, I'm going to jump," Duffy explained.

"What about him?" Christian said gesturing over his shoulder to the cabin where Schloss sat.

"You take him to wherever it is that you're supposed to take him," Duffy said.

"But I don't understand," Christian answered totally bewildered.

"You don't have to." Duffy stood up and returned to Herr Schloss seated in the cabin.

When Duffy returned to the cockpit he was dressed in the same clothes he'd had on when he met the submarine, only now a parachute smock and harness had been added to the outfit.

Worried by Cathy's non-appearance, Emily made short work of clearing up. Some regulars becoming upset by the uncharacteristic attitude displayed by Emily that night. Oblivious to their demands and protests Emily finally ushered the remaining hangars on out of the door.

"Blimey, that was quick." George, the landlord, said as he entered the bar.

"It's Cathy, George, she's all on her own." Emily said.

"Don't worry, I'll finish up. You get off home, Emily, there's a good girl."

"Thanks George you're an angel." Emily kissed him on the cheek.

Flattered, George watched the pretty young woman as she hurried out of the front door of the pub. If he was only twenty years younger . . . He thought to himself.

Emily almost ran the short distance up the hill to the flat. Taking the stairs two at a time, she reached her front door on the first floor of the semi detached house, opened the door and rushed in. The light in the sitting room was on, so was the wireless, but Cathy was nowhere to be seen. Hurriedly, she went to the bedroom, as she opened the door the light flooded into the room. There was Cathy, fast asleep, her blonde hair sprayed across the pillow.

Relieved and now feeling very tired Emily undressed and slipped into the sheets beside Cathy. As she did so Cathy's arm went around her shoulder, a little kiss, warm and sincere was planted gently on Emily's neck.

"Goodnight, Em." She said sleepily.

"Night, night, Cathy." Emily replied feeling the warmth of Cathy's body next to hers.

Sean Duffy, complete with parachute, stood next to Christian in the cockpit. His arm on Christian's shoulder, his eyes peering out of the canopy into the dark night.

"We're almost there." Christian said looking into Duffy's face, "you had better get ready, Sean."

"Thanks, Christian." Duffy said patting the pilot on the shoulder.

"Sean?"

"Not now, Christian." Duffy said. "One day I'll explain everything." With that, Duffy went to the fuselage of the aircraft; he wished Schloss good luck then opened the door of the Junkers.

The howl of the wind as the door was opened lasted a few seconds before it was closed firmly by Schloss. Duffy was gone into the black night.

Christian banked the aircraft, there below him, just barely visible in the improving light, were two parachutes. Instinctively he turned towards Schloss, but the German sat unperturbed in the cabin of the Junkers, still in the full regalia of an American General.

"What the hell…" Christian's mind began to race.

Relieved as the canopy blossomed above him, Duffy let out a huge breath. Gently he began to float earthwards towards the countryside. The other parachute spiralled towards the trees to Duffy's right. He watched as the chute disappeared into the woodland below him, a huge grin on his face.

The ground now rapidly came up to meet him. Preparing for the shock, Duffy bent his knees, his legs giving way, his body in a tight roll; he made a perfect landing. Quickly, he gathered in the parachute, folding it into a neat bundle by his feet. Once the air had been spilled, Duffy un-strapped himself, then checked his surroundings. All was quiet. Duffy took out a small shovel from his rucksack, carried the chute into a small wooded copse and buried it.

Once the chute had been concealed, Duffy squatted on the ground listening for any sounds. The only sound he heard was the crash of waves on the shore some distance away. 'Jesus, Christian, you're good,' he said quietly. 'Bang on target.' Hurriedly he left for his destination.

Duffy covered perhaps a mile before he came to the edge of the village. Skirting the main street, he entered the garden of a building. He passed through some trees and a wire fence. As he approached the building his eyes scanned the windows at the rear. Deciding he had located the correct one, Duffy picked up some small pebbles and threw them gently at the glass of the window.

When the third pebble had struck its target, Duffy saw the curtains move followed by the window being opened. The naked torso of a young woman leaned over the windowsill, her dark hair highlighting the creamy bare flesh of her body.

"Who is it?" The girl whispered in the darkness.

"Darling girl." Duffy whispered back.

"Sean, is that you?" Where have you been? What…."

"Mary just open the door, there's a good girl." Duffy grinned.

Mary giggled, "ok but keep quiet." Then her head disappeared back into the room.

Christian, realising that radar must have picked him up, made the transmission.

"Hello, this is Patriot two calling do you receive me, over?"

"Hello, Patriot, we receive you loud and clear, please identify, over."

Christian did as he was asked then asked to be patched through to Northolt.

"Hello Patriot, this is Northolt. Do you have your visitor, over?"

"Yes, visitor on board. Can you vector me in, over?"

"Hello patriot, no trouble." The voice cracked over the earpiece. Christian was given the correct co-ordinates ready for his approach.

Back at Northolt there was a frenzy of telephone calls. Commander Thompson received his, the phone on his bedside table disturbing his sleep.

"Sean, where have you been?" Mary asked as she silently closed the door to her bedroom in the upstairs of the inn located in the pretty countryside of Pembrokeshire.

"In purgatory, darling girl." Duffy whispered as he slipped the housecoat she had put on, gently over her shoulders. The temporary covering fell in a heap on the floor, exposing Mary's now totally naked body. Duffy's mouth went to the girl's neck, her fingers busily undoing the buttons on his trousers. Duffy led the girl to the warm waiting bed, as Mary turned her back towards him, Duffy smacked her exposed bottom firmly.

'Ouch!' Mary pouted, before her mouth spread into a delicious smile. Furiously Duffy shed the remainder of his clothes. Lying naked awaiting his body Mary giggled.

'Sean Duffy, you naughty man," she said as Duffy lowered himself to her.

'And you Mary darling are a very naughty girl…thank God!' He grinned.

Christian banked the Junkers in a tight turn as he passed the gasometer in Harrow, levelling her out as he made the final approach. His eyes shot a glance at the fuel gauge, each one showed empty, the needles not registering. As he began to lose height the port engine coughed then spluttered before coming to a complete stop. As Christian passed the hedge on the airfield perimeter the starboard engine also cut out. Gliding the aircraft in on one engine, the Junkers touched down safely. Gunther Schloss let out a sigh of relief.

An American Colonel seated next to Commander Thompson in the jeep, watched as the Junkers taxied to a stop along with the others in the little convoy. The vehicles had made their way to the standing area in front of the huge hangars. Patiently they waited for the General to appear.

"Thank you son," Schloss said in a perfect American accent. "You did a fine job."

Christian stared at the man, now completely in character.

"Good luck."

"General, sir, welcome to England." The Colonel said as he saluted sharply. "We have a car waiting to take you to Ike's headquarters." Pointing to the saloon that had arrived dead on time.

"Thank you, Colonel." Schloss said. "It's sure good to be back in England."

"Sir, may I introduce Commander Thompson, British Naval Intelligence," the Colonel said gesturing towards Thompson.

"Pleased to meet you sir." Thompson said shaking the General's outstretched hand, his eyes studying closely the General's reaction.

"Good to meet you Peter, I've heard a lot about you." The general smiled.

"Sir, if I may," the Colonel pointed towards the waiting car.

"Certainly son," The General moved towards the car then hesitated before he got in turning to face Thompson. "Hope to see you soon, Commander Thompson." He said, before getting into the waiting car, assisted by the nervous Colonel.

Thompson smiled, "I'll look forward to it, General."

The car pulled away leaving Thompson with his thoughts.

"Cocky bastard wasn't he, sir?" Harry Milburn said.

He's a general, what do you expect, Harry," Thompson smiled.

CHAPTER 25

Duffy slipped out of the young barmaid's room at first light; silently he left the grounds of the inn via the garden. It was chilly; a fresh sea wind had picked up, forcing Duffy to walk quickly to keep warm. It took him forty minutes to reach the beach hut where the bike had been concealed.

He changed in the hut, placed his other clothes into the rucksack, then hauled the bike across the sands, leaving the hut once again padlocked. When he reached firm ground Duffy mounted the bike, kicked it into life and started the long journey back to Ruislip.

Mary snaked her arm out of the covers instinctively looking for Duffy's body from her half sleep. When she found no response her eyes opened fully. The space in which Duffy had occupied was again empty. She sat bolt upright, a sulky pout on her mouth. "The bastard's done it again!"

Mary thought about the night before, the unexpected arrival of Duffy, their passionate love making, and a smile spread across her face. "Cheeky sod," she said aloud, as she dived beneath the covers again. The warmth invigorating her senses. With the smile still on her lips she drifted back into warm sleep.

Duffy gunned the motorbike through the lanes until he reached the A477. Confident that no police would be active at this hour of the morning, he opened the throttle, speeding away from the sleepy hamlet and the pretty young barmaid. He wanted to put as much distance between him and the drop zone. If he were lucky he would be half way home before anyone discovered the body of the parachutist, dressed in the uniform of a Wehrmacht Major. That would be the time that Sean Duffy would disappear.

Christian, totally exhausted by the trial of the last few days, went through the motion of the debrief with his CO. Satisfied on the basics, the CO had allowed Christian to get some much needed sleep. The full written account of his operation could be submitted the following day, just prior to his official debrief from the intelligence services. Christian knew only too well what that would involve, another patronising meeting with Commander Thompson.

Sleep came easy to Christian the sheer physical and mental stress of the operation had used what surplus energy that may have existed. Once in his bunk sleep came instantly.

General Popowski had been whisked away to a comfortable billet at Eisenhower's HQ. Later that morning he would be driven to Patton's headquarters at F.U.S.A.G. where he would meet Patton together with Montgomery and Bedell Smith. Confident in his own ability to fulfil the role he'd been asked to play, Gunther Schloss slept peacefully. So good had been the preparations Mosel had enforced, Gunther Schloss dreamed that night in American English.

Once through Carmarthen Duffy took the A40 stopping at Llandoveny on the Northern perimeter of the Brecon Beacons for some much needed sustenance.

He ate a hearty breakfast washed down with a steaming mug of tea at a small roadside café, his reception more cordial than his previous visit to the area.

The General was woken by a Captain that morning. His breakfast brought on a tray to his bedside, fresh orange juice, ham and eggs and real coffee.

"Good morning General, I'm Captain Johannes Petrovski, or Jonas as most people call me." The Captain said with a huge smile, borne out of years growing up in the laid back Californian sun. "I'm your aide whilst you are here in England."

The General noticed the Californian accent in the young blonde Captain's voice.

"Where you from son?" He enquired.

"San Luis Obispo, sir."

"Your surname's Polish, though."

"Yes sir, my gran daddy was from the old country."

"Do you speak Polish?" the General asked a warm smile on his face.

"Only a little sir," the Captain responded looking slightly downcast for the first time. "Not much call for it in L.A. sir." He mumbled almost apologetically.

"Good," The General replied, "Then we can talk in English, now what are the plans for my day, Jonas?" He smiled.

Upon the recognition of his nick name the young Captain beamed a huge sunshine smile. "Well, sir. . ." he said confidently as he began to inform the general of his itinerary for that day.

At nine o'clock that Saturday morning, Mrs Constance Williams, a retired schoolteacher, was walking her dog Scruffy in the woods between the hamlets of Jamestone and Lamphey.

The dog ran into a clump of trees, Mrs Williams called several times for the dog to come to heel, however, the little mongrel refused to answer to her calls. Annoyed by the dog's disobedience she began to walk through the trees following the excited barking of the dog. As she came to a small clearing, there under a huge elm tree sat the barking dog, his tail wagging in frenzy.

"Scruffy, you naughty boy, come here." She commanded as she strode towards the dog. "Come here, you bad boy." Mrs Williams scolded as she picked up the lead still trailing from Scruffy's collar. As she tried to walk away the dog pulled on the lead still barking furiously. Instinctively her eyes followed the dog's line of sight.

A cold shiver ran down her spine, she sensed something hanging above her head, slowly her eyes came upwards. There, hanging a few feet above her head was the lifeless body of a parachutist, straddled on the branches of the elm, his boots swaying gently in the onshore breeze.

A shrieking scream came from her mouth…

Two farmers on a horse and cart heard the scream as they passed the copse. Dismounting the farm vehicle they rushed to the scene finding Mrs Williams crumpled on the woodland floor, the barking dog, and the lifeless body of the parachutist.

By the time the body had been discovered by Mrs Williams, Duffy was approaching the urban sprawl of Gloucester. Refreshed by the breakfast he was making good time; with a clear road he should be back in Ruislip by eleven.

It took half an hour for the police to turn up at the now crowded scene in the small copse. Several locals, the two farmers, two constables and the whole platoon of the local home guard were there. A WVS volunteer and two boy scouts handed mugs of tea to the gathering melee. A reporter from the local weekly paper was interviewing Mrs Williams, now fully compos mentis after her fainting spell. The senior policeman on the scene had discussed the formalities of the discovery with the Captain of the Home Guard, a retired counsellor, and both had decided to bring the Army into the equation.

Eisenhower had made his apologies to the General via one of his many aides. The Supreme Commander having been summoned to Whitehall was unable to greet the new arrival to the planning committee personally. Unperturbed, the General had made his way to the waiting car, which now took him and his new aide Captain Jonas Petrovski, on the long journey to F.U.S.A.G. HQ in England's East Anglia.

Schloss, confident in his role as the American General, chatted busily to the young Captain, the torturous sessions with the brutal sergeant at Mosel's head quarters in Berlin was paying dividends.

On the journey the General was genuinely impressed with the mass of ordnance that headed towards the coastal areas of this irrelevant little island as Goering had called it. The whole of England seemed to be one enormous army camp. A fortress within a fortress, Schloss thought to himself.

When he arrived at Patton's headquarters the sheer scale of the enterprise engulfed him. Thousands of tanks, artillery pieces, aircraft and all the other vehicles of destruction filled every field. For ten miles he saw nothing but the military might of a determined British force, swamped by an American army fortified by the industrial might of the largest economy the world had seen. How could Germany possibly withstand the onslaught that surely would come, he reflected quietly to himself.

As the car drew up to the main carriage drive of the secluded country house the General turned to face the aide Jonas, who sat next to him.

"God," he said, looking dumbfounded, "I didn't realise we had so much…is this it all?"

"No sir, the whole of East Anglia, Essex, the Thames estuary and the south coast of England is just like this, and more arrives every day. We could put two million men into Europe in a single push," Jonas said excitedly.

"Jesus, the Germans don't stand a chance," the General gasped.

"By the time the balloon goes up, sir, we'll probably have half as much again."

The General sat back in the deep leather upholstery of the car, if only the German people knew, he mumbled.

"What was that, sir?" Jonas looked at the old man; saw the graveness on his face.

"Nothing…nothing Jonas, just a thought."

When the car stopped outside the main entrance to the house, two MPs showed him up the steps into the main lobby of the house. Dark ancestral faces stared back at the General as he mounted the huge stairs, every painting telling a history of the grand house. He was shown into a huge room, probably a ballroom due to its size. He counted eight chandeliers flooding the walls with light, a huge table with maps spread across it. Two others the size of billiard tables with miniature models of areas of the French coastline stood to one side of the room.

To the other side of the room stood a party of officers, all Generals, drinking coffee and smoking huge American cigars. About ten paces away stood Monty talking to Bedell Smith as far from the tobacco smoke as he could get in the crowded room. The General, overcome by the mass of military genius contained within the single room, could find no words to explain his feelings; virtually the whole of Allied Command was present.

Montgomery looking over the top of his teacup saw the General's entrance.

"General Popowski, so good of you to come," he said gracefully, extending his hand.

"Of course you know Bedell," Monty said nodding in the American's direction.

"Yes sir, of course." The General took Bedell Smith's hand.

"General Popowski," Bedell acknowledged.

The general was introduced to all the other members of the elite group. General Omar Bradley was in discussion with Air Vice Marshals Tedder and Harris. They all smiled at the General before turning once again to their private conversation.

"General Patton will see you now, sir." Jonas interrupted.

"Yes, yes of course, excuse me gentlemen for the moment."

"Listen, Popeye." Monty said casually, "I'd like to get your opinion on one or two things. Perhaps you and I could have a little chat when you finish with Patton."

"Yes sir," the General smiled nervously. "As soon as I've seen Patton." The mention of his name alone brought an uncontrollable shiver to his knees.

"Are you alright, old boy?" Monty squinted at him.

"Yes sir, probably the journey, the flight, I'll be ok in a minute," He lied.

He was shown to a large purposeful room, dotted with maps, the aide announced him.

"General Popowski, sir."

"General, so good to see you." Patton smiled, standing up to greet him, the huge hand extended in a greeting. "That will be all, Frank."

"Yes sir." The aide answered closing the door behind him.

Once he had gone Patton grinned at the General, exposing the wide set of dentures.

"Popeye, how you doing?"

"I'm fine thanks, George." The General said taking in the importance of the room. "Boy you sure came up in the world since North Africa."

"Yep, top of the tree for a fighting man, not bad for an ex cavalry officer."

"That lot outside," the General nodded over his shoulder, "they all under you?"

Patton looked beyond Popowski to the door. "All except Bedell, yes, you could say that, although Monty reckons he's still running the show." Patton sat back in his chair, his eyes examining the General. "So how do you like England?"

"I'm impressed with what I've seen so far, it's a lot better than forty two."

"I love this place, but don't tell those guys out there," Patton grinned again. "So much history, this crummy little island just reeks of battles." Patton again scrutinised the man in front of him.

"Is there something wrong?" The General asked.

"No, it's just...you lost a lotta weight, Popeye."

"Limey rations," The general smiled.

"Yes, of course," Patton grinned.

The General leant forward.

"So come on George tell me what its all about?"

"The invasion – I've got a part for you and your boys, not the main show...." Patton hesitated to watch the reaction, he could see the earlier expectancy drop.

"....but it's important, and it's a fighting role."

The Generals eyes looked up, "So what is it?" He said looking happier at the mention of a fighting role.

Patton stood, then went to a set of curtains that hung on a plain wall. He pulled the cord to open them, like a dignitary at the opening of a new hospital wing, or a department store. "This," Patton said pointing to the huge map of the area around the Pas de Calais – "Operation Plantagenet. The second front, the invasion of occupied Europe."

The General stood up in amazement; there in front of him was the plan of attack, for the greatest amphibian assault in the history of warfare.

"Four parachute armies," Patton continued, pointing to the map with a billiard cue, "Will land here, here and here." He pointed to each location, tapping the map with the chalk end of the cue before continuing. "The four American beachheads are here. Sherman, Grant, Lee and Stonewall." Patton paused for effect. "The British here, Marlborough, Gordon, The Canadians here at Wolfe."

"Wow, that's impressive George, where do I go in?" the General asked moving closer to Patton.

"The problem we have, Popeye, is all the German armour is placed around here." Patton pointed out the area on the map. "It looks like Von Rundstedt knows we're coming...we need to make him move all of his armour out of the area. Fool him into thinking we're going in somewhere else..." Patton looked directly into his eyes, Schloss could feel the burning stare, it only lasted for a second before the grin returned to Patton's face. "A classic feint, Popeye."

"Where?" The General asked.

Patton moved to another map showing the whole coastline of France. "Here." He pointed. "The bay of the Seine."

"Looks plausible." The General said, "But where exactly?" He asked.

"That's what you're here for General." Patton said, "you were the best Staffer we had, are you still up to it?" Patton almost demanded.

"Yes, sir." Schloss answered as a funny thought, ridiculous as it was real, came into his mind: here he was another ex corporal being asked to change the face of Europe.

Duffy arrived back at the bungalow he rented in Ickenham just before midday. Silently he crept into the building, collected a few clothes then left quietly over the back garden fence, heading to where he had parked the bike a couple of streets away. Carefully he checked to see if he had been followed, satisfied all was well he kicked the bike into action.

Duffy booked into the Bull Hotel in Denham using the name Michael Reilly, paying in cash.

Gunther Schloss spent the whole of the afternoon in the company of the bombastic Patton. Moments of nervous tension regarding the correctness of his performance were interspersed with the pleasure he felt at being able to fool the General about his real identity and purpose. By the time he left Patton's office, Gunther Schloss, now every bit General Alexander Popowski, felt weary, but elated. Now if he could convince Monty with his performance, then he would be home and dry.

Christian followed the CO into the briefing room at RAF Northolt. Commander Thompson was already there, seated behind the desk like a head master, once again playing the role of judge, jury and executioner.

"Good afternoon, Flight Lieutenant, please be seated." Thompson said not looking up. In front of him Christian could see the report he had given to the CO an hour earlier. Christian sat down.

When Thompson had finished reading the report, he looked at Christian, his eyes searching for any uncertainty. Christian returned an innocent Look, not allowing Thompson to see the emotions that spiralled from the depth of his stomach.

"Seems fairly routine," Thompson said sitting back in the chair, his fingers flicking the cover of the folder that held his report shut. "Anything else to add?"

"No sir, that's it. Fairly routine, as you said."

Thompson was about to say something when almost on cue, Harry Milburn entered the room. Thompson saw the look on Harry's face and sat forward. Harry went right to Thompson's side, leant over and whispered something in Thompson's ear. Christian watched as the confidence Thompson had shown just a few moments ago began to fade from his face.

"That will be all, Flight Lieutenant," Thompson said pushing Christian's report to one side.

Christian stood to leave, not wishing to stay any longer than necessary.

"Sean Duffy."

Christian turned, the turmoil returning to his stomach. "What about him?"

"He's a friend of yours?" Thompson's stare was hard.

"Not really, he's a friend of my..young lady…a girl I've been seeing…why?"

"He's been found dead, killed apparently in a parachute drop…dressed in the uniform of a German Major." Thompson emphasised the last point, his voice almost an accusation. Christian stared in disbelief, his face betraying the true nature of his friendship, his association by guilt.

"But…but how?" Christian stammered.

"We don't know the exact reasoning just yet…but we will find out. That's all, Flight Lieutenant."

When Christian made it to the fresh air, he lit a cigarette. The lighter shaking uncontrollably in his hand. Christian's feeling of remorse was halted by a memory of the night. Two parachutes. He pulled hard, the need for nicotine reducing the Players into a stub in no time. He ground the butt into the tarmac; still confused he made his way back to his quarters.

Thompson's matter of fact declaration regarding Duffy's demise upset Christian; he did not see Yvette as she entered the building he had just left.

Thompson was sitting side on to Harry Milburn, the two men talking quietly together as Yvette entered the briefing room. The CO nodding in her direction as he passed her in the doorway. Thompson looked up.

"Yvette, please take a seat." He said pointing to the chair in front of the desk, as he turned to face her.

"Harry." Yvette said as she sat down.

"Yvette." Harry smiled, as he also turned to face her, his eyes betraying the reason for Yvette's presence, the sadness informing her of bad tidings to come.

Swallowing hard, Yvette spoke.

"Commander?"

"Thanks for coming…how are you feeling? Everything ok?" Thompson asked pleasantly.

"Fine sir, although I have a feeling you haven't asked me here to check on my general well-being," Yvette said bravely.

Thompson smiled, hesitated to speak then sat forward in his chair.

"Yes of course, very perceptive of you, you're right…I've got something for you."

Yvette's heart sank. Her fingers began to nervously play with her skirt.

"A job, Yvette," Thompson said finally.

"But I've only just got back," Yvette mumbled, her eyes filling with tears.

"Yes, I know." Thompson said sincerely, "but its of the utmost importance, I wouldn't have called you here today unless I had an overriding confidence in your ability."

"Can somebody else do it?"

"No, Yvette, I'm afraid I couldn't trust anybody else with this one."

Yvette sat upright, her arms folded in defiance, the simple act not to show fortitude but to control the trembling fear that invaded her whole body.

"What is it?"

"France again, not Rennes, but the Pas de Calais. Back with your own circuit."

Thompson paused to see the reaction, there was none. Continuing, he said. "The information you overheard from the conversation between Mosel and Rommel about Normandy…"

"What about it?"

"Well the General Staff think it's important, and so does Winston."

"The Prime Minister?"

"Yes, well the short of it is, we are going in through Normandy as planned, however, its been scaled down." Yvette looked up at the news. "It will now be a feint, a ruse to make Von Rundstedt and Rommel move their armour south."

"So where will the main action take place?"

"The Pas de Calais," Thompson confirmed.

"But that's madness," Yvette exclaimed. "They won't fall for it."

"We believe they will, we have something on the burner…we're convinced the Germans, when…" He hesitated again. "When they discover the information we've planted, will react accordingly."

Yvette tried to take it all in, it was incredible. "When do I have to…"?

"This week," Thompson said firmly.

"But…but it's so soon," Yvette mumbled.

"The sooner the better, Yvette." Thompson's smile disguised the betrayal he was planning. It was now his turn to feel the nausea.

Yvette tried to make it back to her quarters, still feeling unsteady on her feet. Her body was not responding, while her mind filled her head with thoughts of impending gloom. Her eyes wet with tears, she staggered against the side wall of one of the outbuildings and lit a cigarette, letting her body slide down the brick surface until she sat propped up against the structure. With her elbows on her knees, her head sank between them and, dropping the cigarette, Yvette began to sob openly. The grey smoke from the burning butt wafting into the cool breeze.

General Popowski had met again with Montgomery, but this time the conversation was longer, more in depth. If anybody could see through the charade Schloss was acting out, then it would be Montgomery; he had known Popowski better than anybody else. Monty had queried one or two of the General's replies, but he seemed unperturbed, putting the slight mistakes down to the tiredness the General must have felt after the long journey. By the time he was shown to his temporary quarters in the north wing of the great house, Gunther Schloss was a nervous wreck.

Christian had been excused of all duties by the CO, so he collected his twenty four hour pass from the adjutant's office before making his way to Emily's house, the thoughts as to Duffy's possible demise still bouncing awkwardly within the confines of his mind. Whatever the situation, he was determined not to say anything to Emily, at least until he was sure of the answer. Anyway, he needed all her attention now. Feeling guilty about his selfishness Christian gunned the Morris towards Ruislip.

When Emily opened the door and saw Christian there she almost jumped for joy, her tummy full of butterflies. She grabbed his neck with both arms, the mouths meeting in an avalanche of kisses.

"Oh, Christian, it's so good to see you." She beamed.

Christian placed his hands on her bottom before his arms lifted Emily up, she giggled as she planted several kisses on his neck. Christian started to carry her towards the bedroom door.

"Where do you think you're going, you naughty man?" She giggled.

"Where do you think?" Christian replied.

"No, no we can't." Emily said suddenly.

Christian pulled his head back to look at her. "Why?"

"Cathy's still here." Emily whispered.

"Oh, I forgot," Christian put her down, and as he did so Emily took his hand and led him into the sitting room.

"Hi." Christian said to Cathy who was sitting on the sofa reading a magazine.

"Hi Christian."

"How are you feeling, Cathy?" He said as Emily went to put the kettle on.

"A lot better thanks." Cathy almost whispered turning her head away slightly so as not to show the depth of her jealousy now that Emily's man had returned, safe and well.

Christian's further attempts at conversation fell flat; an embarrassing silence pervaded the room. Neither Christian nor Cathy daring to speak, in case the emotions ran over.

Fortunately Emily broke the silence.

"Who's for tea?" She asked innocent of the silence that had developed.

"Not for me thanks, Emily," Cathy said closing the magazine. "I think I'll just pop into Ruislip, do a bit of shopping."

"Wait, Cathy. Christian and I can come with you."

"No, it's ok, Emily, you two have got a lot of catching up to do, anyway," she said confident now. "I need to walk, it will do me good."

Emily put her finger under Cathy's chin lifting it to look into her eyes.

"Are you sure Cathy?"

"Yes, yes," Cathy said turning her head slightly away, "I'll be fine…promise."

She smiled bravely.

Cathy left Christian cuddled up to Emily.

"Do you think she'll be alright?" Emily asked, ignoring the kisses Christian was putting on her neck.

"She'll be fine," Christian said softly as he started to nibble Emily's ear.

"I hope so." Emily said thoughtfully.

Christian pulled his head from her ear to look at her; he smiled, stood up and took Emily by the hand, leading her silently to the bedroom.

Frankie Cavenaugh could not believe his eyes, on the late news section of the Saturday Evening newspaper, he read the snippet of late news regarding the discovery of the body of a parachutist in Pembrokeshire.

"My God," he exclaimed. There in black and white was the name – Sean Duffy. An evil grin spread across Cavenaugh's face.

When they had finished their lovemaking, Christian lay on his back smoking. Emily, her face on his chest, her fingers playing with the blond hair surrounding his nipple.

Christian drew heavily on the cigarette, blowing out the smoke in an exaggerated fashion. Emily lifted her head, her eyes now on his.

"What's wrong, Christian?" She whispered.

"Nothing, Em. Honest,"

"Come on Christian....talk to me," she asked firmly.

Christian took a huge draw on the Players before answering.

"It's Monica and the girls."

"Oh," Emily said softly.

"It's the Germans, they've taken them hostage." Christian stumbled.

"Oh, Christian, I'm so sorry." Emily said, feeling guilty over her jealousness.

She took his face in her hands and kissed him gently, before lowering his head to nestle between her breasts, stroking his hair, like a mother comforting a child. Christian began to cry softly, the tears running down the swell of her chest.

"It's ok, darling." She comforted him, her hand still stroking his hair, her grip firmer now.

When Cathy returned about two hours later she noticed the upstairs curtains to Emily's bedroom were closed. Silently she opened the door, and as she closed it gently, she noticed a note on the mat by the door. Bending down, Cathy picked up the note and read it.

Sorry to hear about Freddie,

Meet me at the Barn Hotel, Room Sixteen at ten o'clock.

I will explain later, Love Sean.

Cathy read the note again, at first she thought of dismissing it, then she read it for the third time. It obviously wasn't meant for Emily, she was still asleep in her bedroom with Christian, and anyway, Christian's old Morris van was parked outside. Perhaps, she thought, it was for her. Cathy remembered the day in Runnymede by the river, their embarrassment at the affection they both felt, the obvious connection.

'What the hell', Cathy thought. Even if Duffy only wanted her body, it would be good to hold a man again, and the thought of Sean did not offend her, even if it was a bit sudden, a bit close to the loss of Freddie. Cathy shrugged her shoulders, looked at the closed door to Emily's bedroom and decided.

Quietly she bathed, put on a cream frock, adjusted her best silk stockings, then fastened the pretty gold heart shaped pendant on her neck. A spray of Emily's honeysuckle in her hair, a last glance at the mirror, then she left silently closing the door behind her. In her pocket was the note she had found on the mat.

Gunther Schloss had to perform his charade yet again that evening. Now that the matinee had gone reasonably smoothly, he prepared, like the actor he was, or had become, for the opening night's performance.

Although the conversation, once they were all seated at the dinner table hosted by Patton, was on a more personal note, the questions still came at him thick and fast. Only Montgomery, seated next to him, continued to speak of military matters. His concerns were mainly directed at Schloss, as to the ability of Patton to lead such a momentous task as the invasion of Europe. Within earshot of some of the Americans' most senior high command, Schloss deflected Monty's claims diplomatically, much to the amusement of Bedell Smith who sat opposite. The only problem Schloss felt was the constant stare of Patton from the head of the table.

Mosel read the report from one of the agents he had secreted close to the area of Patton's F.U.S.A.G. command.

The whole of the allied command, except for Eisenhower, was present at the dinner. The various command cars having been noticed as they filed through the outer security ring, some ten miles away from the actual dinner table. Eisenhower apparently was suffering a cold brought on by the ever-changing British weather. Confidently Mosel smiled to himself, the goose was soon to lay the Golden Egg.

Mosel looked up as Steiner entered the room.

"Good news from our agent in Norfolk," he smiled. "The Goose is in, Hans, dining with all the hierarchy at the farm."

"Yes, good news," Steiner said hesitating.

"What is it, Hans?" Mosel noticed the look in the young Leutnant's eyes.

"A copy of the London Evening News, sir." Steiner held the flimsy message in his hand; nervously he put it in front of Mosel. "It's Duffy, sir, seems his parachute…"

Mosel read the report. "My God, Hans," he said quietly. Mosel sat motionless for a minute or so, Steiner hovering over his desk, not daring to speak. Mosel sat upright; he pushed the flimsy to one side. "No matter, Hans," he said at last breaking the prolonged silence. "His job has been done."

"But sir, how will we know when the goose is ready to fly?"

"Kawolski, Hans…We have his family remember…Duffy, sharing the flight back with him….I'm sure Major Duffy would have spoken of such an eventuality…I'm sure." Mosel said, not believing a word of it.

When Christian and Emily awoke from their slumber, they were astonished to find no sign of Cathy. At first Emily was upset, the lack of bath water and the smell of honeysuckle made her realise that Cathy must have returned while they slept. Probably embarrassed by Emily and Christian's use of the bedroom, she had slipped out for the evening, maybe going to the mess at Northolt. But as the evening wore on, Emily became more and more unsettled by Cathy's absence.

Cathy had indeed gone back to the base. Doubt over her planned liaison had forced her to stop at Northolt to gain Dutch courage. The three gin and tonics she had consumed in the mess gave her the courage to pursue the secret meeting.

Slightly tipsy, she took the keys to Freddie's roadster. Driving less than proficiently, she pushed the sports car towards Ruislip and the Barn Hotel next to the station.

Cavenaugh was sitting in the back room of the public house in Hanwell when the door opened about a foot, the fat neck of Porrick leaning through the gap.

"Did you do as I said, Porrick?" Cavenaugh asked.

"Yes Mr Cavenaugh, sir," replied the gorilla.

"Good man, Porrick, have a pint on the house."

"Thanks Mr Cavenaugh."

As his man closed the door to fetch his humble pint, Cavenaugh sat back in his chair and grinned.

Duffy awoke with a start in the blackness of the hotel room. The lack of sleep over the last few days, had led him to be unsettled, his normal alertness had deserted him. Almost in a panic, he washed and shaved, time was critical. The paranoia at his lack of steadfastness ground away deep inside the pit of his stomach.

As Cathy parked the car the earlier bravado, fortified by the need for closeness, and the large dose of alcohol, drained away. Hesitatingly she hovered in the car park. Her needs as a woman prevailed, adjusting her dress; she strode purposefully into the reception of the quaint little hotel.

Gunther Schloss, in his role as General Popowski, made his apologies for his early retirement that evening. Having stayed courteously answering questions over after dinner drinks; he now made his way to the sanctuary of his quarters. Un-surprised by his early retirement, the gathering at Allied High Command F.U.S.A.G accepted his rationale. "The man must be dead on his feet," remarked one staffer to another. Patton on the other hand was more concerned by Popowski's departure, not because of the charade he had enacted, but more to the point, what Monty had said to him.

Once in the room, Schloss took off his dinner jacket, loosened his tie, and thanked his God for the bravery, the fortitude he had shown that day. Consumed by tiredness he undressed fully, slipping into the bed sheets in the pyjamas provided, complete with his rank embroidered onto the sleeves, and drifted into contented sleep.

After the spiritual uplifting of another gin and tonic, Cathy made her way to room sixteen. She knocked on the door, her arm supporting her as she leant against the door surround, but she received no response. Gently she turned the handle, the door gave way. Slowly she entered the well-lit room. By the bedside table was a plate of fresh sandwiches, in an ice bucket was a bottle of reasonable white wine.

Staggering now in an ungainly fashion, Cathy approached the bed. On the pillow was a small hand written note. "Have been delayed, love Sean,"

"Bastard," she said aloud. "Oh what the hell." Cathy picked up the bottle of wine and poured herself a drink.

Thirty minutes and half a bottle of wine later, Cathy stood unsteadily, walked towards the door, and switched off the light. Stumbling back to the bed, she fell, turning as she did so to lie flat out on the covers, the gold pendant glinting in the half-light, as she collapsed into alcohol induced sleep.

Emily was worried, it was past midnight, still there was no sign of Cathy. Distraught she begged Christian to look for her.

"She's probably at the base."

"Christian, you'll have to drive there," Emily said. "I'll stay here just in case she turns up."

"Alright Em, I'll go, but I bet she's safe and sound, she's probably had a couple of drinks and crashed out."

"Oh, I hope so, I couldn't bear it if something's happened to her." Emily whispered her face mixed with sadness and fear.

Christian held her tightly, then kissed her gently on the forehead, he turned to leave. "Don't worry, I'll find her."

Christian drove the Morris to the base, his eyes watching the pavements for any sign of Cathy. When he arrived at the base, he went straight to the mess. A few stragglers were still at the bar, their playful antics frustrating the steward who was trying to close up. Christian saw Faye Williams, a WAAF friend of Cathy's, sitting at a table in the corner talking to a young pilot officer. He strode towards her, and as he approached Faye looked up, smiling at him.

"Christian, Hi." she said, but when she saw the look on his face the smile disappeared.

"What is it?" She asked.

"Hi, Faye, have you seen Cathy tonight?" Christian asked pensively.

"No but somebody said she was in earlier. She had a few drinks and left."

"You don't know where she went?"

"No but the steward might know, is everything alright, Christian?"

"I hope so, Faye, thanks."

Christian went to the bar to talk to the steward. Faye sat silently for a while, Christian's words had alarmed her. The young pilot officer saw her reaction, and put his hand on hers, She smiled at him, then turned her attention back to Christian who was now talking to the steward.

"Yes, she was in earlier sir. Had a couple of gin and tonics then left at about ten thirty."

"Do you know where she went, did she leave alone?"

"I think she must have been meeting somebody." The steward said as he polished a glass. "She was dressed up, as if she was going to a party or something, but she left alone."

"What makes you think she was meeting somebody?"

"She kept looking at her watch as if waiting and she was all dressed up as I said, sir."

"Thanks, steward." Christian said, his mind racing now. Who would Cathy have been meeting? He kept asking himself. Christian turned to face the steward again. "Did she order a cab?"

"No sir, she had some keys with her, I think.."

"Car keys?"

"Yes sir, I think so." The steward stopped polishing the glass.

"Freddie's car." Christian said aloud. He almost ran to the car park, where Freddie's roadster was always parked, it was gone.

Room sixteen at the Barn Hotel was in a block away from the main building. Silently the man in the dark coat approached the door from the first floor landing. Gently he turned the handle, and the door opened in a silent arc. On the bed stretched out lay the fully clothed body of a young blonde woman. The man stepped inside then shut the door quietly behind him. He stood for a moment allowing his eyes to adjust to the sudden darkness, before approaching the bed.

Cathy sensed the figure as it approached, her head still thick with the alcohol. Slowly she opened her eyes, turning her head as she did so towards the door, the gold shaped pendant illuminated around her neck.

"Sean, is that you?" She mumbled half asleep.

'Yes, darling girl.'

The man stopped for a moment before continuing towards the bed, as he stood over the now waking Cathy, his shadow covering her face.

Consumed by the darkness, the silence, the alarm bells in Cathy's mind began to ring.

"Sean are you still there…I can't see you?'?" She whispered, her voice concerned, and a little edgy. No answer came. The fear took over, then she saw him in the half light as he moved towards her, his eyes filled with hatred. A scream formed in her throat, as a huge hand pressed down hard on her mouth blocking the scream.

Cathy's eyes bulged as she tried to force the cry from her lungs, but no sound would come, instead the hand pushed harder. She tried to force herself up, every muscle in her body pulsating with the strain. She felt the man's knees dig into her stomach as he moved on top of her, crushing her down. Her lungs almost at bursting point, her eyes wide with fear.

Cathy began to shake her head, her hands desperately trying to hit, scratch, grab, anything that came close enough. A blow hit her stomach, knocking some of the fight out of her. The excruciating pain caused nausea to rise, and for a second all resistance stopped.

Something glinted in the light; she saw it and panic spread again. She tried to fight off the assault as the knife came to her throat. The resistance faded, slowly the flaying hands became still, her breathing subsided. Cathy's eyes now still, stared up at the man, the tears glinting in the darkness. Slowly he took his hand from her mouth, the young woman's body rose in one last gesture of defiance.

"Why?" a whisper gurgled from her mouth as the stream of blood poured from the corner of her lips. Her chest heaved, as the last gasp of air left her lungs, the air causing a gurgling sound in her throat, then the light in her eyes faded, as her life left the body.

The pillow and bedclothes around her neck were dark, the stain from the blood spreading out in an ever widening circle. The man now released all pressure from the lifeless body. As he stood up, he wiped the blood off the twin bladed commando knife, staining the bedclothes. Putting the knife back in his coat pocket, he took out a glass jar, slowly he unscrewed the top, carefully he held the colourless liquid, his hand still.

"Filthy whore." He cursed as he threw the liquid over the young blonde's face, the splashes burning small holes in the pillowcase as they landed, 'you just couldn't wait to be rid of me, opening your legs for the first man that came along, and he a traitor to boot, you're just a feckin whore Emily Cassidy.'

The man replaced the top on the glass jar, carefully wiping the edges with a cloth. When the jar was safely back in his pocket, he moved to the washbasin. Casually rinsing his hands in the cold water. He dried his hands on the towel, then moved towards the door. Silently he opened the door, checking the corridor for any signs of life. Confident in the secret of his identity, he took a last look at the lifeless body on the bed; the gold heart shaped pendent glinting again in the new light.

"That will teach you to fuck with me." His voice hard, the emotions of what he had done not showing. "You're just like the other two, whores the three of you." He cursed in a distinctive Irish accent.

Christian was now very concerned by Cathy's disappearance; he was about to get into the Morris when the figure of Commander Thompson came towards him from the shadows of The Admin. Building.

"Ah, Flight Lieutenant, just the man." He said. "Come with me."

"Not now, Commander," Christian spat.

"That's an order, Kawolski."

"Listen, sir, I can't stop, I'm looking for somebody."

"Now, Flight Lieutenant," Thompson boomed.

"Fuck you," Christian cursed as he got into the Morris. He started the engine driving off, his tyres screeching as the Morris headed for the gate. As Christian reached the barrier he braked hard. A Corporal on duty at the main entrance approached the Morris, Christian unwound the window.

"Lift the barrier, corporal," he shouted.

"Sorry sir, orders." The corporal opened the door of the Morris.

"Do as you're bloody told, man."

"Sorry sir, I've been told to detain you, you're not allowed to leave the base…Sorry, sir."

Christian got out of the car, as a jeep with two MPs roared to his side.

"Sir." One of the MPs said, gesturing to the jeep as he got out. Reluctantly, Christian got into the front seat, the MP who had got out now went to the Morris as Christian was driven back to the main buildings.

Emily was beside herself with worry now, Cathy had still not turned up, to add to her insecurity Christian had now been gone for over an hour. Nervously she had paced up and down the living room carpet. Going to the bedroom, she had peered out of the window, desperate for any signs of either of them. As she returned once again to the living room, she heard a gentle tap on her front door, flushed with relief Emily rushed to the door.

"Christian where….Sean! What are you doing here?"

"Sorry girl, a bad time?" Duffy looked shocked.

"You could say that, come in."

"What's up?" Duffy asked removing his coat, laying it on an armchair in Emily's living room.

"It's Cathy…she didn't come home…Christian's gone to look for her, that was over an hour ago…Oh Sean, I'm so worried."

"Hey, it's alright." Duffy said, taking the young woman in his arms. The warmth of her body causing the feelings he had for her to soar. "Don't worry they'll be fine." He said pulling his head back slightly to look into her eyes.

"What's happened, Sean?" Emily asked out of concern.

"What do you mean?"

"Your face. It's all scratched."

"Oh that, I walked into a rose bush in the blackout."

"Come to the kitchen," Emily said. "I'll dress it for you."

"Don't worry, Emily, it's only a scratch."

"Do as you're told." Emily smiled the maternal instinct coming to the fore, as she gently led the protesting Duffy to the kitchen.

"Ouch." Duffy winced as Emily cleaned the deep cuts, when she had finished Duffy followed her back to the living room.

"Still no sign of them," Emily said, the worry once again returning to her face.

"Do you want me to go and look?" Duffy asked.

"No Sean, I'd only worry about you then, stay with me please."

"Of course I will." Duffy said as he sat on the sofa. Emily sat next to him the smell of her hair filled his nostrils.

After about an hour, Emily fell into a troubled sleep, her head on Duffy's lap his hands gently stroking her blonde hair. Duffy brushed a slither of hair from Emily's face, then he noticed it was missing. The small heart shaped pendant, the one she always wore, the one he had given her, was nowhere to be seen.

Christian explained his outburst to Commander Thompson. Thompson, although in need of some other explanation, reluctantly agreed to let Kawolski return to his search. Christian then left heading back once again to Ruislip and Emily, promising Thompson he would return first thing in the morning.

As Christian's Morris pulled up outside Emily's house, Duffy gently eased Emily's head onto a cushion. Standing slowly, he made his way to the bedroom. Standing in the dark, the door slightly ajar, Duffy watched as Christian entered the flat. Christian went into the living room as Duffy slipped, unnoticed, out of the door.

Walking in the rain towards where he had parked the bike, Duffy pulled up the collar of his dark coat, his heart heavy as he trudged through the darkness.

CHAPTER 26

It was the chambermaid who found the bloodless body of the young blonde girl that Sunday morning. The relief Manager had heard her screams. Trying to understand the hysterical girl's rantings he had followed her eyes to room sixteen. The sight that met his eyes caused him to vomit. When he had completed throwing up, he staggered with the sobbing chambermaid towards the main hotel block.

The barman, who had been stacking shelves when he heard the screams, now rushed to take the girl who was hanging desperately to the relief managers' arm, allowing the manager to phone the police.

"It's the Relief Manager at the Barn Hotel, come quickly, there's been a murder." He stammered down the phone.

"If you could just give me some details," The voice on the other end responded calmly.

"Listen to me," The manager screamed. "There's been a murder, a young girl…her throat…"

"Don't worry sir, we'll send a car…now where are you calling from?"

"The Barn Hotel."

Tommy Boyle was reading his Sunday newspaper when he received the phone call from the duty sergeant at Ruislip.

"My God Emily," was all he said as he dropped the phone.

"Sir…sir, are you there?" The voice of the sergeant pleaded as the phone swung by its cord.

"Tommy, your break…." Mary, his wife, tried to call as the door slammed shut.

Tommy shook with anticipation as he rushed to his car, started it and sped off towards the Barn Hotel.

When he reached the hotel a crowd had already gathered, the police cars attracting passers-by. Hotel guests still in their nightclothes had been woken by the ringing bells of the police vehicles.

"Get this lot out of here." Boyle shouted at a constable as he pushed his way through the throng. Sergeant Jim Watson CID saw Tommy's approach.

"What's happened, Jim," Boyle asked.

"You had better see for yourself sir." The sergeant said as he made his way to the room. As they neared the door, Watson stopped, putting his hand in front of Boyle in warning. "It's not a pretty sight, sir."

"I've seen it before, Jim," Boyle said brushing him aside.

When Boyle reached the door, the sheer scale of the carnage stopped him briefly. Swallowing to contain the nausea, Boyle stepped inside.

No matter how many times Tommy Boyle had been at a murder scene, each one brought its own horror, its own perversion. What Tommy saw disgusted him, made him shake with fury at the pointlessness of the exaggerated butchery. "My God!" He whispered as he leant against the door. The blood, like a tidal wave, had spread from the bed, staining the carpet as it oozed towards the door. The albino like white body, devoid of blood, lay like a statue, white and lifeless on the bed.

As Tommy's eyes took in the scene, they registered on what had once been a pretty young girl's face. Blackened and burnt to the bone by the acid. The skeletal head stared back at him, one eye un-burnt looking imploringly at Boyle, "Why?" it seemed to say. Like a ritualistic act, the burning liquid had stripped the face.

Boyle turned his eyes away a moment, taking a deep breath of clean fresh air, he then fully entered the room. Standing over the body, he tried to imagine what the face looked like. He had seen this scene enacted out in all its gore once before, at Hammersmith in 1939.

Boyle saw the blonde hair, and instantly his eyes went to the girl's torn throat. There on a gold chain, stained by blood, hung the heart shaped pendant, just like the one Molly had worn back in Hammersmith. Just like the one Mary McGrath had worn in Dublin, just like the one Emily Cassidy had worn.

"I'm sorry, honey." Boyle wept, the tears rolling down his cheeks. "I should have warned you, protected you." He whispered as the salty tears seeped into the corner of his mouth. "I knew it would happen," he continued his shoulders shaking. "I'm so sorry, girl."

"Sir?" Watson interrupted Boyle's thoughts.

"What?" He said, as he wiped the tears from his face.

"It's the manager sir, we've located him. He saw the girl last night, he was probably the last one to see her alive." Watson said quietly.

"Show me." Boyle said pushing past Watson in the doorframe. When they reached the bottom of the stairs Boyle stopped to face Watson. "Sorry Jim, I…I didn't mean . . ."

"It's ok sir. I understand." Watson put an arm on Boyle's shoulder, "You know who she is don't you sir?"

"Yes Jim, I know who she is." Boyle turned again, heading for the main reception area.

Christian woke that Sunday morning with Emily's head on his chest, both their bodies stiff from the fitful sleep on the small sofa.

Gradually gaining consciousness, Emily shot up. "Cathy," she said as she rushed to the bedroom, it was empty. Emily searched the whole flat in vane; no sign of Cathy's safe return was to be found.

Emily began to cry. Christian took her in his arms, comforting her as best he could. He glanced at his watch, "Christ," He said, noticing the time. "I've got to go, Emily," he said, staring into Emily's tearstained face. "Thompson wants to see me."

"Oh Christian, don't leave me." Emily sobbed.

"I've got to, Em, It's an order, I must go," he said pulling away from Emily. "Listen, Cathy's probably back at the base by now…sleeping off a hangover…just you see." He kissed her forehead, before pulling away to leave. Emily had not mentioned Duffy's sudden appearance.

Tommy Boyle went into the Manager's office to escape the morbid crowd. Shutting the door behind him, he cursed his fellow man for their grisly fascination.

Taking a deep breath Tommy began his questions.

"You saw the girl arrive Mr. Er…."

"Grimwald."

"Mr Grimwald," Tommy said as he wrote the manager's name in his notebook.

"What time was that?"

"About ten thirty, she had a drink in the bar."

"Did you notice anything unusual about her, her attire, attitude?"

"No, she was very calm, well dressed, as if she was waiting for someone."

"What makes you think that?" Tommy asked.

"Well, she kept looking at her watch."

"Ok, Mr Grimwald, what happened next?"

"She finished her drink then left via the front door. I assumed that whoever it was that she was going to meet had failed to turn up."

"You're convinced she was meeting somebody?"

"Yes, Inspector, as I already said…she was a nice pretty thing, obviously not one of those."

"Those?" Tommy raised his eyebrows.

"Tarts, Inspector. This is a respectable establishment," the manager said looking down his nose at Boyle. "I would not let a tart in here." He confirmed.

"She didn't book the room herself then?" Boyle asked.

"No, it was booked over the phone, a man with an Irish accent, well spoken, educated."

"Did you see him?" Tommy stared at the manager a glint of hope in his voice.

"No, I'm afraid not, he must have taken the key when I went to check on the kitchen."

"What time was that?"

"Just after eleven fifteen."

"Are you sure?"

"Yes, I had just told the barman to ring the bell. I always check the kitchen at that time…one of my routines." The manager said confidently.

"A routine?" Boyle asked, his mind now exploring all the possibilities of what the manager had said. "Have you noticed an Irish voice recently. Perhaps somebody at the bar, probably close to closing time? Just before you check on the kitchen."

"No not….you think…but that's…"

"Yes sir, I think whoever booked the room had been watching you, checking on your routines."

"Oh," The manager whispered, the confident smirk disappearing from his face. Boyle allowed the thought to sink for a minute before continuing.

"How was the room paid for?" he asked.

"What, sorry…Er…an envelope, cash," the manager mumbled.

"An envelope? Do you still have it?" Tommy asked, sitting forward.

"What, oh…yes . . .I think so…I put it in the bin."

"What bin?"

"The one behind the reception desk," the manager stammered.

Boyle shot up, opened the door, outside stood Sergeant Watson.

"Jim, get the bin from behind the reception desk, inside should be an envelope."

"Yes sir," Watson said.

Boyle shut the door again.

"What colour envelope?" Boyle asked the manager.

"Oh, Er…buff . . .letter size."

Tommy Boyle opened the door as Watson knocked, the bin in his hand.

"Thanks Jim." Boyle said, peering into the bin. "Is this the one?" Boyle asked holding a buff envelope up by the corner.

The manager put on his glasses to look closer. "Yes that's the one I recognise the name that's printed on the back, Rawlingson's Dairies."

"Got you, you bastard." Tommy mumbled under his breath. "Put this in a bag, Jim."

"Evidence sir?"

Boyle smiled, "The final piece of the jigsaw, Jim. The evidence that will put the noose around the bastard's neck."

"Jim?"

"Yes sir?"

"Get the barman in here." Boyle turned to the manager. "That will be all, Mr Grimwald," he said, dismissing the manager from his own office. The Manager, his face showing indignation, left the office.

"So who is it, sir?" Watson asked when the manager had passed out of earshot.

"Sean Duffy. It's an exact replica of a murder I was involved in Hammersmith in 1939. I suspected Duffy then, but I couldn't prove it. Now I can prove all three murders, Jim. Duffy did them all. The sick bastard. I've got him." Boyle exclaimed.

"Sir," Watson said as he closed the door.

"What is it, Jim?" Boyle asked.

"You had better sit down, sir," Watson said quietly.

"What is it, Jim?" Boyle asked again as he slowly sat down. The look on the sergeant's face told him something was wrong.

"It wasn't Duffy, sir."

"What?" Boyle stood up, "but…"

"Sir, the Sunday papers, didn't you see…?"

"What about them?" Boyle demanded.

"Duffy, the body of Sean Duffy was found early Saturday morning…in Pembrokeshire…dressed in the uniform of a German Major…His neck…his neck broken by the tree, his parachute landed in."

"What? But…." Boyle was dazed. "But it can't…" He whispered.

Christian had asked everyone he saw at the RAF base in Northolt, as to any news of Cathy. No one had seen her since she left the mess that night. As Christian left the adjutant's office, he bumped into Thompson.

"Ah. Flight Lieutenant, nice to see you're on time, briefing room three now."

"Yes sir," Christian said meekly.

"Are you alright Flight Lieutenant?" Thompson asked.

"It's my friend, sir. She still hasn't turned up."

"Oh sorry to hear it. What's her name?" Thompson asked.

"Cathy, sir."

"Freddie Moreland's girlfriend?"

"Yes sir, She disappeared yesterday…no one's seen her since."

"Poor girl." Thompson said quietly.

Tommy Boyle was still in shock when the constable entered the room.

"What is it, constable?" Watson asked.

"We've found two notes, sir." The Constable passed the pieces of paper to Watson. He read the two messages, his face becoming pale.

"Where did you find them?" Watson demanded.

"One under the pillow, the other," the constable swallowed, "the other in the young ladies pocket…sir?"

"What is it, Jim?" Boyle said looking up.

"You're not going to believe this, sir," Watson said as he passed the notes to Boyle.

"Bloody...." Boyle said as he read the notes. "But...how?"

As Christian followed Commander Thompson into the briefing room he saw Yvette sitting in one of the chairs, looking pale.

"Of course, you know Yvette," Thompson said as he sat behind the desk.

"Yes sir, Yvette," Christian nodded.

"Flight Lieutenant Kawolski," She acknowledged, her voice quivering.

Christian sat down. As he did Thompson leaned forward on the desk and spoke.

"We're sending Yvette back to France, north west Paris to be exact."

Christian turned towards Yvette, he saw the shudder as Thompson spoke, her hands went to her lap, her fingers playing nervously with her skirt.

"You're going to fly her in?" Thompson said. Christian didn't hear his words, his mind still on the trembling girl's eyes.

"What? Sorry sir?" Christian tried to concentrate on Thompson's words.

"Your mission, Flight Lieutenant, you're flying Yvette in...tonight."

"Tonight? But..." It was Christian's turn to feel the shudder.

"Yes tonight," Thompson said firmly. "You leave at midnight."

Christian was about to answer when Harry Milburn burst into the room.

"Harry you're late." Thompson said coldly.

"Sir, I need a word." Harry said, his face grave.

"What is it?"

"Its private, sir."

Thompson rose from his chair, huffing as he did so. The two men went to the corner of the room. Christian his ears straining, tried to listen to their conversation. Yvette her eyes staring at her fingers on her lap, showed no sign of recognition.

"What is it?" Thompson demanded.

"There was a bit of a hubbub in Ruislip this morning...The Barn Hotel...a girl was murdered," Harry whispered.

Thompson shot a glance at Christian then turned to face Harry again.

"Who?" he asked.

"I don't know yet, but apparently, it was a copycat of the murders in Hammersmith and Dublin back in 39."

"Shit!" Thompson exclaimed, glancing again towards Christian as he spoke. Christian pinned his ears back, something was going on, something bad.

"Does our man know?" Thompson whispered, now looking directly at Harry.

"I don't think so, sir."

"Get on to him straightaway. You know where he is?"

"Yes sir," Harry replied.

Thompson sat down again, "Sorry about that, where was I?" He smiled. "Ah yes, Flight Lieutenant, from now to take off you're confined to base."

"But sir, my friend." Christian pleaded.

"Ah yes, Harry will enquire on your behalf, now..."

"But sir, my girlfriend...She's a friend of Cathy's. I said...I would look for her. She's all alone sir. Probably worried sick."

"Don't worry you can phone her after our meeting." Thompson grinned.

"She's not on the phone sir, if I could..."

"Out of the question, Flight Lieutenant." Thompson dismissed Christian's protest. "Give Harry her address, he'll pop in and see her soon, make sure she's alright."

Reluctantly, without a choice, Christian gave Milburn Emily's address. Harry promised he would visit as soon as he could, reassuring Christian a little, as he left to make a phone call.

Cavenaugh in the back room of the pub in Hanwell answered the phone when it rang. Without saying a word, he listened. Slowly a huge evil grin spread across his face.

The phone also rang in the bedroom where Sean Duffy slept at the Bull Hotel in Denham.

Duffy awoke, one eye opened as he stared at the buzzing phone by his bedside. Suddenly alerted, he sprang up sitting on the edge of the bed, his hand hovering over the phone. "Who the hell," he said to himself, hesitating to answer.

Slowly Duffy lifted the receiver. He did not speak, he just listened. Duffy let the phone drop; he had not uttered a single word. He hurried to dress, time was short, soon they would find out.

The General was allowed to sleep in, it was ten thirty when his new aide, Jonas, woke him, his breakfast on a silver tray.

"Good morning sir. Ham 'n' eggs." The Californian smiled. "Orange juice, coffee."

"Good I'm hungry." The General sat up in bed, the aide bolstering the pillows for him. "Thanks, Jonas, what's on the schedule for today."

"You have a meeting with Patton, er, sorry, sir, General Patton." Jonas apologised for his slip. "Then with Field Marshal Montgomery after lunch. Oh and General Eisenhower is on his way. He'll see you as soon as he gets here."

"Ike's coming...I thought he had a cold."

"Yes sir, he does, but I guess it's important. He wants to see you urgently."

"Are you ok, General?" Jonas added seeing Schloss' face harden.

"Yes son, I'm fine, hey is this real coffee?" He asked taking a sip.

"Sure is, sir."

"Wow that's good, it reminds me of Boston."

"Boston sir…but I thought?"

"I went to Boston when I was a kid, that's the first time I had coffee," Schloss lied, realising the error. "You never forget your first coffee."

"Yep, I guess you're right sir."

'When did you have your first coffee? Where?" The General asked.

"I dunno sir, S.L.O.B, I guess, till I got called up, I ain't never been out of Obispo."

"Well….good ham this, Jonas." The General said, slightly nervy.

Duffy almost ran up the stairs, breathing heavily he knocked loudly on the door.

"Sean, what…have you heard anything? Sorry, come in," Emily said.

"Are you ok?" Duffy asked his hands on Emily's shoulder.

"Not too bad…It's just I haven't heard anything about Cathy. Christian went to the base…He hasn't come back yet…I just…"

"Listen, Emily." Duffy looked into her eyes "pack some things…now Emily?"

"But…Sean, what's wrong? Is it Christian?"

"Don't ask questions, Emily, we haven't got much time. I'll tell you when we get there," Duffy said his eyes firm.

"Where? I can't go anywhere…Christian…"

"I'll tell him later," Duffy lied. "Listen, Emily girl, you just have to trust me on this." Duffy tried smiling at the girl.

"But…"

"No buts, here I'll help you pack," Duffy said as he led the girl to the bedroom.

When the briefing was over, dejectedly Christian made his way to the mess hall. Yvette, totally distraught at the thought of returning to France, stayed behind in the briefing room, her empty stare unsettling Christian.

He selected a table in the corner and hardly touched the Spam, powdered eggs and baked beans on his lunch plate. He pushed the food around the plate, his mind on the sudden operation. The look on Yvette's face had filled him with foreboding, and as if in a trance he stared straight ahead.

Two young pilots, flushed with the certainty of youth, sat at the other end of the table.

"Did you hear about the murder in Ruislip?" One said being serious for a moment.

"No, what happened?" asked the other, the fork full of beans, hovering just in front of his mouth.

"A young blonde girl was murdered, acid thrown in her face."

"Jesus," the one with the beans exclaimed, his mouth open again.

"Yes, apparently they couldn't recognise her."

"Wow."

Christian, slowly coming back to reality, looked up at the two young men. "Cathy, poor Cathy," he said quietly.

"Yes, the only way they could identify her was by a gold pendant which she was wearing on her neck."

"What did you say?" Christian barked at the young man, the horror of the reality hitting him like a blow from a fist.

"A pendant, sir, she…she wore a heart shaped pendant."

Christian dropped the fork, the utensil banging loudly on the plate as it fell. Ashen faced he stood up, his knees weak.

"Emily, no, please God no." He blurted as he walked unsteadily away. "Please God, no!" He kept muttering.

"Flight… Flight you ok? Flight." The young pilot asked as Christian walked away.

Duffy almost bundled the protesting Emily on to the bike, kicked the machine into a roar, and sped off in the direction of Denham. Emily, her thoughts in turmoil, held Duffy tightly around the waist. Her eyes full of tears imagined all the bad things that might have happened to Cathy.

Boyle was flabbergasted at the conflicting nature of the evidence. On one hand he had the murder, with all the evidence pointing to Duffy. Circumstantial, ok, but the notes, which had been found on the girl, were from Duffy. The envelope containing the payment for the room came from Rawlingson's Dairies, where Duffy was the Manager. His presence around both murdered girls in 1939. On the other hand, he'd read the newspaper article reporting Duffy's death. Duffy couldn't have died, then resurrected himself, then driven all the way from Pembrokeshire, then committed the murder at the Barn Hotel, or could he?

Boyle looked up.

"Jim, get me the West Wales Police, Pembrokeshire."

"Sir?" Watson asked, "but why?"

"If we don't know its Duffy, how could they?" Boyle beamed.

"Sorry sir, you've lost me." Watson shook his head.

"What if the body they found in Pembrokeshire wasn't Duffy."

"But the papers, sir."

"They could have been planted, Jim."

"I see, yes of course, you're right." Watson scratched his head. "We've only got their word for it that it's Duffy."

"Exactly, Jim." Boyle was buzzing now. "Listen Jim, you've met Duffy, you know what he looks like."

"Yes sir, I could identify him," Watson said, knowing what was coming next.

"I'd go myself, Jim, but I've got a meeting tonight, hopefully with the final part of the jigsaw."

"Sir?" Watson looked up.

"The murder weapon, Jim, at least the weapon that was used to kill Molly and Mary, and Jim, I'm assured Duffy's prints are on it."

"Ok, but what about here?"

"I'll have to spare you for the moment, Jim, anyway, forensics will be busy all day."

"It's a bloody long way, sir," Watson mumbled

"I know Jim, I know," Boyle agreed.

Christian had begged the adjutant to let him go to Emily's and find out what had happened. Although he was sympathetic, the adjutant had no choice but to refuse Kawolski's plea. Shattered by events, Christian stood in the light drizzle trying to light a cigarette, his hand shaking. Frustrated, he threw the now soggy unlit Players to the ground.

"Problems, Flight Lieutenant?" It was Harry Milburn.

"Harry, thank God." Christian said as he took out another cigarette. Milburn held the light for him; he blew the blue smoke into the cool air. "Any news about Emily?" he asked.

"Sorry Flight Lieutenant, no answer."

"Oh my God." Christian began to shake again, the pain suddenly appearing in his right knee.

"We still haven't found young Mr Moreland's young lady, either."

"Cathy?"

"Yes, it's more probable that the murdered girl was her."

"No…no." Christian said, "Emily wore the gold pendant, not Cathy."

"Sorry Flight Lieutenant, that's all I know." Harry didn't mention the note he had found at Emily's house that would have screwed everything up.

"Thanks anyway, Harry," Christian mumbled.

When Duffy arrived at the hotel room with the disconsolate Emily by his side, the girl demanded an explanation. Reluctantly Duffy told her as much as he dared. She listened silently as he explained. When he got to the part about Cathy's murder at the Barn Hotel, Emily broke down.

"Poor Cathy." She sobbed.

"It was meant to be you, Emily." Duffy told her.

"What?" Emily's head shot up, the eyes wide, the sobbing silenced for a moment. "But why?"

Duffy took Emily's face in his hands. "It was you he was after," he told her. "It was the pendant that made him mistake Cathy for you."

"Oh, Sean." Emily burst into tears again. "Hold me, Sean, please hold me," she begged. Duffy took the weeping girl in his arms, holding her tightly.

"Why was Cathy was wearing your pendant?" Duffy asked her softly.

"She found it in Freddie's things. She…she thought Freddie had bought it for her." Emily's voice began to catch as she tried to speak between the tears.

"How did Freddie come to have it?"

"Christian…they, they wouldn't let me see him…I gave it to Freddie to give to Christian. He must have for…forgotten."

Duffy tried to console Emily. "Come on, be a brave girl."

"Oh, Sean. It's…it's so awful, just so awful."

'I know darling girl,' Duffy smiled thinly.

General Popowski was in discussion with Patton, regarding the proposed details of the troop movements prior to D.Day when an aide announced the arrival of the Allied Supreme Commander.

"George," Eisenhower said as he strode into the room, his presence in accordance with his rank.

"Ike," Patton smiled. "Of course you know General Popowski?"

"Popeye, how are you?" Eisenhower offered his hand.

"I'm fine sir, thank you." The General accepted Eisenhower's huge hand. Eisenhower took his gloves and coat off, then laid his cane on the table.

"Listen, guys, I'll come straight to the point. I've just left a meeting with the British Prime Minister. He feels Alexander needs just one more push at Cassino to break Kesselring's line. Alexander's had a tough time, with all his best troops taken away from him. He's confident in his plan." Eisenhower paused, "and so am I."

Eisenhower's eyes went to Patton, who just grinned, then he looked to the General, whose reaction Ike found more interesting. "The plain fact," Ike continued, "is that Alexander's got fifty thousand spare troops raring to go. Politically, I agree with the Prime Minister, if Cassino breaks then so will Rome. Hitler must reinforce Italy, that will mean less German divisions for you to face, George."

"Suits me, Ike," Patton replied.

"Winston reckons that Rome could fall before we go in to Calais, that would be a big boost to our guys here. As well as the men in Italy."

Eisenhower looked directly at Popowski. "In short, Popeye, I'm sending you back."

"But my work here, sir?"

"I'm sure George can spare you, the troops we're going to use are the Poles, Popeye…You will lead them, under their own flag." Ike paused for the reaction; the one that came was what he expected.

"I won't let you down sir, It's not France but, well, Rome seems good to me."

"Good man." Eisenhower slapped Popowski on the shoulder. "You leave this week."

"Thank you sir."

"Right, Popeye, you've got a lot of packing to do, I probably won't see you again until after Rome, Good luck, General."

Schloss saluted smartly. "Thank you sir."

"Now if you don't mind, I need a word with George."

"Certainly, sir." The General left the room.

Once outside Gunther Schloss smiled to himself. "Two birds with one stone, the Fuhrer will be pleased."

Eisenhower smiled at the grinning Patton. "Good job, George, good job."

Commander Peter Thompson got the call from 'C'. Popowski was to be taken back the same way he came in, Kawolski must be the pilot.

Thompson made another call, "It's on, this Thursday."

CHAPTER 27

Tommy Boyle's day had been eventful to say the least. He returned home for a short while, ate dinner, then changed to prepare for his meeting with Phelan's men.

Jim Watson had finally got his travel permit, and as Boyle was getting ready, Watson boarded the overnight train that would take him to Pembrokeshire. With any luck he would be able to identify the body sometime tomorrow, call Boyle, then make the long journey back home.

Tommy felt sorry for Watson, his wife Gladys was not the most accommodating woman, no doubt Watson would suffer the venom of her tongue for the enforced trip when he got back. 'Thank God I've got Mary,' he smiled to himself.

Happy with his state of mind and his full stomach, thanks to Mary's ability to turn the most meagre supplies into a sumptuous meal, he set off on what he believed would be the penultimate meeting prior to solving the case that had loomed over him ever since 1939. It was time to lay the ghosts to rest.

Duffy finally got Emily to sleep; the poor girl's devastation at the tragedy that had befallen Cathy had then been compounded by Duffy's revelations. It was guilt, tinged with fear that sat heavily on her mind now.

When Duffy had explained his reason for leaving her alone that night, at first Emily had begged him to stay. Duffy had assured the girl that there was no danger as long as she stayed where she was. Reluctantly, Emily had agreed. Now, Emily's tortured mind at last got some respite.

Duffy kissed the pretty girl's forehead as he left, the anger burning deep inside, and revenge filling his thoughts.

Christian walked slowly towards the black shape of the Lysander. Yvette trudged beside him. The sparkle of life had left her being, her eyes, wide and staring, conveyed the look of hope lost.

As Yvette reached the aircraft she stumbled, but Christian caught her arm stopping the fall.

"Are you alright, Yvette?" he asked.

Yvette scanned the surroundings with her eyes. Her sadness and fear were plain to see. "I don't think I'll be coming back," she mumbled.

Christian was about to speak when a jeep carrying Commander Thompson screeched to a stop alongside the Lysander. For a brief moment, a glimmer of hope showed in Yvette's eyes; but Thompson's words switched the light out. The mission was to go ahead, its importance now upgraded.

At five minutes past midnight the Lysander lifted into the black night, its wheels reluctant, like Yvette, to leave the safety of England's soil.

Tommy Boyle parked his car next to the Greenford Hotel. The lights in the building had been extinguished some time ago. The whole area was cloaked in the black night. After about five minutes Boyle checked his watch, using a small pencil torch. Peering through the darkness beyond the windscreen, he could see no signs of Phelan's men. After another ten minutes of patient waiting, Boyle was about to start the car when he saw a flicker of light about fifty paces away. Boyle got out of the car, pulled up the collar on his Mac as the rain began to fall and headed in the direction from which the light had come.

Walking slowly, carefully placing one foot in front of the other, Boyle felt his way through the blackness. He had covered perhaps forty paces when he saw the light again. A yellowy ghostly face illuminated by the match used to light a cigarette appeared, then disappeared.

"Hello," Boyle called softly.

"Mr Boyle?" A voice with a distinctive Irish accent answered.

"Yes, where are you?"

"Do you have the money, Inspector?"

"Yes, do you have…"?

"Show me the money first," the voice said, hardening.

Boyle took out a white envelope from his inside pocket, opening the top to reveal the bundle inside.

The match light appeared again. Boyle could now see it was the red haired man he had seen in the bar in Ireland.

"The envelope."

"The evidence." Boyle said firmly, shining the pencil torch in the man's face. The red head smiled, reached inside his coat and took out a bundle, slowly pulling back the cloth to reveal a double bladed commando knife, the bloodstained metal shining in the torchlight. Gingerly the swap was made, and the man counted his money.

"It's all there."

"Just checking, Mr Boyle." The red head grinned as he turned to walk away. Boyle took the evidence, carefully wrapped the weapon back in the cloth, and then made his way back to where he had parked the car. This time he used the torch to show the way.

As Boyle reached the car door he heard a noise behind him. He turned, and pointed the torch in the direction of the noise. Boyle saw the blow coming. He managed just to pull his head back slightly, as the blow fell glancing off his skull. Shocked by the suddenness of the attack rather than the pain, Boyle stumbled, then fell to the ground. Unable to react quickly enough to regain his balance. Boyle waited for the decisive blow, the torchlight illuminating his assailant. It was the tall man, Donal, a vicious grin on his face.

As the man stood over him, Boyle prayed to God and his wife Mary to forgive him, and waited for the blackness that would come. A thud resounded through the darkness. Donal, his face contorted in pain, the whites of his eyes turning upwards in his head, fell next to Boyle, his eyes only inches from Boyle's face. Boyle tried desperately to comprehend what had happened, urging himself to stay conscious. But he lost the battle, and blackness crept over him.

The flight had been fairly uneventful; the only moment of excitement had come just as the Lysander flew over the coast of France. Christian was flying just above the cloud base at two thousand feet and had spotted a night fighter, the moonlight glinting on the canopy showing the German's position. Christian dived the Lysander into the security of the clouds losing the ME110 in a matter of seconds. Now, according to his calculations, Christian should be about two miles from the drop zone. Losing height, he brought the aircraft through the clouds, levelling out at three hundred feet. There in front of him was the flash of light as the beacons illuminated his final approach.

Christian brought the Lysander down, its wheels touching the soil of occupied France. When the Lysander came to a complete stop Christian pulled back the canopy. Three men in dark clothes came running towards him, an assortment of weapons clutched in their hands.

"Monsieur, welcome to France," said the voice of the largest of the three.

"Yvette, so good to see you," smiled the man, Yvette alighted from the aircraft, then kissed the man on both cheeks.

"Good to see you, Marcel," she said, looking slightly more in control than she had earlier.

The large man turned to Christian, smiled, then extended his hand.

"Good luck, Monsieur."

"Yvette," Christian called to the girl. She stopped, turning to face him.

"Good luck," Christian smiled. Yvette stared at him for a moment, before the large man took her by the arm. "Come, Yvette, we must go," he said. With that Yvette turned away, following the three men into the darkness.

As Christian applied full throttle, the Lysander gathered speed; ready for take off, he was haunted by Yvette's silent stare.

Slowly a dim fuzzy glow appeared. As he blinked his eyes the light came again, this time more strongly. Tommy Boyle came slowly to consciousness, the pain on the side of his head expanding as his senses returned.

"Where…where am I?" Tommy tried to sit up, a hand gently pushing his body back to the softness of the mattress.

"It's all right, Guv, you're in hospital," a kindly voice told him.

"But, but . . ." Tommy tried to speak, his mind slowly coming to terms with his predicament, "How did…. How did I get here?"

"You were found unconscious by your car in the car park of the Greenford Hotel. You've been the victim of an attack."

"The evidence."

"What evidence, Guv?"

"In a towel, the knife wrapped in cloth, have you got it?" Boyle pleaded.

"Sorry, Guv, all we found was you, no sign of anything else, except of course the two bodies."

"Two bodies!" Boyle exclaimed.

"Yes sir, one shot through the back, the other shot through the head, very messy." The man, a sergeant from Ealing CID, said.

"Bloody hell!" Tommy's mind was in turmoil.

"Looks like you've got a guardian angel, the man that called us explained everything, then disappeared…pity, we would like to talk to him."

"I've got to get back." Tommy tried to sit up again.

"You stay exactly where you are Tommy Boyle," Mary said.

"Mary, what are you doing here?"

Duffy crept back into the room and, seeing Emily was fast asleep, he took off his shoes, then his coat. Putting the coat over him Duffy tried to make himself as comfortable as possible in the chair.

"Sean…Sean is that you?" Emily whispered.

"Yes…go to sleep, girl," Duffy said softly.

"You can't sleep there," Emily whispered, "Come to bed."

"I daren't."

Emily pulled the cover exposing her nightie and her bare legs.

"Please Sean, come to bed…hold me, please."

"Ok darling girl," Duffy grinned. Slowly he undressed, then slipped into the bed next to Emily. Cuddling up to her back he could feel her backside, cooler than the rest of her, as she snuggled it into his groin. Duffy leaned over and kissed her bare arm gently then nestled his head into her sweet smelling neck, the smell of honeysuckle filling his lungs. With his arm around her waist, both fell into warm soft sleep. Sean Duffy was suddenly happier than he had ever felt in his life.

Dawn was just beginning to break over the small hamlet of Ickenham, as Christian brought the Lysander in to land. Meanwhile, Yvette with Marcel and the two other men had made their way to the safe house in a small hamlet just north west of the outer suburbs of Calais. The journey had taken an hour and, desperate for sleep, Yvette lay on the bed in the attic of the small cottage, feeling a little easier, a little safer, as she closed her eyes.

Steiner had interrupted Mosel's sleep. He read the flimsy with the message that the aide had brought to his bedside in the small anteroom just off his office. He smiled.

"The goose will bring the egg to us this week, Hans, good news, yes?"

"Yes sir, but I think you had better read on."

Mosel read the rest of the decoded message, his eyes concentrated. When he had finished he looked up at Steiner.

"The magpie demands that we bring the woman and the two children to the airfield. He's asking, no, demanding," Mosel corrected himself. "An exchange, he wants a protected flight from there to neutral Sweden."

"Yes sir," Steiner said. "What are you going to do sir?"

"Agree," Mosel smiled. "If Kawolski brings this off…he deserves it."

The crowing of a cock brought Yvette from her deep sleep. Slowly she opened her eyes, and as she did so her body stiffened. Pointing directly at her head Yvette saw the barrel of the Luger, a row of fat fingers gripping the weapon. Her eyes widened as she followed the line of sight over the barrel towards the podgy face, a face she knew. Yvette's heart began to beat harder, nausea began to rise, her body began to shake. Small, cruel, eyes stared back at her, the mouth stretched in a wicked grin.

"Good morning, Mademoiselle Margot, or is it Yvette?" Obergruppenfuehrer Von Ebstein smiled wickedly at the girl. "Welcome back to France. This, Mademoiselle, is your last visit – hands up."

Sick with fear, unable to move, Yvette began to cry.

When Emily awoke Sean Duffy was already up, stripped to the waist he shaved in the small mirror above the basin in the hotel room. Duffy stared at her reflection in the small shaving mirror, her big blue eyes wide, her golden dishevelled hair laying on her bare shoulders, her arms above her head in a stretch.

"Good morning Sean." Emily spoke through a stifled yawn.

"Good morning to you darling girl," Duffy smiled at her in the mirror.

Tommy Boyle was discharged from the cottage hospital in Hanwell that morning. Driven by a constable, and accompanied by his ever-faithful Mary, they made their way towards Ruislip.

Despite Mary's protests, Boyle made the constable wait whilst he changed, then the two men got back into the police car, heading towards Ruislip Police Station.

When he reached the office, he read the copy of the report of his assault the night before, which had been delivered by the sergeant from Ealing Police Station. Still confused, Tommy had questioned the sergeant intensely. It was only then that he was able to piece together the memory of the events of the night before. Someone had saved his life. But why? Boyle kept asking himself.

The ringing of the phone on his desk interrupted Boyle's thoughts. Slowly he lifted the receiver.

"Boyle."

"Sir. It's Sutcliffe at Forensics...the body of the victim found at the Barn Hotel..."

"Yes," Boyle said.

"We've just got the report from the autopsy...according to the dental records we've just received...."

"Yes, go on," Boyle prompted.

"The body is not that of Emily Cassidy."

"What!" Boyle exclaimed. "Whose is it, then?"

"A young WAAF officer, based at Northolt, her name's Cathy Fry."

"The other girl, Emily's friend, but why?" Boyle said aloud.

"Sorry, sir?" said the voice at the other end of the line.

"Carry on," Boyle said, his mind now in overdrive.

"Well, we were a bit lucky there, seems both young ladies used the same..."

"Emily!" Boyle shouted. Without listening to the rest of the caller's sentence, he replaced the receiver. If it wasn't Emily...then she was still in danger.

Christian awoke from his brief sleep at noon, tired and hungry. He readied himself for what remained of the day. With any luck he could complete his briefing by late afternoon, then take what was left of his twenty four-hour pass and visit Emily. In the meantime he would also check to see if Cathy had turned up. He was sick with worry as to who the body found at the murder scene in Ruislip belonged to. He prayed to God that it was neither of the girls, especially Emily.

After he and Emily had taken breakfast, Duffy went to the main hotel reception and paid in cash for another two nights stay at the hotel. When he and Emily returned to the room, the girl began to regain some of the spirit that had seen her through the nineteen years of torment she had endured so far in her life. She demanded that Duffy told her everything he knew. Duffy sat on the bed next to her, and reluctantly he began the story, which started in Dublin in 1939.

When Duffy had finished over an hour had passed. Emily did not interrupt at any stage, only her eyes told of the emotions she felt as Duffy unveiled the whole story. Emily stood up, and looked at Duffy.

"Sean, I need to be alone."

"I understand," Duffy said. "I've got to go somewhere...will you be ok?"

"Yes...yes I'll be fine," Emily said, her face pale and blank.

Duffy kissed her, then he left.

Emily took a towel with a few wash things that she had managed to bundle into a vanity case the night before, then made her way to the bathroom located on the landing. Finding it empty, Emily locked the door, then poured a hot steaming bath.

When the bath was full, Emily slipped beneath the hot soothing water, as she laid her head back she began to cry.

Boyle was still at his desk that afternoon when he received the call he had been waiting for. It was Jim Watson from Pembrokeshire.

"What's the news Jim?" Boyle asked pensively.

"I've seen the body sir," Watson replied.

"And?"

"It's not Sean Duffy sir,"

"Are you sure, Jim?" Boyle tried to contain his excitement.

"Certain, sir."

"Good work, Jim, make your way back as soon as you can." Boyle smiled as he put the receiver down, then he picked it up again dialling the CID room.

"CID." The voice responded.

"Geoff, It's Inspector Boyle…make out a warrant for an arrest."

"Who, sir?"

"Sean Duffy."

CHAPTER 28

After the briefing, Christian asked if he could visit Emily, Thompson shook his head.

"Sorry, Flight Lieutenant, it's out of the question, you're flying again tonight."

"What!" Christian stared at Thompson in disbelief. "But my girlfriend and Cathy."

"No news on either yet, as far as we know. According to the police the identity of the girl found murdered in Ruislip doesn't fit either girl. As for your flight. . you will fly the Lysander to F.U.S.A.G. HQ in Norfolk tonight, rest, then bring General Popowski back to Northolt tomorrow. On the following day you'll fly him back to Italy in the Junkers 52.

"Italy?" Christian said alarmed.

"Yes, Flight Lieutenant, Italy – any problems?" Thompson asked.

"No sir," Christian replied quietly, "none at all."

Yvette was handcuffed then taken on a long journey to Gestapo headquarters northwest Paris. As soon as she arrived at the grey gaunt three-storey building, she was taken to the basement. There the beatings began immediately. Von Ebstein conducted the initial onslaught, his thin lips stretching every time the blows landed on Yvette's naked body. After an hour, Von Ebstein passed this responsibility to one of the guards. As he refreshed his thirst with wine, the screams from the basement almost drowned the tunes of Wagner that played on a gramophone.

Commander Thompson received a call late that night, just as he watched Kawolski's plane take off from the airfield at RAF Northolt. He picked up the receiver as the call was put through.

"Thompson?"

"It's Harry, sir."

"What is it?"

"Our man, sir, he's making a move."

"Right, Harry, get there as soon as possible, and Harry…"

"Sir?"

"For God's sake stop him Harry… I'll get there as soon as I can." Thompson put the phone down, a worried look on his face. He turned towards the adjutant who stood next to him. "Get me a car could you, George, it's urgent."

"Yes sir."

When he had left, Thompson picked up the phone, as the operator answered he spoke.

"Get me Ruislip Police Station, Chief Inspector Boyle."

"Yes sir." The girl replied.

Boyle took the call in his office; Thompson had just caught him as he made to leave. Thompson told Boyle where he could find his murderer.

Christian landed at F.U.S.A.G. Headquarters after the short flight, and headed toward his billet close to the building in which Gunther Schloss slept that night. Happy that the nightmare would soon be over, Christian looked forward to a long cool pint, his mind flickering to the possible fate of Emily.

Duffy parked the bike in a side street, and made his way slowly to the rear of the building. He sat silently in the dark, waiting until all the lights in the main buildings were switched off. Satisfied that all was well, Duffy approached the window, which overlooked the back yard, from the small ground floor back room.

Slipping a knife into the gap, Duffy slid the catch back, and slowly raised the lower half of the sash window. He hauled himself over the windowsill, closed the window silently, drew the curtains then sat in a chair behind the desk, facing the door of the small room.

Boyle got into the police car at Ruislip station with an armed constable by his side. Another car containing two CID men, also armed, followed Boyle's car as it sped off.

Commander Thompson waited for the car the adjutant had secured to arrive, frustrated by the delay. He glanced at his watch impatiently. "I hope Harry makes it in time," he said to himself.

Duffy heard the goodbyes as the last of the voices left the room in front of him. As the main door was closed, Duffy reached into his pocket. He saw the light under the crack of the door disappear, then the footsteps as somebody approached the door to the small back room.

Harry Milburn cursed to himself as a small convoy passed at the junction by the Red Lion, in Greenford, banging on the steering wheel in frustration at the delay. "Come on, come on." he kept repeating.

Duffy saw the door handle as it began to turn, slowly the door opened, a hand reaching for the light switch.

Harry Milburn could stand it no longer, shoving the car into first gear; he sped forward, just managing to slip between two trucks. The driver of the second shaking a furious fist at Harry, as he watched in the rear view mirror. Now free from traffic restraints, Harry gunned the motor down towards the junction.

The light came on as the man entered the room; Duffy was ready for him, his eyes anticipating the sudden flood of light.

"Duffy, what the Feck…?"

"Come in and sit down, Frances," Duffy smiled.

"What's all this about, Sean," Cavenaugh said, his eyes fixed on Duffy's, His voice dropped as he saw the gun in Duffy's hand.

"Sit down and shut up," Duffy commanded.

Terrified, Cavenaugh did as he was told.

With his eyes firmly fixed on the quivering shape of Cavenaugh, Duffy slowly reached inside his pocket. Cavenaugh made to move, but Duffy was ready for him, he raised the gun, the barrel pointing directly at Cavenaugh's eyes. Knowing his chance had gone, Cavenaugh eased himself back into his seat. Duffy took the wad of papers and threw them onto the desk, followed by a pen.

"Sign it," Duffy said gruffly.

"What is it?" Cavenaugh asked nervously.

"A confession," Duffy snarled.

"A confession to what?"

"The murders, Frances, the murders you brutally conducted on the poor bodies of Mary, Molly and a pretty little friend of mine at the Barn Hotel in Ruislip the other night. You know the other places, of course," Duffy continued. "Hammersmith and Dublin in 1939."

"But, but..." Cavenaugh stammered at Duffy's revelations.

"You picked on the wrong girl, Frances."

"But….but….now listen, Sean."

"Sign it!" Duffy shouted at the shaking Cavanaugh.

"Go Feck yourself!" Cavenaugh screamed.

"No…Feck you, Francis," Duffy said as his finger cocked the trigger.

"Wait, wait! For God's sake, wait!" Cavenaugh cried. "I'll do it, I'll do it," he sobbed.

"Sign now," Duffy commanded.

Weeping loudly Cavenaugh picked up the pen, then with his hands trembling he signed the paper. When he had done it, Cavenaugh pushed the papers towards Duffy.

"You won't get away with this, Duffy, I'll find you and as God is my judge…"

"God's not your judge or jury, Francis, I am." Duffy said with a grin, his hand raising the gun once again to Cavenaugh's terrified face. "I'm also your executioner." Duffy's finger increased the pressure on the trigger.

"Jesus, no!" Cavenaugh screamed.

"Put the gun down Sean," Harry said as he burst into the room. "He's not worth it." Harry's gun was now pointed at Duffy.

"Oh! But he is Harry." Duffy grinned. "He is."

"Put that gun down, Duffy," Tommy Boyle shouted as he entered the small room, followed by the constable.

"Ah. Inspector Boyle," Duffy smiled. "Just like the cavalry, fucking late as usual."

Duffy stared at Cavenaugh, a wicked grin spreading across his face.

"Now, Sean." Harry barked.

Slowly Duffy let the gun drop. The constable rushed to Duffy, took the gun and replaced his own. Boyle stepped forward.

"Sean Michael Duffy, I'm arresting you…."

"What the hell's going on here?" Commander Thompson boomed.

Everybody looked towards the new arrival.

"Jesus, Peter… I was wondering when you would show up." Duffy grinned.

"Sorry, Sean, bloody RAF car stalled." Thompson returned the grin.

"What's going on here?" Boyle asked confused.

"He forced me to sign that," Cavenaugh blurted. "I didn't do it, the blonde girl, Duffy forced me."

"How do you know it was the body of a blonde girl?" Boyle said, turning to face Cavenaugh. "That information hasn't been released yet."

"Because this is your murderer, Inspector." Thompson said moving forward, "Francis Cavenaugh, he also murdered Molly and Mary back in 1939."

"And who are you?" Boyle asked.

"Commander Thompson, S.I.S." He showed Boyle his identity card. "And this is my colleague Harry Milburn. Sean Duffy," Thompson said looking towards Duffy, "also works for SIS."

Boyle looked dumbfounded, "But…but I thought…"

"If you check with your forensic department, Inspector, you will discover that they have just found some fingerprints at the murder scene, my guess is they will match this man, Francis Cavenaugh."

"How the Feck…" Cavenaugh spat.

"The tap by the basin in the room." Thompson smiled.

Cavenaugh knew the game was up, and made his move. He rushed forward for the constable's gun. Duffy anticipated his move; his fist buried itself under Cavanaugh's jaw. The man seemed to rise in the air, as he fell backwards into the chair, his eyes spinning, he lost consciousness.

Boyle sat down; he took a handkerchief from his pocket and wiped his brow.

"I don't understand. I was sure…"

"Who do you think killed Phelan's men last night?" Thompson interrupted.

Tommy Boyle looked slowly at Duffy, realisation beginning to form.

"He saved your life," Thompson added.

"But Mary, Molly…"

"He tried to save them also, we suspected Cavenaugh, but until yesterday…"

"The knife, you took it," Boyle gasped.

"We needed to be sure." Duffy smiled.

"Emily?" Boyle asked.

"She's fine," Duffy said. "She knows everything."

"Everything?" Thompson raised his eyebrows.

"Everything," Duffy grinned. "She had a right…"

CHAPTER 29

Francis Cavanaugh was taken to Ruislip Police Station where he was formally charged with the murders of the three young blonde girls. He confessed sobbing openly,

Boyle caught up with Duffy just as he; Commander Thompson and Harry were about to leave.

"Duffy…Sean. I'm so sorry…I was sure…"

"It's ok, Inspector, you weren't to know," Duffy conceded gracefully.

"May I?" Boyle said extending his hand.

"Sure why not." Duffy grinned.

Thompson turned to Duffy as they left the Police Station.

"Sean… will Emily say anything?" He said a worried look on his face.

"I don't know, Peter, I don't know," Duffy said.

Christian pulled back on the stick, lifting the Lysander into the clear blue sky of Norfolk, with the impostor Gunther Schloss seated directly behind him.

Emily, sitting alone in the bedroom at the Bull Hotel in Denham, had made her mind up. Worried by Duffy's prolonged absence she waited, desperate to see him again.

Boyle took the file out of the cabinet, opened it and stared for a few moments. With tears running down his unshaven face, he sighed. Closing the file, he put it into another drawer in the cabinet, this one marked Solved. "Rest in peace. Molly," he whispered, as he closed the drawer. Taking his hat and coat, Boyle opened the door to the office. Glancing over his shoulder, he took a long hard look at the empty room then slowly closed the door.

As Boyle passed the front desk, he placed a letter on the counter, then walked outside into the clean fresh air.

When Duffy entered the hotel room, Emily rushed to greet him, her arms snaking around his neck, holding onto him as if her life depended on it…as it had.

"Oh Sean, I was so worried." She sobbed.

"It's all over now, Emily, you're safe now," he whispered to her.

"Oh, Sean, I'm so happy you're safe," Emily said kissing his mouth repeatedly.

Duffy pulled his face gently from hers, looking deep into her beautiful big blue eyes, stained with tears. He spoke softly.

"It's not over just yet, Emily. I've got one more trip to go."

"I know, Sean," she whispered. "I'll wait for you. You will come back, won't you?"

"You try and stop me." Duffy grinned.

Christian brought the Lysander to a complete stop beside the Junkers 52 that had been wheeled out of the hangar to test its engines. A jeep pulled up as Christian and Schloss climbed out of the aircraft. The Jeep took Christian with the general in the back to the CO's office. Confined to barracks, both would rest that day. The take off for the flight to Italy had been brought forward, and they would take off that night.

When Boyle got home, his wife wasn't expecting him. "Tommy, what are you doing here?" she asked.

"Mary, I've got something to tell you."

"What is it, Tommy?"

"How would you like to go back to Roscommon…to live."?

"What."

"I've resigned, well retired actually."

"Oh, Tommy." She smiled, as she hugged her man.

Emily seemed like her old self as she and Duffy ate a light meal in the hotel's restaurant. When they had finished, Duffy escorted her to the door of their room. Outside the room, Duffy kissed Emily gently on the cheek, his eyes saddened, as he made to leave. Emily put her arms around Duffy's neck, pulling him to her, her mouth went to his, she kissed him long, hard and deep.

"Come back to me." She smiled as Duffy slipped away, a spring now in his step.

When Christian entered the body of the Junkers, he made his way to the cockpit to go through his pre-flight take off routine, before the jeep that carried Gunther Schloss arrived. When Christian entered the cockpit he was astonished to find Sean Duffy seated in the co-pilot's chair.

"Sean, what are you doing here?"

"I've come to make sure you don't do anything silly, Christian, we don't want to lose Gunther, now do we." He grinned.

"You know?" Christian said quietly.

"I've known all along Christian, It took Thompson a little while longer."

"Commander Thompson?" Christian turned in his seat. "He knows?"

"Yes, Christian, he knows."

"What…what am I going to do?" Christian said quietly.

"Exactly what you are told to do…"

"What will happen to me…Monica…the girls?"

"You'll all be safe…I have a plan," Duffy grinned.

"Sean?"

"Yes, Christian."

"Whose side are you on?"

"Mine, Christian, mine and Ireland's." Duffy grinned an even bigger grin.

When Gunther Schloss had been seated Christian flicked the switches to the engines, one by one the props turned.

"What's the weather like for the trip?" Duffy asked.

"Fine, a slight tail wind, should be a nice smooth flight."

"Thank God for small mercies." Duffy whispered as the Junkers took to the air.

"Well sir, what do you think?" Harry said to Thompson in the tower, as they watched the heavy Junkers disappear.

"I think Hitler and his chums are in for a big shock, Harry, a very big shock."

Yvette sat on the cell floor, oblivious to the darkness and cold. She stared at her shoes for a long time. "Think, Yvette, think." She cursed her tortured mind. Slowly the rationale came to her. Yvette moved her swollen, almost indistinguishable bloody fingers, the nails missing, each one pulled slowly, sadistically, from her fingers. Yvette somehow managed to take off the shoe, she took a deep breath, then tried to loosen the heel, finally the heel gave way. She peered into the void, as she did so her heart sank, the shoe was empty, the cyanide pill was missing.

Frantically she stubbed painful fingers, clawed at the other heel, it too was empty. All hope faded, as she began to sob; yet no tears came. Yvette knew then that she had been betrayed. With what strength she had left, now beyond the level of human endurance and suffering, she called for the guard.

When the guard arrived, she told him to fetch Von Ebstein. Yvette had made up her mind – she would talk.

Once the Junkers had passed the coastline of England and was out in the Channel, Duffy leaned towards Christian, his finger tapping against the map in his hand.

"Make for here," Duffy shouted above the noise of the engines.

Christian looked at the map, his eyes focussing on the point to which Duffy's fingers were pointing.

"Norway?" Christian said his eyes wide in disbelief.

Duffy nodded.

Christian banked the aircraft then set his new course.

The radar on the south coast picked up the change of course. Immediately, they reported the change in flight path, to their centre at RAF Uxbridge, they in turn relayed the message to the tower at Northolt. Commander Thompson received the call from the CO as he sat in the officer's mess, sipping a pint of bitter.

"Shall I scramble a flight of Spitfires?" The CO asked excitedly down the phone.

"Wait until Harry and I get there, don't do anything until I arrive, do you understand.

"Yes, sir," the CO replied.

Harry stood to leave. "Where are you going, Harry?" Thompson asked. "Sit down and finish your drink."

Christian leaned towards Duffy who saw the movement, cocking his ear he listened.

"You know they will have seen our change in flight path, the radar at Ventnor, on the Isle of Wight, will have been monitoring us. They'll probably send up a couple of Spits to see what's happening."

"Yes I know," Duffy said. "But not for a while, with any luck we'll be out of range by the time they catch us."

"How can you be so sure?" Christian yelled.

"Trust me, Christian," Duffy grinned. Duffy stood up, leaning towards Christian; he spoke normally in his ear. "I'm just going to check on our cargo, see how he is." Duffy holding on to whatever he could find, made his way to the belly of the Junkers. When he reached Schloss, he unscrewed the thermos flask he was carrying, poured a cup of coffee, then passed it to Schloss.

"How are you doing, Gunther? A hot coffee for you."

"I'm fine thanks, Major Duffy, thank you." He said taking the hot brew. "Major."

"What?"

"How come you're on this plane? The British?"

Duffy smiled. "The silly fools think I'm working for them."

"So you're... a double agent?" Schloss asked.

"No Gunther, I'm an Irishman...the Brits," Duffy continued, "have ravaged my country for over four hundred years, stealing our land, making prisoners of my people. Now when their backs are against the wall, they want our help...funny people the English."

"But Ireland fought with the British in the First World War."

"Yes, Gunther, then we had no choice, since then we've become a republic. Now we can choose who we want to fight with."

"So you have chosen Germany then?" Schloss looked pleased.

"For the time being, Gunther. For the time being," Duffy smiled.

Thompson met the CO in the tower, with Harry in tow. The CO seemed frustrated by the delay.

"What's the situation now?" Thompson asked.

"Well, their last position was here." The CO pointed to a map. "Radar have lost them, but if they continued on the same flight path, they should be about here." He pointed again.

"So they haven't turned anywhere at the moment?"

"No sir, but if we don't move now they will be out of range for our fighters, do I have your permission Commander Thompson?" The CO asked.

"Don't worry," Thompson said casually. "I anticipated this, I've got a couple of Mosquitoes on standby at Duxford. They will be able to intercept and, at the same time, they should be able to fend off any Jerry escorts."

"Commander?" The CO asked, his face troubled by the events. "I've known Flight Lieutenant Kawolski since he came to this country in 1940, he's a brave man, an excellent pilot...what I'm trying to say...is Christian a traitor?"

"We don't know yet...he might just be a bloody hero." Thompson spoke quietly, his mind focussed on the mission. "We'll just have to wait and see."

Duffy made his way back to the cockpit, seating himself back in the co-pilot's seat; he began to send a message in code.

"Who are you sending that to?" Christian asked.

"Best you don't know, Christian." Duffy said, his face serious for once.

Half an hour later at an airfield on the northern shore of Germany, Mosel received the message he had been waiting for.

> The goose has flown, stop.
> The golden egg is on board, stop.
> Bring family, stop. Exchange stop.
> No tricks, stop.

"Good news, sir?" Steiner asked.

"Yes Hans, we have it, tell the pilot to get ready. Tell him to head for here." Mosel pointed to the map.

"But that's on the border of Norway and Sweden."

"Yes Hans, I know..." Mosel turned to look at the young lieutenant. "Put the woman and children on board."

"Yes sir," Steiner smiled, happy that the family would be safe.

"Oh, and Hans?"

"Yes sir?"

'Send this message to fighter command." Steiner took the flimsy, he read it, his face changing colour. "But sir…" he protested.

"Send it Hans…now."

The two Mosquitoes took to the air from their base at Duxford on the Essex and Cambridgeshire border. Their course for the intercept was already plotted. At the same time two ME 110s, all that could be spared, also took to the skies, their plots also confirmed.

"How long now?" Duffy asked Christian.

"About an hour."

"Can't this think go any faster?"

"Probably a bit more, if we go to its maximum ceiling. But there's a problem," Christian said, pointing to the sky above the canopy.

"What?" Duffy asked.

"No cloud cover up there…if we get jumped, I've nowhere to hide…I can't outrun them in this thing," Christian shouted above the engines.

"Bollocks."

Mosel and Steiner boarded the Junkers together with the little family. Once seated, the engines ready, the aircraft taxied for take off. The young woman seated towards the rear of the plane, held each child close to her. Her arms encircling the girls in protection. The two young blonde children, Anna and Maria, struggled to peer out of the small window, unaware of the possible danger, the excitement at flying a new experience. The girls Ooh'd and Aah'd as the Junkers took to the sky.

Duffy peered out of the canopy, his eyes searching the sky. Christian had banked the aircraft, now they were heading eastwards. Duffy knew this would be the dangerous part.

Christian knew it too, and although he was confident in his ability, he also looked at the sky for the sign of fighters. His search was less animated, since he didn't want to worry Duffy unduly.

Christian saw them first, two black dots approaching from a southeasterly direction. He put the Junkers into a steep dive. Duffy felt the reaction; his eyes went to the sky. Now he saw them. Duffy gripped the armrests tightly as the aircraft's nose dropped sharply.

Christian saw the cloud to his left. He banked, heading straight for it. Duffy watched in frightened anticipation as the dots became larger. The distinctive shape of aircraft about to attack appeared

"What are they?"

"ME110s," Christian answered.

"Is that good?" Duffy asked.

"Better than 109s, yes."

The Junkers bounced as it hit the clouds at speed; within seconds the canopy was screened by grey cloud. Christian put the Junkers through various turns, dives, climbs, everything he could think of to lose the pursuing craft. "If only the cloud holds out," he thought.

The co-pilot of Mosel's plane came to Mosel's side.

"Sir, our fighters have made an intercept, the Polish pilot has taken evasive action, what should they do, sir?"

"Just follow," Mosel said, "Nothing else, just follow."

Christian's fears were realised; the cloud suddenly came to an end. As the Junkers came out of the cloud into clear blue sky, the Me110s were still with him. Slowly the fighters pulled alongside.

Christian peered at them over Duffy's shoulder. The lead pilot in the ME110 rotated his finger, signalling Christian to turn and follow him.

Duffy saw the signal. "What will we do?" he asked.

"Nothing," Christian said, "They can't touch us." Christian looked over his shoulder to where Schloss sat in the fuselage. "They want him alive."

Duffy smiled, Christian was right.

The ME110 again signalled for Christian to turn.

Christian shook his head. Suddenly the two ME110s banked sharply away.

"What the hell?" Christian exclaimed.

"The cavalry," Duffy smiled.

Christian followed Duffy's line of sight. To his left two Mosquitoes screamed in. One of the RAF planes gave chase, the other hovered beside the Junkers. Christian watched as the first Mosquito closed in on the trailing ME110. The burst of cannon fire smashed into the slower German machine, a trail of black smoke came from the stricken fighter. It banked sharply then fell from the sky, the trail of smoke following it until it disappeared into the blue water below. The other 110 skulked for home.

The second Mosquito pulled back to realign itself with the Junkers.

"Get down!" Christian screamed to Schloss, who sat terrified in the belly of the aircraft. Schloss didn't need a second opinion, he unbuckled the seat restraint to lie flat on the floor, and as he did so, a line of bullet holes appeared in the fuselage.

Christian banked the Junkers in a steep turning dive. The Mosquito followed. As he levelled out at sea level, the Mosquito pulled alongside, the other RAF plane also joining in.

"That's it, we've had it," Christian said disheartened.

"Not at all," Duffy said.

Christian looked at him, he was smiling. Then the two Mosquito pilots waved, and peeled off for their return journey to England.

"You knew, didn't you?" Christian asked.

"Yes," Duffy said, "A little show to convince our Jerry friends, which reminds me . . . ." Duffy said, looking over his shoulder at Schloss, who was still sprawled on the floor of the aircraft. "I'd better see how yer man is, I bet he's shit himself."

"You bastard." Christian grinned, and Duffy returned the gesture.

Thompson was still in the tower at Northolt, where he received the verbal message from the CO.

"We caught up with them, shot down one of their escorts, the other buggered off."

"And?" Thompson said.

"One of our chaps managed to get a burst off at Kawolski's plane, but lost him in cloud…low on fuel. Both Mosquitoes had to return…I'm afraid he's got away."

"Good." Thompson smiled.

"Pardon, sir?" The CO enquired totally confused.

"Don't worry. perhaps when all this is over you might read about it one day." Thompson turned to Milburn. "Come on, Harry, we've got a beer to finish."

Christian brought the Junkers down, making a perfect landing. He taxied the aircraft back into position, ready for an immediate take off.

Two cars pulled up some twenty yards from the cockpit, Mosel got out of the first car, Steiner by his side,

"Time for my little show." Duffy said as he unstrapped himself. He went to the belly of the aircraft, drawing his Walther pistol as he did.

"Come on, Gunther, you're almost home," he said, as he dug the pistol into Schloss's ribs.

Schloss was hauled towards the door of the aircraft, his mouth open wide in protest. As Duffy opened the door he pushed the terrified Schloss in front of him, his pistol pressing into Schloss' temple.

Mosel stood alone by the door; Steiner had remained by the car.

"Sean," Mosel smiled.

"Ernst," Duffy returned the compliment.

"I see you have my package, I trust the egg has not been broken."

"Its in perfect condition, Ernst, now where's my package." He said, pushing the gun harder against the confused Schloss' temple.

Mosel smiled again, "Hans," he called not turning, his eyes still on Duffy. Steiner went to the other car and opened the door. Monica, her face uncertain stepped out of the car, followed by her two daughters, their faces beaming with excitement.

"What's happening?" Monica turned towards Steiner, her blue eyes pleading with him.

"You're free, Monica. You and your children are going to Sweden." He smiled.

"Freedom…really?"

"Yes madam…and there's another thing."

"What?" Monica asked.

"Your husband's flying the aircraft."

"Chr…Christian!" Monica mumbled, the tears forming in her eyes.

"May I escort you?" Steiner smiled, holding his arm towards the young woman.

Christian, still in the pilot's seat, could not believe his eyes. "Monica," he breathed. When he saw the girls, the tears welled in his eyes, tears of joy.

Steiner brought the small party to the aircraft. Duffy stood to one side to let them board. As soon as Monica and the girls were seated and strapped in, Duffy lowered the gun. Tapping Schloss on the shoulder he spoke.

"It's time for you to do your duty, Gunther. Good luck," he said genuinely.

As Schloss stepped from the aircraft, Christian applied full throttle, his feet on both brakes, the aircraft shuddered as it tried to escape. Mosel shook hands with Schloss, pointing towards the waiting car, and as Schloss departed, Mosel turned to face Duffy.

"We could still shoot you down Sean." He said his face serious.

"I know, Ernst." Duffy said, "But I've got a high powered VHF set on board, tuned into the frequency at Northolt. I could let the Brits know of your little plan."

"But you won't?" Mosel smiled.

"Nor will you, Ernst," Duffy grinned as he closed the door.

Steiner now at the front of the aircraft, saluted Christian, then smiled, mouthing the words good luck. Christian, elated, returned the salute and the smile.

As the Junkers Took to the sky, Duffy returned to the co-pilot's seat.

"How long?" He asked Christian.

"Ten minutes." Christian smiled.

"I wonder what the beers like in Sweden?" Duffy grinned.

Gunther Schloss was debriefed at ABWEHR Headquarters; he told the excited audience gathered, including most of the German high command, what he had learnt, including Alexander's proposed push in Italy.

The High Command, Himmler in particular, were still suspicious. However, two events took place that convinced them of Schloss' authenticity.

Firstly, Yvette confessed, her confession corroborating with the information Schloss had provided. Beaten and tortured almost to the point of death, Yvette had told her captors of the feint that would take place in early June somewhere near the bay of the Seine. The main invasion taking place one week later, at the Pas de Calais.

Secondly, Alexander did attack again at Cassino, although the possible amphibious assault didn't take place, the main assault did, exactly as Gunther Schloss had predicted. On the 18th May 1944 the Poles attacked and captured the monastery, fighting as an independent force; the Poles raised their flag on the monastery itself.

Rommel, convinced that the main assault would take place in Normandy, cancelled his planned fortifications of the beaches, based upon the information Schloss had revealed. Although he had strengthened the area to stop glider landings and flooded the back areas of the beaches, only a few of the precautionary measures Rommel had undertaken were put into effect.

Most of the heavy guns designated for Normandy, such as those at the Melville battery, and the Point de Hoc, failed to arrive. Had they been in place, the Allies would have suffered many more casualties on the beaches. More importantly for the Allies, the Germans kept all their heavy armour in the area of the Pas de Calais.

Yvette, near to death was transported to Dachau to await execution.

D.DAY PLUS NINE

Mosel sat alone at his desk, his career in tatters. In front of him on his desk lay the iron cross, first class. He had won it as a young Lieutenant on the cruiser Falkenhiem during the First World War. The addition, presented to him by the Fuehrer himself, of the Oak leaves, sword and diamond cluster lay next to it. Nine days after the Allies had landed in Normandy, led by Montgomery, as Gunther Schloss had predicted. The proposed main invasion by the fictitious F.U.S.A.G., led by General George S. Patton in the Pas de Calais, had failed to materialise.

The egg had gone bad.

Mosel looked up as Steiner entered the room.

"Any news Hans?" He asked expectantly.

"No sir, the area around Calais is quiet still."

"Ah!"

"Sir?" Steiner said softly.

"What is it, Hans?"

"Von Rundstedt, Rommel….they've demanded the armour be sent south… The Fuehrer agreed sir."

"It's over then, Hans….I've been deceived.."

"What will you do sir?" Steiner asked.

"Wait," Mosel said. He reached into the drawer of his desk, took out an envelope.

"Your orders, Leutnant Steiner." Mosel said, as he passed the envelope to Steiner who read the document enclosed.

"But sir. My place is with you," he said forcefully.

"Orders, Leutnant, are to be obeyed."

"Yes sir." Steiner saluted, tears in his eyes.

"You have never disobeyed any of my orders Leutnant Steiner, I don't expect you to start now."

"Sir." Steiner turned to leave.

"Hans…." Mosel said, his eyes had a paternal look. "Hans, good luck my boy…now go."

Steiner left the room with tears in his eyes. He took the car to the airport and the waiting aircraft. Leutnant Hans Steiner had obeyed his final order.

Mosel sat back in his chair, waiting-It wasn't long. The doors burst open. Obergruppenfurhrer Manfred Von Ebstein stormed into the room followed by two SS guards.

Mosel smiled, "Manfred," he acknowledged.

"Ernst," Von Ebstein returned.

"Somehow I thought it might be you." Mosel smiled again.

"Who else," Von Ebstein grinned, the thin lips curling in triumph.

"Captain Ernst Mosel, Kreigsmarine, you are under arrest, hands up." Von Ebstein said quietly but viciously, as he raised his Luger.

"On what charge?" Mosel asked.

"Treason," Von Ebstein barked.

'C' sat opposite the Prime Minister in the subterranean offices under Whitehall, a triumphant smile sat unusually on the mouth of the head of the British Secret Service.

Churchill finished reading the report in front of him and closed the file. He then took another headed 'Captain Ernst Mosel,' opened the buff cover, staring intently. After a moment, Churchill removed his spectacles, then rubbed his tired eyes before looking directly at 'C'

"A resounding success, sir. I'm sure you would agree," 'C' said, expecting a confident yes from the Prime Minister.

"The deception was complete, the consequences of fate were a good ally. Yes 'C', history will support us in the option we were forced to undertake…but in the depth of our conscious, in the autumn of our lives, will it bring us the same feelings of exuberance, or will the stain of deceit, the betrayals, the vanities, come back to haunt us? Will it be Valkyrie?" Winston continued. "Or Satan in the guise of an angel, that welcomes us upon that long journey."

"Sir." The Prime Ministers statement dumbfounded 'C'; confused he tried to continue, "But surely…."

"There is no glory in what we have done 'C'," Churchill interrupted. "Our only consolation is that it was the result of necessity." Churchill returned the spectacles to the bridge of his nose. Changing tack, he asked, "Yvette…do we have any news 'C'." he asked.

"No sir." 'C' looked down, "The last we heard she was alive….but in Dachau."

"What of General Popowski?" Winston asked.

"Good news on that front." 'C' brightened, "He was picked up by our forces just north of Rome." 'C' hoped this information would lift the spirits of the Prime Minister, he was wrong.

"A wicked web 'C', Poles, Germans, even our American friends…a wicked web."

Churchill's hand went to the stamp on the desk in front of him, he picked it up hovering a moment over the open file, before he banged it firmly on the front page. The red ink stained the paper with a single word – "Destroy!"

Winston put the stamp back on the table and sat back looking at 'C'.

"The profanity of eagles 'C'," he mumbled. "The profanity of eagles."

THE END

NOW

The red BMW pulled up outside the RAF memorial in Coopers Hill Lane, in the small village of Englefield Green in Surrey.

The old man walked through the beautiful gardens to the memorial itself, followed by the two blonde girls.

It took him about five minutes to find what he was looking for. There, amongst all the names of the men and women who had given their lives for freedom whilst in the service of the RAF. was the name he was looking for. That of Flight Lieutenant Freddie Moreland.

The old man prayed for a while before taking one pace backwards. He saluted smartly, then turned towards the girls and walking hand in hand, they returned to the road. Once back on Coopers Hill Lane the party turned and walked towards a white stone cottage.

Rose Cottage had hardly changed since those balmy sunny days back in the late spring of 1944. The old man and the girls took a steep path through the garden to the rear of the cottage, its walls swathed in ivy, its porches and windows edged by rose bushes.

Another old man welcomed them, his hair still full, fair but splattered with grey, a huge grin spread across his face.

"Christian." He offered his hand.

"Sean." They shook hands. "These are my grand daughters, Katra and Emilia."

"And beautiful they are." Duffy smiled, the girls smiled coyly back.

"Come, tea's ready." Duffy showed the way.

When tea was finished the two old men took a stroll in the garden. Passing the millponds and a small clump of fruit trees they came to the edge of the garden. Below them the hillside fell away steeply to flatten out in some fields below them. The River Thames cut through the Runnymede countryside towards London, just visible in the haze beyond. A British Airways 747 taking off from Heathrow banked overhead as it began its climb.

"Emily loved this place," Christian said quietly. "She always wanted to be here."

"She is, Christian."

"What?" Christian looked at Duffy.

"Come with me." Duffy said. He led Christian to the other side of the garden. There shaded by a cedar tree, lay a gravestone, looking out over the wonderful view. The two men stood looking at the headstone.

Christian's eyes filled with tears. "I did love her, you know," he said turning to Duffy.

"I know you did." Duffy put his hand on Christian's shoulder. "She loved you too…that's why she let you go…"

"But I don't understand." Christian said.

"She did, she knew you would never leave Monica and the girls."

"But the murder . . ." Christian exclaimed.

"It was poor Cathy," Duffy sighed, "She was buried next to Freddie at St. Martins, the church in Ruislip."

"But Emily…"

"I married her." Duffy said. "She was a good wife, we had no children, she couldn't have them, not after she lost your baby."

"My baby?" Christian shot a look of disbelief at Duffy.

"Yes, she was pregnant with your son…she miscarried."

"But…I…I didn't know, Sean."

"She didn't want you to…it…it would have complicated things."

The two old men returned their eyes to the grave.

"When did she go?" Christian stammered.

"Three months ago, when I contacted you in America."

"I did love her, Sean," Christian said softly the tears falling.

"Me too, Christian," Duffy said, his tears also falling. "Me too, Christian."

Aftermath

Hans Steiner returned to the little village by the chateau, his beautiful wife bore him two daughters, one named Helena after his mother, the other Yvette. Steiner and his partner run the little café that Anne Marie's uncle had once owned.

Tommy Boyle, police inspector, retired with his wife Mary to the beautiful Irish countryside near his hometown in Roscommon.

Harry Milburn succeeded his boss Commander Peter Thompson RN when he retired. An East German sentry killed Harry as he crossed the Berlin Wall in November 1963.

Yvette Granville survived Dachau and now lives quietly in a little village in Somerset.

Gunther Schloss was executed as a traitor in May 1945 just two days before the German army in Europe capitulated. His body was exhumed and laid next to his brother Alexander in the family cemetery on Long Island.

Frankie Cavenaugh was convicted of the murders of three women, two of which were prostitutes, and hanged in 1945.

Captain Ernst Mosel was executed on June 15th 1944 for treason, no trial took place. SS Obergruppenfurhrer Von Ebstein fired the final bullet that killed Mosel. Von Ebstein himself was captured by Polish troops with Montgomery's 21st Army group. He was convicted of war crimes and hanged.

Phelan was murdered in a Belfast bar in 1950. His murderer was never found.

MikeTiernan